The Nostradamus Conspiracy

The Nostradamus Conspiracy

Eric E. Shore

Writer's Showcase
presented by *Writer's Digest*
San Jose New York Lincoln Shanghai

The Nostradamus Conspiracy

All Rights Reserved © 2000 by Eric E. Shore

Writer's Showcase
presented by *Writer's Digest*
an imprint of iUniverse.com, Inc.

For information address:
iUniverse.com, Inc.
620 North 48th Street, Suite 201
Lincoln, NE 68504-3467
www.iuniverse.com

ISBN: 0-595-12624-3

Printed in the United States of America

Dedication

To my parents, who I wish were still here to read this book, and to my sons, Brett and Matthew who I hope still will.

Foreword

Nostradamus, in his Centuries, predicted that sometime between 1997 and 2007 a war would begin. It would be initiated by a man in a blue turban, and flow from Persia (now Iraq) to engulf the rest of the world. He even describes nuclear and biological weapons, and predicts that after a long war in which most of the world would die, there would follow a thousand years of peace.

He also said also that whether his predictions came to pass or not was up to us…

Acknowledgements

I'd like to thank Sherron Miller, who's encouragement helped me to finish this book when it languished on my computer disk, and the following people without whose encouragement and assistance this book would never have been possible:

Prologue

The gentle wind caressed their bodies as they lay naked on the beach where they made love. She lay on her stomach with her head nestled into his right shoulder and he on his back, watching the smoke from his cigarette disappear into the blackness with only the occasional flicker of a star to note it's direction.

She pretended to be asleep while he stared into the starlit sky searching for...what? He could never quite put his finger on it. He knew this was wrong—they didn't belong together. They had met by accident less than a month ago while she ate alone at a table next to his at a small restaurant in Tel Aviv. She was an American and thus represented everything he despised most in the world, yet here they lay. He had tried to leave earlier in the week, but couldn't. Each time he picked up the telephone to call a taxi, the sound of her soft voice whispered to his subconscious or her clean, lightly scented smell drifted through his mind. He stayed.

"Jenn," he whispered, and looked down at her to see her reaction. There was none. "Jennifer," he called again, slightly louder, extending her name and lifting her cheek. She opened her eyes and smiled. Her startling green eyes reflected the starlight and once more caused him to pause in wonder.

"Hello, my darling," she said softly, not moving.

"Jenn, we have to get up. It will be light soon, and people will be coming onto the beach again."

"Yes." It was her only answer. There was still no movement.

"Jennifer," once again he tried to reason with her, but not very hard.

In answer, she lifted her head and, moving slightly upwards over his chest, placed her mouth over his, while rolling onto him. They kissed deeply, then she began moving her lips along his neck to his ear, then down his neck to where it met his shoulder. He inhaled deeply through his teeth as the tingle spread through his body. Her hands began to play over his chest, then finding their way to his abdomen and finally coming to rest between his legs where she began to gently massage him into erection. With great but gentle strength, his tightly muscled body rolled her onto her back and he began his own manipulations of her body until she began to moan deep in her throat.

"David," she whispered, "now, take me now." He did, and their bodies rose and fell as they had done so often during this past week, each seeming to know what the other wanted and needed. They reached a climax at nearly the same instant, her vaginal muscles contracting as he drove into her one last time.

"I love you, David," whispered Jennifer, her moist blonde hair flowing outward and spilling from the blanket onto the sand.

"I know," he replied, and I love you too," he returned her whisper. Still, he knew that they would have to part soon. She had to return to the United States, and he had his work here. She could never be a part of what her did. He knew it even if she didn't, but pretended that the time would never come.

He had never felt like this toward a woman before. He exhibited a gentleness that she drew out of him, that he never knew was there. His other "encounters" were usually rough, with him taking and them giving. This was different. They gave to each other.

At eight o'clock they sat in the coffee shop at the Tel Aviv Hilton sipping coffee and staring at each other. They had been inseparable for nearly a week, but his time was drawing to a close.

"Jenn," he began.

"I know, darling," she answered, "you have to leave." It was a statement. She understood, she accepted, but she never acquiesced.

"I have no choice, my love." He held her left hand, gently kissing each of her finger tips. "We'll see each other again," he lied, then turned his eyes away from hers so she wouldn't see them well up. "I'll finish my business in about a month, and come to New York. We'll meet there, and you can show me around." Her face lit with hope as he kissed her once more, paid the check, and said goodbye.

"Shalom", she said. I'll be waiting for you in New York.

✳✳✳✳✳✳✳✳✳✳✳✳✳✳✳✳✳✳✳✳✳✳✳✳✳✳✳✳✳✳✳✳✳✳✳✳

Mohamet Azziz sat in front of his laptop computer, a state of the art model that was illegal to export from the United States to Syria, so it wasn't. It was imported from France, where it was bought from the U.S. Azziz neither knew nor cared about these things. He clicked on a bookmark in his Web Browser, and the form he was looking for appeared in front of him. With practiced dexterity, he entered the name and account number of the first bank from two pull-down menus, then did the same with the bank and account number to which he was transferring the money. He wasn't told the User ID or Pass Phrase, the computer took care of these for him. He then typed the amount of money to be transferred, in American dollars, clicked the "Submit" button, and when the screen told him that the transfer was successful, he exited the program and turned off the computer.

The process had become routine, and Azziz followed it without variation. He was already dressed, so he simply took the worn brown briefcase from the closet in his hallway, and walked to the bank branch only six blocks away where he withdrew three hundred and fifty thousand American dollars, filled the briefcase with the bills, and left. Nothing was mentioned at the bank.

Nouhad Hazzar removed the worn briefcase from the locker at the bus terminal where Azziz had left it, and carried it along one of the few paved streets in this area of town. It was hotter than usual, and the sweat began to make his clothes stick to his body as he approached the large iron gate blocking the entrance to an ornate dwelling that he had never actually been allowed to enter. After ringing the bell, a large man in jeans and a tee shirt, whose weathered face was covered with a beard and hair halfway to his shoulders, took the briefcase without saying a word, then shut the gate. Hazzar walked back to town. His job was done.

In the house, the quiet man in jeans walked to the living room where he removed his shoes before crossing the Oriental rug, and placed the briefcase on a table in front of Osama Bin Ladin who opened it and smiled. Things were as they should be.

****

It was dark on the road to the Eretz Tov Kibutz, and less than a week after two people held each other on the beach. The thirty-eight children in the slightly battered, universally yellow school bus were laughing. Their teacher, a small woman with dark hair and olive skin tried unsuccessfully to quiet them. It was the fourth time they had made this particular field trip, and it was a good thing the driver knew the road as well as he did, or the sudden curves and rock strewn shoulders would have made the drive more exciting than the time they had in town. As they headed northeast around a curve, a waving lantern brought them to a complete halt. The driver peered through the darkness trying to detect what the emergency was that delayed them. Suddenly, in front of the his startled gaze, the shadow in front of them carefully placed the lantern on the ground, lifted a tube about eight centimeters in diameter from the ground and placed it into a steady position on his right shoulder.

"No!", shrieked the bus driver, and frantically tried to get the bus into "Reverse" as the end of the tube flared briefly. The middle aged Israeli army reservist had seen the flare from shoulder launched weapons before. He knew he was already dead, and before anyone else even knew the incident had occurred, it was over. The bus erupted into a blinding yellow-white ball of light and heat, leaving both vehicle and passengers as little more than a molten heap or metal, cloth, flesh and bone.

On the road ahead, a tall, dark man lowered his hood and surveyed his work, then returned to his jeep and drove away.

"No," thought the sole occupant of the jeep, "she could never be a part of this."

✸✸✸✸✸✸✸✸✸✸✸✸✸✸✸✸✸✸✸✸✸✸✸✸✸✸✸✸✸✸✸✸✸✸✸

A month later, Jennifer sat in a small bar off of Seventh Avenue with her third martini. He had never come. Somehow, she knew he wouldn't, yet hope made her come to New York and wait. Well, it was time to leave. She had a life to live, and it would seem that David was to be just another memory.

The Metroliner sped her south from New York, her thoughts now turning to other matters. She had no way of knowing that halfway around the world, her lover sat at an outdoor café sipping cappuccino and thinking of her. His life couldn't include her. Still, he dreamed.

Chapter 1

Date: Sunday, 07-Jul-01 06:21 Zulu

>

> From: usa_1\num_1_usa@terra.gov

> To: rus_1\ num_1_rus@terra.gov

>

> Subject: Re: Sandman

> We are aware Sandman leaving soon. Will terminate on arrival.

Take no further action.

>————————End Message. No reply needed.—————--

It was unusually warm in London, which usually remained cool even in July. Mark Harmon strolled slowly along the periphery of Hyde Park, approaching "Speakers' Corner". On any Sunday, in all directions, people could be observed literally standing on "soap boxes" to espouse their disparate views of the world. It was a routine Sunday event here, and one that tourists always flocked to—perhaps the truest exercise of free of speech.

He had arrived here, only days earlier, for a conference sponsored by the Royal Society of Medicine, of which he was an affiliate member. He had joined through The American College of Physicians, but this was the first time he had actually gone to London to attend one of their conferences. Actually, the conference was just an excuse to get away from home for a little while.

This was one of his favorite places. Contrary to the notion that the British people were cool and aloof, he found them to be a warm and friendly people. They were usually helpful, and always ready to discuss shortcomings (yours, not theirs) over a pint of Bitters, while taking a few pounds in a dart game from an unsuspecting "Yank."

Crossing Piccadilly, Mark strolled leisurely into the lobby of the Hyde Park Inn, where the conference was being held. He crossed the large Oriental rug covering the newly installed Italian marble floor, and entered the bar.

Although not much of a drinker, he had come to enjoy having one or two shots of tequila before dinner since he arrived. After all, he rationalized, he had no real responsibilities now, so a slight amount of inebriation was a feeling to be cherished, not scorned. The first sip always tightened his throat, but he was now swallowing the remainder of his second drink, and already feeling the euphoria it produced. He delighted in the pattern of free association that followed, and usually wondered at the apparent clarity of his thoughts, while realizing, somewhere in the front of his brain, that these thoughts would seem substantially less brilliant after the effects of the alcohol wore off.

Sitting and staring at his glass, a figure caught in his peripheral vision, attracting his attention. He quickly swung his head to the left to get a better look, but whoever it was had already become an apparition, disappearing through the ornate stained glass doors of the hotel "Pub."

"Oh well," he said to no one in particular, and ordered another. As he finished the last of his second drink, and awaited the arrival of his third, his thoughts wandered once more, along the meandering path of free association. Here he was in London, by himself. He could go anywhere or do anything he wanted, yet he was spending his time sitting in a bar drinking. "Why?" The question popped into his head repeatedly, and rattled around until it began to take on a rhythm of its own.

Gathering himself together, he rose from his seat, pushed back the heavy wooden chair and, tossing a couple of five pound notes onto the bar to pay for his drinks, walked back out the door, through the lobby, and into the street. It was now well past noon, and even the unusual warmth had faded into the overcast so characteristic of this city. A chill began to fill the air, so that Mark was forced to reposition the collar of his jacket for protection against the wind as he walked.

Fifteen minutes later, he had crossed the park, and stood diagonally across from Buckingham Palace. Soon, he knew, the customary crowds would begin to gather for the "Changing of the Guard." He had witnessed the spectacle before, and had no wish to see it again, so he turned left and began walking along the edge of the park back toward central London. The slight chill in the air had erased the trace of inebriation created by the tequila, and he mentally relived his last evening at home.

✷✷✷✷✷✷✷✷✷✷✷✷✷✷✷✷✷✷✷✷✷✷✷✷✷✷✷✷✷✷✷✷✷✷

It was late the evening before he left, when Mark maneuvered his BMW Z-3 along the West River Drive. His foot pressed the accelerator pedal further toward the floor, and the car responded by lurching forward with the tires squealing as he rounded a curve. He rarely felt anxiety or fear, except when he went home. At five feet ten inches, he was solidly built, but his longish dark hair and deep brown eyes gave him a soft appearance that, along with his quiet manner added to a visage that some mistook for weakness.

He had been inducted into the Gamma Club only three hours earlier, sitting alone at dinner because Meredith was "too busy" to come.

The evening ended, as most Gamma meetings did, with a speaker. She described in detail how the cutbacks in funding were causing difficulties for various government agencies, but both words and titles evaded him. Mark's attention, had focused upon the speaker, rather than the speech. She was breathtaking in the truest sense of the word. He actually found himself consciously expelling a breath he had taken several seconds earlier, and he was unable to disengage his eyes from hers. They were nearly "Kelly green" with microscopic flecks of an indeterminate metallic color sprinkled around an iris of midnight black. Her skin was a creamy cafe'-au-lait that comes with exposure to the tropical sun, and all of this smooth perfection was surrounded by brilliant sandy blonde hair.

His mind returned to his route, which he navigated at a pace that was most charitably described as "spirited," to his comfortable "California Modern" style home in the suburbs of Philadelphia.

"Well, it's about time!" his wife, Meredith said, somewhat sarcastically, as he entered the house. "Tomorrow, I'll go out for the evening and leave you." Mark felt the muscles in his chest contract, and his gut begin to cramp. This was their standard dialogue. He knew better than to answer because he knew she wouldn't listen and didn't care.

Theirs had been a cool relationship for several years now. Neither would admit that the love they once shared had long since evaporated. It was the only situation in his life where Mark was willing to accept less than control, and the only one in which he was never sure if he had been the victor or the vanquished.

They began their usual arguments, with his attempt at calm making her more angry. Her shrieking was one of the things that most annoyed him. Why did she have to scream everything? Too tired to argue, Mark went upstairs, and changed into a blue scrub suit, taken from the hospital. These served him as pajamas, and were even acceptable to wear to WAWA during the warm summer months.

"Why must we always fight?" he intoned wearily. Why can't you just say "Hello," or "Hi," or "how was it?"

"Why are you so sensitive?" she asked for the thousandth time. "You know that's just me. Besides," her voiced trailed off, "I'm tired. I've had a hard day."

"She's always tired", Mark thought to himself. How could someone who slept so much, and worked so little, be so constantly tired?

"I'm sorry if your day was bad", he said in a quiet and weary tone, and went downstairs to get a snack and watch TV. A few years ago, they would probably have made up and then made love, but no more. Their sex life had devolved to once or twice each month, with whole months sometimes slipping by without any desire on her part. He wasn't sure whether it was a lack of interest in him, in sex itself, or perhaps another man, but there appeared to be no cure for it. He wondered sometimes, why he had never had an affair with anyone during more than a decade of marriage, but that wasn't him.

After about an hour of television, he turned to reading, followed by playing around with his computer. He had been doing that for so long, that even he thought of himself as a "computer nerd" sometimes. Sleep began creeping up on him at last, and when his attention began to wander, he went upstairs, turned off the light that his wife habitually left on, and went to bed. He was to leave for his conference in the morning and, as always, sleep came less easily to him when he was troubled. Their deteriorating marriage and the increasing severity of their financial problems, kept him staring into space longer than usual. Unnoticed by him, he slid into a sleep whose dreams, though unremembered, left him sweating when he awakened in the morning.

Chapter 2

Smoke curled around the glistening hair that lay flat against the skin above Mustafa's ears. It had been pressed into place under the black chord which, only minutes earlier, held his red and white checkered *kaffiye* in place. It had been a trying day, and he was oblivious to the odor of sweat, dirt, and cordite that emanated from his body. He was a warrior fighting in a holy cause—a *Jihad*. Without a thought, he dismissed the dark haired girl (to refer to her as a woman would have been adding several years to her age) lying naked on his bed. For a moment, she sat there, leaning back with her outstretched arms behind her, arching her back. She was thin, and her ribs showed as she took one last deep breath. Her small, firm breasts rose with her chest emphasizing the dark areola and erect nipples. Even at her age, she knew she was seductive, and used it to her advantage. She rose, dressed in the crumpled uniform lying on the floor, and left without a word. These were facts of life.

Walking to the table that sat at one end of his room, he returned to studying a map that had nearly as much grime on it as ink. His group, *"Bloody April"*, had several missions planned, and he needed to be prepared.

Slowly, he lowered the harsh Russian cigarette from his lips and exhaled. As the fetid breeze grudgingly moved the smoke across the room and out of the open window, he stared at it, allowing his thoughts to wander back to his youth in the United States.

He remembered how happy his father had been upon arriving in "America". This was the *real* Promised Land!

"Maybe this taking of our land by the Zionists was a sign from Allah that they were to move on and prosper." Mustafa never believed it.

"You must learn English," his father constantly admonished him during that first year. "No accent!" bellowed his father in thickly accented English. "I want to hear no accent. You are an American now, and there must be no doubt in anyone's mind."

Slowly, because though of above average intelligence, he never had any particular facility for languages, painfully because of the pain in his father's eyes if he were to mispronounce a word, and resentfully, because all of this should not have been necessary, Mustafa learned to speak English as though he was born to it. His accent was mid-Atlantic, but in his mind, he was Palestinian! He was the master of his land, or would have been, had not the Zionists taken it from them with the help of the people whom his own father wanted him to emulate. He would occasionally use the term "Israeli", but never called the country Israel since, in his mind, it did not really exist. He was only eight years old, but a hatred of everything American grew, unchecked, in his soul. It grew to the point where it became all consuming. It grew until the combination of his hatred for the Americans, their Israeli "stooges", and the entire "West", crowded any but the most erotic thoughts from of his mind. So great was this "passion", that each small satisfaction of it, each hostage killed, each building destroyed, each American or Israeli or even Britain lying in shreds after a car bombing, created a sensual pleasure he could obtain in no other way!

His mother had died in childbirth, and was buried not far from Jafa. When his father died, he returned to his "homeland". There, during a visit to Jordan, he met Yasser Arafat, a man he greatly admired, and an older man who was introduced to him as Mohammed Al-Rakar, but whom he later came to know was George Habbash. Here were men who not only hated, but allowed their hate to prod them to action. It was from these feelings that he accepted his first "mission" for the PLO.

A school bus would be crossing the intersection, only a few kilometers from Jafa at 1300. There were to be no survivors. He would draw his "first blood" against school children, to prove to the Zionist pigs that so long as they were in Palestine, not even their children would be safe. He understood the barbarism of his act, but rather than being repulsed by the thought, or even remorseful, he reveled in it. After all, the blood of the children was not on his hands, but on those who refused to leave his country. He was only carrying out Allah's wishes—*"Allah Achbar!"*

As the last of the tobacco burned out against the long filter of his Russian cigarette, he returned from his reverie, gulped the remainder of his cold coffee and rose from the chair with slight difficulty. Sometimes, when there was a storm coming, he could feel the shrapnel in his right knee. He knew that it had been skillfully removed many years ago, but it caused pain none the less. It was a pain that he used to generate additional hate, as if that were necessary.

"Mustafa!" the door opened only partially, and a beard whose appearance had been carefully tailored to resemble that of Chairman Arafat, entered the room, followed by a face for which the covering of a beard was a blessing. Turning, Mustafa made the slightest gesture with his head, indicating his permission for Abdul to enter.

"Yes?" Mustafa asked, wearily.

"There is a call for you at headquarters." Abdul's left shoulder rested against the door jam, apparently awaiting some sign of friendship, but his casual demeanor evaporated rapidly as Mustafa's stare made it quite clear that this was not to be tolerated. "There are no friends," he would remind himself. There were only his superiors, whom he was expected to obey without question, and his inferiors, from whom he would tolerate nothing less.

"Thank you. I'll be there in a minute", and the return of his attention to the papers on the table made it clear, that Abdul's presence, no longer necessary, would no longer be tolerated.

Mustafa carefully replaced the two pieces of paper he was holding into the well-oiled leather pouch, then tied the pouch with a strip of sheepskin cut for this purpose, and returned it to its hiding place behind a brick in the mantle. Satisfied that, after spreading a small amount of dust which he always left for this purpose, his hiding place was once again secure, he donned the camouflage jacket that was his favorite attire, and stepped out into a cooler night than he expected. The slight chill brought some alertness back to a brain that had been made lethargic by nicotine, sex, and Ousso, of which he had become fond while in Greece. He stepped a little more lively as he approached the large tent that was thought of as "Headquarters".

Inside, light was provided by several rows of hanging light bulbs, covered with repainted cones directing all the light downward, leaving the top of the tent in a relative twilight.

With the casual rigidity of one used to command, Mustafa crossed the few meters of open space to the Duty Officer's desk and asked, simply, "Where?" The D.O. inclined his head in the direction of a telephone handset that had been left lying on the desk. Still wondering whether to demand the respect due his rank, he decided to let this small infraction pass. There were other things on his mind.

"Al Assad." Mustafa stated his last name in a matter-of-fact manner. It was the only acknowledgment anyone needed at the other end. After a short pause, in which he could picture the person at the other end checking a meter to see if there were an energy drain which might indicate a "tap", he heard the hollow tone of a "secure" line respond, "*Allah Achbar.*"

No name was needed. The voice at the other end of the line was one he knew only as Hassan, but he knew it well. There was no mistaking that rasp, the authority it commanded, or the cruelty behind the words. Mustafa had tried many times to visualize the face behind the voice, but each time the vision eluded him. He knew, without ever meeting Hassan, that while he, Mustafa, fought for a holy cause, Hassan fought because he loved the fight. More to the point, he loved the kill. It was the thrill of slaughter that drove Hassan and men like him. Alas, this was a necessary evil at this time, but when their victory was assured, men like Hassan would be disposed of. At times, when a tiny bit of his hatred wore thin, he wished this could be over so he and his people could get on with their lives. These men would be eliminated. He had been assured of that.

"Tonight", Hassan, followed by a click at the other end. There was no further need of discussion, the place of meeting was always pre-arranged by the date and time. Anyone intercepting the call, even if he knew that a meeting had been arranged, would have no way of knowing where and when unless he, too, possessed the small red notebook which rested alongside the leather pouch behind the brick.

Mustafa hung up the phone, turned, and without acknowledging anyone else in the room, thrust himself through the wooden door of the headquarters tent. He strode determinedly past the "Mess Hall" to his quarters where he loosened the brick and withdrew the notebook from which he would decode the place of meeting.

Chapter 3

The lights dimmed in the "Situation Room", and the large horse-shoe shaped table became a shadow. The opposite wall dissolved into a map of the world, zoomed rapidly to the Persian Gulf area, and then zoomed again to show a variety of ships, planes and troops of several nations, all neatly labeled by the computer. From time to time, the tag or the symbol on the map would flash and change to indicate a change in strength, condition or position.

From their location in the "nuclear proof" shelter beneath the White House, they could be in contact with virtually anyone, anywhere in the world. Satellite communication and surveillance allowed them to be aware of the movement of even a handful of men or equipment belonging to any nation. The satellite cameras were so accurate, they could read the name tags on the uniforms of foreign troops.

Standing behind one leg of the table and only a few yards from the behemoth screen, was another shadow that nearly disappeared into obscurity next to "The Wall." Pressing a button on the lectern behind which the shadow stood, a flashing square appeared around a group of ships, heading in a northwesterly direction. In the center of the group of ships was a larger rectangular shape with an American flag at its center, and bearing the label—"U.S.S. Enterprise". This was the flagship of the carrier battle group which had been escorting American flag as well as "tag along" neutral vessels in and out of the treacherous Persian Gulf region.

Officially, the United States had been neutral in the tensions between Iran and Iraq, but unofficially, while the U.S. wanted the Shiite Fundamentalist government in Iran changed to a more moderate one, Saddam Hussein had become a much greater threat. He coveted the ancient Persian throne, and would do anything to make it happen. Even the Russians, who normally side with anyone who opposed the U.S. were on the same side. Several years earlier, they had tried to make their relations with their southern neighbor more normal, but repeated attempts by the Iraqis to subvert "Moslem" Azerbaijan, and thereby ferment rebellion within the old U.S.S.R., finally convinced President Gorbechav that this was an unworkable course.

Then there was the SCUD missile, intended for the Kurds in Northern Iraq, that detonated in southern Azerbaijan with its chemical payload killing an entire village. Saddam tried to blame the Americans, whom he said launched it from within his country to make it look like he did it, but no one believed that, and the Russians, not wanting to show a chink in their armor, didn't even admit it happened.

Since then, the U.S. and the "Confederation of Independent States" (read USSR) had clandestinely worked together for the first time since World War II. Now, as is wont to happen in world affairs, Iraq's invasion of Kuwait in 1990 caused sides to change and positions to realign. Friends had become enemies and foes emerged as allies. Iran and Iraq settled into a tenuous peace with Iran clandestinely aiding Iraq against the "infidels" while outwardly remaining part of the multitude of nations opposed to Saddam Hussein.

"The carrier group which you see in the middle of the screen", began a soft female voice without preamble, and just a trace of the steel personality that lay behind it, "is lead by the U.S.S. Enterprise. It is comprised of eighteen ships including several destroyers, light cruisers, and guided missile frigates, as well as four mine sweepers, two helicopter carriers, and two troop carriers. It is being escorted by Sub-Pack Echo, the flag of which is aboard the U.S.S. Stingray, and is comprised of six,

Los Angeles class, nuclear powered attack submarines and two Trident missile subs".

"Approximately six hours ago, the British tanker "Esquire" was attacked by six small, but heavily armed Iraqi gun boats operating out of a base near *Bandar 'Abbas*. It wasn't sunk, but was burning hotly when it called for assistance from any nearby ship. Until now, we hadn't known that Iraqi boats were based or allowed to operate from Iranian soil."

"The Enterprise, having received their distress call, launched four F-14 fighters, and ordered the guided missile frigate "Martin Luther King" to break away from the group and come to the assistance of the burning tanker, which was then only fifty kilometers from the battle group. Accordingly," continued the compelling voice "these units moved into position to render assistance." A smaller square in the lower left corner of The Wall illustrated the action being described by the speaker. "Being the first to arrive at the scene, the F-14's found six gunboats turning for another attack, and six more surface contacts showed on their radar screens, not more that two kilometers behind them. The F-14's split into two flights, with the first initiating an attack run against the gunboats, during which five of the boats were sunk, and one was left burning. The second flight", continued the voice from the shadow, "flying top cover for the first, encountered four Iraqi MIG-23's, which they dispatched with sparrow missiles, long before they became any real threat."

"At this point", the voice paused, to allow the situation to sink in, "with the planes and ships having returned to the convoy, Rear Admiral Scheinhotlz, the battle group commander, was made aware of ten incoming silkworm missiles. At the end of the battle, none of the American ships were damaged, but two neutral ships were left burning. Within ten minutes, a second salvo of missiles was launched, falling wide of their mark, but coming within the short range radar of the convoy".

"At fourteen thirty hours, Greenwich Mean Time, Admiral Scheinholtz contacted Admiral Langston, commanding the Gulf fleet, to request authority to launch a counter-strike against Iranian shore installations, as well as the military airfield outside of Basra, in Iraq, from which the aircraft took off. The time is now 15:10 ladies and gentlemen." The lights were raised. "Any questions?"

With the lights raised to a level at which everyone could see clearly without obscuring the screen, sixteen people stared first at the startling Kelly green eyes of the speaker, and then quickly turned to wait for the only person in the room whose vote counted.

President Andrew Dalton, whose detractors usually referred to the current White House staff as "The Dalton Gang", sat quietly for a few moments before speaking.

"Thank you, Miss. Lynch", he stated flatly. He was not a man to bandy praise about. "Please summarize our political, diplomatic and military options, as you see them, before I open the topic for discussion." At this, his eyes, of equal clarity but with a frayed appearance about them, met Jennifer's. He wanted *her* appraisal of the situation, and *her* recommendations, not those of her bosses or inferiors. The silence remained unbroken, until she spoke.

"What we have here, Mr. President, is a failure to communicate." For an instant the silence remained unbroken, and then, as if by mutual consent, each seemed to finally catch onto the joke. Laughter erupted until it was brought under control by the firm voice, and slightly watery eyes of President Dalton.

"Ladies and gentlemen, please!", he repeated several times in a half hearted manner, until he finally had their undivided attention. Turning then to Jennifer, he continued "Miss Lynch," and he once again resumed his *Presidential* demeanor, "would you please proceed with your analysis". It wasn't a rebuke, exactly, just a reminder of who she was, and where they were.

"Certainly, Mr. President. I actually do mean, however, that we have here an extreme failure to communicate to the Iraqi's just how solid our commitment is to the protection of shipping in international waters, and to the protection of American property and lives around the world."

Our reputation, held over from the days of Viet Nam, gives our enemies hope that in the end, we will "cut and run" like we did before, if only they can hold out long enough, and kill enough people. That's why they're threatening Kuwait again, after our last round there, and why we are always being taunted." She paused for a moment. "We're dealing with a "Market-Place" mentality which assumes that what is being said is always open to negotiation. We would probably lessen the chances for a full scale war in the Middle East, if we take a strongly offensive posture."

"I know," quipped Bruce Javitz, "let's nuke 'em and end this bullshit once and for all!" Javitz, who encouraged the idea that he was an indeterminate relative of the late Senator, was a last minute compromise at the Democratic National Convention in Honolulu. He was placed on the ticket as the candidate for Vice President, primarily to influence the Minority vote—a growing, vociferous segment of the population. At the same time, he helped Dalton, for whom he had great respect, but major disagreements, to carry areas like New York, Philadelphia, and key districts in California.

"Please, Mr. Vice President", continued Lynch, "it isn't necessary to eliminate one's enemies to make offensive action on their part too costly to initiate."

"If you understood the Arab mentality, you would know that there is no cost too high to pay for revenge or face saving, even if it means fifty million deaths!" Martin Daimler, an easy confirmation for Dalton as Secretary of Defense, continued to address Jennifer. "They believe that dying in the service of Allah is the surest way to heaven, and that Allah would never allow an Infidel victory."

"Understood, Mr. Secretary." She had to retrench. "But what I am saying is that if we choose the military option, we ought not to engage in a limited response. There ought to be a large, decisive initial blow that would leave Iraq and possibly Iran incapable of striking back militarily, while bolstering, at the same time, the positions of the moderate Arab states in the area." She paused for just a second before continuing.

"What I am *not* saying is that we ought to choose the Military option. It's my job to present you with these options as I see them, and then to allow you to make your own analysis and decisions."

The President looked around the room. Jennifer had handled Javits adroitly, without his help. She would have made a fine politician, but her interests lay in other directions. "Please continue," said the President.

"Thank you, Mr. President. As I was saying, I believe we need a strong response to this situation, but that an armed incursion would be inappropriate and counter-productive." "What we need," she continued, "is an act that would so devastate and demoralize Saddam, that he would give up his dreams of world domination, while at the same time not provoking a *Jihad.*

"And just what did you have in mind?"

Jennifer's mouth was becoming dry, so she paused for a drink, then continued.

"Although we've been trying to keep a close watch on what has been happening at each of the terrorist training sites, and where the trainees are being sent, this has become increasingly difficult. Due to cutbacks in our budget, we lack the necessary "assets." Her rancor was lost on no one. "For this reason, we increased our cooperation with the Israeli Mosad, our CIA's counterpart in Israel. Unfortunately, Mosad operatives have now become emboldened so that, despite orders from their Prime Minister, they have taken it upon themselves to assassinate a man named Al K'Arrim, one of the architects of the Air France Hijacking in which three hundred people died."

"Unbeknownst to us, the Mosad had, likewise, developed a working relationship with the F.S.B., Russia's Updated version of the old KGB. As strange as this sounds in light of all of the decades that have past, we must remember that the Israelis are a pragmatic people. They will accept a thing on its own terms, and in this case, there turned out to be a common enemy."

"Is this going someplace?" Dalton was becoming annoyed with her increasingly pedantic approach.

"Yes sir," answered Jennifer, haltingly, "but I need to finish the background. Bear with me for a few more minutes." Dalton nodded his ascent, but remained impatient.

"You will recall", continued Jennifer, "that after "Desert Storm", things seemed to settle down for a short period. Since then Hussein, not having been removed from power, has repeatedly threatened everything from re-invasion to an attack on the US, itself." She paused again for effect, then concluded with, "and you'll remember that with the Chinese espionage coup discovered in '99, some of our most advanced nuclear weapons and missile designs have been for sale on the open market— another victory for budget cuts." She had to get this last jibe in, and no one answered because most of them had been in government when the events took place, and had taken part in the financial castration of the very agencies that could have prevented that disaster, or at least limited its effects.

"Two weeks ago, a message was intercepted by a Russian agent in Kabul, in which reference was made to "The Apple." He thought nothing of this, but passed it along to his superior who, in turn, passed a seemingly innocuous message to his Israeli counterpart—standard procedure. Itzchak Cohen is a man of uncommon insight, but more importantly, in this case, he is not a sabra. He was born and raised in Manhattan, and lived on Long Island until his early thirties, when he decided to emigrate to Israel, and enter service in the Mosad. It was fortunate for us that he did, because he was able to put together things that would by-pass the average Israeli. He began to believe that references in that and other messages, referred to New York, and to some activity involving it, most likely destructive in nature."

Jennifer remained quiet—this was the test. If they believed her, then she would get the resources she needed to fight this situation. If not...well, the consequences in destruction and loss of human life were staggering.

"Why can't we simply bomb the training camps?", asked Marshall Lakewood. The general was the Army Chief of Staff, and represented his branch of the service among the "Joint Chiefs". "Wouldn't that crimp their style for a while?" The general was a superb tactician and military strategist, but his grasp of Middle Eastern thought was lacking by several degrees. It was not by chance that, though senior, he was by-passed by the President in appointing Admiral Stuart Hallsey to be Chairman of the Joint Chiefs.

Hallsey was a brilliant man, and one who never, under any circumstances underestimated his adversary. He took every opportunity to learn the way his enemy thinks, and to put himself into his place. "Know your enemy as you know yourself...," Sun Tzu had said, and Hallsey never forgot it.

"Don't be such an asshole, Marshall!", Hallsey began, looking disdainfully at Lakewood. "It's the excuse those bastards would need to claim that the United States is bombing innocent women and children, and that such acts more than justify what they are doing. No! Any military response we take has to address the immediate situation, without widening the current conflict beyond its present boundaries."

"I think Admiral Hallsey has a valid point", the President began, and I would prefer to limit our discussion, today, to what our response to this one particular attack should be. We can address the larger situation at another time."

"But", began Jennifer, not understanding why the President was choosing to limit their alternatives even before she had presented hers. "Mr. President, I..."

"Thank you, Miss Lynch." It was clearly an order from the Commander-In-chief to sit down and shut up. She did.

"Admiral, I believe you were going to suggest an alternative reaction to our present situation."

"Mr. President," the others waited, "I think we should take out a military target of major importance to the Iraqis, but only one that either took part in the attack, or could have taken part in the attack. Specifically, I believe we should attack the base from which the gunboats operate, and the base from which the missiles were fired". He paused for a deep breath. "That way, there is an immediate connection between the two events, and even the Iranians can't say that we were the aggressor, without first admitting their culpability in the attack."

"Discussion?", asked the president.

"Mr. President," Jennifer began, "I think we really ought to consider other options in light of the information which I presented earlier."

"Thank you, Ms. Lynch." The President had again dismissed her remarks, and returned to the remainder of the group.

"Very well then, ladies and gentlemen, I can assume that…" His voice trailed off as he watched several symbols converge in the area of the Indian Ocean, and the border of the screen began flashing red.

"Sir!" A young ensign had entered the room, red, yellow and blue security badges dangling from his uniform, and handed the President a single piece of paper.

"Thank you, Ensign." The young man turned about face and left the room.

Looking up from the message, the President cleared his throat and began, "I have just been informed that there has been another attack on a convoy moving north in the Indian Ocean, and under the protection of our flag. No military or American Flag vessels have been damaged, but one neutral has been sunk, and one more is burning. I think our decision has been made." The mood in the situation room was now resolute. "See to it Admiral Hallsey."

"Yes sir, Mr. President", responded Hallsey, assuming his full military bearing. The President, however, had already left the room before the sentence was complete. "Yes sir", repeated Admiral Hallsey to the absent President.

One by one, in silence, they all left their seats and the room except for the petite figure at the other end of the table. Jennifer stared at "The Wall" without moving, for several minutes. Then, with no further hesitation in her movement, left the room as well, but with other things on her mind.

Chapter 4

Mark had left Philadelphia's International Terminal in overcast weather, and a more overcast mood. When he had attempted to discuss the problems in their marriage and possible solutions with Meredith before leaving for the airport, she had retorted that she had no intention of rehashing all of the things they had been through so many times before. They had agreed, several times, to see a marriage counselor, but she never seemed to find time to go, nor had they separated. In essence, since their sex life had long since disintegrated into an occasional physical engagement at her whim, and had lately ceased to include even this small token of affection, their relationship had degenerated into that of roommates who had a common interest only in their children.

Mark had begged her to accompany him to London, saying that they needed to renew their relationship without interference from parents, children, friends, or anybody else. She found this argument to be specious, and chose to remain at home, simply wishing him a "good time." What was worse, he was afraid she really meant it!

Wandering aimlessly around London, now, he began to feel the evening cold begin to bite through his inadequate jacket, and cause the chills that he sometimes experienced, even at temperatures that didn't seem to warrant it. Realizing that he had been walking for hours with only two glasses of Tequila for nourishment, he looked around to get his bearings. Unfortunately, the street names gave him no clue as to the direction from which he had come, nor which way to go to return, so he decided to hail a taxi.

He felt even more morose when the door to the boxy black London cab opened to deposit him, once again, in front of the covered marble, from where he made his way back to the bar for more "nourishment." He knew this had to stop, but he went in none the less, and spent the next several hours making sure that he would feel no cold.

When he finally arrived at his room and entered, it took most of his will to simply remove his clothes and drop them on the floor. The small amount of remaining will was distributed between asking the operator to awaken him at nine thirty the following morning and falling onto the bed. His final thought, as he sunk into the oblivion of an unaccustomed alcoholic stupor being—" 'tis a consummation devoutly to be wished." He wasn't sure why, but it seemed appropriate at the time.

When the telephone rang the following morning, Mark grabbed for the handset three times before actually grasping it.

"Sir", intoned the cheerful voice, "you asked to be awakened at nine thirty."

"Thank you", retorted a slightly befuddled and definitely fuzzy voice, and then he tried twice before finally replacing the handset in its cradle. "Shit!", thought Mark, and rolled over to return to his stupor.

By eleven-thirty, Mark's eyes began to focus on the small brown travel clock he had carried with him for nearly fifteen years. He knew there were better, more accurate, and modern clocks he could carry in his bag, but somehow, he always brought this one.

"Well", he thought, "guess it's time to get up." He felt fairly well at this point, albeit somewhat weak, but the moment his head left the pillow, the alcohol regained control, and his flight to the bathroom and the waiting toilet bowl could only be judged a draw.

After about an hour of clinging to the cool porcelain of the bowl, he finally began to feel as though living might be a tolerable alternative. When he returned to his room, he found that he had neglected to place the "Do Not Disturb" sign on the outer handle of the door, so the maid had evidently cleaned, made the bed, and left, while tactfully avoiding the "person" in the bathroom for so long.

Staring at himself in the mirror atop the dresser, the only words that would come to mind, escaped his dry lips in a whisper—"Oh Jesus!" He rarely stared at himself in a mirror, but the haggard, unshaven face staring back at him was not what he usually expected to see when he did. "Shit!", he repeated his earlier remark and, taking his toilet kit with him, returned to the somewhat rank bathroom, emerging, about forty minutes later, showered, shaved, teeth brushed, and feeling more himself (although he doubted that he would feel really well for at least another twenty-four hours).

He dressed in a tweed sport coat and gray trousers, and put his burgundy Bass Loafers back on (he always traveled with them because they went with nearly everything). Finally, he gathered his wallet, keys, and sundry "junk" he had accumulated (OK, he was a "pack rat" and he knew it), stuffed these into his pockets, and left his room to attend the afternoon scientific sessions.

"*Newer Antibiotic Prophylaxis in Rheumatic Valvulopathy*" the white cardboard sign read beside the entrance to a curtained off area of the large convention center where the lecture was scheduled to begin in ten minutes. Carelessly, Mark found an empty seat and slid his slightly larger than usual girth into it, commenting to a not yet looked at colleague about the upcoming lecture.

"By the way", began Mark, holding out his hand, "I'm Mark Harmon."

"Basil, Sir. Richard." intoned a mass of tweed in the next seat, as though presenting himself, last name first, for indexing.

"Pleased to meet you," returned Mark, just as the lecturer began his dissertation.

"With the advent of the third generation broad spectrum antibiotics, a new era dawned in the Prophylaxis of Valvular Vegetations and Endocarditis." Mark made little attempt to stifle a yawn, and began doodling on the yellow legal style pad provided for him in his symposium packet. By the end of the half hour lecture, Mark's headache had returned, and he was considering returning to the bar for a "hair of the dog." "Why not," he thought to himself, and passed through the marble lobby, now bright with sunlight streaming through the large, partially curtained windows, and through the vaguely remembered stained glass doors into the hotel pub.

"Tequila, straight up", and nearly as quickly as the words left his lips, it appeared in front of him. First one, then another drink found its way to his stomach, returning him to a state of comfort. "Time to get out of here," he thought.

He had just exited the front door to get some air, when a limousine discharged a dark man, in his mid-fifties, onto the cement in front of the hotel door. Although Mark paid little attention, it was only seconds later, when the man collapsed at his feet.

Quickly, Mark dropped to the man's side, and rolled him over as the physician in him took control. Feeling no jugular pulse, he initiated a routine that had been so ingrained that he never actually realized when he began. The man was clutching his fist across his chest, as though to help him stand the pain he must be in. With great strength, Mark pried the arm away from the chest in order to begin compressing the heart and, when the man's fist opened, took the matchbook he had been grasping when he fell and placed it in his own jacket pocket, thinking only of the man's life. As he placed the heel of his hand against the unconscious man's sternum to begin CPR, he noticed the small, but spreading, deep red stain in the middle of an expensive white shirt. Tearing it open, Mark tried, unsuccessfully, to compress the wound with his hands, while yelling at no one in particular to call an ambulance. Minutes later, the ambulance came and went, leaving Mark to stare at his blood caked hands. As people, gathered around and began hurling unintelligible questions, he wandered back into the lobby to return to his room, when a hand lightly but firmly grasped his right shoulder.

"Sir." Mark turned, finding himself face to face with a rather pink faced young man wearing the uniform of a "Bobby". "Sir," repeated the officer again, "would you be kind enough to come with me for a statement." the words framed a question, but the lack of a rising inflection at the end of the sentence made it clear that this was a direction rather than a request.

"I really don't…", began Mark, cleared his dry throat and continued, "don't know anything officer. I was only walking out of the door when it happened. I'm a doctor, you see, and…". He was cut short by the young policeman who explained that he was a material witness, and would need to give a statement anyway.

"OK, but would you mind if I cleaned up a bit?"

"Not at all sir, however I'll have to accompany you to your room."

"No problem", said Mark, come on", and he led the way through the lobby to the "lift", and together went to Mark's room.

Across the street, in a "Westminster Blue" Jaguar, binoculars were deposited on the tan leather passenger seat, and a gloved hand punched a series of numbers terminated by the "SND" button on the cellular telephone without lifting the handset.

"It's done", the voice betrayed no hint of affect. "There was a man by his side, who grabbed him as he fell. I have no idea who he is."

"Find out!", ordered the voice at the other end, and static filled the passenger cabin of the car. Again the gloved hand stabbed at the handset of the car phone, this time at the "END" button to disconnect.

Three hours later, after a comfortable but thorough interrogation, he was returned to his hotel, where he resumed his retreat. This time, he walked determinedly to the coffee shop for some much needed food. Later, after transferring a few pounds to the concierge, he returned to his room with a new bottle of Jose Cuervo Tequila in a black plastic bag tucked under his arm.

The man he had tried to save earlier today had been the oldest son of a wealthy middle-eastern family, in London on holiday. The police had no motive for the killing, but were always suspicious of any crime involving someone (especially someone prominent) from that part of the world.

"I can't believe it!", thought Mark, and turned to look at himself in the mirror. For the second night in a row, weariness overcame him as he undressed. Once again, he spread the contents of his pockets on the dresser, this time managing to fold his clothes, only later remembering that they had to be given to the Valet in the morning, to be cleaned and pressed. He lay back and was asleep before he realized he had even closed his eyes.

Awakening brought Mark Harmon no closer to being refreshed. He was again hung over, and was half way to the bathroom when he actually looked around. Strewn about the room were various pieces of his clothes, bags, and belongings, several drawers were left, not quite open, but slightly ajar, the overall effect being somewhat disquieting. It was as though someone had searched his room while he slept, tried to make it look as though they hadn't been there, but had finally given up and let the few remaining things lay where they fell.

His first reaction was to snatch his wallet from the dresser to examine it. All of his money, credit cards, etc., were in place. The pictures of his family were undisturbed, and none of his other possessions seemed to be missing. His memory of how he had left them when he had undressed the night before was clouded by an alcoholic haze, so he had no idea whether they had been rearranged. He was confused after two days of unaccustomed drinking, a murder, and the realization that someone had been in his room last night while he slept. Mark sat in the deep blue, tufted, high backed chair next to the small table in his room, cradled his forehead in his hands, and shut his eyes. "Perhaps," he thought, "when I open my eyes, it will all go away."

Chapter 5

"O230:00," read the deep red digits of the clock on the bulkhead just above the thick glass plates separating the bridge crew of the Enterprise from the nearly absolute blackness of the night. No stars were visible through the thick clouds that lay less than three thousand meters above the gently rolling flight deck. The only light came from the Enterprise and her companion ships gliding silently through the Indian Ocean, south of the Persian Gulf.

John Vincent, Lieutenant Commander, U.S.N., stood the watch on the bridge. He had done so, at this time, for the last several weeks. He was the second of his family to have chosen a career in the navy, having grown up as a navy "brat." His father served before him, through three wars, and retired as a Chief Petty Officer. John's light complexion and sandy colored hair gave little hint of the southern Mediterranean origin of his family, or the "e" that originally adorned the name—"Vincente."

At the moment, all was quiet. Only the small number of the flight deck crew needed to make ready for the impending arrival of the two electronic surveillance helicopters ("Essies") were moving about below.

On the bridge, no one even noticed the eerie reddish or greenish color imparted to people and equipment alike by the overhead lights and the glowing LED's of the myriad instruments on the panels.

"Bridge, C.I.C.", even the tone of the intercom merely broke the silence without shattering it.

"Bridge, Vincent", the reply left Commander Vincent's lips before he had even realized he had recited his half of the formula.

"Commander, Emory here." Vincent could picture the owlish face of Robert Emory, made even more so by the round glasses he wore, staring at the banks of radar, sonar, and computer displays, below, as he kept the part of the watch under his command.

"Go ahead, Bob." Vincent replied.

"Sir", began Emory, "I'm picking up our inbound "Essies" about three *klicks* out, but there are six "bogies" approaching just above the surface, from land, well behind them." Vincent frowned, but said nothing.

Hearing no reply, Emory continued. "This has been confirmed by both Essies, and they are standing by for orders." The finality at the end of the sentence reminded Commander Vincent of the weight of command. The next fifteen seconds seemed like an eternity. If he acted prematurely, he would seem a rash fool to the Captain and the Admiral, as well as the crew (not to mention himself). On the other hand, if these were real incoming "bogies"....

The hesitation was unnoticed by anyone but Vincent himself.

"Boson". A slight hesitation again, followed by, "Sound General Quarters, and alert the fleet!"

Then, without hesitation, Vincent's index finger depressed the square blue LED on the right arm of the swivel chair in which he sat, and suddenly, as the harsh sound of the ships klaxon shattered the blackness, he spoke into the concealed microphone—"Captain, to the bridge!" Soon, the responsibility for what lay ahead would be squarely on the shoulders of those above him, and he would again be merely "following orders." He hoped he was correct, but he hoped he was wrong just as much.

As he awaited the arrival of the Captain, he noted with some satisfaction that the running lights of the Enterprise, as well as all other ships within his direct view had been extinguished, and that the fleet had become nearly invisible unless one knew where to look.

On deck, partially dressed sailors were preceded by their fully dressed shipmates to "Battle Stations", while below, other officers and crew proceeded to theirs.

Captain McCarthy (Buck, to his few close friends) raced down the companionway and through the hatch to the bridge, trying to complete buttoning his shirt while still holding his cap tucked under his arm. It would be only about a minute before Admiral Scheinholtz would follow suit and rush into C.I.C., knowing that the ship was being taken care of, and that his duty was to command the battle group.

"What's up, John?", demanded the Captain, as the blare of the klaxon finally ceased.

"Sir", began Commander Vincent, after exhaling the deep breath he had taken to calm himself, "C.I.C. reports six incoming bogies bearing 045 degrees relative, at just under Mach one." He paused to catch his breath. "Additionally", continued Vincent, "There are four more bogies about ten *klicks* behind them. Identity remains unknown, sir." The outward calm resulting from years of training and simulation, as well as the attack that took place only days earlier, belied the tension John felt inside.

"Right", answered the Captain in an equally matter-of-fact tone, coming from years of combat experience. "Let's find out!"

Now seated in the swivel chair so recently occupied by Vincent, McCarthy quietly addressed the seaman seated forward and to his left.

"Helm", he began, "evasive action".

Depressing the green button under his index finger, he spoke to Flight Control;

"Launch intercepts." Within seconds, pilots and aircraft that had been awaiting some order, were airborne and being vectored by the worlds most sophisticated combination of shipboard, airborne, and space based combat tracking and navigation systems to their targets.

"Buck!" The raspy voice of William Schienholtz sounded hollow as it echoed across the bridge from the wall speaker.

"On the Bridge, Admiral", responded McCarthy.

"Buck", repeated Admiral Scheinholtz, "I'm in C.I.C., and we're showing multiple bogies at 050 relative. I've ordered the group to disperse, except for our destroyer escort."

"Understood, Admiral", responded McCarthy, and the tone in his voice became a standard "battle calm."

Two decks below, "Wild Bill" Schienholtz's face reflected the soft red and green lighting of the displays and readouts that he had been so intently studying. On a miniature version of "The Wall", he watched as the American F-14 "Tomcats" approached their targets, and waited tensely for some word. Slowly, two groups of four blue triangles closed with the twelve red circles, about 200 kilometers northeast of their position. There was nothing to do now but wait. The ships' air conditioning, functioning perfectly, did nothing to prevent the little beads of perspiration that formed on the Admiral's forehead. Minutes passed, and time seemed to stand still. "They're so close" thought Scheinholtz to himself, "why can't they see them?"

As though in answer, the speaker boomed with the voice of a young pilot whom he never recalled having met—"Tally Ho!" The recognition of the enemy, as old as combat aviation, brought a small, unnoticed smile to the corners of Scheinholtz's mouth. He had been a pilot himself when he was younger. His mind sat briefly in the cockpit of the F-104 over Korea, then returned to the Combat Information Center of the Enterprise.

"Enterprise, Cobra leader", bellowed the speaker. "Five…, no make it six Silkworms closing rapidly, with six Phantoms about twenty klicks behind. Beginning attack!"

"Weapons Control", McCarthy directed his remarks.

"Weapons Control Aye", answered the lieutenant currently manning the weapons console.

"Activate A.D.S." intoned McCarthy, and a one square meter transparent panel mounted just forward, and to the left of the helm and radar displays sprang to life, showing the relative positions and identification of all participants in this "game".

"All systems green", replied the young officer, whose face was obscured by the shadows of the bridge. "All weapons on full automatic and locked on target. Targets still one-eight kilometers beyond range at this time, but continuing to close". The tension in his voice caused it to crack. He wasn't "seasoned" but despite the fear, his training prevailed.

"Activate E.D.S. and I.D.S. systems now" returned McCarthy, and within ten seconds, six drones were launched carrying electronic defense systems, infrared defense systems, chaff, and sundry other defensive gear to confuse enemy aircraft and missiles before they could reach their target. Along the Starboard rail, the Aegis anti-missile systems continued tracking.

"Bridge, C.I.C.", "Silkworms spreading out following defense drones, but Enemy aircraft continue to approach." Almost simultaneously, the slightly tinny echo of the radio speaker blurted "Enterprise, Cobra Leader, beginning engagement!"

The next three minutes were the entire time occupied by the battle that was unfolding more than eighty kilometers from the fleet. During this time, all otherwise unoccupied eyes on the bridge were riveted upon the A.D.S. panel, and listening to the voices of the pilots and crews comprising the blue triangles on the screen, engaging the red triangles.

"Snake, you and Fox take the two to the north, we'll try to split off the other four."

"Roger. Let's go, Snake, it's party time!"

"Coming around now, almost have…there! Tone on bogie one!" Seconds later—"He's gone to Allah."

"Bogie two is in paradise now, also!" The voice appeared to be that of the pilot called "Snake", but no one could be sure at this point.

"Cobra leader, Fox, here comes the cavalry!"

"Come join the fun, guys, but three bogies are already gone", replied another, as yet unidentified voice". The A.D.S. board confirmed, all but one of the incoming Phantoms were gone, and all silkworms had been sufficiently deflected by the E.D.S./I.D.S. systems to pose no further threat. "Coming around for the shot on Bogie six. Too close, going to guns. A little more, a little more...there!" And the last red triangle disappeared from the screen.

"Enterprise, Cobra leader, we're coming home."

"Roger, Cobra, well done!", replied Captain McCarthy, finally allowing himself the luxury of sweating.

"Maintain General Quarters, turn into the wind and stand down A.D.S." The captain relaxed for the first time in several minutes.

Below, in C.I.C., Admiral Schienholtz picked up a red telephone, flipped the cover from the digital keypad and, after entering a six character code, said simply—"patch me through to the Pentagon." Seconds later, the booming, unmistakable voice of Stuart Hallsey, Admiral, Chairman of the Joint Chiefs of Staff, confident of the President, and a lifelong friend of Bill Scheinholtz answered—"This better be good, Bill!"

Five minutes and thirty one seconds later, Hallsey expelled a breath he felt like he had held throughout the entire description of the battle. His only reply—"Stand by for orders, Admiral," and the line assumed that slightly static laden tone that tells you that you are secure and haven't been cut off, merely placed on "hold". Buck Scheinholtz held.

The minutes dragged on until the hollow tone of the "secure" line returned. "Recall all aircraft. Head due south, and, once out of range, exit the gulf." The line went dead.

Steinholtz stared at the handset still clutched in his hand. He was in command of more sheer destructive power than was used in all of World War Two. At a word, that pip-squeak country could be made uninhabitable, or a surgical strike could vaporize military and industrial targets, while leaving the general population untouched and unharmed. The entire gamut of response was at his fingertips, and he was to turn tail and run. Not until the silence was shattered by the harsh quality of the intercom did he replace the handset, straighten up, and remember that he was an officer in the United States Navy. He had been given an order, for reasons he didn't understand, but his duty was clear.

"Captain", the word had difficulty escaping his throat. "Signal all ships to come about. Make due south." His finger moved to the lighted, touch sensitive blue square, and with the lightest of touches, turned off the intercom and ended any possible discussion. Then he turned, ducked as he passed through the hatch, and strode down the companionway to his quarters, where a half liter of Stolichnaya vodka, provided to him by a Russian Admiral he had befriended in Murmansk, made the gnawing feeling in his gut bearable, but just.

Chapter 6

Date: Monday, 09-Jul-01 1834:00
>
> From: kwt_1\num_1_kwt@terra.gov
> To: rus_1\ num_1_rus@terra.gov
> cc: usa_1\num_1_usa@terra.gov
>
> Subject: Re: Sandman
>
> Sandman not problem now. Proceed with operation. Wonder if any
   info passed during resolution.
>————————End Message. No reply needed.————————

Mustafa's "shrapnel" began to hurt again as his Jeep bounced along what barely passed for a road. The boulder strewn terrain was nearly invisible in the moonlight, but light was not necessary, which was good since the captured Israeli Jeep that he now drove was running without headlights. He knew the road well. He was traveling toward a point at which a centuries-old olive tree bordered a sharp twist to the right. There were no further thoughts in Mustafa's mind than those of reaching his destination.

With each bounce, the pain in his leg grew, and his determination to ignore it grew equally. He was alone in the Jeep. He knew the drill. He would park the Jeep just off of the road around the bend, past the olive tree. There, he would walk due south, about thirty meters to a large somewhat flattened boulder, next to which there would be a small, irregularly shaped rock. Under the rock would be a goatskin pouch, similar to the one in Moustafa's wall cache. Within this pouch would be his instructions, sealed, yet another time, within a waterproof plastic bag.

Mustafa had driven for nearly thirty minutes before he spotted the enormous knurled tree he had been looking for. He maintained his speed until the last moment so anyone following would be unaware that he was about to depart from his current route, then swung the rear of the car both around the bend, and around to the opposite direction. His speed, carried him over the rough terrain and slightly into the woods. To anyone following more that a few meters behind, he would have seemed to simply disappear around the bend, and never reappear.

Sitting for a moment to collect his thoughts, Mustafa had just begun to painfully swing his left leg out of the Jeep, when a raspy voice sounded from behind a knoll, invisible in the inky blackness that enveloped them. He froze as they exchanged appropriate signs and passwords. This was the man with whom Mustafa had talked earlier this evening. He had arranged the "drop", and was the man whose face Mustafa had envisioned so many different ways, depending upon his mood.

"Allah Achbar", The voice intoned quietly from within the night.

"Allah Achbar", Mustafa replied, but with just a hint of the uncertainty and confusion he felt . "I didn't…, I wasn't…", he cleared his throat, and began again, when he was cut short by the disembodied voice.

"You are surprised that I am hear, yes?"

"Yes", was all that Mustafa could manage. With all his training, and despite his refusal to accept the reality, he remained in awe of his superiors, and thought of them, when he thought of them at all, in the same way a peasant thinks of the baron, upon whose land he would live and die. He was theirs, by right, to command. To disobey, he had been conditioned, was as unimaginable as his own death.

"You have been summoned here for a special purpose tonight. There will be no message for you to read." As the voice paused, the transient glow of a cigarette lighter silhouetted the hill behind which it remained, only its relative position now revealed, as though to demonstrate trust.

Resuming, "In two days, you will pack a small bag, containing nothing personal, and board the local bus that will carry you to Tarabulus, from which you will be driven by your contact to Beirut. Once there, you will register at a hotel selected at random by you, and send a message, through the regular channels, to alert us to where you are staying, and by what means you can be reached." The voice paused, and the slight glow behind the knoll informed Mustafa that he awaited the exhalation of smoke before his directions would continue. "That is all for now." He had been "dismissed", like a child at school. It was final.

Turning, without any word, Mustafa retreated to the familiarity of his Jeep, started the motor on his second attempt, and drove, slowly at first, then gaining speed, back onto the road and in the direction from which he had so recently come. He had things to do before he left for Beirut. They must be done quickly, but give no hint of anxiety or anticipation. Nothing out of the ordinary, just a routine trip on even more routine business.

Already, Mustafa was beginning to formulate his cover story. he would complain, loudly, about having to travel that distance, to see his cousin in Damascus. He hated having to go there, but under the circumstances (which he had not yet thought of), what could he do?

Arriving back at his base camp, he went immediately to guard post number 4, where he knew that Miryam would be on duty. Each time he thought of her, his manhood would become evident, and perspiration would begin to appear on his forehead and armpits. She was a soldier, a comrade in arms in a holy cause, yet the mere thought of her sent a tremor through his body. As Mustafa opened the door to the guardhouse, Miryam and an unknown private snapped to attention. They were young, and the glory of military life had not yet worn off.

"Sergeant!" Mustafa snapped, looking at Miryam, "you are relieved of this duty. Come with me. "He turned and walked into the cool, dry desert night knowing that Miryam would be in step behind him, and would continue to follow him until he gave her some other order. He was always amazed at the gullibility of these young people, and their ability to be led. "Stupid!", he had thought to himself many times. None the less, he would not trade his current position for a more equitable one. Miryam was following him into his hut where she "halted" as he shut the door.

"Disrobe!", he commanded, and without question, her combat fatigues began dropping to the floor. Mustafa had poured himself a glass of Ouso, then followed it with another. She fell into his arms as he launched himself into her body with an abandon that suited neither of them, but that each one wanted in their own way, and for their own reasons. He for the release of tension and emotional control it provided, she for the personal and political advantages it could hold. Each loved the act itself, but would not have been there had not the other motives existed. They weren't considering that right now.

As minutes seemed to stretch into hours, and time took on a new meaning, their hands probed, stroked, kneaded, and caressed various parts of each other's bodies. They had been together before, and each knew secret places on the other that raised ecstasy to a new level each time they made love. Slowly, their sweat soaked bodies began to move rhythmically, together. He rammed in and out as she attempted to hold him inside her as long as she could. Time after time, their arms entwined, they reached the precipice, and stepped back. Only now, when neither of them could bear more excitation without bursting, did they allow themselves to peak, he with a deep inspiration through his clenched teeth, and she with a low scream, muted by her mouth against his left shoulder.

Two hours later, Mustafa awakened, to find his bed once more empty except for himself. He knew she had returned to her post where no explanation would be required. Rolling over, he raised himself, with some difficulty, to his right elbow and, after finishing the remaining part of a glass of Ouso, he lit another of his Russian cigarettes, and settled back to allow himself the luxury of a blank mind. Minutes passed, with Mustafa observing smoke curl to the ceiling and spread out into a barely visible mushroom, which dissipated if not added to. "Enough", thought Mustafa, crushed his half smoked cigarette against the butts remaining in the bottom of the chipped ashtray, turned out the light, and was almost immediately asleep.

When he awakened, after showering, brushing his teeth, and putting on a pair of fatigues with just the right amount of "worn" look to them, he left his hut and went to the mess hall for breakfast. There, his table awaited him. No one would be sitting there until he did, and then, not until invited—"R.H.I.P.". Today, no one was invited. His breakfast consisted of coffee with cream and three teaspoons of sugar, bread and a soft goat cheese. It was a meal he preferred, and was waiting for him nearly every morning.

Slowly, while eating, his mind began to clear of the previous evening's activities, and to concentrate on the tasks at hand. First, he needed an excuse to suddenly leave camp to visit his cousin in Damascus. That should be no problem, his cousin was known to have developed a "bad heart", and that would be good enough.

Next, his mind ranged over what he would pack to take with him. Having no specific instructions, he knew that what he took would only be used temporarily. He would be given further instructions later, and his area of operation would determine his attire. Opening the worn chest of drawers that had served him for many years, he withdrew a khaki shirt and dark green pants, as well as a pair of jeans that were just worn enough to be comfortable. These, he placed in the soft brown leather bag he would carry, along with a white shirt, dark red tie with a "University" stripe design, and a carefully folded blue suit and black shoes. Topping the bag were his underwear, socks, sneakers, and toiletries. the entire bag weighed only a few kilos, and would fit neatly under the seat of a bus or airplane. He knew better than to ever have to wait in lines for his baggage.

The time had come. Mustafa went to the headquarters area and, when nobody was paying attention, lifted the handset of a telephone and pretended to be listening. After speaking quietly to the dial tone for several moments, he loudly proclaimed that he saw no reason that he should have to leave to attend his cousin, whom he was not overly fond of anyway. None the less, after allowing the non-existent relative to speak for several more seconds, and failing several attempts to interrupt, he reluctantly, but loudly agreed to come to Damascus and make sure that his cousin got well after his "heart problem."

Cursing his fate, Mustafa left the headquarters tent and returned to his own hut where he assessed his performance. "Not bad", he thought, although he may have protested too much. "Well, never mind", he answered himself, it was believable, could be made confirmable, and would be questioned by no one.

By 07:30 the next morning, after "entertaining" both a petite lieutenant and a corporal at the same time, he boarded the antique and somewhat unstable blue bus that would carry him to Tarabulus. Placing his pre-packed leather bag beneath his seat with its end touching his ankle so that any movement of it would alert him, he sat back to close his eyes and rest. Rest and food, he had been taught, were always at a premium and were to be savored even if not needed. One never knew when one would have to do without either, so make use of them whenever you can. He did.

By 11:30, the bus on which Mustafa traveled was rolling along on paved roads, so the ride had become much smoother. Awaked by the lack jolting to which he had become accustomed, he found himself about to pass through the center of the city of Tarabulus, and into the slightly more run down district where the bus usually made its stop.

At exactly 12:12, his hand slapped at the bell resting upon the slightly dusty, but otherwise clean counter in the nondescript "Bed and

Breakfast" type of Inn that he preferred. There were so many of these in each city, that they were hard to keep track of. They went into and out of business regularly, and kept little or no records of whom their guests were. Their primary interest, confirmed by his conversation with the slightly built, balding man with the cigarette dangling from his mouth, was with payment, and the rules designed to keep the building intact, and the police away. Everything else was of no concern to them.

The room to which he was directed, was at the rear of the second floor hallway, next to the single bathroom. He liked the location, but found the lack of a second stairway mildly disturbing. He liked another escape route, but remembered that every additional route of escape was also a potential entrance for an enemy. "Well, no matter."

With great care, he took the neatly folded suit from the bag, and hung it in the closet along with his white shirt, tie, and the leather jacket he had included at the last minute. The remainder of his belongings he left in the bag, then tossed it onto one of two threadbare chairs in the room, and left, making sure to not only lock the door behind him, but to wedge a small piece of dust between the door and the jam. Finding it on the floor on his return would alert him that the door had been opened in his absence. In that event, he would not enter the room, but simply continue on to the bathroom as though he was another guest. Upon completion of his "business", he would leave the Inn and all of his belongings behind and find another place to stay. He would be uninterested in who entered the room, only in that it was entered, and that he needed to abandon that location.

Walking the two blocks to a small druggist shop he knew from previous visits to Tarabulus, he went inside and bought a pack of cigarettes. He paid for them with a bill of small denomination, upon which he had previously written information about his whereabouts and methods by which he could be reached. This done, he casually crossed the street to have a glass of wine, and read what passed for news in the paper he had just purchased.

Within twenty minutes, a battered, elderly light blue Subaru glided to a stop a meter from the curb. The driver, an olive complected youth whose lack of facial hair defied convention, politely requested that Mustafa accompany him. With exaggerated nonchalance, Mustafa finished the last bit of his second drink, folded his paper under his arm, and got into the car on the passenger's side where, saying nothing, he simply sat back waiting to find out where he was going.

Ten minutes later, after driving in some curious circles that were apparently suppose to confuse him, Mustafa was deposited in front of The Palace, a hotel with much local color and flare and directed to room 302.

The door opened into a passageway which led to small, but comfortable sitting room. So far, there had been no words exchanged, and only an occasional gesture. This changed when a portly man, in his early fifties (or so Mustafa guessed) entered the room and sat in one of the heavily upholstered chairs.

"Sit, my friend." It was said courteously, and quietly, but the aura of command demanded obedience.

"You are about to be given an assignment that will help change the way the world perceives us, what it gives us, and the way we exist." There was a pause before continuing, then, "You have been chosen because of your dedication to our cause, your ability to follow orders, but most of all, because of your success in past missions. If you are compromised, the mission cannot be allowed to suffer. You will be killed quickly, painlessly, and replaced with another. You understand that this is a necessity. It has nothing whatever to do with you personally. If I were to fail in my part, the same fate would be mine." There was another pause to allow this to sink in. When Mustafa's mouth began to open, the other man raised his hand slightly, and further discussion was cut off.

"When you leave here, you will be given instructions for the pickup and delivery of a package. You will make whatever arraignments you find necessary to deliver this package to a locker at Kennedy International Airport in New York, then, after a short stay in a hotel of your choosing, will return here. You are cautioned not to allow the contents of the package to fall into anyone's hands. Should such an eventuality seem likely, you will destroy it, along with yourself, if necessary." Yet another pause. "Is any of this unclear?"

"Clear", intoned Mustafa with finality. His head was spinning with questions, but no answers were offered. Why was he chosen instead of an expendable courier?

"It has been a pleasure meeting you, Mustafa", stated the portly gentleman in soothing tones. "I hope we have a chance to discuss our mutual parts in this venture at some future time."

Mustafa knew that he had been dismissed. He rose, and re-entered the small anti-room, Where the man who had originally answered the door, handed him a small white envelope, on the outside of which was printed in neat Arabic—"Destroy after reading". It seemed an unnecessary instruction.

Standing outside the door again, the same car awaited him. Once inside, the driver handed him a slightly worn leather wallet, in which he found an Israeli passport, several credit cards, a driver's license, and five thousand U.S. Dollars, as well as small amounts of local currency. The driver pointed to the floor next to Mustafa where a valise was sitting, and drove to the "frontier", where Mustafa was transferred to a boat, thence to another car, which drove him to Tel Aviv and directly to Ben Gurion airport.

By 16:00, Mustafa was abroad El Al flight 251 for Paris, and within several hours, was crossing the North Atlantic abroad the Concorde in supersonic luxury. Terrorists weren't supposed to be traveling First Class, so it was felt that this was the best way to get through the United States Customs.

By 21:00, Eastern Daylight Time, Mustafa was ensconced abroad the Metroliner bound for Manhattan from Washington, DC (where his flight had landed), and had phoned ahead for reservations at the Plaza.

If this mission were as important as everyone said, then he might as well go "First Cabin" all the way.

As Mustafa sat in the ornately upholstered chair opposite his valise, he rubbed his eyes, took the last of his Russian cigarettes from the silver case he so loved and, after lighting it, inhaled the smoke deeply into his lungs. He reached back into his memory, visualizing the few terse sentences he had committed to memory earlier in the day. By 09:00 of the following day, he was to deposit a briefcase he would receive in a locker at Kennedy International Airport. He had no key. the locker would be left slightly ajar, and he was to close it and allow it to lock automatically. There were no more instructions except those for the meeting to obtain the briefcase, and that he was to leave within five days.

Mustafa had all night in Manhattan, a thought he savored. Though he hated the United States and everything it stood for, there was still no more exciting city anywhere in the world. Nowhere could be found the variety of people, things, places, sounds, smells, and sights.... No other city had built (he remembered the phrase with some difficulty) "canyons of concrete" that literally blotted out the sun and produced echoes for kilometers (miles, he mentally corrected himself, he was in America now).

After showering, and changing into clothes he found in the valise which fit surprisingly well, he opened the Yellow Pages to look for clubs. He felt the need for some entertainment, preferably female. It took only minutes to find what he wanted and, without further rest, he stepped out into the humid evening air, and began the universally frustrating task of hailing a taxi.

Chapter 7

Date: Wednesday, 11-Jul-01 17:26 PM

>

> From: usa_1   \num_1_usa@terra.gov

> To: sov_1   \ num_1_rus@terra.gov

> cc: isr_1   \num_1_isr@terra.gov

> gbr_1   \num_1_gbr@terra.gov

> ira_1   \num_1_ira@terra.gov

>

> Subject: Re: Sandman

>

Sandman gone, but message lost. Am attempting to intercept. Please advise if you are aware of present location.

>————————End Message.————————

When Mark Harmon lifted his head from his hands, he found that more than a half hour had passed. Slowly, he began to gather his thoughts. For nearly an hour, he ruminated upon the previous day's events, looking for some rationale, but none came. He understood why he was behaving the way he was—he was feeling sorry for himself. That's what was causing him to drink to excess. He knew that the murder was startling, but shouldn't have caused him the amount of disquiet he felt. It must have been having his room searched that left him afraid. Realizing this would lead nowhere, he decided to call home to say hello to Meredith and the kids.

"Let's see", he said to no one in particular as he gazed at his watch by way of judging the time back home. With the fiddling he'd been doing in his room, showering, shaving, the breakfast he had eventually ordered served by room service, and the coffee he had consumed, it was just after 1:00 P.M. in London, which left it about 8:00 A.M. at home.

After giving his credit card number to the overseas operator, he listened as the telephone at his home rang several times before being answered.

"Hello? "Meredith's voice seemed strained. "Leave your brother alone!", she shouted to one of the boys before he could even reply.

"Hi, love", he began, and awaited her reply.

"Mark, how nice of you to call." No amount of sarcasm in her voice could keep the sound of it from being comforting after his recent ordeal.

"How are you?", her voice softened slightly, and he breathed a sigh of relief. This was not to be an argument.

"Boy, have I been through the ringer in the last twenty-four hours", he began, but was cut short by her again breaking up some squabble between their sons.

"Mark, I've got my hands full getting the boys off to school right now, why don't you call back a little later."

Anger, resentment, hurt and frustration, all of the emotions that only she could elicit from him at one time, welled up inside him. Here he was, thousands of miles from home, and she simply couldn't make any time to talk to him.

"OK, Love. Talk to you later", with which he replaced the telephone handset in its cradle, and stood up to put his jacket on. No sense fretting about it, it was as it was.

Dressed, feeling somewhat better, and with less apprehension, he closed the door to his room, made sure that it was locked, and walked to the elevators where he stood for only a few moments before the doors opened. Inside, to his amazement, was Jennifer Lynch. He wasn't sure he remembered her name, but those eyes, surrounded by her thick blonde hair had haunted him since he first saw them.

"Hi!", he said with genuine delight. He had found a friend, a fellow traveler, and someone he could, at least, talk with for a little while. "What are you doing here?" he asked, still delighted that she was.

"Excuse me?" Jennifer appeared to have difficulty placing him, then with only a small glimmer of recognition, continued "Oh, yes, how are you?" Her voice conveyed that certain element the busy executive has when faced with an "underling" whom they are supposed to know, but don't remember, but for whom politeness and politics demands a measured response.

"Boy am I glad to see a friendly face here", replied Mark. "Are you busy now? May I buy you lunch?"

"Sorry, I am sort of busy." The elevator doors opened again, and two elderly people entered to stand between Mark and Jennifer, and the doors. This seemed to make her uneasy, and there was no further discussion until they reached the lobby. When they exited the "lift", Mark reminded her of their meeting at GAMMA, and again asked her to join him, at least for a cup of coffee. He seemed harmless enough, and it was probably the only way she could get rid of him.

"OK", she answered, finally, "but only for a few minutes. I really do have to be someplace important."

Sitting at a small table near the window of a nearby restaurant, Mark and Jennifer exchanged pleasantries inquiring about what each of them had been up to. He, of course, related that things were going well, he was in town for a medical symposium, his wife was home, being somewhat indisposed ("besides", he added as an afterthought, "someone has to take care of the kids"), "and what about you?"

"I'm doing some research for a report I have to write", answered Jennifer with some degree of honesty. "Say", she stopped for a moment as if trying to remember something then, as her face unclouded she asked, "didn't I see your picture in the Times this morning?" Without waiting for him to answer, she continued. "Sure, you were the one who tried to save that man who was shot!—the Sheik's son."

"Right", answered Mark, realizing that this was the first time that Jennifer seemed genuinely interested in what he was saying. "He was shot, and I didn't even know it until I pulled his jacket apart to try to do CPR".

Even as Mark was taking a breath to begin his next sentence, a movement at the street corner caught Jennifer's eye, leaving her feeling uneasy.

"Mark…" She stopped without continuing. She was about to explain that she had to leave now, and that she would, perhaps, see him another time, when the glass next to their table shattered, leaving sharp sparkles over their clothes and hair. Mark was too stunned to move, but Jennifer grabbed his jacket sleeve and pulled him to the floor.

"What the…", Mark began.

"Shut up!", commanded Jennifer, and peered tentatively over the low sill to see if anything of value could be noted. "Let's go!", and again she grabbed his arm and propelled him through a small hallway at one end of the lunch counter, and toward what she hoped was the back of the restaurant.

"Where are we going?", Mark asked, trying to stop for a moment in the darkened, grease stained hallway. She wouldn't allow it. With a surprisingly strong grip for a woman her size, she once again drew him along and, when he hesitated again, issued a simple, impossible to defy command—"MOVE!"

Once outside, she hesitated for a moment, trying to decide what to do. "Look", she began, "get away from here as fast as you can, without being seen."

He grasped her sleeve to prevent her from running away and said "wait a minute!" "Where are you going?" "What's going on?" "Why…". His question was cut short by a large, swarthy man appearing at the corner of the building, at the entrance to the parking lot in which they were standing.

"Damn it!" whispered Jennifer through clenched teeth, and turned to Mark. "Too late! Get into the car." Without waiting for a response, pulled him into a dark green Range Rover parked only a few feet from where they stood. Ignoring Mark completely, she selected two wires from under the dash and ripped them from their places. Touching their ends produced a deep roar from under the hood in front of them, following which Jennifer put the car into gear, released the parking brake, and accelerated directly at the man they had seen, who had, by now, been joined by another.

"Hey, watch it!" yelled Mark. There was no reply except for a dull thud followed immediately by a shudder as the heavy Range Rover threw one man over its hood, while brushing the other aside, and crushing him against the concrete rear wall of the restaurant.

Using the accelerator instead of the break, Jennifer swung the rear of the car around to the right, pointing the front down the drive leading to the street. She accelerated again, this time into traffic, and blended with the other cars going around the "circus" before she seemed to relax a little, then reached into her pocket, and withdrew a pack of "Ovals". "Want one?", she asked, offering Mark one of the English cigarettes.

"No thanks", replied Mark, who simply stared at the woman sitting beside him driving the car. For the first time, he noticed that the upper part of her left sleeve had a dark stain surrounding the shoulder area. "You're hurt", he stated matter-of-factly, and reached to examine the area.

"It's nothing", Jennifer answered.

They drove for nearly twenty minutes, reaching the countryside, before Jennifer pulled off to the side of the lane and stopped the car. Exhausted, she allowed her head to fall back against the headrest and her eyes to close for a few seconds, before sitting upright again and beginning to think. The stain on her jacket had grown larger by this time, and yet another attempt to examine his new patient was rebuffed. "I have to think," she said, then opened the door and, stepping out of the car, collapsed onto the cinders that bordered the lane.

Mark ran around the front of the car and knelt beside her. There was a shredded area of flesh on her left shoulder, which had continued to ooze blood. It was superficial, but the loss of blood had been significant enough to cause her collapse.

After being unable to find anything to bandage the wound with, Mark reached under her skirt and removed her slip. He tore a strip from the bottom, and folded the rest into a tight ball, thrust the result under her sleeve, and made it into an effective pressure dressing by tying the torn strip around it. He then scooped her up without noticing any weight and carried her away from the car and into a nearby, partly ruined, stone shack. Once inside, he laid her on his jacket but decided to wait until she regained consciousness, before calling the police.

While waiting, he found an outdoor spigot at a house not far from where they were and, after wetting another piece of her slip that he had torn from the main portion, returned to clean her wound. Carefully, he removed her jacket, then the left side of the blood stained silk blouse, and finally her left bra strap, and attempted to clean the wound. No matter how he tried, her jacket and blouse kept getting in the way.

"Oh, fuck it!", Mark said to no one in particular as he simply removed her jacket, blouse, and bra. He then proceeded to clean the wound, being grateful that she wasn't awake to feel the pain. He followed this by brushing all of the glass first from the wound, then from her arms, neck and breasts, and finally shaking it out of her clothing which, he knew, she would have to put back on since they had nothing else.

Once the wound was cleaned and redressed as best he could, he replaced her blouse and jacket, but was unable to replace her bra which was now part of the dressing, having been deemed by Mark the least important part of her clothing. With Jennifer's redressing completed, Mark took a blanket he had found in the Range Rover, covered her with it, then lay back and, himself, fell into a deep but troubled sleep.

It was dark when he awakened, to find her lying next to him, her eyes open and examining him with what he felt to be curiosity, more than anything else.

"Good evening", she smiled and winced with pain at the same time as she turned more in his direction, "did you have a tiring day?"

After less than five seconds of being awake, Mark was roaring with laughter. It was merely an emotional catharsis, but enjoyed it none the less. He hadn't had a good laugh in a long time, longer that he cared to remember, and he wasn't going to surrender this one without a fight.

Jennifer laughed along with him, easily, tossing her slightly matted blonde hair our of her eyes. At that moment, she looked like a schoolgirl who knew she had just been slightly naughty, but had gotten away with it. Mark felt a growing warmth for her, then was jolted back to reality by the thought that this schoolgirl had just been shot, and had, herself, probably killed at least one and maybe two of her assailants with the car. The laughter subsided, his smile softened to a more serious, though hardly stern, countenance, and after a few moments of silence, he asked simply—"Who are you?"

The question seemed to take her by surprise more than it should have, and she took a few seconds before replying. "You know who I am", she began, slightly uneasily.

"No!", Mark interrupted, "I know your name, and that we've met before under different circumstances, but", and he paused, trying to phrase the question in a more precise way, giving up, and repeated, "who are you?"

There was no immediate answer, and Mark assumed, correctly, that she was attempting to formulate one to placate his curiosity, without actually telling him anything. When she began to answer, Mark held up his hand to stop her. "Look", he said, I don't want or need any bullshit. I'd rather you simply didn't tell me than to lie to me. "I'm not going to lie to you", lied Jennifer, "why should I?" "I don't know why we were being shot at, but I can tell you that I work for the government, and there may be people who don't want me to complete my work and file my report. I can't think of anything else." She waited for his reply. There was none, and the silence became palpable.

"Well", she began again, "say something."

"I'm cold", he said, "and hungry, let's go find something warm to wear and hot to eat."

They walked slowly, with the blanket drawn around both of them. Mark supported her now and again when her weakness made her nearly stumble. After almost twenty minutes, a bend in the road brought them to a farmhouse where a look inside found a large family sitting down to dinner. Before Mark could stop her, Jennifer said simply, "follow my lead", and knocked on the door.

"See who's at the door, Jack", said a deep tenor voice from inside. When the door opened, "Jack" turned out to be an offish looking teenager who yelled back into the other room, "couple of strangers, Dad", and, without saying anything else, stood blocking the doorway, awaiting instructions.

From the other room, Mark and Jennifer could hear the sound of chair legs being scraped along a wooden floor as "Dad" moved back from the table to attend to the strangers.

"Help you mate?", inquired "Dad", as he appeared in the lighted opening behind Jack. He spoke to Mark, ignoring Jennifer's presence entirely.

"Good evening sir", Mark began tentatively. "We've had an accident with our car a little way back, and would greatly appreciate it if we could use your telephone and, perhaps, clean up a little."

"Well, I don't know…" From the other room, a woman's voice echoed through what Mark imagined to be a short hallway, asking who was there.

"Couple O' strangers", began "Dad". "Want to come in." "Say they had an accident down the road." His clipped sentences were beginning to irritate Mark, who was about to try to bulldoze his way into the house. Jennifer seemed to sense his intentions even before he was aware of them himself, and stepped in front of him, assuming her most demure posture—the little girl who needs help.

"Please sir", Jennifer's voice became a throaty whisper, "won't you help us?" There was no help for it., "Dad" let them in. By now, Mrs.

"Dad" was standing just behind them and to Jennifer's right, with Jack behind him and to her left. Mark was left to enter in her wake.

Once inside the house, the dried blood on Jennifer's left shoulder became evident.

"Oh, my God", exclaimed the gaunt figure standing behind "Dad", she's hurt!". And with this, Jennifer was whisked off to attend to her wounds, leaving Mark to fend off questions from "Dad".

"So, where's your auto, mate?" No name was offered, so Mark decided to change that by offering one of his own.

"I'm Mark Harmon", said Mark, offering his hand, which was taken, tentatively.

"Stevens", and a slight squeeze of his hand was all that was offered by way of a handshake, "Luke Stevens", and their hands separated.

"Thank you, Mr. Stevens." Mark turned to see what became of Jennifer. "We really appreciate your help."

"Want to call a doc?", inquired Luke, obviously uneasy with the couple's presence, and anxious to return to his supper after they left.

"I'm a doctor." answered Mark. "I've attempted to bandage her shoulder as best I could, but I had no antiseptics or clean bandages."

"I'm sure we have some", and Jack was through the hall and into the rear of the house, before Luke could say anything. When he returned, he was carrying a metal box with a slightly scratched red cross across its cover. "Here", and he handed it to his father, with a smile, then noticed the scowl on Luke's face, and wondered if he should have asked before he fetched the first aid kit. "Here, Doc", and Luke hesitantly handed the kit to Mark.

"She won't be needin' that", and each turned to see Jennifer and "Mrs. Dad" return.

"Yes", and Jennifer smiled warmly at her hostess. "Martha has helped me re-bandage my wound, and has leant me a blouse and jacket."

"You're very kind, Mrs. Stevens", and Mark again offered his hand, this time taken with a more positive attitude.

"That's all right. Just a Christian act", and released his hand with a slight hesitancy that made Mark wonder about her intentions.

"Mr. Stevens", began Mark again, "is there a bus that will take us into the nearest town?"

"We'll hear of no such thing." Once again, Martha Stevens was to assert her prerogatives. "Jack will drive you into Harwich, and from there you can get the bus to Ipswich".

"That's most kind of you", returned Jennifer, "but really unnecessary. We'll be fine if you can tell us where to get the bus." "Nonsense!", and it was settled. Jack was already putting on his jacket, and it seemed obvious that, posturing aside, this was a matriarchal household.

They followed Jack around to an insubstantial shed on the side of the house, where an older, but well kept Ford wagon was "stored". With practiced care, Jack slipped into the driver's side and, after starting the engine, slowly eased the car from its tight quarters, to allow his two passengers to enter.

Once they were all inside, Mark could see Jennifer wince, even in the darkness, as they bounced to the road, not far from the "garage". Jack accelerated smoothly once on the road, and was soon up to whatever speed he was up to (the speedometer had apparently stopped working some time ago, but the quality of the roads in this area left no room for speed, anyway).

They drove for about fifteen minutes before anyone spoke. Jennifer glanced, repeatedly, over her shoulder, occasionally peering into the rather murky blackness searching for…, Mark wasn't quite sure. "There it is", thought Mark, he wasn't "quite sure".

"You're a good driver, Jack", Jennifer's voice, though mellow, seemed to splinter the heavy silence. Jack smiled, taking his eyes from the small area washed by the headlights just long enough to look at Jennifer.

"Thank you, Misses", and he returned his eyes to their task.

A curious feeling spread through Mark when Jack mistook Jennifer for his wife. He wasn't sure what it was, but he recognized its presence.

"No", he decided, and put the thought that was emerging well back into his consciousness where, he felt, it belonged. None the less, Jennifer seemed to edge slightly closer to him after this, and he felt only momentary remorse at surrounding her with his left arm. He was careful not to put any pressure on her injured shoulder.

For another twenty minutes, they drove along, Jack rambling slightly in his description of the country to these "Yanks", his evident pride in his family's farm, and sundry other things holding no immediate interest for Mark and Jennifer who were now comfortably nestled together. Finally, lights began to appear in the distance, grew larger, and became a town.

Harwich was almost exactly what Mark expected—a rustic town which, were it not for a slightly shabby appearance, would have been quaint. Being near the sea gave it a nautical flavor, with signs marking the locations of various shops dealing with boats and their accouterments, while the neon over a diner added the "neo-shab" (the term came to Mark's mind, and amused him) that disturbed the English town's tranquility.

Stopping in front of a wooden sign reading "The Prancing Pony", Jack looked at them both (although he had difficulty giving mark his share with Jennifer so close), smiled again, and announced that they were "here". They looked slowly around, and then asked where they would be getting the bus from.

"It's about two blocks up, Misses", related Jack, but there won't be no bus along again until tomorrow, maybe."

"But I", Jennifer corrected herself, "we thought there was a bus from here tonight."

"Well, Misses", Jack looked somewhat uncomfortable, "there ain't no bus tonight. There may not even be one tomorrow. I'm not sure. That's why I brought you to "The Pony". I sort of thought that you could, at least, sleep here and get some food, until you can get the bus."

Mark wasn't at all disappointed with the idea of spending the night with Jennifer, although he felt guilty about it. His thoughts wandered back to Meredith, at home, but this did nothing to re-enforce his resolve, so he waited to see what Jennifer would do.

"That's all right", and Jennifer was quickly out of the car, and standing in front of the door, lit by two incandescent bulbs in an aging fixture above it.

Jack smiled again (he reminded Mark of a puppy), and led them into the inn. It was, again, as Mark expected. They were in a lobby of sorts, with a small sitting area. To their right were several heavy armchairs covered with dark green fabric which allowed for no part of their original upholstery to show through. There was a sofa covered in the same material, and a coffee table, which seemed to have been dropped, rather than placed.

To their left was the registration desk where a hand bell, sitting on the noticeably dusty synthetic marble top, was sufficient instruction. Mark reached out, striking the protrusion from the top, and filling the lobby with echoes of vibrating brass.

Nearly a half minute elapsed before a rotund man, looking to be in his mid fifties, emerged from a hidden door behind the counter and to the left.

"Yes?" He seemed annoyed to have been disturbed. Before Mark could answer, Jack blurted, "Room for Mr. and Mrs.!"

Mark was about to correct him when Jennifer followed with, "Yes, and may we have a king-sized bed, please. My husband and I are very tired." She looked his way and smiled, while her eyes said "shut up!" He did.

When the manager, now doubling as the bellman came around to take their non-existent bags, they thanked Jack, and Mark attempted to place a ten pound note in his hand. Jack took a step back, looking indignant, then said that he was a good Christian man who didn't take money for helping out. Mark suggested that the ten pounds might do to put "petrol" into their car, in place of that which they had burned getting here.

"Well", began Jack, "I guess it's OK", and quickly stuffed the crisp note into his left trouser pocket, said goodbye, and returned to the car. The last they ever saw of Jack was his taillights dwindling in the distance.

The ancient lift stopped trembling at the third floor. Mark and Jennifer trailed a short distance behind the manager/bellman until he halted in front of a poorly lit door to room "316". The brass numerals were, like the rest of the inn, slightly tarnished, but an attempt to keep them in good condition was obvious.

"Thank you." Mark handed the man two pound notes after the obligatory tour of the room. "Whew!", and Mark sat on the bed after closing the door behind their "host", "I'm exhausted." Jennifer sat in a high backed armchair across the room without answering. She was staring at nothing in particular.

More than five minutes went by before either moved, and then it was Mark, realizing that his bladder hadn't been emptied in several hours. When he returned, Jennifer was draped in the bedspread. Her clothes lay in a heap at the foot of the armchair she had so recently occupied.

"I'm exhausted too", she stated flatly, "and I need a shower so badly I can smell myself." Not waiting for a reply, Jennifer and the bedspread marched themselves into the bathroom and closed the door. She emerged about fifteen minutes later with her hair wrapped in a towel, and another draped from mid-chest to mid-thigh. Her wound, now cleaned better than before, didn't look nearly as bad as it had earlier.

"Here, let me look at that", and Mark gingerly pulled her shoulder toward him for examination. "Not so bad", he opined, and redressed it with some extra bandages that Jack had left with them.

"There", and he completed his task with a flourish. "Now", Mark stated, "it's my turn", with which he piled his clothes, underwear excluded, on the floor next to hers, and marched to the bathroom again.

The mirror remained fogged from Jennifer's shower, and after closing the door, he took off his underwear and, moved the assorted hotel soaps, shampoo, comb, etc., placing them on the counter next to the sink. He then stopped long enough to survey himself in the, now, partially cleared mirror. He wasn't sure he liked what he saw, but he was as he was. Still, for being past forty, he didn't look bad. If only he could loose that slight stomach he had since his youth. he knew it wasn't a function of his weight, only genetics. Still….

The needlepoint jets of hot water first burned as he stepped under them, and then began to beat his aching muscles into submission until they relaxed. Slowly, the weariness that he was trying not to feel, began to spread throughout his body. Only then did he become aware of the pain. It was more than an ache, he hurt nearly everywhere. "I'm too old for this sort of thing", he thought, and was surprised to find himself talking out loud. His voice sounded deep in the echo of the shower stall, and he began to experiment with bits of songs he remembered.

"I've got sunshine…", he began again. "Time, goes by, so slowly, and time…". Soon, he was singing old songs that he had loved, but forgotten that he even knew. Then he smiled. He hadn't sung in the shower in years. Not since, well, he couldn't remember when. "I think", he began, "it was because I didn't want to wake Meredith in the morning." Well, whatever caused him to stop those many years ago, had caused him to start again tonight. He was enjoying himself enough that he had to remind himself where he was, and to get out of the shower.

By the time he had toweled himself dry, and put his underwear back on, Mark was beginning to consider his situation. Only hours earlier, he had been sitting at a lecture in a London hotel. Now, after being shot at, chased, stealing a car, and being tired, hungry, and in pain, he was in a hotel room with the most startlingly beautiful woman he had ever seen. The problem was, he didn't know why. "Why him, why her, why here…, why anything?!"

Grabbing the last remaining dry towel, he wrapped it about his waist and flung open the door, "Jennifer! There are a few questions I…". She was sound asleep in the bed, her shoulder length blonde hair tossed about her on one of the pillows, and the lights on all over the room. He considered waking her, but decided against it. There would be time enough in the morning to get answers. He was dead tired, and aching all over. When he looked about for another place to sleep, there appeared to be nowhere sufficiently comfortable, so he climbed under the sheets on the opposite side of the bed, taking care not to notice her nudity as he lifted the covers. He was asleep before he ever realized he hadn't turned out any lights.

Chapter 8

Mustafa had been to three clubs in the last six hours. All but the first were havens for the young. He liked young girls.

Carelessly, his arm hung around Debbie's bare shoulder, and his right hand was massaging the breast it cupped. She had put up no protest when he had begun his massage. She simply accepted it, during the ride back to the hotel. She had sat down next to him at the bar after seeing the roll of bills that he had drawn from his pocket. "Rich", Debbie had decided. She wasn't a "hooker," exactly, just a "free spirit" who expected to receive expensive gifts for superior services.

Mustafa's gait was somewhat disturbed by the combination of marijuana, cocaine, and alcohol he had consumed during the last several hours of "club hopping", but he needed little support, simply encouragement. Together, they rode the three floors to his room. He would never stay above this level, as it provided him with an opportunity to escape a pursuer via stairs, as well as elevator. They were alone in the hall. it was nearly five o'clock in the morning, and still they "shushed" each other all the way to his room. With slight difficulty, Mustafa fumbled about in his jacket pocket trying to dig his room key out. "Maybe it's in here", giggled Debbie, her short blonde hair whipping across her eyes, as she reached into his right pants pocket and began to kneed his genitals. Mustafa fumbled faster.

Once inside, Mustafa turned and lowered Debbie's sleeveless knit top to her waist, exposing her breasts. He cupped one in each hand and, making sure her nipples were between the index and third fingers of each hand, began to massage while he his fingers together until he was sure she felt pain. He knew the "type", and knew that this small amount of pain would excite her, while more would cause her to back away.

Debbie moaned deep in her throat, closed her eyes, and threw her head back. He kept massaging her breasts, squeezing a little bit harder each time, until she unzipped his pants, pulled them and his silk underwear down to his ankles, and moved her massaging to his testicles while she drew him into her mouth and down her throat. Slowly, she rocked her head back and forth so that her teeth scraped, very lightly, along the shaft of his penis, sending shivers throughout his body. He knew that he would erupt soon, and wanted to prolong it as much as possible. He released her breasts and, slowly withdrawing his glistening, lipstick streaked penis from her mouth, lifted her off the floor and threw her onto the king sized bed, where he proceeded to remove the remainder of her clothing. Her legs hung limply over the edge of the bed as he lowered himself to his knees and began to stroke her thighs, lightly at first, then with greater strength, always moving slowly up her legs. With each passing minute, her throaty whimpers became louder, and her hips moved in greater circles. By now, she had thrown her legs around his neck and shoulders, and he had begun to work his tongue slowly up her left thigh toward the blushing red "lips", surrounded by wispy blonde curls.

As he proceeded, Mustafa got onto the bed, swinging his hips around so that Debbie could again pull him into her mouth. This time, he "pumped" in and out of her lips, driving his now throbbing organ over her tongue and into her throat. His tongue now found its way onto her clitoris, moving in small circles then back and forth, while his fingers moved rapidly into and out of her vagina. The vibrations of her moaning again sent a shiver throughout his body, while he felt the muscles of her vagina contract against his fingers, then felt himself spurt into her throat several times. She swallowed with vigor and continued to suck for more as he pulled out of her mouth, swung around, and thrust himself as hard as he could into her vagina. She screamed, but he covered her mouth with his own as he pumped harder and harder into her. With each thrust, her screaming became more frantic as her pain increased. She tried to roll out from under him, but his weight pinned her to the bed. Again, Mustafa felt himself about to erupt, but this time, he withdrew from her vagina and, gripping her right shoulder, rolled her over onto her stomach. Then, from atop, he rammed his penis into her rectum with such fury that her shriek escaped the pillow, into which Mustafa had pressed her mouth, and filled the room. He tightened his grip on her right breast, while holding the pillow more tightly to her mouth, each thrust ripping her anus a little more. He couldn't see it, and wouldn't have cared, but small drops of blood dripped from her, lubricating his penis as it slid in and out. Finally Mustafa reached the climax that only the combination of sex and torture could bring to him. His body shuddered, and he collapsed on top of her.

Her screaming had ceased a little while earlier, and he assumed she had fainted from the pain. When, after a minute, his sweat slicked body slid off of hers and rolled onto the bed, he was unable to arouse her. Even a cursory examination revealed the reason for her quiet—she had died some time during his last efforts, while he pressed her face into the pillow to mask the sounds of her torment and fear.

Mustafa sat on the bed, lit a cigarette and turned on the television. He glanced at the clock, and found that it was nearly 6 AM. Well, he would need to perform his mission, so distractions were out of the question. Looking back over his shoulder at what used to be a young girl named Debbie, he stood and pulled her further up onto the other side of the bed, then covered her with the sheet and blanket. She looked peaceful. The dead always did. After placing the "Do Not Disturb" sign on the outer handle of the door, he returned to the bed, quietly lay back down next to her and slept another 5 hours, awakening just before eleven o'clock.

After a long shower, he returned to the room, and called for Room Service, ordering Eggs Benedict for himself, and a Continental breakfast for Debbie, along with a large pot of coffee. He had shaved and dressed by the time breakfast arrived. "Shhh..." he cautioned the waiter, nodding toward Debbie on the bed. "I don't want to awaken her yet. We had a long night," and he winked as he handed the waiter five dollars and signed the check. "Yes sir," the waiter said softly, looking at the apparently sleeping Debbie, "I understand," and shared a knowing smile with Mustafa.

As the waiter left, Mustafa sat at the table that had been wheeled into the room, ate a leisurely breakfast, and left after watching the news on CNN. His head hurt, and there was still a slight fog by the time he left, but he knew it would pass quickly. The Koran warned against the use of alcohol and drugs, and Allah made him pay dearly for his follies with one hangover after the other when he did this. Still, since he would never take the chance of doing it in his own country, he indulged himself among the infidels. He left the room and Debbie by noon. He had no intention of returning to either and, with the "Do Not Disturb" sign on the door, she might not even be found until the next day. By then...

The doorman hailed a taxi in return for a dollar tip, and it deposited him, per his instructions, at 36th Street and 7th Avenue. The day was sunny and warm, although the height of the buildings kept most of this area of Manhattan in shade. It would have been pleasant, had the air not carried the noxious odor of auto exhaust. It was this smell, more than anything else, that represented the United States to Mustafa in his subconscious. He walked quickly, not because he was in a hurry, but because the throng of which he wished to become a part moved at this pace. He was dressed as he expected the average New York executive to be—in a Brooks Brothers' gray business suit and Ralph Lauren tie. His Balley shoes were as comfortable as he could buy, and he topped it off with mirrored sunglasses. As he passed several windows, he looked into each to survey his appearance. He was pleased with what he saw.

He entered the concourse of Pennsylvania Station, and his senses became more attuned to the sights and sounds around him. Twice, the hair on the back of his neck stood up warning him of possible surveillance, but each time he was unable to detect anyone nearby, so he dismissed the thought.

For fifteen minutes, he sat in a seat near one of the tracks, waiting for the brunette with the flowered suitcase to show up. She was late, and that was something that couldn't be excused.

"There!", Mustafa thought. "There she is." He was sure of it. Through the years of clandestine meetings and escapes, he had developed a sixth sense about people. Perhaps it was the tentative way she walked, or the way she carried the suitcase, or the way her eyes darted, constantly, from side to side. Whatever it was, he knew her at once. With practiced ease, Mustafa stood and walked, not toward her, but in an intercept path so that he would seem to meet her merely by chance. They closed to within a meter before speaking.

"That suitcase looks heavy, may I help you with it?" The words were not his, nor was her response hers, but both had to be correct, or no transfer would take place.

"Not so heavy, but I would appreciate the help."

Mustafa took the hard leather handle of the suitcase, and walked a short distance with the girl, until he said, "I have to go the bathroom, please wait", then disappeared into the Men's Room with the suitcase. When he emerged without it, he was wearing a light brown wig, his olive skin tone giving him the appearance of somebody who had recently returned from a sunny climate, and wearing a blue sport coat with his gray pants. The briefcase he carried was black leather with brass hardware, the combination to which he already knew. His mirrored glasses had been replaced with slightly blue tinted ones to match his jacket. The effect was equally fashionable, but the person was not the same one who had entered the Men's Room earlier. He walked quickly, emerging from the station to begin his trip to the Airport.

Mustafa placed the briefcase on his lap in the taxi. After staring at it for a moment, he used the combination that he already knew, and gently opened the lid. Tissue paper expanded and rose to meet him. Before removing the paper, Mustafa patted the middle of the wad, to ascertain the location of whatever was inside and, feeling the mass sitting near the middle, carefully pulled sheet after sheet from the briefcase until only a central core was left. This he gingerly lifted, and held for a moment sensing its weight. In his grasp, the tissue stuffed piece split in half, and both halves nearly dropped to the floor before being caught "in the nick of time". Sweat poured from Mustafa's face, but his hands remained steady. He wasn't sure what these things were, but he had been told that they were the most valuable things he had ever been entrusted with. He waited about a minute, catching his breath, before completing the unveiling. There, in front of him were two highly polished, but perfectly ordinary looking bowls. Lifting one to the light, he examined it carefully, looking for its value. Nothing struck him as important, so he replaced the paper, placed the two bowls together as they had been, and rewrapped them with the remaining tissue paper. He replaced this package into the briefcase and turned the wheels at each latch so that they were again locked. He knew that if they were opened in any but the correct manner, the resultant explosion would leave little intact within about thirty meters. He had worked with this case before. He had returned to a hotel room in Madrid, to find it (the room) gone. He remembered that sight each time he opened a briefcase.

Chapter 9

Mark awakened slowly, without opening his eyes immediately. He was passing through that time when the only thing of which we can be sure is that we are. His dreams had been troubled, but even now, they were disappearing from his consciousness. He knew that in a few seconds he would open his eyes and all would be forgotten, so he savored each moment spent in this netherland until the pale light of dawn from the slightly open window intruded upon his reverie.

Opening his eyes, the first sight that greeted him was the flowing blonde hair on the pillow beside him. In a burst of memory, the pervious day came rushing back to him. As he lay there, Jennifer rolled back toward him, the sheet slipping from her bare chest revealing her breasts. The nipples were full, and the areolae only marginally darker than the surrounding area. Mark felt himself becoming aroused, but pushed it from his mind. Tactfully, he drew the sheet up over Jennifer's chest, and slipped out of bed. His clothes lay in the pile in which he had dropped them, so it was easy to find them and get dressed. As he did so, he heard Jennifer stir and finally awaken.

"Good morning", he offered. She opened her eyes and just stared for a moment, perhaps going through the same process as Mark, then smiled.

"Umm…", Mark began again, "I think I'll go into the bathroom and let you get dressed. Then, maybe, we can find a restaurant". With which, he finished buckling his belt, slipped his Bass loafers onto his feet, and walked into the bathroom where he proceeded to empty his bladder, and rinse his mouth out with water. There was, of course, no toothpaste, no toothbrush, and no shaving equipment, still, he felt a little better.

After leaving what he hoped was an adequate time, he made small noises with the door to let her know that he was coming out, then re-entered the bedroom to find Jennifer just slipping into her skirt. By the time he was fully into the room, it was about her waist, zipped, and buttoned. "Your turn", he remarked, and angled his head toward the bathroom.

"Thanks", she smiled and went into the bathroom to try to accomplish the same things as he. When she returned, she appeared to be cleaned, refreshed, and neat as a pin. He marveled at her ability to rebound from yesterday. Still, there were questions that needed to be answered.

"What's going on?", Mark asked. He didn't really expect a direct answer, but he asked the question anyway.

He was right. Jennifer just stared at him then returned his question with another question—"What does it look like to you?"

"I think things are out of control, I think I should be very scared, and I think we should be getting out of here."

"Right", and Jennifer brushed against him, leaving small tingles where she had never even touched. A slight blush escaped anyone's notice but his, and he followed her into the windowless hallway and shut the door behind them. Before they left, she returned to the room and placed the "Do Not Disturb" sign on the door. Mark was beginning to wonder at her thoroughness as much as at her beauty.

Outside, they walked along a narrow cobbled street until reaching a small marina where fishing boats and small personal yachts were tied up alongside docks floating on metal pontoons. The air was more crisp than Mark had expected, and laden with intermittent smells of food cooking—the fishermen preparing their morning meal before heading out to sea. He found himself grateful for the stimulation.

There appeared to be no restaurant in sight, but a gently swinging sign, "The Brass Rail", caught their attention. It was a pub that was probably frequented by the local sailors. It wouldn't be open for business at this hour, but if anyone was there, they might know where some breakfast might be obtained.

A knock on the door brought no response until the third attempt, when one of two heavy, weathered doors creaked slightly open, and a gravelly voice asked, rudely, what they wanted.

"Excuse us, sir", Mark began, "we're trying to find a restaurant, or someplace to eat. Can you help us?" "Go away, it's too early!", and the voice began to shut the door when Jennifer placed her face into what was left of the opening.

"Please, sir", Jennifer intoned, "we really are hungry, and need some help." The door stopped moving, then reversed itself. As light flooded through the opening, it fell upon a face as weathered as the door. He looked back and forth from Jennifer to Mark, staring mostly at Jennifer, then seemed to soften. "All right then, come in", and the door was swung the last few degrees.

Once inside, it took more than a few seconds for Mark and Jennifer's eyes to adjust to the relative darkness. But even a short examination revealed a well kept establishment. The bar was worn, but highly polished. There were the expected fishing nets hanging from the ceiling, interspersed with large ceiling fans to move the hot smoky air from one part of the room to another. The walls, mostly brick, were covered with various fish, interspersed with pictures of old sailing vessels and the occasional portrait of a ship's captain.

"Jonas". Their examination was interrupted by their host.

"Excuse me?" Mark turned toward the source, noting that the voice had become stronger and less gruff. "Jonas, my name is Jonas Sykes. I own this place. Who might you be?" He spoke to Mark, but his eyes never left Jennifer.

"I'm Mark Harmon", replied Mark, his hand extended, "and this is…".

"Jennifer Lynch", interrupted Jennifer. It was her hand that Jonas took first and, with unexpected gentility, pressed lightly to his lips.

Mark's hand, left extended, was now grasped with surprising strength, then released.

"Well now, Miss, I know most people around here, and I would certainly remember you. American." He stated it flatly. "We don't see many yanks around here, and those we do see aren't usually wandering the docks at dawn. So, tell me, what do you really want?"

"We really want breakfast", began Jennifer, and we'd be most grateful if you could tell us where we might find some.

"Well, I might be making some myself, and you'd be welcome to some of it, maybe."

"We can pay for it", and Mark was stopped by the look of disdain in Jonas' eyes.

"You're my guest, Miss", retorted Jonas, as his eyes returned to Jennifer. "Guests don't pay."

"I humbly apologize for my companion", declared Jennifer, casting a stern look at Mark, "and gratefully accept your hospitality."

They were led to an oversized, heavy oak table in the back of the establishment, near a large window, facing east to the docks, through which the early morning light streamed. Mark and Jennifer were quiet for awhile, noting that most of the boats had already set to sea. Only a few pleasure craft, and two trawlers were left bobbing in the gently undulating water. They sipped from two large mugs of very hot, very strong coffee that had appeared almost immediately upon sitting down. Sykes had disappeared into the kitchen as soon as they had been seated, so they sat quietly and stared from the sea to each other, and back again for several minutes before Mark could wait no longer.

"Who are you?", he initiated the conversation without preamble. Jennifer sat quietly for at least a full minute before answering, parted her lips just slightly, twice, as if to speak, then finally began.

"My name is Jennifer Lynch."

"Damn it!" roared Mark in a whisper, so as to not be overheard by Jonas Sykes, "I know what your name is. I want to know who and what you are. How is it that you can do the things you can, and why am I here!?"

"Calm down, Mark. I'll answer your questions the best I can, and I won't lie, but I have to do it in my own way, or else it will make no sense and, please, don't interrupt me until I'm done." She stopped, hesitating a few seconds as if to make some final decision, then began.

"My name really is Jennifer Lynch." A brief hesitation again, the snapping of some conditioned bond, and she continued. "I am a Special Assistant to the President of the United States. My specialty is Foreign Affairs and Security, and their impact on U.S. policy."

Another swallow of her coffee, now more tepid than hot, and Jennifer continued. "Several days ago, there was an incident in the Persian Gulf involving a number of ships. You probably read something about it in the papers. Their reports, as usual, told little of the real story. The important part, however, was that there was a request from the fleet commander to retaliate against the Iranian shore positions. From a military standpoint, this made perfect sense. From political standpoint, it was a "no win" option because even if we were successful in taking out the shore batteries, it would still arouse the local population against us, and that could spread into uprisings against our moderate and liberal Arab friends. Unfortunately, the President was convinced by the Military that the attack was needed, and the rest you read in the news." She paused, and another sip of coffee followed, allowing her to gather her thoughts. "My feeling was that there had to be another way. The stakes are too high for us to make a mistake in the region now. That's why I was sent to Europe to explore some possibilities for future actions, and report back to the President. Only a handful of people know who I am, and fewer still know why I'm here. I didn't want to tell you because that knowledge would put you into imminent danger."

They looked at each other, thought about the preceding twenty-four hours, and both began to laugh uncontrollably. "I'm glad you didn't tell me before", Mark forced out between his sobbing laughter, "someone might have tried to hurt me!" Jennifer began to choke on the small amount of coffee she had in her mouth, small dribbles wandering down her chin where she failed to contain them through her own laughter.

"Glad you're having a good time, mates", and Jonas pushed his way backwards through the swinging doors that separated the kitchen from the remainder of the restaurant, holding a large tray laden with food.

Mark looked at Jennifer, began to say something, then shut up. "Boy, that smells delicious", he remarked, as the tray was placed at the opposite end of the huge table.

"Should be", declared Sykes, "it's my own recipe. Orange juice, a seafood omelet, biscuits, bacon, and more coffee." A large white cloth covering was removed from the tray to reveal more food than they could have eaten in two sittings. The aroma made them remember how hungry they really were, and their salivary glands went into overdrive.

Twenty minutes later they found themselves stuffed, satisfied, and filled with an apparently never ending flow of stories about the sea, the port, and the "Life and Times" of Jonas Sykes. Not once, during the entire time did either Mark or Jennifer get a chance to interrupt, and neither really wanted to. Far from the surly curmudgeon who met them at the door, they found Sykes to be jovial, and generous. It wasn't until after the meal, and another refused offer to pay, that he turned somewhat wary. Jennifer asked him about the possibility of chartering a boat, or perhaps getting passage on a boat headed south, or even to France, across the Channel.

"Why would you be wanting to go to France by boat, anyway?", Sykes asked, "Most folks fly or take the shuttle under the channel. It's much faster, and there is an airfield not far from here." Mark, who had not considered going to France, wondered the same thing.

"Well", and without hesitation Jennifer explained that Mark and she wanted something more "romantic" and exciting than a plane ride, and they were hoping to slip over to Le Havre for a night without anyone finding out. Jonas grinned slyly, and Mark marveled at her ability to "lie on the fly".

"Well now", Jonas was still grinning, "I don't know as I ought to be helping you, but old "Bull" Trumble has been known to cross the Channel now and then if there was a piece of change in it for him. I suppose it wouldn't hurt to ask him."

"Where can we find him?" Jennifer asked in a nonchalant manner.

"Right now, you can't. He's out with the others. But he'll be back about eight tonight. You might want to stop by then."

"We just might", and Jennifer rose and, instead of extending her hand again, leaned over and kissed Jonas on his left cheek. Her lipstick left a slight smudge mark, but it was quickly lost in the blush on Jonas Sykes' face. Mark shook Jonas' hand firmly, then they went back out of the heavy wooden door through which they had entered, and found themselves again at a corner of the harbor.

"Well, where to now?" Mark looked around and then back at Jennifer. "We seem to have most of a day to kill".

"Yes, don't we", returned Jennifer, and they began to amble back in the direction from which they had come. There wasn't much in the way of conversation during their walk. Both seemed to be lost in their thoughts, and neither seemed ready to share them. They soon found themselves back at the hotel.

"I think we'd better go back to the room", Jennifer stated. "I don't think it's a good Idea to be wandering about attracting attention."

"Why not?", asked Mark. "What are you afraid of?"

"It's not fear", replied Jennifer, her eyes darting about, "it's caution." With which she hooked her left arm through his right, and allowed him to lead her in the direction she had chosen.

Chapter 10

Mustafa deposited of the briefcase in the designated locker without a problem, but instead of returning to his room at the Plaza where Debbie's body might already have been discovered, he obtained a room at the airport Hilton using a different set of credit cards and credentials. He had booked a Mini-suite and, walking through the drawing room into the bedroom, deposited his clothes onto one of the two queen size beds, and decided to indulge himself with a bath.

He allowed the water, as hot as he could bear, to play over his body. Each ripple caused a small searing pain, he used to strengthen his resolve. As the bath cooled to a more normal temperature, he began to feel his muscles relax and his head lay back against the cool edge of the tub. There was s short period when he thought he might drift off into sleep, but this passed.

As he looked down at the body laying just under the clear water, he noted each scar, and remembered how it was obtained—each battle, bullet, or bit of shrapnel. With each memory, there flooded into his mind both satisfaction and hatred; and even the hatred was satisfying. He leaned back and reached to his right where a small water pipe, a "hookah", filled with a fruity wine, sat on the floor. A moderate amount of hashish sat in its bowl. He lifted it to his lips and, with the butane lighter that he had bought in his other hand, he lit the irregularly shaped, dark brown chunk in the pipe and inhaled deeply, holding the wine filtered smoke in his lungs as long as possible. Slowly, second by second, the world began to slow down, each second feeling like an hour. His mind soared, and his body seemed to melt into the water. He was relaxed, and aroused at the same time. He was invincible, the ultimate warrior, who couldn't quite muster the energy to move.

Years later, Mustafa dragged his body from the bath, leaving the water to sit. He toweled himself off, dressed in the light weight navy blazer with the University stripe tie and tan pants, and went downstairs where he had a delightful dinner, made more so by the effect of the hashish. Appetizer, soup, entree, desert, Mustafa knew he would never have been able to consume all of that food but for the drug. After paying for the dinner by signing his room number to the check, he left the table and returned to the ornate elevator that took him to his floor and his room, undressed, and fell across the bed.

Morning came with sunshine and little memory of the night before. Mustafa arose, and went into the bathroom where he emptied the standing water in the tub, showered, groomed himself, then returned to the bedroom to dress. He wasn't sure what he was going to do now. He had been given latitude in when to return home, so he could spend more time here, go to another city, or travel around. He chose the later. New York was a great city to visit, but he liked other places better. Besides, there was Debbie…

He packed the single bag he had purchased, along with some new clothes to replace the ones he had left at the Plaza, then carried it himself to the cashier's desk where he paid his bill. Then, without yet being certain where he was going, took a cab to Pennsylvania Station, where, on the spur of the moment, he boarded the Metroliner for Washington. A half hour later, he decided that he would leave the train in Philadelphia. He wasn't sure why, but it seemed the prudent thing to do. "Always do the unexpected," and the most unexpected thing was, obviously, something which even you didn't know you were going to do until the time you did it.

He left the train at 30th Street Station, walked up the stairs and, standing under the high stone canopy, entered a cab that took him to the airport. There, he purchased a one way ticket to Paris, and proceeded to the international terminal to await its departure which, he had been assured, was imminent. It wasn't, but by 1600 he was ensconced in a first class seat in an Air France Airbus 300, lifting off across the Atlantic.

After a long and uneventful flight, Mustafa left the airport in a taxi and held his breath while the small blonde driver negotiated the Paris traffic with an aplomb he had never been able to fathom. Finally, they cruised down the *Champs-Elysées* and turned onto the Avenue George V where Mustafa had planned to stay at the hotel of the same name. He always tried to vary his hotel when he traveled on "business", but he had to admit that he was especially fond of this one, and tended to return to it more often than he should.

Entering through the glass doors, he crossed the lobby to the Reception desk and was greeted by a smiling young lady with very red hair, "*Bon jour, Messier.*"

"*Bon jour*", replied Mustafa, "*Jé voudré mon salle. Jé sui Messeur Adam.*" The name was, of course false, but it had been some time since he had been here, and few people would remember him by another. The room reservation had been telephoned in from the train station in Philadelphia.

The suite to which he was led by the bellman was appointed in Louis XIV furniture, heavily gilded with gold, on large, ornate oriental rugs. His King size bed faced a writing desk with a leather padded surface, next to which stood the ubiquitous television/radio combination. A trip to the bathroom revealed the remembered gold hardware on the sink, tub and bidet, and the well known *George V* white terrycloth robe hanging on the door, waiting for the next guest to become its owner.

Mustafa hung his small wardrobe in the closet, undressed, and once more stretched out across a strange bed. "When", he wondered, "will I be in a bed of my own. When will I be home?" On that thought he fell into a peaceful sleep, untroubled by the world around him—the violent world he helped to shape.

Chapter 11

Once back in their room, Jennifer replaced the "Do Not Disturb" sign on the outer doorknob and, crossing to the opposite side of the room, slumped into the large padded chair, leaving Mark to first sit, then lie on his back across the large, freshly made bed. Both felt weariness overcome them, and they realized that neither had physically recovered from their ordeal of yesterday (although Jennifer seemed to be doing a fairly good job of it).

"Jen…", Mark began, and smiled inwardly at the affectionate shortening of her name that he had just performed without realizing it.

Jennifer crossed the small space between them, sat on the bed next to Mark, and ran her hand gently over his head and left cheek. The fingers of her right hand caressed his ear and, as he stared, once more mesmerized by the depth of her eyes, she leaned forward and gently pressed her lips against his. He reached up with this right hand and found her head, with which he pressed their lips gently, but more firmly together. Without realizing when it happened, their mouths opened, and his tongue darted in and out of her mouth as a deep moan left her throat and vibrated through both bodies.

Mark began to gently roll to his left, and Jennifer followed, their mouths never parting, but their hands beginning to explore each other. Before he could more than fumble with the buttons of her blouse, he felt his belt unbuckled, and her hand reach under his shirt and begin to gently move across his chest, then drop to his abdomen, and finally come to rest between his legs. With each circle she made, she scraped her nails lightly over his skin, then finally began a practiced massage that spread tingles throughout his body, each nerve standing on end. More quickly than either of them expected, they were lying naked across the bed, their clothes once again in a heap on the floor. Only the bandages that remained on Jennifer, still concealed any skin.

Mark allowed his lips to press against the right side of Jennifer's neck, his tongue making small circles as he moved to the front of her neck, and began to slowly descend onto her chest. Without thinking, his right hand cupped her left breast and kneaded it gently upward as his mouth closed over the nipple. His tongue continued the circles as he drew her breast further into his mouth. Forgetting the pain in her shoulder, Jennifer's mouth opened, allowing a deep moan to escape, as she rolled onto her back arching it upward, her chest expanding to show her ribs as she inhaled deeply. Minutes or hours passed, neither could tell which, as each took turns bringing the other to the brink, then backing off.

When she could take no more, she drew him into her, their bodies locked together moving rhythmically. Faster and harder he stroked, her hips rising to meet him each time, until both of them seized in a seemingly endless orgasm, then lay motionless, their bodies covered in a fine sheen testifying to both their effort and their ecstasy.

More than ten minutes passed before either of them spoke. Mark felt a twinge of guilt, remembering his wife for the first time in two days, then shrugged it off. "They hadn't been married in years...they were more house-mates sharing children than spouses...they were no longer friends, and had long since ceased being lovers." These rationalizations all passed through his head as he lay there. Finally, he answered himself. "No", "this felt right".

Jennifer was lying to his left with her eyes closed, as he looked over at her. How old was she? Twenty-five? Thirty? Thirty-five? He couldn't guess, and couldn't care less. She was all that he had dreamed about for most of his life, but never dared to dream he could have. He wanted to hold her, protect her, and share himself and his life with her. He hadn't felt this way in years and yet, there was something unsettling about her. Something surreal about the way in which she did things she shouldn't be able to do. This warm, soft, child lying with her eyes closed beside him had made more passionate love than any mistress he could have imagined, and yet had killed at least two men yesterday as easily, and with no more thought than he would have given to a laboratory animal. He leaned over and once more gently stroked her hair. She opened her eyes and smiled at him and, even as his world lit up, he had to know.

"Jen", he hesitated not wanting to ask again, fearing both the truth and a lie, but needing to know, "please, what's going on?"

"I don't know. I honestly don't know." Jennifer looked troubled. It was the first time Mark had seen that expression on her face, and it bothered him. He realized that he had come to think of her as having a resourcefulness that would get them out of any problems they found themselves in, and now he had to admit to himself that it might not be true.

"What do you mean you don't know?"

"Just that", Jennifer replied, "I thought I did, but I've been thinking about it, and the whole thing doesn't make sense." She paused, apparently considering how to phrase her next sentence, or exactly what to say. "I assumed that since my mission was so sensitive, that it was me they were trying to kill at the restaurant. It made sense then, but it doesn't now. Listen, Mark. I was a registered guest at the hotel. They could have gotten to me any time they wanted to, and I had been there for two days before you even arrived." Again, she paused, emphasizing her uncertainty. "Then too, killing me would have served no particular purpose for them beyond sending a message, and that they would have done quietly. Besides, someone more capable would have been sent in my place…"

"Not more capable, love", Mark interrupted, better trained, perhaps, but not more capable."

Jennifer's face lit with a smile. "Thanks", she began again, "but believe me there are plenty of people more capable in this type of an operation. It's just that it wasn't supposed to become this type of an operation. This was a fact finding mission. The information that I gathered wasn't even going to be used in its raw form, but included with that from many other sources to form a policy. They should have been feeding me "disinformation", not trying to kill me, and certainly not by gunning me down in broad daylight in a restaurant!"

Mark sat quietly. He had no response to her uncertainties, only a mounting fear that what she was saying was true because, if it was, there was only one other person being shot at and chased, and he didn't like that idea at all!

"It was me, wasn't it?" Mark stated it as a fact, even though it was phrased as a question. "There wasn't anybody else there but us, and if it wasn't you, then it was me."

Jennifer looked at him oddly. "Why you?", she asked quietly. "Do you have any enemies that would want to kill you?"

"Hell no!", bellowed Mark. "Why the hell would anyone want me dead?"

"Still", Jennifer continued, "there has to be something. Have any of your patients told you anything sensitive lately?"

"Neither lately, nor before. There's nothing, I tell you."

"Have you been talking to anyone while you've been here?"

"You, and a very proper British internist, that's all…", but the look on his face puzzled Jennifer.

"You've thought of something?", she asked.

"Well, remember when we met you said that you had been reading about the man that was killed in front of the hotel, and that you had seen my picture in the newspaper?"

"Yes", Jennifer answered tentatively, and rolled further onto her right elbow, propping herself up to look more squarely into Mark's eyes. Her hand had absent-mindedly begun to stroke his arm while she thought. It had to be him, yet she was unable to understand the connection.

"Well, I don't know if you remember it, but that man was the son of Sheik something-or-other." Maybe that is the connection."

"Yes", answered Jennifer again, "but if that was the case, it would still make no sense. It you had saved him, then there might have been a motive, but he died just as he had been intended to. If he had had time to tell you something that you shouldn't know, then there might be a motive, but you say that he was essentially dead when you got to him. In short, there is still no motive."

"I don't know, Mark stated flatly, and I don't care", and he rolled onto his back, hooked his left arm around Jennifer's back, and gently pulled her to him where she lay, each sleeping lightly, her cheek resting against his chest, for more than two hours.

Mark awakened to find that Jennifer was already awake, but hadn't moved. She smiled at him, lightly brushed her lips against his chest, then rolled off of the bed and began gathering her clothes up from the floor. He watched her with more than passing interest, wondering if he should pull her back into bed with him, but decided against it. they might make love again, but not now.

"Jen…", Mark hesitated, not quite knowing what he wanted to say, but liking to hear the sound of her name.

"Mark, listen to me." Jennifer Lynch, while only partially dressed, none the less had resumed the dignity of the Presidential Advisor. She spoke with authority, and without realizing it Mark's mind switched gears, even as he lay under the sheet watching her dressing in front of him. "We have to get out of here", she finished.

"I know, we're going to cross the Channel with "Bull", tonight."

"No, I mean right now. This minute". The urgency in her voice startled him, so he said nothing, but waited to hear what else she had to say.

"Mark, pay attention. We've just spent a restful night in a hotel, had the best breakfast I've personally had in years, and capped it off the best way I could ever imagine. We've been behaving like lovers off on a holiday, but we're not. We're fugitives Mark. There are people trying to kill us, and it doesn't make a damn bit of difference whether it's you or me at this point, because we're both in it together, whether we like it or not." When Mark still didn't answer, she continued. "We had no trouble finding this town or the hotel. We were brought directly here because it is the only place near where the car went off of the road where transportation is available, and this is the only hotel in the town. By now, the police have found the car we stole, will begin asking questions, and will be led directly to us. Also, whatever the police can do, our friends with the guns can do also, perhaps even more quickly as their methods are more," she hesitated for a moment, "persuasive. We can't wait for them, and we can't go to the police because they're going to want to know about the stolen car and two dead men in London."

"Like I said", Mark began, swinging his legs off of the bed and reaching for his clothes, "we have to get out of here now!" He slipped his legs into his pants and, as he was buttoning his shirt, stopped for a moment, looked at Jennifer and asked, "but where are we supposed to go, and how do we get this cleared up?"

"Getting it cleared with the police won't be easy, but it can be done if I can get in touch with my people in DC", and Jennifer stopped to think. "The rest of it...", and her voice trailed off as though the uncertainty left her speechless.

Chapter 12

Leaving the docks, Mark and Jennifer strolled along the small ribbon of road that wound past the town. The sun had risen beyond its ten o'clock position, but the dust and quiet was making them more uncomfortable than the heat could have alone. They hailed each passing truck (Jennifer insisted that they not attempt to "hitch" a ride with cars since their occupants were more likely to be people they didn't want to). Finally, a geriatric Ford with shocks sufficiently worn to cause a "list to port" stopped, and the burly driver, a single gold tooth dotting his smile, asked where they were headed.

"Where are you going?", Jennifer responded before Mark could. "When you're unsure how to answer a question," she remembered, "answer with another question."

"*Down the rroad, Miss*", answered the Ford in a decidedly Scottish brogue. She was about to give it another stab when Mark surprised her by responding first.

"Excuse me, sir," Mark began hesitantly, then gathered steam, "my wife and I are trying to abandon our tour party. We drove all the way from London, but our car broke down, and we're afraid they'll track us here." He paused to assess the effect of his statement. He knew it sounded somewhat phony, but he was determined to "tough it out" anyway. "Do you know any way that we can get to Le Harve without anyone finding out…at least for a few days?"

"*Well now*", began the Ford, "*Wouldn't be wantin' to escape more than yerr frriends, would ye?*" A glint escaped the Ford's eyes and his gold tooth shone in the pale sunlight. Mark assessed the situation more quickly than he was wont to do, then decided (without consultation), that he had chosen the right track.

"Well", and Mark's conspiratorial smirk told the Ford that he had been right all along, "we wouldn't want to meet anyone from the government, if you catch may meaning", and Mark relaxed for the first time in five minutes. Ford took the bait, and was drawn into their mini-conspiracy with a missionary fervor.

"*I can trruly underrstand*", replied the Ford. "*I've haad occasion to want to visit frriends accrross the channel m'self.*" His smile remained unchanged, but his eyes darted about, engaged in assigning risk value to everything they observed.

"*It just so happens*", continued the Ford, "*that there is a small aircraft to which I have access.*" He paused to allow this to set in. "*Of course*", he proceeded, "*therrre arre cerrtain costs involved....*" "Snap", Mark heard the bait being taken and knew that lady luck had smiled upon them.

"We certainly understand that gaining access to an aircraft involves some costs", he had the hook and line, now the sinker, "but we certainly hope you'll allow us to compensate you for your trouble."

"*Well now, I would na a had it any otherr way laddie.*"

"Done", thought Mark, and noticed that Jennifer was staring at him oddly.

They boarded the elderly Ford, and names were neither offered nor requested. After an hour bouncing along the unpaved road, they turned onto a side road beginning in an opening between two parts of the same cyclone fence. At first, Mark thought it was a farm, but as they approached a large flat area, it turned out that this was what originally gave the name to an "air field". It consisted of a large, very flat grassy field with a row of squat buildings and one aging Quonset hut at one end. In front of the buildings were rows of light aircraft, tied to the ground by thick ropes attached to stakes reminding Mark of the pitons used in mountain climbing.

They drove around the periphery of the field until they reached the Quonset hut.

"*Well, here we arre laddie.*" And the old man hopped out more spryly than Mark had expected, and led them around the back to a door which was dwarfed by the size of the building.

They walked through the door, their footsteps reverberated through-out the metal walled cavern, and wended their way between a "V" tailed Bonanza and an antique J-4 ("Jenny"). After stooping to walk under the sloping wing of a twin Beach (affectionately known to pilots as a "Bamboo Bomber"), they were led through a frosted glass door lettered "Baron's Flying School" and into an office. It was sparsely furnished with a metal desk, two five drawer pull-out file cabinets with unlabeled drawers, and a worn green vinyl sofa with chairs to match.

"*Sit*", stated the surly Scot. It was a command, despite the polite nature of his voice. They sat. "*I'll be rright bachk*", and he disappeared through a door they hadn't noticed. leaving them to sit for several minutes.

"*This is Ian*", the Scot returned, "*I leave ye in his hands. Now about our arrrangements…*"

Twenty minutes later, the still anonymous Scot left, satisfied. Mark had really developed a liking for the man. Scoundrel was the only word he could think of to describe him, and he liked that too. Ian then explained that they would be flying an American Piper 180 (vintage 1975). It was a four seat aircraft, whose gear remained "down and welded." Throughout all of this, Jennifer remained quiet, leaving the arrangements to Mark.

They found the cream and blue Piper sitting tied next to a Cessna 172, untied it, then entered by climbing on the black strip on the right wing and through the only door in the aircraft. Jennifer entered first, sitting in back. Next Ian entered, sliding across the right seat into the left, thus taking his rightful place as Pilot in Command of the aircraft, followed, finally, by Mark who sat in the right or co-pilot's position.

From a leather bag Ian kept on the floor, he withdrew a "kneeboard", to which was attached a worn checklist from which he began reciting and checking.

There was no control tower, so after announcing his intentions to anyone who might be listening on the appropriate frequency, they rolled across the field, turned into the wind, and accelerated until the small aircraft became light on its wheels, stopped bouncing, and lifted gracefully into the air. Mark never tired of the sensation of flight. Each time an aircraft lifted into the air, he felt his heart leap, and the adrenaline flow.

In seemingly no time, England was fading behind them, and the coast of France loomed larger by the minute. Ian reached over and gently pulled on the "T" shaped throttle to reduce the power. Slowly, they began to sink toward the water beneath them. Soon, the light chop became more visible, and the occasional small boat became much more identifiable. Mark and Jennifer weren't sure what was happening, but before they could wonder much longer, they were level at 300 meters.

Ian noticed Mark's quizzical look, smiled, and answered simply, "Radar". Mark nodded, and nothing more was said by anyone until they noticed that the shore of France had receded behind them.

"Would it be possible to take us past Le Harve toward Paris?" inquired Jennifer politely from the back seat.

"Sure, Miss, but it will cost you more money. Petrol, and all—you understand..." She did, and produced a fifty pound note. Ian smiled, put it into his shirt pocket, and continued flying. Eventually, they seemed to be tracking the road from Le Harve to Paris. Just as Mark thought that he could make out the outline of a city far ahead, the piper banked sharply to the right, and its wheels were rumbling over the grass of another field.

"Far as I go, mate", said Ian as he reached across Mark and unlatched both the upper and lower latches. The door, now unrestrained, popped open about three inches, increasing the volume of noise admitted by the low roar of the engine.

"Where are we?", asked Mark.

"About ten kilometers from Paris", answered Ian. "You should be able to get a ride from here."

"Thanks," replied Mark, then climbed out onto the wing, pushed his seat forward, and reached into the rear seat to help Jennifer out. "We really appreciate...", began Mark, only to be cut short by Ian's closing the door and waving them off of the wing.

Within seconds after climbing off of the wing and stepping back, the Piper roared again, and lifted into the deepening blue sky, disappearing quickly, at nearly tree top level, in the direction from which they had come.

"Well, where to now?", asked Mark absent-mindedly as he surveyed the field they had landed in, the surrounding farmland, and the nearby highway.

"We have to get to Paris", stated Jennifer flatly. As she began walking towards the road, she looked back and said, "come on", tossing the order over her shoulder and continuing on her way. Mark was left with no choice except to follow.

"Wait a minute!", shouted Mark while jogging to catch up with her. "How do you expect us to get to Paris?", he continued slightly out of breath. "I have no more money, I don't think you have much left either, neither of us speaks French, and we are wearing the same clothes we've had on for three days." His breathing slowed to normal, and he found that he had clamped his hands on her shoulders while waiting for a reply. He could see her wince from the pain, but she stared at him quietly, apparently waiting for him to calm down.

"To begin with," began Jennifer, I have some money left. Not a great deal, but we can get more in Paris." She paused, not for effect, but as though she was considering how much she should divulge. "We can buy new clothes, get a room, some rest, and begin to figure things out." She looked down, began to walk toward the road again, then turned toward him and waited a few seconds before continuing. "Look, I told you I work for the government. There are places we can go to in Paris, and people to whom I can turn for help. Maybe we'll also get some answers. But first, we have to get to Paris, so come on." She held out her hand and waited once more.

Mark wasn't sure why, but he trusted her. He took her hand, and together they walked to the road. They found it surprisingly easy to get a ride into town. The elderly couple that picked them up seemed to have no fear of strangers. The driver, *Messier Monsard*, it turned out spoke fairly fluent English, since he had been with the Resistance "during the War." His wife, a gentle woman with white hair tied in a loose bun, spoke no English, but *Pierre* would occasionally translate for her when she felt the need to enter into the conversation. He seemed to enjoy the role of being able to do something that she could not. More importantly, however, was that they seemed to accept the "car broke down" story, and gave them a ride without further inquisition.

"Where do you want to go in Paris?", asked Pierre.

"*Tois Tois Cenc Rue de Martin*", replied Jennifer immediately, following it with the explanation that "My aunt and uncle live there, and we are staying with them."

"That is one of the better neighborhoods", responded the elderly Monsard with a smile."

"My family is wealthy," Jennifer said, and left it rest at that.

A few minutes later, Mark and Jennifer were deposited in front of a well preserved brownstone, and climbed the discolored but immaculate steps to a wooden door painted a deep forest green. The Brass "lion's head" knocker hung just below eye level for Mark, who was about to ask Jennifer who lived here when she reached past him and knocked three times.

The door opened, and a woman with reddish brown hair and an aquiline nose poised between brown eyes ("handsome" was the word that came to mind for Mark) that looked to be in her mid forties opened the door. "*Oui?*", asked the woman as she spoke through the door, open only about three inches. The latch chain was visibly holding the door from opening any further.

"*Je m'apell Jennifer, é mon'tant es Madam Liber*". Jennifer's French appeared from nowhere, the accent seemingly correct to an untrained ear.

"*Entre Vous*", replied the woman. The door closed momentarily, and Mark could hear the chain being slid across the latch, then it opened, and they entered a small foyer, lit by an undersized hanging brass chandelier with three "flame shaped" bulbs. Behind the woman, a narrow staircase rose against the flowered wallpaper of the right wall, turned left at a landing that crossed above and in front of them, then rose another flight in the opposite direction on their left. The wall with the landing was broken by a small window with faded white curtains, in front of which stood a vase with bright yellow flowers that seemed incongruous against their drab background. Along the left wall was a closed door that Mark supposed to be a closet, followed by a squared archway.

"Please", said the woman in heavily accented English, and led them through the archway into the living room. There was a small step down, bringing them onto a worn but well cared for Chinese rug, surrounded by various pieces of furniture covered in fading flowered fabric. "sit, please", and the woman left, abandoning them to find their own seating arrangements.

Jennifer walked to the sofa, in front of which stood an antique mahogany coffee table. The sunlight entering through the windows made the room more cheerful than the other parts of the house they had seen, buoying Mark's spirits as he sat next to her.

"Where are we?", Mark asked quietly, his eyes darting furtively around the room.

"A *safe house*", replied Jennifer. Then she added, "a place where we can rest and get some help".

Mark said nothing. He was feeling tired, and not inclined to trust anyone or anything. He had lost track of time. How long had it been since he had stood in an elevator and asked a beautiful young woman to join him for a cup of coffee? How long since he had disappeared from his hotel. "My God", he thought, "I haven't spoken to Meredith or the boys in days!" He had better let Jennifer know that there were people he needed to call, he decided, and had just begun to voice this when a "bearishly" large man entered the room.

"Jenn!", he thundered, his voice booming in English, accented somewhere between England and France, and his smile revealing his obvious pleasure at seeing her. Mark was totally ignored for the moment, as the two hugged.

"Porter", began Jennifer, turning to face Mark, "this is Mark. Mark, Porter." He was left unsure whether Porter was the first or last name, but it didn't matter.

"Hello", and Mark offered his hand which he soon found engulfed in Porter's.

"Hello", Porter answered, then returned to Jennifer.

They spoke quietly for a moment, then she turned to Mark and asked that he wait a few minutes. "I'll be right back", she offered. "Please try to sit and relax. We're safe here, and there are things I must arrange before we can go any further." He was about to protest when she squeezed his hand then, taking Porter by his arm, they disappeared together, leaving him no choice but to wait for their return. He sat, picked up a surprisingly new magazine from the table in front of him and felt like a kid glancing through a comic book, being unable to decipher the French text.

About fifteen minutes later, Jennifer and Porter returned. They were smiling, but not in a way that Mark thought of as jovial. "Mark", Jennifer seemed tentative, "Porter needs to ask you some questions. It won't take long, but we need to know certain things to help us clear this up."

"Come with us, old man", and Porter led Mark with Jennifer following behind, through a small door, at the rear of the staircase, and took an elevator to the basement. They wended their way through old crates, piles of old clothing, and a rarely used workbench, and through another door into a brightly lit antechamber. A hallway led off to the right, and straight ahead was a door that led them into a room that staggered Mark by its appearance.

The room into which Mark was led was large and well lit by fluorescent fixtures recessed into the acoustic ceiling behind translucent panels. A gray Berber carpet covered the floor, upon which a modern but comfortable grouping of furniture including a taupe sofa, three chairs, and a central coffee table of glass and chrome was arranged. Mark sat on the sofa with Jennifer, while Porter sat in the chair to his right. He had just begun to look around when his attention was returned to Porter.

"Well, old man", Porter's use of that phase was beginning to become annoying, "let's go over what has happened." It was Mark's first *de-briefing*.

Chapter 13

Lt. Commander Donald Allen, "Jaguar," banked his F-14 Tomcat left to 340?, his wingman following behind and to his left. They were only ten minutes into their mission, and were still "playing" with their aircraft. *"Oh I have slipped the surly bonds of Earth, and danced the skies..."* the thoughts echoed in his mind as wisps of clouds passed beneath them, no waves were visible from their altitude. Allen had loved flying since he saw his first airplane. He took flying lessons during high school, with his parents' grudging permission, then delighted in being selected for flight training after graduating from The Naval Academy. Now, high above the Persian Gulf, alone except for his wingman who, to his delight, maintained radio silence, "Jaguar" searched the sky around them constantly, without any conscious thought of doing so. His trained eyes spotted nothing, but that was no surprise. In this day when air warriors could be separated by a hundred miles, vision only played a role at the end of the battle, when an aircraft had closed to short range with the adversary or missile. This was the eighteenth mission "Jaguar" had flown in the last month, and each had ended uneventfully, with the bone shattering bounce that characterizes a "good" carrier landing. There was about an hour left before turning for home, when the slightly raspy sound of his headphones blasted his reverie into shreds—"Sky Raider, this is Searchlight", then repeated "Sky Raider, Searchlight".

"Searchlight, Sky Raider", replied Allen, his senses now alert, "I copy."

"Sky Raider, Searchlight, I'm painting four bogies at zero eight zero degrees relative" (the "e" in zero being stretched into an "eee" to distinguish it from other letters over the radio). "They look like 31's, but we can't be sure."

"Roger, Searchlight, will intercept and identify."

"Cobra, Jaguar", Allen awaited a reply from his wingman.

"Roger Jaguar", answered Cobra.

"Follow me to zero six zero", and didn't wait for a reply before banking his wings into the morning sun, knowing with absolute certainty that his wingman was glued into position to his left and behind. As his nose turned through 045?, they both began their roll out to steady up on their new course.

"Scorpion, you got anything yet?", Jaguar addressed his REO sitting behind him.

"Negative", replied Scorpion, you painting anything Hornet?", he asked his counterpart sitting behind Cobra.

"Negative also."

"OK gentlemen", began Jaguar, "let's…"

"Tally Ho!", interrupted Hornet, "straight ahead."

"Roger, I've got him", answered Scorpion, about fifty klicks with eleven hundred closure."

"Searchlight, Sky Raider, we've got our bogies, closing now."

"Roger, Sky Raider", came the instant reply, "remember, be friendly. Do not, repeat do not fire unless fired upon."

"Killjoy!", answered Jaguar with a bravado he really didn't feel. He had been in combat only once before, over Libya. The Libyan pilot had been no match for him, and the adrenaline rush carried him well beyond any thrill he had yet known. Even so, he could taste the acid welling up in his throat, "the taste of fear", he thought.

"Cobra, Jaguar. I'm gonna break high right, you go low left. We'll see if we can split 'em and converge." "That's a Rog", and each aircraft headed into a different part of the sky, intending to converge at a pre-arranged location.

Only seconds passed before four specks in the distance became darts, then aircraft speeding towards them. As the enemy aircraft approached, the formation broke apart with one pair of MIGS following Jaguar, while the other two followed Cobra. Turning sharply, the MIG behind Jaguar began to narrow the gap, only having to slow so that he could narrow his turn to try to get inside of his prey's turning radius.

Jaguar, the sweat beading on his forehead, banked high and left then, with an abrupt "wingover," was pointed at the ground. He prayed that Cobra would be where he was supposed to be. The bitter taste in his mouth, and the burning in his throat reminded him that he was no superman. Behind him, the flight of MIGS was falling slightly behind.

As they passed through eighteen thousand feet, Jaguar looked to his right. There, at about two o'clock, was Cobra, trailing two MIGs on his tail.

"Jaguar, Cobra", the radio crackled.

"Roger Cobra."

"Jaguar, I've got you sighted. I'm coming around behind you to…" His voice trailed off then erupted with, "He's firing! Break right! Hard right!"

As the two closed the first part of their figure eight, Cobra turned toward the number two MIG behind Jaguar. "I've got missile lock!", he announced nervously, "firing, taking the shot, I'm firing now…"

Jaguar had just locked onto the trailing MIG behind Cobra as he banked into a climbing right turn, then fired almost simultaneously with Cobra. Two bright orange plumes erupted in he sky, now only four planes bored holes in the air.

"OK Cobra", the radio erupted, "follow me up on a *six*". A pause, then, "you'll be able to get my tail then break hard right while I come around and under yours."

Jaguar began his climb, with the other MIG following behind him. He was losing ground to the faster MIG, but at least he had a plan. He twisted, just as a row of cannon fire ripped through a section of wing that, fortunately, contained no vital structures. Thirty-five thousand, forty thousand, then the MIG erupted into an expanding yellow-orange ball, behind him.

"Time," he thought, and kicked his left rudder peddle as he pulled his stick back and to the left. He was suddenly pointed as the ground, then felt the "G" forces tearing at his consciousness, and the sky turning pink, as he swung through the horizontal plane to begin his climb back under the last MIG.

"Cobra, Jaguar," he bellowed, break right, NOW!"

Cobra broke right without answering, and Jaguar waited until the indicator flashed red and the tone echoe in his ears to indicate "missile lock" before pulling the trigger. He saw the missile climb ahead of him and, breaking right to join up with Cobra, turned to look at the exploding MIG as Scorpion simply exhaled, "whew!"

"Searchlight, Sky raider", and Jaguar heard the immediate reply—"Searchlight."

"Searchlight, strike four, they're out of the inning. Now tell me, where did they come from?"

"Need to know, Sky raider", answered the carrier, referring to the term used when some piece of information isn't important for someone to possess, "come on home."

"Roger", Jaguar sounded both tired and excited, if that is possible, then turned for the carrier, and home, Cobra behind and to the left.

Back on the Enterprise, Rear Admiral Scheinholtz sat, alone, in a padded leather chair, overlooking a glass tabletop display. The computer had just finished showing the "players" in the recent air battle, the positions of the other ships and airborne aircraft in the fleet, and surrounding shore and terrain. He stared blankly at the various, moving, multicolored symbols, a tepid cup of black coffee remaining only half finished in his right hand. Sweat was beading on his forehead, and his eyelids were half closed as his mind wandered through the various response options at his command. He surmised that the aircraft had originated within Iraq, yet these were not Iraqi MIGS. Neither the Russians nor the Americans ever gave their latest technology to other countries. The aircraft that the Iraqis were flying were at least one, and usually two generations behind what the they were flying themselves, and these were the latest.

"Lieutenant!", barked Sheinholtz and, without waiting for the obligatory reply continued, "get me the stats on the MIG 31." With that he returned to his reverie, awaiting the arrival of the information he had just ordered. It arrived within two minutes in the form of a large bound, five ring notebook, within which were dozens of white sheets of paper, each covered in plastic, with statistics about most of the armament in the Russian armory. It was already opened to the page bearing the information on he MIG 31. He filled his coffee cup to the brim again, then returned to his seat to read the technical information on the MIGS. He needed to digest it completely. There was something wrong, something out of place, but he couldn't quite put his finger on it.

"Prepare to receive returning aircraft", the P.A. system blared, as something clicked in Wild Bill Sheinholtz's mind. He reached for the red telephone, lifted the handset and, after a slight pause, raised it to his left ear. Seconds later, a hollow voice at the other end said "yes…". After a slight hesitation, Schienholtz said simply, "get me Admiral Hallsey", then sat awaiting a reply. The thought of what he was about to discuss left butterflies moving around in his stomach. There was no other logical explanation.

"Hallsey!" the name was barked with a vehemence of one who had not wanted to be disturbed. "Sir", began Sheinholtz, establishing for his old friend that this was no casual call but one he considered to be of immense importance, "four bogies downed in the last ten minutes." "Congratulations, Bill, but why the call instead of a report?"

"Sir", Sheinholtz hesitated, then continued with renewed conviction, these were MIG 31's. They came from the direction of Iraq but *intel* makes me believe they were flown from somewhere else by Russian pilots."

"That's a serious charge, Admiral", the use of Sheinholtz rank for the first time signaling a change in the tenor of the conversation. "Why would the Russians, especially with their present difficulties, want to engage us in an area they have specifically kept out of?"

"I'm not sure sir, but I doubt they gave 31's to the Iraqis, and I doubt they would have had time to train them if they had. Worse, they seemed to know exactly where we were coming from and what we would do. In short, I think it seemed important enough to them to stop us from completing our mission that they were willing to risk lives, even direct confrontation." A pause followed, then, "But Stuart," and he hesitated once more, "We were only flying a routine mission. Why would they do that?"

"Let me think, Bill, I'll call you back soon." The line went dead, leaving Sheinholtz holding the handset to his ear but hearing nothing. He sighed, put the receiver down and, poured himself some "medicinal" brandy after returning to his cabin, then drifted slowly into a troubled sleep.

Chapter 14

Sergey Ivanavich sat at his ornate desk in the Kremlin reading page after page of endless reports. His job as FSB liaison officer for the Kremlin elite gave him more than prestige, more than power, even more than access to information that few other men in the world shared. More than all of these, it gave him a three bedroom apartment on Kosminsky Prospekt, not far from where he now sat. He was important. It showed in the "trappings" around him.

Sitting just to the right of the nearly antique brass telephone on his desk was a squat black phone. It was a "secure" line. To Sergey, it meant that there were probably no more than two or three "bugs" placed there by the Americans, the British, the Israeli's, his superiors. Even this made him feel more important.

His desk always looked busy but neat. Just the right number of papers was spread out on his desk. Too many would make him look disorganized. Too few would make it look as though he hadn't enough work to do or he was lazy.

To Sergey's right was a tray with "incoming" mail, next to which was another tray with incoming "communications". From the list of these that he read day after day, it sometimes seemed that Russia was coming apart at the seams. The once solid "superpower" had become splintered into multiple pieces. Sergey understood this, but it didn't seem to register in his conscious mind. To him, all was as it was because to consider otherwise was unthinkable. The USSR was all he

had ever known, and he couldn't conceive of its not existing. He plod-
ded on through the days work.

"*MOST SECRET*" read the scarlet Cyrillic lettering on the folder in
his hand. Opening it, there was a description of an "incident" in which
four Soviet MIG 31's had "accidentally" engaged American F-14's over
the Persian Gulf and had, subsequently, been destroyed. Sergey stared at
the report. He was startled, not only by the destruction, but by the presence of the MIG's in that area. There had been explicit instructions
from the President himself that all perceivably provocative military
action be refrained from in that area of the world. That meant no over-
flights without notifying the Americans, and certainly no engagement.
Why, then, had such an engagement taken place, and by whose orders?

The fighters had left an air base named after an obscure bureaucrat
and, after over-flying portions of Iraq and Iran, engaged the Americans
in international airspace. This would have required refueling over Iran
and, had they been successful, doing so again on the return trip, all of
which would have required (at least tacit) cooperation from the
Iranians. *The Iranians were cooperating because they had deliberately
caused the airliner to squawk a military code so that they were "mistak-
enly" shot down by the American missle cruiser.* Something didn't make
sense, yet to question it would place him in an exposed position.
"*Nyet!*", thought Sergey, "I'm not going to get involved in this one. It's
over anyway".

There the matter would have remained except for the interference of
Fate which, in this case, took the form of a ringing telephone. Sergey
looked at the black handset through four rings before picking it up.

"*Drastedje Sergey Ivanovitch*", said the clear baritone voice at the
other end of the line.

"Mr. President", Sergey answered deferentially, and waited for
President Yelenkov to continue.

"Sergey", continued the President, "What is this bullshit about some
of our MIG's being shot down in the Persian Gulf?"

"Sir", replied Sergey hesitantly, "I've only just read the report myself."

"Well, what about it?", "Yelenkov's" irritation was becoming obvious. "What were they doing there? Who gave the orders? "The president's voice was becoming shrill. He never used to get like this, thought Sergey, still, he was the President.

"Sir, I don't know, but I'll find out."

The line clicked and went dead. Sergey found that he had risen to his feet, and remained standing, holding the telephone handset. The sweat that had not had time to form before, now found its way down his forehead and onto his face. He sat down and, replacing the handset onto its cradle, began shaking furiously, then his mind fell into gear. His shaking stopped as abruptly as it had begun, and his manner became calm. He knew better than to ask direct questions of the military. There would be a chain of orders leading off into the sunset. No one would be traceably responsible. There never seemed to be any origin for an action with an unfavorable outcome, yet all orders were always legitimate. "Perhaps this is our greatest weakness", he considered, but still needed a starting point for his investigation.

The Americans were basing most of their activity off of naval vessels, so any observation at those sites was impossible. He would simply have to visit the Russian air base from which the attack had been launched.

Three hours later Sergey was comfortably ensconced aboard an Aeroflot twin engine Tupalov and working his was through his fourth vodka.

"Another!", he barked to the stewardess. It arrived with a smile, one never offended a high ranking government official. It just didn't pay.

"Will there be anything else General?", inquired the very Slavic appearing young lady who was the stewardess aboard this flight.

"*Nyet!*", barked Sergey, and downed his last drink, then faded off into a world where spies and saboteurs were only the stuff of novels.

This is where the reader finally becomes suspicious that there was more to the story than even the jaundiced eye could see. There was something aboard the plane that the Vincences shot down that was so damaging to so many governments, that the Ianians were ready to sacrifice their own plane and all the passengers and crew to protect it. The Americans were willing to be the "Bad Guys" and shoot the plane down, and the Soviets were willing to risk losing four of their most advanced fighters to keep the American pilots from flying into an area in which they might observe what they shouldn't. Wakefulness was slow in arriving, and the plane was nearly at the terminal building when Sergey completed rubbing his eyes and straightening his clothing in preparation for leaving the aircraft. There were no customs or "papers" checks for Sergey. Everyone at the station knew he was coming, and not to interfere with him. He walked down the "airstairs" (there were no "jetways" here) and crossed the steaming tarmac to the un-air conditioned terminal, and from there to a waiting dark, late model Mercedes limousine. As soon as he entered, the car moved smoothly away without a word having been said. This was just as well. Sergey had to think.

"Take me to the "Air Station", Sergey said to the driver quietly.

"Sir", responded the driver, "I was told to take you directly to the hotel."

"Son", Sergey smiled at the young driver, "do you know who I am?"

"Yes sir!"

"Then don't argue with me, just do it."

"Yes sir!", and the big car swung around in the opposite direction and, two streets later took a hard left and headed out into an area of rock and scrub bushes covering low hills.

Ten minutes later, Sergey displayed his Identification Papers to the guard at the gate, then proceeded to the headquarters building. "Perhaps they aren't quite ready for me", thought Sergey to himself. Maybe he would be able to catch some log entry or form that had remained unaltered.

The squat cement building gave no indication as to what lay inside. Once through the outer door, Sergey was led down several nondescript hallways and through a simple, green metal door that opened into an office nearly as ornate as his own at the Kremlin. He stood, amazed, taking in the surroundings with distaste. This was a field command. These trappings were reserved for areas where visitors were to be impressed, not for soldiers.

Across the room, a heavy-set balding colonel rose quickly to his feet, crossed the several meters of floor space and maneuvered around a table with surprising agility, to shake Sergey's hand. His manner was obsequious, and would have been funny in another surrounding. Here, it was out of place. People like Colonel Markov brought the military to its lowest common denominator.

"General", began Markov, "how nice to see you." His moist hand and slight squint belied his jovial greeting. "We weren't expecting your visit until tomorrow." "That, at least", thought Sergey, "was the truth."

"I thought I'd stop here before going to my hotel so that I could get a small head start", Sergey stated as matter-of-factly as he could, while observing the colonel for any other signs of uneasiness. "Would you be kind enough to have someone bring me the flight logs and orders for the last week? I'll wait for them here", and Sergey walked around to sit in the colonel's chair at his desk, making it obvious that he had just appropriated the office for his use. "Oh, by the way Colonel, would you have someone bring me some tea and sandwiches, I may be here for awhile." It was an order, not a request, and carried with it the suggestion of the unspoken word—"Dismissed!"

Colonel Markov left to do as he was "asked", while Sergey settled back into the leather chair to await the papers he had requested. It took nearly fifteen minutes for the tea and sandwiches to arrive. He was eating when a sergeant brought two large folders with the ubiquitous "CLASSIFIED" stamp on each. "Thank you, sergeant", and Sergey took the folders and placed them to one side. They could wait a few minutes before he began.

Two hours later, his eyes beginning to burn from reading column after column of print, Sergey leaned back and rubbed his forehead and neck to relieve the muscle strain. He had gone through the flight log and orders thoroughly. It was there, he knew it, but couldn't find it. He was missing something, but he didn't know what. Everything seemed to be in order. Still, there was a nagging feeling that it was, somehow, "wrong." He closed the folders, determined to begin again in the morning. He placed into his pocket a list of documents he had compiled as he read through the material in the folders (he wanted to be sure it was all there when he asked for them in the morning). Then standing, and leaving the folders on the desk, he walked out of the door to find his guard waiting to escort him back to his car.

"Lock the office and place a guard at the door", Sergey ordered and, after observing it being done, retraced his earlier steps to the waiting Limousine, got in, and simply allowed the driver to take him to the hotel without further conversation.

The hotel was an older building, with some of the "charm" of Ashkhabad remaining. From the aging lobby, he was shown to his room. It had worn furniture, an overhead fan that moved little air but at least kept the flies stirred up, and one overhead light fixture. The remaining light came from two bedside lamps as well as one next to a winged chair with the fading fabric that sat next to the open balcony doors. He thanked his "aid", threw his things on the chair, and closed the door. Ten minutes later he lay between the rough but cool sheets, drifting into a troubled sleep. Something was missing, but he was too tired to think of it tonight. He would think of it in the morning when he was rested, "in the morning, in the morning…", his mind repeated.

He awakened to the disorientation he always felt on the first morning in a new city. His eyes opened to the unaccustomed brightness, and he spent several seconds watching a fly walking across his night table before lifting his head. "Ashkhabad!", thought Sergey with disgust, and swung his feet onto the thinning oriental carpet, rubbed his eyes, and began his daily ablutions.

Breakfast consisted of black coffee, strong to the point of being harsh, toast, and some undefined meat that he ate out of hunger rather than appreciation. He read the newspaper as he drank the remaining coffee, then called for his car. Within thirty minutes, he was ensconced at a desk in a different office. Colonel Markov had thought ahead this time and had him moved to a private office rather than giving up his own, but the same stacks of reports were in front of him. Even their order and pilings had been maintained.

In front of him sat another cup of black coffee and a pile of black bread and butter. He drank the coffee and pushed the bread and butter aside. There was something in the reports that had troubled him last night, and he was unable to put his finger on it. He began reading again, from the beginning.

Two hours later he pushed the papers back, still uneasy, and still without the answer that eluded him. He would have to call the president today to give him a report. What would he say? He began again.

By lunch, Sergey had enough of the piles of paper to last the most hardened bureaucrat for days. Stretching, he ambled through the green metal door and down the hall to what appeared to be flight operations, "OPS" as it was known to the flight crews. He stood there, being as unnoticeable as possible, watching the goings-on around him.

"Excuse me, Captain", he began, as he addressed a young pilot signing his flight log. "Can you explain to me what you just signed and what its purpose is?"

The pilot, seeing Sergey's ID badge, answered quickly as sweat beaded up on his forehead. "Well sir, before each flight we sign the aircraft out, and after each flight we sign it back in again, accounting for the time flown, mission, crew, fuel, and so forth."

"And is that your signature?", asked Sergey, knowing that it was.

"Yes sir", replied the pilot.

"And why have you signed it in both the official block, and right below the last line of your report?"

"Well sir, these reports have been known to be changed, *added to* if you know what I mean, and I don't want that to happen to my reports."

"Do many of the pilots do that? Sign in both places, I mean?"

"Everyone", stated the young officer flatly. It doesn't take long to learn how things work around here." He hesitated for a moment, wondering if he should continue, then decided he had little to lose. "Sir, fuel, ammo, even spare parts are easily sold in the black market here. Sometimes things are added to a flight report as having been expended when they weren't, in order to account for their disappearance."

"Hmm", thought Sergey to himself.

"Well sir, if there's nothing else, I'd like to get some rest before my next flight. We all go up at least once daily since there aren't enough of us, and it maintains proficiency."

"Of course, Captain, and thank you for your help." He watched the young man stride away with the "cocky" air that fighter pilots have all over the world, sighed, got another cup of coffee, then returned to his desk. Something was beginning to take shape in his mind, but it wasn't yet clear. He would find it…today.

By fifteen hundred he had it. "*Boigemoi!*" It was so obvious once found that it jumped out at him and shouted "STUPID!" for not having seen it before. There were two piles of reports on the aging wooden desk in front of him. Of all of the paper in both piles, two sheets were perfectly executed. There were no duplicate signatures, there were no deviations from one to the other. The exact amount of fuel that the pilot had signed for was pumped by the crew chief, and takeoff and landing times were exactly the same in both pilot and tower logs. The reports were perfect except, of course, that the planes reported as having landed, had actually been shot down.

It came as no surprise to Sergey, then, that neither the pilot nor the crew chief were known to anyone at the base, and the tower controller who prepared the tower log that day had been transferred ("You'll have to check with headquarters to find out where, General").

Slowly, he reached for the telephone on the desk in front of him, removed a small black cube from his briefcase, and from it, extracted two thin cables which he attached to the telephone handset in a practiced manner. With determination, he dialed a telephone number that was known to only a small number of people, waited until several rings had passed, and was about to hang up when the familiar voice rang hollowly from the other end, "*Da?*"

"*Drástetze tzovarich President,*" began Sergey after flipping a switch on the black cube, "I have something here that I think you should be aware of. I'll be returning to Moscow today, and I'd like to meet with you when I get back. It's important." This was all that needed to or could be said at this time, despite the scrambling device. The rest would come later.

Chapter 15

Dinner at the "Safe House" in Paris was served formally. Porter sat at one end of a long, ornately carved oak table, obviously designed for more people. Jennifer sat to his right, and Mark to his left. Crystal chandeliers cast soft but adequate light upon gold rimmed Wedgwood china with sparkling silver flatware and flowing Baccarat crystal. The table could have been set for royalty.

As he and Jennifer sat down, Porter pulled his chair closer to the table, and a liveried waiter brought iced vichyssoise and hot bread to the table, while filling each wine glass with the deep color of "Nuit St. George".

"Cheers!", began Porter, raising his glass and sipping from it before either of his "guests" had a chance to join him.

"Well, old man," began Porter, knowing that it irritated Mark, but with a slight twinkle in his eye. "Are you feeling better?"

"Yes, thank you. I took a nap, and when I woke up, I found that my clothes had been cleaned and laid out for me, with some new things to boot. How did you know my size, and find things that fit me so well?" Mark knew it was a stupid question when he asked it, but the sheer relief of what seemed like un-relievable tiredness made him continue to babble. His mouth had a mind of its own.

"And you, Jen," Porter redirected the conversation. "How are you feeling now that you've had a rest?"

"Fine," lied Jennifer, her shoulder continuing to throb. "What's after the soup?" Neither tiredness nor pain made her babble.

Porter ignored the question, and the conversation continued on a casual vein throughout the meal. With the arrival of desert and coffee, the waiter seemed to disappear, and the conversation once more took on more ominous tones.

After about twenty seconds of complete silence during which Jennifer and Porter stared at each other, and which seemed to Mark to stretch into minutes and hours, Porter cleared his throat, began to speak, and then cleared his throat again.

"Mark," Jennifer interrupted Porter's halting beginning, "I have to leave you for awhile." I should only be gone...," her hesitation branded what followed as a guess, if not a lie, "...a short time. A few days at the most. You'll be safe here, and I'll be back as soon as I can."

"I'm going with you," Mark stated flatly. "I don't know these people, and you may need me. Besides, where are you going?" His confusion showed through. He was about to be deserted by the one stable point in the last few days—the one person whom he had come to depend upon.

"No, you can't come with me this time. I promise I'll be back soon." Mark began to sweat.

"Where are you going?", he asked again in more shrill tones.

"Mark...," Jennifer began, but was cut short by Porter, now asserting himself.

"Listen Mark," Porter's voice was quiet but demanding. "Jennifer once knew a man who has now shown up in Paris. He's...", Porter paused trying to find just the right words, "...on the other side. We need to know what he's been up to , and Jennifer is the only one whom we think would be able to get," another hesitation, "...close to him", concluded Porter.

"What does that mean?", Mark asked hesitantly, looking from Porter to Jennifer. "Jenn...", and he stared at the green eyes he had come to trust in a space of only a few days.

Tears welled up in Jennifer's eyes and, without answering, she rose abruptly and left the room. Both men sat staring at the pocket doors left open as she fled to the stairs, neither saying anything for a few seconds.

Mark rose to follow her but Porter's surprisingly strong grip on his arm restrained him. "Don't," Porter directed. "Give her some time." They both sat down, and the silence became unbearable.

"I'm going to talk with her," Mark stated flatly and, not waiting for a reply, rose and walked calmly to the stairs. He climbed past the first landing to the second of three floors, and stood for a minute listening to hear any sign of her. "Jenn?," he called out tentatively. Getting no answer, he tried again, louder this time, "Jenn!?" After a few moments, he saw her standing at the partly open third door on the right. The light was dim in the hall, but even so, he could see she had been crying. He walked quickly and pushed his way past her before she could protest.

"Mark," she began, "I…" He cut her short. "Listen Jenn," he said as forcefully as he could manage, "you don't have to do anything you don't want to do." He paused, was it really true? He decided that it sounded convincing so he would continue. "They can't send you after some spy and get you killed. I won't stand for it!"

She smiled slightly, a mental vision of him standing in front of her, his arms spread, protecting her from enemies. "Look, Mark…", and her voice trailed off. "it really isn't like that." She hesitated, then continued cautiously, "This…man, is someone I knew a long time ago. I…, that is we…," she searched for a delicate way of explaining it. "Mark, we were lovers." She stopped at that, waiting for a response.

Mark wasn't so much stunned as taken aback. he knew she had a life before him. Christ! He was a married man! Still, what she was being asked to do, ordered to do, really, was beginning to sink in.

"These bastards are sending you back to screw him again for infor-mation!?" The thought brought waves of nausea, his recent dinner rose just past his stomach and into his chest. "How can you let them do this to you? Don't you have any pride? I won't let them!" his voice was becoming louder and more shrill, but hr was unable to stop himself.

His head rang from the way it snapped as she struck him. It wasn't a "love tap." With one motion, she had stopped his speech dead in its tracks.

"Shut up!", she commanded. "Why, you goddamned ignorant, arrogant...," she searched for the words, "son-of-a-bitch! You have no conception of what's going on here and what's at stake!" She was screaming at him, a decidedly uncharacteristic thing for her to do. "Who the hell do you think you are?", she continued. "What do you mean *You* won't allow it!? How *dare* you !" Finally, realizing that her voice was rising to a screech, she stopped, forcibly slowed her breathing and inhaled then exhaled deeply. After regaining her composure, she sat on a light antique stool that stood in front of a dressing table, still holding the blouse she had been packing when he walked in, and stared alternately at him and the floor.

Mark stood frozen to the spot. He was transfixed. She had been the rock upon which he anchored his life since a man was shot in front of his hotel, and now she seemed to be coming apart. He didn't know how to react. He didn't move.

Slowly, Jennifer rose and walked toward him. Very tentatively, she dropped the blouse onto the floor, then reached out and placed her hands on his chest, staring up into his eyes. She seemed, suddenly, to have gotten smaller. His mind always saw her as tall, yet the top of her head reached only to his chin. Without a word between them, he gently pulled her towards him then, after a soft peck on her forehead, they kissed deeply. One long sensual kiss that lasted for days, then they stood in the middle of the room holding each other. There was nothing left to say. There was nothing left to do.

After a few more moments, Jennifer bent over, retrieved the blouse she had dropped and, after placing it in the lavishly expensive valise on the bed, closed the bag and carried it toward the door. Mark's eyes followed her, but he never moved. Silently, after one more look back,

Jennifer disappeared through the door frame, down the hall, and was gone. Mark remained standing in the same spot, his body still tingling from the feel of her pressed against him. Then he remembered to breathe.

Once more, Mark and Porter were seated at the dinner table. The two men talked about nothing in particular, simply to pass the time while finishing their coffee. Neither mentioned Jennifer.

The dishes had been removed, the tablecloth was gone, and the rich, highly polished wood grain was visible again. Their chairs were pushed back, and they faced each other, diagonally across the corner of the table.

"Dr. Harmon," began Porter, more formally than before and with more respect, "I've never seen Jennifer react that way before, and I've known her a long time." Mark studied the older man with growing curiosity. He sounded tired and surprised in the same sentence.

"I'm not sure what you mean," Mark answered without thinking.

Porter didn't answer. He remained still, staring at a blank spot on the wall, then he sat up, straightened his chair and continued. "I'm not sure where you fit into all of this, or even if you do. There doesn't seem to be any real connection," he ignored Mark's question.

"Connection with what?" Mark sat, looking and feeling confused.

"Look," and Porter weighed his words carefully, "do you follow the news very carefully?"

"As carefully as most people," Mark answered hesitantly, not knowing where this was going, "why?"

"With relations warming up between the Russians and us, we've begun to share information, and look at other countries and sources of potential trouble. As you are no doubt aware, the largest potential source of trouble in the world, right now, is terrorism." Porter paused for effect. Seeing none, he continued. "The man Jennifer knew a long time ago is someone whom we believe to be a part of that shadow world that we've never been able to really penetrate well. Recently, he showed up in the U.S., stayed for a short while doing nothing in particular that we could detect, then boarded a plane to Paris. He's been here for a few days now. It was pure luck that you and Jennifer showed up when you did. I don't think we would have even thought about her except for your arrival."

"Great," thought Mark, "wasn't it lucky for us?" "What's all this got to do with us," Mark asked out loud?

"As I said before, I'm not sure it has anything to do with you or Jennifer, but her arrival here was serendipitous, and we'll use it." There was a short pause, then Porter continued, "Now Mark, tell me about yourself."

"Excuse me," queried Mark? "I'm not sure what you mean."

"Look, old man," and Porter's eyes twinkled slightly, "I've told you more than I really should have about what's going on, so the least you can do for us, and yourself, is to cooperate. We need to know as much about you as possible, in order to see if there is any connection whatever. We can find out much of it by investigation, but that takes time and we're never sure we have enough of that, so please...," Porter spread his arms out in front of him, palms out, as a gesture of request. Perhaps it was at this moment, Mark sensed that Porter's role was more than just that of a proprietor of a "safe house." He seemed too connected, and this house was too elegant.

"OK," and Mark began to expound on his life and, seeing no impatience on the part of Porter, he slowly became more serious, giving a description of his early life, his education, his social life, etc. When he reached his marriage, he hesitated. He wasn't sure how far to go, what he should say, or how to say it.

"Continue," Porter urged.

"Meredith and I were married after my residency, after only a few months of knowing each other. In retrospect, that was probably not a good idea, but we did it anyway." Mark continued from there. He hadn't intended to go into lurid detail about his failing marriage, his wife, their children, and the problems he was trying to contend with in his daily life. Somehow, though, they seemed so far away and unconnected to his present situation that it was more like telling a story than talking about himself. "And that's how I wound up in London, a few days ago," Mark concluded.

"And how did you meet Jennifer?" Porter immediately zeroed in on this somewhat vague point.

"That's not really important right now, and I'd prefer not to discuss it if you don't mind."

"But I do mind," Porter's demeanor was more rigid now. He was the interrogator. "I need all the information you can give me." He waited.

"No, it's not." Mark was equally determined to keep the details to himself. Sensing the amount of resistance he was meeting, and also sensing that Mark was correct about it being unneeded information, he let the subject slide away and continued in another vein.

"How much do you know about the man who was shot in front of your hotel?" Porter asked.

"Only what Jenn told me, and what I've managed to read in the papers," replied mark, quizzically.

"He was the son of a sheik, whose kingdom would consist of mostly sand if it weren't for the fact that there is a lot of oil under that sand." Porter paused, took a drink of water, and continued. "Rumor has it that he was in London to deliver information to someone. We believe it was to have been the Russians, but we're not sure what it was, or why the Russians would be interested, or why he chose London. We're not even sure it was the Russians he was delivering it to. In short, Mark, we don't know anything about it, and we find that very scary in a world where a mistake can cost millions of lives."

Mark simply sat. There was no immediate reaction, since he still didn't see the relationship between the man Porter was describing and himself.

"The point," continued Porter, nonplused by Mark's indifference, "is that for some reason, you seem to be in the middle of this. Everywhere you go, events seem to follow you. Why?" He could tell by the look on Mark's face that he had hit his target this time.

"How the hell should I know?" Mark couldn't believe this was happening. He looked around, feeling trapped. "Look, I'd like to leave. I don't think I should be involved in all of this."

"You're right," sighed Porter, "but you are, anyway." He stood up and began to pace back and forth in front of a large wall mirror, then stopped and looked directly at Mark. "Listen." His tone had changed. This was no longer a discussion but a command. "Jennifer couldn't see the forest for the trees, but I can. She assumed that she was the target of those attacks. She was wrong. I believe they were each aimed at you, but I don't know why. It must have something to do with the Sheik's son, but I don't know what. Now think!"

"I don't know!" Mark stood up and, leaning on the table, was screaming at Porter. "Look, you people are insane! I'm a doctor. I was in London for a symposium. I walked out of my hotel and a man collapsed in front of me. I did what I could for him, then met Jennifer for a cup of coffee. After that, all hell broke loose, and you know the rest. Now how can I be involved?" It was the first breath he took. Mark slumped back into his chair, the effort seeming to leave him weak.

After a few moments passed, Porter spoke again, more gently this time. "OK Mark, let's begin again."

Chapter 16

It was past six thirty in the evening when Jennifer found herself standing across the desk from the registration clerk at the George V. She had tried to be as unobtrusive as possible. She arrived at a time when, she knew, most people would be dressing for dinner, and most of the hotel staff was either off duty, or preparing for things to come that night. Still, her startling looks drew appreciative stares from the scattering of men in the lobby.

"*Je suis Jennifer Marshall,*" she stated flatly.

"*Oui, mademoiselle,*" and the clerk handed her the plastic card that has come to substitute for a door key around the world. An elevator carried her to the fifth floor, and a bellman, carrying her single valise, led her to the door of room 512 where they were both deposited. She glanced briefly around then, not wanting to begin the job she was sent here to do, slumped into the large cushioned chair sitting in the corner next to an expensive table, and flipped on the T.V. The news commentator was babbling on about local events, and Jennifer didn't feel like straining her mind by translating it, so she just sat there.

After about five minutes, she lifted herself out of the chair and began to undress. She had been wearing a tailored suit that she had been provided with (along with the rest of her clothes) by Porter. Her wounds still ached a little as she pulled off the jacket, but not as much as she had expected. Standing in front of the mirror in her underwear, she surveyed the effect. She liked it. She was never in doubt of her looks, and knew, instinctively, the effect she had on men. She had seen it, since she was a little girl, and now frequently relied upon it to accomplish what she wanted. She felt no regret at this. Some people have exceptional intellect, some are born wealthy, and others are beautiful. Jennifer would use whatever tools she had at her disposal to accomplish her job and, in this case, nature had provided her with exceptional intellect as well as breathtaking beauty

Within a few minutes, she had ascertained the time that "*Messeur* Al Assad" was dining in the main dining room that evening, and began changing into a filmy white lace blouse, a slightly shortened beige skirt, and black panty hose. Her bag and shoes had been perfectly accessorized by Porter's staff. She piled her hair up and, liking the accentuating effect this had on her neck and breasts, decided to wear it "up" this evening. The crowning effect came from a diamond choker, also provided courtesy of the U.S. government. She knew they were synthetic diamonds, but also knew that they were, in any real sense, indistinguishable from perfect stones. She was stunning. She looked at her gold "Fred" watch and, seeing that it was nearly eight o'clock, decided that this was as good a time as any to get started.

The same elevator she had taken to her room deposited her in the lobby. She surveyed the scene. This was a European hotel in the "Grand Tradition"—marble floor, high ceilings, brilliantly lit crystal chandeliers flooding the entire area with a slight pinkish glow that cast an aura of luxury upon everything. Clumps of guests stood around the room, many not sitting so that they didn't wrinkle expensive clothing until it was seen by the right people. Jenn wouldn't want to live in this world permanently, but it was fun to visit.

She walked slowly, with practiced grace, toward the large "French doors" that led into the dining room while looking in all directions to see if Mustafa had arrived yet. Not seeing him, she approached the Matre d'Hotel who, staring appreciatively at her, as is every

Frenchman's time honored right, led her to a small table by the wall, from which she could survey the entire room without being noticed.

"*Vin*," She told the waiter who had asked *mademoiselle* if she wanted anything to drink before dining. "*Chateau Neuf du Pape*," she added, quickly as he was turning his back. She was on an expense account.

A different waiter came for her order. "Nothing with too much garlic," she thought, and ordered vichyssoise, Escargot Florentine, the "*salad de la Maison*," and Dover Sole Verinique. This done, she sat quietly, trying to compose her thoughts when, in the space of a nanosecond, the world ground to a halt.

Across the room, by the entrance, stood Mustafa Al Assad—"David." His six foot, muscular build showed even through his impeccable Armani suit. His thick, midnight black hair with mustache to match, and large, deep eyes always had the same effect on her that she had on men. He hadn't seen her (she had planned that in advance), but she stared at him with feelings she thought were long since buried, stirring in her. After a few seconds, she let out the breath she had been holding, and forcibly tried to relax.

He was being escorted to a seat across the room. A small table, for two, just to the left of the double doors that formed the entrance. It was a seat well suited to his particular tastes. From there, he could see whoever walked into the room before they could see him, and he had an unobstructed view of the kitchen entrance as well. "A real pro.," thought Jennifer to herself, and a small smile crossed her face.

She sat for a while, just watching him. Images of a time long past flooded her mind, and for a few moments, she was floating in a warm reverie that lifted her spirits and made her glow. It was abruptly shattered by the simple bumping of a waiter into her chair as he passed. It would have gone unnoticed during a conversation, but dream worlds are fragile things.

Jennifer sighed, then opened her small black beaded bag and took out her lipstick which she reapplied. No, it hadn't come off with her meal (she hadn't yet eaten anything), it simply needed some gloss. It gave her, she knew, that "just licked her lips" look that men find irresistible. "OK," she thought, it's show time."

She replaced the lipstick into the purse, slung the long silk strap over her left shoulder, and began walking to the ladies' room. Her route took her in a semicircle that would have her pass just close enough to Mustafa's table to be seen and recognized by him, but not close enough for it to appear that she saw him, or was trying to attract his attention. It was calculated, in her mind, down to the time it would take to walk past. She knew he would not react at this time, he was too much the professional to do that, even for her. She could wait.

Dinner was completed quietly. "*L'addition, sil vous plait,*" she beckoned the waiter to her table, signed the check with her room number, and left the dining room. It was too soon to return to her room. She had to give him time to leave the restaurant, follow her, and contact her. She walked out of the front entrance on the *Avenue George V*, turned left to the *Champs-Elysées*, and strolled slowly toward the distant *Arc d'Triumph*. She loved strolling through this area of Paris at night. It was beautiful in a way that no other city in the world was. The gentle summer breeze blew her hair away from her neck and she stood for a moment with her eyes closed, before proceeding. After about ten minutes, she turned and walked, at the same pace, back to the hotel. She hadn't been followed, she was sure of it.

In the lobby, she looked around and , seeing no one she knew or should have known, walked to the elevator and pressed the button for the 5th floor. She stood, once more in reverie, as the elevator carried three other people to their floors before reaching hers. She stepped from the elevator, turned left down the corridor, and thought to herself that she must do better tomorrow. The key card slid into its slot and the small lights changed from red to green. She opened the door to her expensive suite and entered, feeling weary. It was a long time since she had seen the man she had once known as David. She knew that her feelings for him were still buried inside her, and was annoyed at how strong they were.

Slowly, she drifted to the window, in front of which she stood without turning on the lights. "Yes," she thought, "Paris is still beautiful."

"You really ought not to stand exposed in front of the window like that."

The city disappeared from her view as she whipped around, her stance lightening to a defensive posture as she searched the darkness for the shadow from which the voice had originated. An unseen hand grabbed hers and threw her to the bed, where a large dark shape pinned her to it. She opened her mouth to scream, when a distantly familiar voice echoed in her subconscious from the shape above her.

"Jenn," the voice said gently. "Jenn," it repeated softly and, as she relaxed slightly in her surprise, her lips were pressed gently and she felt herself begin to drift away. She was on a beach in Tel Aviv, a million years ago, with a man whom she hardly knew, yet loved desperately. Their mouths parted and each expelled a short breath as he rolled to one side.

The outline of his face and his mustache were just visible in the dim light from the open window. She lay there transfixed for a moment, then ran her hand along his hair his ear, and the curve of his chin.

"David," she said softly. She was not supposed to know who he really was, and she was to call him that as long as he kept up the pretense. She had no thought of this. Her mind knew this was Mustafa, a terrorist killer, but her heart knew him to be David, the man she had loved since that month in Tel Aviv, a long time ago.

"David," she said again softly.

"How are you, Jenn," Mustafa asked, just above a whisper? "I've missed you. "

Without enough warning for him to react, she slapped him as hard as she could manage in their positions. His cheek felt the pain as his head rang loudly. She was still the only one who could surprise him. He reached up to gently rub his face as he sat up.

"How the fuck do you think I am? It's been years! Where have you been! I waited for you in New York, but you never came." She might have been acting, but her words and her anger were real. She stood up and walked toward the window, where she stood looking out over the city again. She wasn't supposed to "blow her cool" like that. He was an assignment, a job. She stood there without looking back. She wanted to hate David ("Mustafa," she corrected herself in her mind) but she couldn't.

"Jenn…," Mustafa began tentatively, sitting up and letting his voice trail off. "Jenn," he said again, "It wasn't what you think. I wanted to come, but I couldn't. There were…," he stopped, searching for the right words, "things stopping me," he continued. She continued to stare into space. Not daring to turn around so that he might see, even in the dark, her eyes well up with tears. "Look, Maybe I shouldn't have come up here tonight. Maybe I should have let the past lie, but I saw you in the dinning room and I had to see you again. I've dreamed about you ever since Tel Aviv. I've loved you since then. Jenn…". Mustafa stopped. He was rambling on and almost couldn't help himself.

"I waited," Jennifer repeated softly. "I sat there at the table drinking coffee and waited, thinking that any second you would round the corner, or walk up the street and sit down at the table."

"Honest, Jenn, I wanted to come, but…."

"Stop!" Jennifer screamed, then calmed down. "Don't say that word. You don't know what honesty means. You're a pathologic liar without morals or scruples." She bit her lip and stopped herself. She was about to give away the depth of her knowledge about him, and then it would be over.

Mustafa stood up and crossed the small room to where Jennifer stood. There was no movement from either of them for what seemed like an eternity then, as she turned to speak, he took her by both shoulders and drew her to him. She tried to resist but before she knew what was happening, they were entwined in a kiss that drew on into the night.

Hours later, they lay in her bed, each staring at the ceiling trying to find the right words. Mustafa reached for his second cigarette before Jennifer said anything.

"What happened, David, why didn't you come?" She knew the answer, but she played her part, now.

"I couldn't," answered Mustafa through the smoke.

"What do you mean you couldn't?" Her words were cool and measured. Her mind was clearing. This was Mustafa, not David. This was a man who kills children, not the lover she had known on a beach, long ago. "If he finds out," she wondered, "will he kill me too?"

"My work," answered Mustafa, carefully, "wouldn't allow it." He paused, then feeling the need to continue, added, "I couldn't involve you in what I do. It's dangerous, and I have to be away for long periods of time." The words felt stale as they left his lips. He knew how they sounded, but what else could he offer her. In all his life, Jennifer was the one real love he had known. He would give anything to be able to live a normal life with her, but it wasn't to be. Even if he wanted to get a normal job and settle down, "they" wouldn't let him. He had become both too valuable, and too dangerous to them.

"David," her words came with greater ease now, "I know you told me that you had something to do with the Mosad, but surely that's over by now. What is it you do?" "Please Jenn, I can't get into that and you know it. It is never over, you know that."

"OK then," Jennifer changed subjects with agility, "let's talk about other things. What have you been doing? Where have you been? Where were you before you came to Paris?" Her questions sounded "girlish" and innocent in exactly the way they were intended to.

Mustafa was quiet for a minute then replied slowly, "Jennifer, you know I can't tell you about my work. I've been...," he paused to choose his words, "away." Then, "And what are you doing in Paris?" Her answer came without missing a beat. It had been scripted the day before in a small brownstone.

"I'm on vacation. I work for the government now, and I was tired, so I decided to take some time off." She decided to change the subject. "Have you been seeing anyone?'

For a moment, Mustafa hesitated, then "no, not in the sense you mean. There have been other women in my life, but there has been no one that has meant anything to me except you." It wasn't a lie.

"Look," and Jennifer changed the subject once again, "I'm going sightseeing today, why don't you come with me?" The idea of being a tourist in Paris appealed to Mustafa, so he agreed.

"I have to return to my room to change, but I'll be back to pick you up in an hour."

"Make it an hour and a half," replied Jennifer, "a girl needs time to fix herself up." There was a smile on both of their faces as he left the room.

Jennifer stood for a minute lost in a short daydream, then turned to the telephone, unplugged the chord and inserted a box no larger than a matchbook between the telephone and the chord, then plugged each end in. The scrambler in place, she picked up the receiver and dialed a number she knew by heart. When a voice she had never heard before answered, she gave no identification (the matchbook sized box did that) but simply stated, "contact," and hung up. She deftly removed the small device from the telephone, returned it to her purse, and undressed for her shower.

She dressed with anticipation, using the first drops from her newly purchased bottle of "Opium" in places she thought the fragrance to be important. "Amazing," she thought, "I feel like a school girl preparing for a date." Makeup in place, hair combed (not much of a chore for her), nails polished, she surveyed the effect and liked what she saw. She knew she was pretty but today she was radiant.

The knock at the door came precisely one and a half hours after Mustafa had left. She opened it, and he stood there in a lightweight beige suit, tailored to perfection, with the perfect accessories. His muscular build was only slightly hidden behind the cloth, and his rugged good looks brought a flutter to her stomach the way he always used to. Without stopping to ask permission, he stepped into the room, put his arms around her and pressed against her as he kissed her deeply. She felt him grow hard beneath his pants, but decided that this was the wrong time—she was hungry.

"OK," she said breathlessly as she broke the connection between them, "let's eat while we still can." Mustafa flashed a broad smile, and they walked to the elevator to go to breakfast.

"Where are we going to eat?" Jennifer was more curious than interested.

We'll have breakfast in the hotel, then I've made dinner reservations at "*Le Tour d'Argent*," replied Mustafa. I know it's a little old, but I always liked it there. She knew the restaurant well. It wouldn't be hard for a dinner and drinks to cost a thousand francs.

They rode silently in the taxi, then walked from place to place as they visited various attractions. They were both unsure what to say to each other. There were too many things each left unsaid out of necessity, so the conversation was limited to trivia. Each knew they had to weigh their words carefully in order to prevent the other form guessing what their true identity and mission was.

Dinner was pleasant, and it passed without incident. There was polite conversation, but neither was giving an inch. It seemed that neither had much to really say to the person with whom he or she had made such passionate love only a few hours earlier. When they arrived back at the hotel, it was nearly midnight. They walked to her room, and he followed her in without being asked. She opened the mini-bar that was hidden beneath the television and asked if he wanted a drink. No, he replied. They stood there facing each other awkwardly.

"Jennifer," he began, then stopped for a minute.

"Yes," she replied, waiting for the remainder of the sentence?

"Jennifer," he began again and, searching for the right words, simply added, "sit down." "Please," he added as an afterthought. "I know I've been quiet all night, but I've been struggling with a dilemma. There are things I need to tell you before we can go on." She began to speak, but he held up his hand, admonishing her to wait until he was finished. There was a long pause, as though he was trying to measure his words with a ruler, then he began again.

"Jennifer, there are some things about me that you need to know. I was never going to tell you these things, but I love you. They may end our relationship before it ever gets going again, but these are things you must know about me. I lost you once because of my work. I was going to leave again, without saying goodbye, because I didn't know how to say it, but I can't. Now that I've found you, by the purest of luck, I can't let you go again." He stopped for a breath, and she began to speak.

"No!" he said too loudly, "please," he added more quietly, "let me finish." Another pause then, "Jenn, I'm not who I said I was. My name isn't David, it's Mustafa, and I'm Palestinian." He paused again, waiting for the withdrawal in her face that he knew would come. Surprised at not seeing it, he continued. "I am not in the Mosad, but a part of the PLO." Again, he waited for her to look at him with astonishment, and this time he wasn't disappointed. Her face showed her surprise, but he couldn't know that it was surprise over the revelation itself, not the information. She wondered why he was telling her so much.

"Look, I know what you Americans think of us, and I won't argue if you ask me to leave, but I thought you had to know. You see, you are the first…," then he corrected himself, "the only woman I have ever really loved, and I could hide what I am no longer. I am not ashamed of who I am or what I do. It is done in the cause of liberty for my people. We deserve freedom as much as anyone!" He was giving a political speech, a thing he had promised himself he wouldn't do.

"Look," he began again, "I know a woman like you will find it hard to deal with these things. They are worlds away from your daily existence.

They are things you read about in your paper, but to me they are real. I've seen children starving in refugee camps. Infants dying during birth for lack of adequate nutrition for the mother. I've seen simple infections kill people for lack of medicine, and illiterate children begging from Israeli soldiers on the streets of a town that once belonged to their grandparents. My father died broken hearted, as a stranger in a strange land because his home had been taken from him by the *Zionists*," the venom with which he used that last word was palpable. He stopped. He wasn't going to describe his exploits. "I...", his voice trailed off, not sure which direction the conversation should take from here.

Jennifer waited, then walked over and stood next to him. Her disgust for him and for his lies to her disappeared, and she felt the flood of emotions he always evoked, washing over her once more. Gently, she stroked his head, ran her fingers through his hair, then tilted her head upward and kissed him.

"Jenn," Mustafa began again, "I'm a Palestinian, and I'm fighting for my homeland." He waited for her reaction and, seeing none, stopped and moved to the "Mini-bar" to make himself a drink. He didn't ask Jennifer if she wanted one, his mind wasn't on niceties. He had expected revulsion, anger, at least surprise, but her lack of any real reaction disturbed him. Somewhere in the back of his mind, an alarm sounded, and his years of training and experience took over from there.

"You don't seem surprised," he commented.

"No, I'm not." She left it at that. If there was going to be any further exchange, it would have to begin with him.

Mustafa's eyes narrowed, though she couldn't see the cloud pass over his face because he was turned away. Was she playing with him? He finished making his drink and turned back to Jennifer, his demeanor back to the warm smile that she remembered. "Why?"

"Dav...", she stopped herself then began again. "Mustafa, there are things about me that *you* don't know." She knew he was suspicious of her, and that she had to give him part of the truth if anything more than two old lovers meeting was to come out of this.

"I know who you are because I work for the President of the United States." She let that settle before continuing. "I was in Paris, and they knew of our past," she hesitated a second trying to find the correct word to use, "association," she continued, "so I was asked to find you and see what you've been doing. It was no accident that I was in the dining room when I was."

Mustafa was expecting something like this, but he felt stunned none the less.

"Were you working for your government in Tel Aviv?" His voice became louder and more shrill than was his wont. "Were you playing me for the fool, making love to me while prying for secrets!?" He became louder still, then stood glaring at her as though to pierce her with a look.

"No, were you?" It was all she could reply for the moment. Several seconds passed, then she added, "I wasn't working at my present job then. It was only later that I found out who you really were." She paused, crossed the room, and began again. "I waited for you in New York, like a foolish schoolgirl. My mind told me I was being stupid, but my heart wouldn't accept it. Perhaps your superiors told you not to become involved with an American. Perhaps you were only playing with me. I came here to finally find out." She was out of breath, and let it stand there.

Mustafa was quiet. He had been angry at an imagined betrayal, and now realized that she felt the betrayal was his. He wanted to grab her and hold her to him. He wanted to make her understand that what he had done was for her own good, not for his. Could she not see this?

"If I had come for you then, you would be running with me now." He stated it flatly, without anger, humor, or remorse, then turned and sat in a striped chair by the curtained window.

"Running where?" Jennifer sighed. "There is no more running. Haven't you heard, there is peace coming to your region. Our two sides are no longer going to kill each other, or supply others who will. It's over." Perhaps there was a double-enténdre there. As she gathered herself to ask him to leave, a faint murmur caught her attention.

"Allah forgive us, it's not over yet." His head was buried in his hands, and his voice was barely audible, yet the words were unmistakable. Mustafa arose and for nearly five minutes stood staring out of the window watching traffic pass more than twenty meters beneath. Without saying more, and with no further opportunity for questions, he turned, gently kissed her, and said he would call her for breakfast in the morning then walked slowly and deliberately through the door and disappeared down the hall.

Jennifer stood for several minutes more without moving, then she too drifted slowly to the window and, after turning out the lights, stood for an indeterminate period of time watching Paris pass by. What he had said, or maybe it was the way he had said it, left her with a chill. She reached over and dragged the blanket off of the bed and wrapped it around her shoulders, but this was a chill she couldn't lose. The lights of Paris now went unnoticed and the traffic unheard, as her mind whirled through a thousand thoughts. It was going to be a long night.

Chapter 17

Sergey Ivonovitch was much more subdued on his departure from the airbase than he was on his arrival. In his briefcase were several documents that were frauds. He knew this, and now he could prove it. More importantly, he had finally been able to trace the origin of the orders for the lost flight back to Moscow. The President had to know, but it wasn't something he could discuss on the telephone.

He was driven to the airport by the same Mercedes that had brought him, driven by the same driver. He used to like the secrecy that his trips involved, but now it was becoming increasingly bothersome. Everyone knew who he was, so why did he have to land at and take off from a commercial airport, when he could have arrived and left from the airbase? Oh, well, things were as they were.

Upon arrival, his single bag was transferred to the waiting plane as he watched and, once more skipping customs, he crossed the tarmac and boarded the same aging Tupolov he had left. It had been cleaned, smelled fresh, and serviced.

"Good morning, General." The stewardess was much prettier this time, and he looked forward to some conversation with her during his trip home. "Good morning," he answered, and allowed himself to be led to his seat. "Thank you," he said pleasantly. What he had found no longer allowed him the luxury of feeling superior.

The noise from the plane's engines rose to a roar then quieted as the plane rolled to the end of the runway awaiting clearance. Finally, they roared again and the glistening silver craft rolled down the centerline of runway 27. Sergey felt himself being pushed back into the heavily padded seat as the craft accelerated. Slowly at first, then gaining speed, the plane reached the necessary speed and the pilot "rotated" the nose into the air. In another instant, the body of the plane shuddered slightly, then followed, with the direction that Sergey was pushed now being down as well as back.

Less than five minutes passed before the plane began to level out, and the stewardess, without being asked, brought a glass of wine to Sergey. "I'd prefer vodka," he said, and smiled when she appeared disappointed. "I'll get you some," she answered, and turned toward the rear of the plane.

Through the worn Plexiglas window, Sergey could see the mountains begin to slide under their wings. The glass of vodka that the stewardess had returned with sat on the table in front of him waiting, but he hadn't touched it yet. He was lost in thought. The flight records, the missing files of the airmen, the orders from an untraceable source in the military from Moscow…

These were the last thoughts Sergey Ivonovitch had. As the aircraft climbed to nearly 10,000 meters over the mountains, a small pressure sensitive switch clicked shut in the hold, a current passed though a wire, and the Tupolov briefly became a bright orange ball that no one but a few natives ever saw again.

The plane would be reported out of radar contact, and word would be passed to "Search and Rescue." Helicopters would be useless at this altitude, and the wreckage would be such small pieces, strewn over such a large area, that it would be possible it would never be found. General Sergey Ivonovitch would receive a medal, posthumously, and be recorded as a hero.

The President would never receive the documents in his briefcase.

Date: Friday, 13-Jul-01 17:26 PM

>

> From: rus_1\num_1_rus@terra.gov

> To: usa_1\ num_1_usa@terra.gov
> cc: isr_1\num_1_isr@terra.gov
>   gbr_1\num_1_gbr@terra.gov
>   ira_1\num_1_ira@terra.gov
>
> Subject: Re: Seeker
>

Seeker gone, plane lost. No further damage possible.
>————————End Message.————————-

Chapter 18

Mark had remained quietly in the room provided for him by Porter. Skipping a lunch he had no taste for, it was nearly dinner time and, much to his chagrin, he had to admit to himself that he was hungry. Still, his mind could not rest. Where was Jennifer? Why had she left so abruptly without more than a cursory explanation? What had Porter asked her to do with this man that she had known so long ago? The word "known" kept rattling about his head. "Known," as in the biblical sense, he wondered? Well, there was no point in wondering about questions he couldn't answer and shouldn't even be asking.

He had finally forced himself into the shower and, having toweled himself dry, was just buttoning his shirt when a knock at the door jolted him from the restful emptiness into which his mind had drifted, back to a reality he really didn't care to remember.

"Yes?" He responded tentatively, then smiled at the naiveté of his belief that he had any control, whatever, over who came and went from this room.

Porter pushed the door open and flowed past it into the room, finally parking himself in a large armchair next to a combination floor lamp and table. He placed the pipe he was holding in the unused ashtray on the table, smiled, and began, "How are we doing today, old man?" Then, seeming to remember how irritating that phrase had become to Mark, finished with a sheepish, "sorry."

"*We*," retorted Mark, "are fine." He paused, then continued, "Where's Jennifer?"

"Mark," Porter sighed, "you know I can't answer that." Then, after a short pause, he continued, "But I can tell you she's safe. By the way, would you like to call your wife and let her know the same about you?" Mark thought there was a smirk on Porter's face when he said that, but chose to dismiss it.

"I guess I should, but frankly I don't think she would even care. Besides, I don't want to get my family involved in this," a short pause then, "whatever *this* is." There was another brief pause then Mark whirled around and, slamming his hand onto the closest surface he could find (an antique occasional table), shouted, "Damn it, Porter, what *is* all of this, anyway?!"

Porter's lips curled slightly upward at the corners, into a smile that would have done the *Gioconda* proud. "What has Jennifer told you, old man?" Porter waited for a reply with equanimity.

"Some," retorted Mark. He knew that he would only receive information if Porter had felt that he already had most of it, and he was simply filling in the gaps. On the other hand, how was he to convince Porter that he already had what he knew nothing about? Well, perhaps it was time for some honesty.

"Look, Porter," and Mark paused for effect before continuing. "I'm caught up in something I don't understand. Only days ago, I was sitting in a bar in London, lonely, brooding over a failed life, and wondering where to go from there. Suddenly, I meet Jennifer, whom I had met once before under circumstances that she can tell you about if she wants to. Then four, maybe five people are killed by us, not to mention how many may have been killed by the other side (whoever they are). We're running from them, the police, and our own people, and I'm not sure who they are either. I've fallen in love with the most beautiful, sensuous, provocative woman I've ever met, who then takes off on "official duty" for a rendezvous with an Arab terrorist whom she had an affair with some years ago, while I sit here in the dark with you. Now don't you think I'm entitled to know why I'm running, from whom, why they are trying to kill me...*us*" (he corrected himself), "and what's going to happen to Jennifer, let alone me?"

Porter sat quietly and looked at him for a few moments, then stood and re-crossed the room to the French Provincial telephone on the table. He lifted the handset and spoke for a few moments in muted tones that Mark couldn't quite understand but, from Porter's frequent glances his way, he was sure concerned him. Having finished his conversation with someone, he returned to the armchair, sat heavily, and gestured with his eyes for Mark to sit diagonally across the coffee table from him, a command Mark complied with slowly but purposefully.

"Mark,..." Porter began, then stopped for a few moments and decided to change gears.

"Dr. Harmon." that was better. It emphasized the gravity and importance of what he was about to say. "We've told you about the Prince that was killed in front of your hotel in London, and asked you repeatedly about what you may have had to do with him or his murder. You've assured us that you were an innocent bystander, just trying to help, and I believe you. I believe you, not because you have an honest face, or even because we've checked you out in the last few hours and probably know more about your life than you do, but because Jennifer says so." He paused for a breath, and the effect came without help this time.

"Jenn is that important," asked Mark?

"Well, yes and no, but she's that trusted by me, and many..." another pause, "on both sides." "Because of that," he continued without interruption, "I'm going to tell you certain things that you are not supposed to know. Before I do, however, you have to understand that knowing these things increases your involvement with them, and may prove even more hazardous to you than even your current situation. The increased jeopardy is something you need to accept before I continue." Porter sat quietly, looking older and more tired than he had looked since Mark's arrival. He just sat and waited, with a patience that Mark marveled at. He must be a good "spook," he decided.

"I accept," Mark replied slowly. "I think I understand the danger, but I suspect it would be more dangerous for me not to know. Besides, I couldn't stand it!" Porter understood.

"A few years ago, while on vacation in Tel Aviv, Jennifer met a man she knew as David Ben Adom, supposedly a minor functionary in the Israeli Mosad." He paused then, in case Mark wasn't familiar with them he completed, "their intelligence service." "They met," he continued, "they fell in love, and he broke her heart by not appearing at a rendezvous as planned. Much later, she learned that David was actually a Man named Mustafa Al Assad—a terrorist."

"Since that time, Jennifer has had no contact with him, nor did she want any. She was hurt and angry, and wouldn't voluntarily have faced him again, except for an emergency situation. Your experience with the Prince, the gunmen, Jennifer, me, and everything that you are asking about is tied up, we believe, with Al Assad's activities during the last few weeks. This culminated with his visit to New York last week, and his arrival in Paris about three days ago." Porter paused again, but in a weary manner, as though he had enough of it all, then completed his explanation.

"Look, Mark, we don't know what's going on, and that's dangerous. It is especially so, because there have been rumors floating around for months that weapons grade Plutonium has been missing from the Russia. Their nuclear security has become more lax during the last few years, after the Union dissolved, and we don't know where it is, or even *if* it is. Combine this with the material stolen by the Chinese from Los Alamos from about '78 through '99, and the possibility of *Extra-national* possession of nuclear weapons is inescapable. Finally, a message was received by one of our allies, relating to some sort of operation in New York, and then Al Assad shows up. It all fits together somehow, but we don't know how. There are too many lives at stake for us not to take all possible steps to find out," a final pause, "including sending Jennifer back to Mustafa Al Assad to try to find out what he knows or did, by any," a short pause, then, *"any* means possible."

Mark sat and stared at Porter. Somehow this entire episode had taken on surrealistic qualities. He was moving as in a dream and, like a dream, seemed to have no control over his own actions, or those of the other people involved. He was an observer as well as the observed, and it was a feeling from which his mind soon withdrew.

"Let me understand this," Mark began slowly. "You're saying that there is a nuclear threat to New York from a terrorist group, of which this Al Assad is a member. Moreover, not only are Jennifer and I somehow involved in it, but you have sent her to see him to find out what is going on, knowing that if what you believe is true, and they suspect that she knows any of it, we may never see her again." Mark paused for a breath. "Is that, essentially, the situation as you would describe it?"

Porter, for the first time since they had met, seemed uneasy. he stood, and began to slowly pace about the room, staring past the paintings on the walls, the curtain covered window, an ornately framed brass mirror, and anything else he could find to occupy his gaze, before he could answer.

"Yes." It was a flat statement, and one upon which he neither needed nor cared to elaborate.

Mark wandered to the bed, lay down on his back and stared at the ceiling, his mind returning to the portico of his hotel in London, a dying man, and a cup of coffee in a small restaurant shortly thereafter, with the most beautiful woman he had ever seen.

Porter, sensing the conversation was over, stood and walked toward the door. As he opened it, he turned to reassure Mark that Jennifer would be OK then, realizing that it would sound patronizing, simply turned and left, silently closing the heavy wooden door behind him.

Mark sat up, his mind an odd combination of swirling thoughts and emptiness. What was there to do? He knew that Porter was right. While he might be able to get away from the safe house, where would he go? If he did find Jennifer, would he help her or put her life into more jeopardy than it already was in?

Inertia and fear kept him on the bed while guilt urged him out the door. Inertia and fear won. He fell back across the bed feeling small and beaten; a feeling that lasted only a few minutes. "Screw this," he mumbled to no one in particular then, grabbing a jacket from the small closet where an assortment of new clothes had been hung, he gingerly opened the door and peered up and down the hall. There was nobody in sight, so he slipped out, closing the door behind him. He had no idea where to begin, so why not with Jennifer's room?

The door was open, so he let himself into the darkened room and quickly closed the door behind him before turning on the lights. Realizing that the light from under the door would give him away, he took a towel from the bathroom and stuffed it against the bottom of the door, then began his examination of the room. There was not much to be seen—the bedspread had remained wrinkled where Jennifer sat, a few scattered papers, towels carefully folded and replaced on the racks in the bathroom, and a closet filled with more clothes than had been provided for him. Not knowing where to begin, he searched the drawers, then the pockets of the clothes in the closet and finally the nightstand and desk. All of his efforts provided no further insight than he had before, so he sat in a chair at the antique desk, rubbing his eyes and trying to think of what he could do next.

As he sat, his eyes wandered to a writing pad next to the telephone on the desk. Could something like that still work, he wondered? Reaching for the pad, he held it slanted against the light from the desk lamp and noticed the indentations where a note had been written on the sheet that had already been removed. He removed a pencil from the drawer and, rubbing gently, produced the message, "GC 417." A small smile bent just the corners of his mouth, realizing that the age old movie ploy still worked. Then another realization developed—he hadn't the faintest idea of what the code meant, or even if Jennifer had written it.

After all, it could have just as easily been written by the previous occupant of the room. Well, if that was the case he had nothing to go on, so he chose to believe that Jenn had written it. Having decided that, however, he still had nowhere to begin.

"GC 417," he kept repeating to himself. A flight number? A locker number? A room number? He had no idea. Taking the note with him, he slipped as quietly down the stairs as he could and disappeared through the foyer and the front door, and found himself in the street. Behind him, Porter emerged from the shadows of the living room and, grinning, reached for a telephone handset, into which he spoke quietly for a few seconds, then returned to his study to ponder the next moves. Mark would be gone soon. Having no way to find Jennifer, he would return to the US (a passport had already been arranged for him at the embassy), and try to forget the ordeal through which he had just passed. If any further problems developed, the pair of agents following him in the CitrÖen would let him know. Also, having run, it was unlikely that Mark would alert anyone. After all, it was his life too. Feeling satisfied with himself, Porter returned to his reading.

On the street, Mark headed to the nearest telephone booth, where he closed the door and began looking through the Paris directory for entries beginning with a "G." He began with airlines, then expanded his search. It was nearly impossible. He didn't speak the language, he was alone, had no money, and no training. Still,....

He began to walk. Eventually, as the hour became late and he became hungrier, he stepped into a small alleyway to take a break without looking suspicious by just standing on the street. In the shadows cast by the setting sun, he nearly fell over the body of a man lying on the cold cement. He hadn't moved, so the physician in him took over, and he leaned down, deftly placing the fingertips of his right hand along the course of the left carotid artery. The neck felt cold, and the pulse was gone. The man had died clutching his bottle of wine, probably slipping from this life into the next without really noticing.

With disgust at his actions, Mark began searching the dead man's pockets and a cloth bag, hung with chord from his waist. It was a virtual treasure trove for one who was walking the street with nothing. As quickly as he could, and without stopping to inventory his cache, he stuffed everything his hands came across into the sack, and left to enter another alley where he could take his time with things.

The sack was now bulging, so he walked to the back of the alley which bordered several buildings reaching no more than three stories, but protecting him from prying eyes, and lay each item out along the top of a low concrete wall. His net worth had now risen by nearly 250 francs, a rather large pocket knife whose blade would lock into position when extended, several buttons, a crucifix that appeared to be silver, and a key to a door whose location remained a mystery. With the discovery of a very expensive wallet, apparently made of ostrich skin, his situation improved immensely. There were more than half a dozen credit cards belonging to "Jacque Moreau," along with nearly 5000 francs and a white plastic card with a blue triangle pointing toward one end, that Mark recognized as the end that was to be inserted into a magnetic reader. It was a card for a parking garage or a hotel room. He had no way of knowing which and, as was customary, there was no identification on it so that people like Mark would be unable to use it. Finally, the wallet contained a receipt from the Hotel Lancaster. He wasn't sure what the receipt was for, but the name of the hotel was across the top. Was that the location of Jacque's room, the door into which the card fit? Mark wondered if he could sneak into Jacque's room when he wasn't using it , if only to get cleaned up and get some sleep. For that matter, he had no way of knowing if Jacque was even alive, since the drunk had the wallet. He needed some food and rest, so he hailed a taxi and, seating himself in the rear, stated simply, "*L'Hotel Lancaster, sil vous plais,*" then sat back to enjoy the ride.

Near the intersection of the *Champs-Elysées* and the *Avenue George Cinc* stood the stately old hotel which had been newly renovated. It wasn't large by modern standards, but its appointments said "luxury." The facade was awash with light as the evening's activity was beginning. "Well," thought Mark, "Now what?" Scanning the area, he could think of nothing more than a direct approach, so he strode into the lobby, and, looking around, found the front desk. "*Messier* Jacque Moreau's room, *sil vous plais*," requested Mark.

"I am sorry *messier*, but is *messier Moreau* expecting you?"

"Of course," responded Mark, and waited for the clerk's next action, having no further idea what he was doing.

"Well I'm sorry, *messier*, but he isn't in at this time" (the smirk on the clerk's face grew wide, he knew that Mark wasn't expected, he had caught him).

"I'll wait for him in the bar," retorted Mark, brazenly, but didn't move.

"That would be a long wait, *messier*, Messier Moreau is not expected to return until Tuesday of next week." The smug look on the clerk's face saying "gotcha!"

"*Merci, messier*," answered Mark looking surprised, "may I leave a message for him?"

"But of course, messier," and he handed Mark a piece of hotel stationary and a pen. The note was gibberish, but it was neatly folded and handed back to the desk clerk in a sealed envelope.

"*Merci bien*," smiled Mark, and turned toward the lobby, glancing over his shoulder as he did so. He noted the clerk turning away then placing the note into the pigeon hole labeled 322. As inconspicuously as possible, he retraced his steps, passed the desk and walked to the elevators where the door to one stood open, He pressed the button for the third floor, and emerged into a tastefully decorated hallway. Finding room 322, he inserted the card, the light on the lock blinked green and, after a short prayer, entered the darkened room and closed the door behind him. The light switch, on the wall where he expected it to be, illuminated one room of a three room suite. "Nice," thought Mark, and walked to the bedroom, examined it briefly, then did the same with second bedroom which had been converted into a study/office. It was obvious that *Messier Moreau* had more money than he needed, and kept this suite for whenever he was in town which, according to the clerk, would not be for nearly a week. He removed his coat and sat in a large green leather armchair next to a round table through which a lamp protruded. He needed time to think. It was in this position that he fell asleep, awakening at about six o'clock the next morning with a bad taste in his mouth, a day's stubble on his face, and a "crimp" in his neck from the way he had slept.

Slowly, coming to the realization of where he was, he stood and looked around the room again, this time in the light of the sun streaming through the windows. "Well," he thought, "I've got to do more than this," and he went into the bedroom, removed his clothes and, after allowing the shower to become hot, stepped into it with a sybaritic pleasure he hadn't felt in years. For a little while, he relaxed, thinking not of his quest, or the predicament he had found himself in, but of how good the jets of hot water felt playing across his back and chest.

Finished showering, he stepped out and toweled himself dry then, finding Moreau's electric razor next to the sink, shaved, and returned to put his clothes back on. "I wonder...," thought Mark, and walked to the closet where he found jackets, slacks, and shirts hanging neatly in rows. He tried them on and found, to his delight, that Moreau was about his size, although just slightly larger in the waist. Well, that could be overcome with a belt. He began dressing, and was searching through a series of drawers for fresh underwear when he came across the holster containing a black automatic, and a box of ammunition and spare magazine. These were neatly tucked next to the underwear he had been searching for. Mark was puzzled by the need for a gun in the *Lancaster*, but thoughts of the last few days made him glad to have found it.

He dressed quickly in his new found clothes, and placed the wallet containing his money (but without Moreau's identification) into the right inside pocket of a blazer he had chosen for today, then placed the gold Cross pen he had found into the left pocket. He felt better. He was clean, properly dressed, and had money. He was also very hungry. As he reached the door to the suite, he stopped. He was forgetting something. After thinking for a moment, he returned and took the gun from the top of the dresser where he had left it, removed his jacket, and slipped into the shoulder holster. It needed some adjustment, but it was right handed and it fit. He then hefted the black Glock, 9mm automatic. Somehow, it felt comforting. He slid the magazine out to check that it was loaded then, after replacing it into the gun, pulled the slide back and released it to place a round in the chamber. He then took the box of ammunition, removed the magazine from the gun, and replaced the top round before returning it to the gun. "You never know," thought Mark, "when that one extra round might make a difference," then placed the spare clip into the jacket pocket, and replaced the jacket. Now he felt ready, and so he left the room and headed for the elevator, just one more hotel guest on his way to breakfast.

He stood in the lobby of the hotel, about to go into the restaurant for breakfast, when he thought better of it. He was living in another man's room, and wearing his clothes. If he spent too much time in plain view in the hotel, someone would eventually ask questions of the guest that no one remembers, and that would be the end of it. With that thought, he walked out of the front door and down the street hoping to find a restaurant or café in which to have his breakfast and think about his next move without worrying about being seen or recognized.

Jennifer turned off the water and stepped out of the shower. Passing the steam clouded mirror, she glanced briefly at her reflection. She never usually thought about her own looks, but when she did, she knew that she drew men to her like a magnet. She smiled briefly at her own vanity then, wrapped in the white terry robe provided for guests by the hotel, and stepped back out into her room to begin getting dressed for breakfast. She had promised to meet Mustafa in the small café up the street. She selected her clothes carefully, not too provocative, yet not too plain, either. It was past 9:30 and they were to meet at 10:00. "OK," she thought, looking at herself in the mirror again, took the light jacket along to protect her from the slight morning chill she expected, and left the room to meet her once and present lover.

Mustafa, like Jennifer, dressed carefully, then walked down the hallway from his room on the fourth floor to the elevator where he waited patiently, thinking not of breakfast at a local restaurant, but of *croissants* shared overlooking a beach in Tel Aviv. He was sitting, overlooking the Mediterranean, feeling warm and happy, staring into the most magnificent green eyes he could ever remember. He realized now, as never before, that he had been haunted by those eyes for years. They had been in his memory awaiting release, and now here it is. He was happy again. Thoughts of missions, codes…were forgotten, as if they were from a dream that was passing away with the night. The elevator arrived, and he stepped into it and rode to the lobby, where he followed the tunnel of his vision to the front door, and emerged onto a sun-drenched *Avenue George Cinc*. The café was only about a block away, so he slowed his pace. He didn't want to be too early or too late. "My God," he thought, I'm behaving like a schoolboy!" With that observation, his pace quickened.

Jennifer, unbeknownst to her, left the hotel only moments after Mustafa. She hadn't seen him and, knowing that there was a slight excess of time, stopped at the Kiosk outside the hotel to buy the morning's copy of *Le Monde*. If Mustafa was late, she would have something to read. It never occurred to her that he would not show up again. It was a beautiful day. She strolled up the avenue with more spring in her step than she had known for a long time. World events would eventually catch up with them, but not today.

Chapter 19

It was noon, but all of the blinds were closed. The small room with pale green walls was deep in shadow except for the brilliant circle of light from the halogen lamp sitting on the aging kitchen table. Metallic puzzle pieces of various shapes and sizes were spread over its surface waiting to be positioned in the container that occupied its center. Herman, a balding man of doubtful significance, appearing to be in his late sixties, adjusted the thick magnifying glasses as a tiny bead of sweat ran down his left cheek. The work was delicate and exacting but he was being well paid. Soon, his bank account would be stuffed, and then he would retire with the respect that he should have had all along.

Deftly, he lifted the newly arrived, highly polished hemispheres from their packaging, and settled them into position facing each other. The alignment had to be exact. Herman knew that his was not the last stop for the assembly of this…"thing," and he suspected that he was not the only one performing such tasks. Still, he was being well paid. Money, he had learned, was the only thing that counted. Soon, he would have more of it than he needed.

Once more he began gently fitting parts together. He glanced at the plans, again and picked up the next piece. When all of the pieces were neatly tucked into their places, he took the second half of the gunmetal blue casing and screwed it gently into place so that the entire assembly was covered by a metallic shell that reminded him more of a large football than anything else.

"Well, it's done." With this, the metal football was placed into a cushioned packing carton, sealed with tape, and left on the table to await the messenger that would take it to its next destination. Herman walked to the telephone, took the small piece of paper from his pocket, and dialed the telephone number it contained. "Yes," a velvet female voice answered. "This is the grocer, your package is ready." Herman hung up. It was nearly finished. When the courier arrived, he would hand him the package, and receive the envelope with his payment. He sat back to wait.

Just under an hour later, the buzzer from the outer door alerted Herman to the presence of someone to see him. "Yes?," he said, pressing the button to the intercom so that he could be heard. "This is the pickup you called for, sir." "OK," replied Herman, come on up."

The knock at the door was answered by a very excited Herman. This would show everyone. He would have a nice house, a car, clothes, vacations…. The young man at the door was not more than fourteen years old, decided Herman. "Here it is," he said, handing the package to the dark complected youth with a bright smile. "Thank you," the youth replied. "Don't you have something for me?," asked Herman. "Oh, yes, I'm sorry. I almost forgot." Herman smiled back at the youth and held out his hand. The boy reached inside his jacket, slowly withdrew a gleaming metal pistol with the long fat barrel indicating a silencer, and the two "spits" that emerged from it were all the payment Herman would ever receive. The thud of his frail body dropping to the floor was small as he crumpled in front of the youth, a questioning look on his dead face.

"*Allah Achbar!*," murmured the veteran of more than twenty missions, then closed the door and left to take the package to its next stop.

Porter lifted the handset of the antique appearing telephone and spoke without dialing. "He's gone." There was a slight pause at the other end then a calm baritone asked "where?" "I'm not sure," replied Porter.

"I had him followed, of course, but there was some traffic, and my men lost him as he crossed the street last night. I have only waited until this morning to call you because the men who were following him thought they had picked up the trail, and so didn't report his loss to me until about a hour ago." Porter paused, then continued, "I don't think he will jeopardize the operation. He doesn't know what he is doing, he has neither money nor papers, and he doesn't speak French. In a nutshell, he is like a fish out of water and, if he isn't killed by some street thugs, he should eventually be easy to find. He'll probably show up in a police line-up or at the Embassy." Porter waited. It was nearly ten seconds before the voice at the other end responded. "We can't allow that to happen. Find him and dispose of the problem." The click at the other end terminated the conversation. Porter stood for a minute thinking, then took the circuitous route back to the hidden operations center.

Standing before the console, he switched it on, placed his palm and fingers on a glass plate, and, when prompted, stated simply "Porter. Omega three alpha." "*Voiceprint and Identification sequence accepted,*" acknowledged the synthesized female voice, "*proceed.*"

Porter thought for another moment about what he was going to say to his operatives, then continued; "To all personnel, operation Dragnet (he winced at the reference to the old TV show, then continued), imperative that subject be acquired and terminated immediately. This is a Code Green alert." Pressing the small rounded rectangle at the top right corner of the touch sensitive keyboard, the screen went blank and the transmission ended. His words would be translated into written form by the computer, and transmitted in a digital burst to the appropriate beepers. No response was required until the orders had been carried out. Then there would be an acknowledgement, which he would transmit back to others. Porter wasn't happy. He liked Mark. Then he turned away to attend to other business.

Jamal sat at the console of his new American computer, carefully entering the message he was given. He was unaware of its significance, but his understanding was unimportant. "**Package arrived. Please advise.**" The message stood for a moment on the screen, then Jamal pressed the send button, and it was replaced with, "**MESSAGE SENT.**" Jamal turned back to his coffee and cigarette.

Chapter 20

Date: Saturday, 14-Jul-01 06:21 PM
>
> From: plo_1\num_1_usa@terra.gov
> To: rus_1\ num_1_rus@terra.gov
> cc: usa_1\ num_1_usa@terra.gov
>
> Subject: Re: Outlaw
>
> Have instructed strike team regarding termination of problem. Am
   planning on retiring
> subject on a permanent basis. Will notify board upon completion.
>————————End Message. No reply needed.————————

The wooden tables of *Café Luna* were covered in the red and white checkered tablecloths the management knew tourists expected, but at this hour locals tended to occupy them. A large number of Parisians were out of the city on holiday this time of year, so even the normal flow of locals had become a trickle. Only two tables were occupied on the sidewalk when Mark took a seat. He wasn't sure what to do or where to go next. Clearly, Jennifer was somewhere in the city, but he had no idea where to begin, or even if he should. Perhaps this would be a good time to reappear in Philadelphia and forget that any of this ever happened. "Be careful what you wish for," thought Mark, "you never know…" His thoughts were interrupted by the waiter bringing him his cappuccino and brioche. It was all he wanted this morning, and fiddling with it gave him time to think. He stared into his cup and stirred it with the demitasse spoon provided.

People who have observed Mustafa walk tended to use the term, "deliberate." It would certainly describe his gait today as he strode to the small cafe and carefully avoided the few occupied tables on the sidewalk to choose one in the shadows inside, next to a side door which provided some cross ventilation in the un-air conditioned restaurant. With this ventilation and the ceiling fans scattered throughout, it approached being comfortable. He summoned the waiter, clad in a short sleeve white shirt, white pants, and a red apron (wondering if it were someone's idea of a joke), and asked for two espressos and two croissants, then sat back to wait. He knew he had to return to Beirut soon, but his life had just taken an unexpected turn. He gazed off into space with his mind seeing the breathtaking green eyes that had haunted his dreams for years. If only he could become something else, they might have a chance, but he knew she could never understand why he had to do what he did. To her, he was a murderer, not a liberator. For just an instant, as he thought of himself that way, he felt a sense of revulsion, it passed almost unnoticed, but an unresolved doubt remained just below the level of his consciousness. It was gnawing at him when he looked up to see Jennifer walking toward the cafe.

She stood in front of the first red and white checkered table and, with umbrellas blocking her view of some of the patrons, searched inside for Mustafa. He would pick a table there, where he could sit in the shadows and see without being seen. As she stepped inside to get a better view, the periphery of her gaze swept past a figure that couldn't be there. Mark sat at the table, staring into his coffee cup, not more than an arm's length away. She had to get inside quickly, without being seen by him. As she glided silently past, Mark briefly looked up and his eyes met hers, but the brief stare she shot his way prevented him from moving or saying a word. He just watched her pass him and proceed to a table somewhere inside. He wanted to follow her, but he knew he couldn't. There was a line of shadow that separated her not only from his vision, but his world. He was mulling this over when the small van pulled in front of the restaurant in an area marked with the white disc, red circle, and red diagonal crossing a large "P" that signified "No Parking." Out stepped a small wiry man with the dark curly hair and swarthy complexion who gently opened the double side doors of the van facing the sidewalk, and left them slightly ajar as he walked down the street. Something was wrong. Mark didn't know why he felt it, but he did. The truck…, the driver…, something within him was screaming, but he pushed it to the back of his mind. He didn't need paranoia to interfere with him now. He stood up and, glancing inside, made a decision he had been dreading. He would just stroll into the cafe, look around, ask where the lavatory was (he had no idea how he would do this in French, but he was going to try), and see who Jennifer was with. He had to know what this terrorist looked like. He would do nothing that would give her away.

Mark rose, threw some unknown but hopefully adequate denomination of francs onto the table, and had walked nearly to her table before he stopped a waiter to ask directions. He paid no attention to the answer, but stared over the man's shoulder at Jennifer and Mustafa sitting and eating a quiet breakfast. For the briefest of instants, his eyes met hers and there was a fear there that he had never seen before. She was terrified that he would give her away. The bronze complected man with wavy hair that sat at right angles from her also looked into her eyes and saw the fear but, looking up, he knew that it was Mark that terrified Jennifer, and he needed to do something about it. He locked gazes with Mark and began to rise when the blast wave that preceded the sound of an explosion, drove Mark, Jennifer, and Mustafa, as well as furniture and other people into the side alleyway so that the fire storm that followed left them unscathed.

Seconds passed, and a quiet that never naturally existed in Paris surrounded the building and the several prostrate figures in the alley. Mustafa was the first to awaken. He lifted his head and dazedly surveyed the rubble. At the entrance to the alley were several charred bodies, clothes blown off of them, some with parts separated, and blood flowing into the cracks of the pavement. Immediately to his left was Jennifer, partly buried under the table they had been sitting at, with a medium complected, well-dressed and semi-conscious man lying just beyond her. He ignored the man, and cradled Jennifer's head in his hand as his other arm threw the table off of her and against a large piece of cement that had once been part of the wall. She was alive and, judging by her fluttering eyelids, beginning to awaken. "Jenn," whispered Mustafa gently. "Jenn," he said again, a little louder this time. Her eyes opened and she stared at him with confusion. "Shhhh…," he whispered again, his finger to his lips. "Don't try to talk yet. I'm going to lay your head back down and take a look at the other end of this alley. It's important." Then he laid her head back upon the cement, and gingerly rose to a kneeling position, scanning the area around them before unsteadily rising to his feet. Slowly, after withdrawing a nickel plated Barretta .380 automatic from a soft, "inside the pants" holster he always wore, he moved cautiously up the alley where several bodies lay scattered about, as though carelessly discarded by some passing storm. Flames and smoke were climbing from the cafe that only moments earlier had been a minor landmark and in the distance, the shrill, bi-tonal klaxon of an emergency vehicle was becoming louder. He re-holstered his gun and quickly returned to Jennifer. She was sitting, just a little disoriented, staring at Mark when Mustafa returned. Additionally, two more patrons, both men in their early thirties had managed to drag themselves through the door and past the piles of rubble, to lie not more than three meters from Jennifer. Mustafa remained unruffled, but determined.

It seemed like hours as Jennifer watched Mustafa pass fleetingly from shadow to shadow as he approached the other end of the alley. There was just the hint of revulsion in his eyes, but no softness, when he returned. He stared at the small band of people that had survived the explosion, turning his stare from one to the other, and finally resting his gaze upon Mark. There was recognition in the stare. Mark was the one approaching when the blast caught them. He was the key. Jennifer watched the slow motion of Mustafa's hand rising from his right side, the Baretta's hammer cocked, and its direction changing to include only Mark.

"NO!," shrieked Jennifer. "STOP!" She tried to rise to cover Mark's body with her own, but her muscles simply wouldn't react yet.

Mustafa kept the muzzle of the small but powerful weapon directed at Mark's head, lying on the cement, as he turned his gaze to Jennifer. She had a crazed look on her face that he had never seen before. Slowly, he lowered the gun, then replaced it into its holster and bent to put his arms around her to comfort her. She slid into his arms, but the remnant of rigidity he felt was testament to the depth of her emotion. "Don't," she stated flatly to no one, then closed her eyes to shut out the world.

The brightly colored lights danced dreamily behind the shifting patterns of shadows that fell across Mark's eyelids. They fluttered open and, for the briefest of instants, he was at home, one arm hanging over the edge of his bed, in that twilight period just before awakening. The image shattered as he slowly focused upon the bricks of a building rising beside where he lay. Painfully, he turned his head just enough to realize that he had no idea where he was. Confusion set in, and he was about to panic when the images of the explosion that threw him against a table and past the door flooded back into his head. "Jennifer!" His mind shouted, but his lips only mumbled as the effort sent bolts of pain through his head and neck. He had been attempting to rise, when the pain forced him back against the wall he had first noticed. It was only then that he saw Jennifer, her long blonde hair with its ends singed and her face scraped and bleeding, leaning against the wall only a few feet from him. She was awake, and staring at the opposite wall of what he now saw was an alley.

"Jenn," he began more softly this time. "What?...."

"Shhhh," she reached out and touched his matted hair, then stroked his cheek. "Don't try to talk until you get more of your strength back." She winced as she withdrew her arm and placed it in her lap.

"What the hell happened?" Mark's confusion broke through her own pain and exhaustion, and prompted a brief answer. "There was a bomb. A car-bomb, I think. Anyway, most of the cafe was destroyed. We were thrown into the alley, along with a few other lucky ones, and we dragged you here so that we could be away from the site of the blast." She sat back to catch her breath.

"We?," inquired Mark. "Yes, we," answered Jennifer with a deliberateness he had come to understand. "Mustafa and I." Mark cringed, as the memory of Jennifer and a vaguely remembered stranger sitting at a table in the back of the now destroyed cafe returned to his consciousness, along with the depression he had begun to feel when he had seen them in the moments before the blast.

"Jenn," Mark had just begun to reach out with his right arm to touch her, when a dark, dirty, but well dressed man rounded the corner with a paper bag in his hand. "*Allah Achbar*," murmured Mustafa, as he knelt beside Jennifer and, after pouring a small amount of liquid into a paper cup he had extracted from the bag, handed it to her. "You are feeling better." It was a statement, not a question. His attitude, as he inclined his head slightly to face Mark, became more brusque, and his smile, so out of place then and there, revealed a cold intensity behind the seemingly soft exterior. He was the soft furry panther, ready to strike at the first sign of his prey's weakness. "That prey won't be me," thought mark, as he pulled himself to his feet and, leaning against the wall for support, extended his right hand. "I understand I have you to thank for being rescued." His extended hand, ignored at first, was reluctantly accepted by Mustafa as Jennifer's glare slapped him across the face.

Eric E. Shore

Mustafa rose to face him. He was slightly the taller of the two, while Mark's broad shoulders made his breadth more apparent. For a moment, the two stared at each other, then briefly back at Jennifer sitting on the ground sipping the warm liquid from the paper cup, steam rising from its lip, then returned to face each other. "It was not I who saved you,…American." Mark's nationality was hurled at him as an epithet. "I would have killed you, but Jennifer stopped me." Mark, for the first time since the blast, remembered the automatic he had tucked under his shoulder and, squeezing his arm against his side, while painful, proved reassuring since it was apparently still in place and undetected. He felt a chill that did not come from the air, and leaned back against the wall. "Why would you have done that?" Mark asked, and waited for a reply. "You are a fool," spat Mustafa. "You have drawn them to you and, because of you, Jennifer and I were nearly killed." "*No mention at all of the other people in the cafe that were,*" thought Mark. "They could not have been drawn by me." It was a flat statement; as much a matter of fact as the sun rising in the morning. "You are very sure of yourself for one so inexperienced. Why is that?" Mark paused before answering. "There could have been no one who followed me, or could plan where to attack me because…," he hesitated once more then, "even I didn't know where I was going until I arrived here."

Mustafa's gaze met a surprisingly steady one from Mark, then he turned away and reached for the paper bag with the hot liquid and cups. As he did so, he reached passed Jennifer, who turned from staring at Mark in silence, to tentatively looking at Mustafa in anticipation of his response. He knelt slightly to pick up the bag and, with a smooth single motion, reached inside his jacket and spun toward Mark, the Barretta cocked, then froze before he completed his turn. As he spun, he faced Mark, holding the threatening black Glock, steadied in two hands, the muzzle a gaping hole directed at Mustafa's head. Jennifer inhaled deeply, then all three stopped breathing for just a moment. "Drop it!," commanded Mark. There was a desperate look in his eyes that Mustafa had seen before in the most dangerous men he had encountered. Slowly, he lowered the Barretta to the concrete and, holding both hands above his shoulders, stood once more so that he was away from the gun, giving Mark no excuse. He could have fired had their roles been reversed. He would have. He had planned to. Mark, he knew, would not, without an excuse.

"Mark!" Jennifer's exclamation was intense, but quiet enough not to startle anyone. She reached out and picked up Mustafa's gun, and placed in beside her then; "Please, put the gun down." Mark's stare remained fixed, and was answered in kind by Mustafa. "Please!" Jennifer said again, looking from one man to the other.

Slowly, Mark lowered his weapon, just enough to become non-threatening, but still able to raise it before Mustafa could attack. "How did you know what I would do?," Mustafa asked quizzically. "I didn't." Again it was a flat statement. This time, however, it implied something more. Mustafa understood, perhaps even better than Mark or Jennifer. Perhaps Mark would have pulled the trigger after all. "Well," Mustafa once again showed his teeth in a wintry smile that left no doubt of his ability to kill without feeling, "I believe you are growing up," and filled a cup with what turned out to be soup, placing it on the ground in front of Mark. "Have some?" Mark looked at Jennifer, then back at Mustafa, and knew that the moment for killing had passed. He didn't know how he knew, but he did. Slowly, still without removing his eyes from Mustafa except for an occasional glance at Jennifer, he returned the gun to its holster and slowly knelt and picked up the soup. Mustafa sat on the other side of Jennifer, and drank his cup of soup, as Mark slid slowly down the wall to warm himself with his. No one spoke again for some minutes.

Charles M. Winston III was the second Undersecretary of State for Intelligence Affairs—"UnSecStat—IA." He came from a wealthy family in Maine and, having completed his undergraduate and graduate education at Georgetown University, found himself serving in the State Department. His quick mind brought him to the attention of his superiors as someone who might go far. His smooth and un-abrasive manner as well as his salubrious speech made sure he was propelled upward more rapidly than would be usual

The telephone next to Winston's bed emitted the irritating electronic tones that had come to replace the jingle of a bell.

"Hello," Winston's voice was husky, and he was mumbling. He cleared his throat and began again, softly, so he would not awaken his wife Dawn, asleep beside him. Without lifting her head, she watched him, and listened. She had been through years of this with him, and the middle-of-the-night telephone calls were always the same. "Hello," Winston repeated again, this time with more authority. "Charles?" The voice at the other end of the line was that of Itzchak Cohen. "Yes," Winston answered again, annoyed at being awakened, but curious as to the reason for such an unusual event and anxious about it too. He was used to being awakened by his own people, not by the Mosad.

"Charles, we have to talk." Cohen sounded nonplused; unusual for anyone from the Mosad, more so for him. "Hold on a minute," answered Winston who gingerly rolled out of bed and, placing the call on hold, went into his study to complete the conversation. "OK," Winston continued, what's wrong, Itzchak?" On the other end, Cohen smiled briefly. His friend Charles was one of the few non-Semitic people he knew to pronounce the "ch" sound in his name correctly. He imagined that it took some practice, and he was flattered that Charles took the time to do it.

"You've heard about Paris" It was a question in the form of a statement. It was a "do you still beat your wife?," kind of question. Answer it "yes," and you are expected to know what the conversation is about. Answer it "no," and you've indicted the competency of your own intelligence organization. Charles was in no mood to be awakened for games. "Paris?" he asked, and waited to be filled in.

"Jesus," said Cohen.

"You're converting?," Charles interrupted him (he simply couldn't resist).

"Listen," began Cohen, again, with more intensity this time. There was a car bombing at a small cafe in Paris, only a few blocks from the *Champs-Elysées*. "So?," Charles answered, unclear why he should be awakened with this information when there are so many bombs and explosions that go off around the world each day. "So," replied Cohen, "we believe that it was intended for Al Assad, but his body wasn't found at the scene. Moreover," he continued, "we have reason to believe that a very attractive young lady, whom we both admire, may have been seen there with him." There was a pause then Winston asked, "and her?" "Don't worry, Charles, her body is missing too." An audible sigh of relief from Winston reverberated through the scrambler.

Winston changed the subject slightly, "who did it?" "Who really knows, these days," answered Cohen. No one has claimed responsibility, but the type of device that was used is usually identified with Bloody April. "His own group?" asked Winston, incredulously. "Why?" "Beats me." Cohen stated. "On the other hand," he continued, "suppose he knew more about something than they were prepared to let him know, and still live." He paused to allow Winston to consider the possibility. "Not their style," answered Winston, after a few moments. "Look," he continued, "give me a few hours to get in touch with my people, and see what I can find out.

Charles Winston III sat in the dark leather winged back chair in his study and closed his eyes. The picture of Jennifer Lynch was still floating in front of him when his wife awakened him at seven o'clock. He was angry that his own body had caused him to lose vital time. He knew it was not something he could have avoided, but it angered him none the less.

After a quick, hot shower, and a few sips of coffee, Winston sat at his desk and reached for the phone. He speed-dialed a number he had long since forgotten, and the firm voice at the other end matched the picture of the young, black Ph.D. that sat at a computer console in the state department. "Hi, Jack," Winston began, "I've got some questions I need answered.

"Paris?" Winston could see the smile on his face, without seeing it. "Well if you knew about it, why wasn't I called!?" Winston was raising his voice when he didn't want to. He calmed down in time to hear the answer. "Sir," the tone was more formal than before, he knew Jack was angry about his earlier explosion, "you are on the list to be called and, if you will check your secure fax mailbox, you will find a written report that has been there for hours."

"Listen Charles," Jack began again, "there doesn't seem to be anything special about this one. None of our assets were involved. It was a routine notification." "Winston was about to explain about Jennifer, then thought better of it. If jack didn't know, perhaps it was better that way for now.

"Any idea who did it?" Winston didn't expect any real answers, and he wasn't disappointed. "Nope, just that it was a stolen van, they used a variant of C-4 that has become popular with Middle Eastern terrorists, and the blast was directed at the cafe. That's it." Winston waited to see if Jack had any more to tell him, then ended with, "OK Jack, if you get anything else in about this, please let me know." The telephone handset once again rested in its cradle, and Winston was once again staring at nothing. Something was wrong, but like so many others, he couldn't put his finger on it.

"Look," Mustafa said as he sipped his tepid soup, "we have to get off of the street, and I don't want to go back to our rooms at the *George Cinc*. Any ideas, Jennifer?"

"I know I'm not supposed to know anything, but I have a suggestion." Mustafa and Jennifer turned to Mark as though they had just remembered that he was there. He was right. They had ignored him when it came to planning. After all, he was a "civilian," and therefore un-knowledgeable. "Yes, what is it?," Jennifer answered, condescendingly.

"I have, shall we say, appropriated a room at the Lancaster. It belongs to a man who isn't scheduled to return until next week. We could go there, have no one know that we are there, and yet still be able to watch your hotel for other surveillance." He stopped talking and waited.

Jennifer looked at Mustafa, then turned back to Mark. "First, how did you manage to get away from the safe house you were at? Secondly, how did you manage to "appropriate" this room and, thirdly, how did you find us?"

Mark smiled. "Getting away from," he stopped himself before she could do it for him, then continued, "the house, was easier than I had assumed it would be. I simply left when no one was looking. After all," he concluded, "it was designed to keep people out, not in. Getting the room at the hotel was luck," and he recounted his encounter with the beggar. "Finding you was pure chance. I went to the café to think because I didn't want to be seen having meals at a hotel I wasn't registered at, and you simply came by." Once more, Jennifer glanced at Mustafa, then returned her stare to Mark. It was Mustafa who began this time. "Impressive," he said, "for an amateur." "I'm not sure that is such a good idea," to Jennifer, this time, "because we may still be observed." Jennifer thought for a moment, then answered, "it's a risk we have to take," then drew herself to a standing position and, after gesturing to Mark and Mustafa to follow her, the three set off, together, for the *Lancaster*.

Chapter 21

Navigating the lobby in their condition was tricky, but no more so than it had been for Mark the first time he entered it. Once ensconced in Moreau's rooms, the three of them sat, without talking, in the "living room" area, the stress seeming to take its toll of all of them. Mark and Mustafa were still staring at each other when Jennifer broke the silence. "OK, what now?" The question was addressed to no one in particular.

"What are you doing here," asked Mustafa? The question was directed, by visual contact, at Jennifer. "I told you," she replied in slow frustration, "I was sent to find you and try to find out what you were up to." She considered how much she should reveal, then decided that if he knew that everyone knew about, him that knowledge would hurt nothing, and might bring more into the open. "You were in New York before you arrived here. Your arrival, departure, and much of what you did there was observed" (a small lie, but the professional in her demanded it), "but we need to know why you were there." The room remained quiet again, while Mustafa thought about this. Jennifer continued, "there are things going on that don't make sense. There are pieces to a puzzle that are missing and, somehow, each of us seems to have a key that we either won't share, or don't even know we have." Mustafa and Mark remained quiet. Each trusted Jennifer, with their lives if need be (she had earned that from both), but their hatred and distrust of each other left them silent.

"Damn it!" Screamed Jennifer, the effort rekindling the throbbing in her head that had begun to dwindle. "Don't you see, either of you?!" The frustration she was feeling became increasingly evident in her manner and voice. Getting no immediate response, she slumped into a deeply padded chair, her matted hair covering some of the green floral print of the fabric, and seemed to give up.

"Look," and both turned to Mark as he began to speak. "I don't trust you," he said staring at Mustafa with hatred in his eyes. "You're a murderer of children, and you don't care whom you hurt. I don't trust you because you have somehow dragged Jennifer and me into something that didn't involve us, and because of everything you stand for." Mark paused for a breath, then continued, "…but Jennifer seems to believe that we have to work together, and I've come to trust her instincts. She may occasionally be wrong, but she would never intentionally hurt anyone" (the images of London flooded back into his mind) "who wasn't trying to hurt her first," he added. "So," he paused again for effect, "since I have the least invested in this beyond my own life, I'm going to begin this discussion. "For the next few minutes, Mark described the journey that brought him from Philadelphia to this room in Paris, in as great detail as he could, but leaving gaps that were evident to Mustafa and Jennifer regarding how they first met, and the details of the safe house. They listened silently, Jennifer already knowing most, but not all of the story, but Mustafa hearing it for the first time, making mental notes of questions as yet unanswered. Mark completed his tale with the simple declaration—"…and that's all I know so far." The silence remained intact for several moments, as each of the others digested his tale, merged it with what each already knew, and tried to make a decision as to how much, if anything, to share with the others.

It was Jennifer who spoke next. She began tentatively, and addressed her initial remarks to Mark, since he was the least knowledgeable of the trio, and had the most to learn to be brought "up to speed." "Mark," but the first sentence was obviously meant for both of them, "I am a special advisor, for national security, to President Dalton." She paused, then added, "and a sometimes *spook*." The small smile that formed at the corners of her mouth made the profession seem almost human to Mark. "London was to be the first stop on a trip to check on some, "irregularities," as they phrased it back home, involving some unusual military operations, when I met you." She looked at Mark to indicate who "you" was, then paused, stood for a moment, crossing to the dresser to look at her reflection in the mirror. Dismayed by what she saw, but too tired to really do anything about it now, she returned to her seat and continued her monologue. "I really hadn't intended for you to get involved in any of this, in fact, you'll remember that I tried to fend you off when you first approached me but," and she smiled a broader smile this time, "you are a persistent devil, aren't you?" "Anyway," she continued, "the shooting at the café was totally unexpected. I don't see how anyone could have known why I was there, that I was going to that café with you, or even how killing me would make any difference to anyone. I hadn't yet had time to make any real inquiries. I had done no investigation, and made no contacts. In fact, I'm still trying to figure out why anyone would want me dead." "Our trip across the channel and our sojourn here reflected more instinct than any directed movements. In fact, I've been impressed with how well you've done on your own," nodding to Mark.

"When I got to the safe house, I was told that Mustafa was in Paris, and that we had to know what he had done in New York, and what he was doing here now. I was asked to meet him because we," there was a slight hesitation that both men detected but neither remarked upon, "knew each other many years ago under other circumstances. It was felt that I might have been the right one to extract the needed informa-tion." She looked at Mustafa, whose eyes had clouded slightly with an inner pain, then added, "I'm sorry." His eyes cleared. He understood. She hadn't wanted to hurt him, or even to take part in the deception, but circumstances forced her actions as they had his. He nodded slightly acknowledging his understanding and empathy. It was one of the things, he knew, that Mark could never feel or understand, and which gave a common bond to Jennifer and him. "I was going to tell you about some of this when we met at the café earlier, because seeing you last night brought back old feelings and memories that I thought I'd buried long ago, but then everything went wrong. First I saw Mark, then the bomb went off. The exhaustion was beginning to show in her demeanor. "Anyway," she concluded," I was sent to discuss the reasons for a recent air battle in the Persian Gulf, some attacks against shipping, and increased terrorist activities, with a select group of people, and to do some investigating on my own. I haven't had a chance do to any of this, so my death would have served no purpose." Her voice trailed off as she shifted in the chair, then lay her head back and closed her eyes, signaling that she had reached the end of her opening round.

Mustafa sat and stared at the other two. There was much that made no sense to him, but he understood what they had not—that the bomb at the café had been meant for him. But why? He had always followed orders, done what was asked, and been loyal to their cause. The people he dealt with were pawns, to be removed from the board or simply, like the "infidel whore" in New York, pastimes to be discarded before they could occasion any harm to him or his cause. But these two were different. Jennifer had returned from a different part of his life. She was a piece of a past that was almost normal, in an odd sort of way. What they had felt, back then, was real. It still is. Each had felt it again last night. And Mark…? Well, he fit in somewhere, Mustafa just wasn't sure where and he begrudged his relationship with Jennifer. But he was still the *agent provocateur*, and his mind raced before he spoke.

"For some time, I have been living in a small village, whose location is no more important to this discussion than the location of that "safe house" you mentioned. About two weeks ago, I was contacted, and instructed to deliver a package in New York. It was innocuous, containing only two metal bowls. I know I was told not to open it, but I admit that my curiosity got the best of me since I felt that such an assignment was beneath me. Still, there had been much made about this being one of the most important assignments in my life, and needing me to carry it out so that there would be no mistakes. After they were delivered, I spent a night in Manhattan then, having a few days until I had to return to my point of origin, and a good deal of money left, decided to spend the time in Paris. It was only my second night here, last night, when we met again," a glance toward Jennifer, then a return to a neutral point of attention, "and the rest you know. Since we left each other, this morning, I have neither contacted nor spoken with anyone." Mark cringed slightly at the phrase, "since we left each other this morning," but kept his thoughts and emotions to himself.

Each of the three now sat in silence, trying to piece together a puzzle with no clear picture of what it would become, nor how many pieces were missing, although each knew that the other two had left information out of their tale. The gaps were obvious.

Mustafa began once more with a question, "Jenn, I'm not sure if your are going to answer this, but I have to ask it anyway," a pause then, "you said that you were investigating the cause of a military action. That was a little vague. Where was it, and who was involved?" This wasn't a demand, it was a request. Jennifer sat silently. She was sworn to secrecy by all the laws and rules she ever heard. And to share classified information with a known terrorist and a civilian was unthinkable! Still, she had never been a stickler for rules, and how were they to ever get to the bottom of this without each knowing the facts?

"All right," she began," then looked at Mustafa and added that what she was about to tell him was not only classified, but that he had to promise her, personally, that he would neither reveal it nor use it. Mark wondered at her naiveté, but said nothing. After he agreed, she continued, describing both the air and naval engagements that had taken place in the Persian Gulf and the Indian Ocean. "That is idiocy," answered a tired Mustafa. "Why would Iranian, or Iraqi boats attack

American shipping knowing they couldn't succeed. And why launch missiles against ships without provocation, knowing that it would bring retaliation against the missile and radar sites?" "And those Russian fighters…?"

Mark knew he was out of his depth in the discussion, and tried to keep quiet, but without thinking, he responded to Mustafa's comments with a simple question, "doesn't it strike anyone that with so much of this seeming unconnected, we're looking at smoke and mirrors?" "What do you mean," Mustafa this time. "Everything that has happened to us, or that we've done, has led us in circles, as though to prevent anyone from looking under the right rock. There is a threatened terrorist attack in New York, the attacks in London, the bombing in Paris, the attacks in the Persian Gulf, all unconnected, but all diverting world attention from anything else. Even," he concluded, "diverting the attention of the people involved—you, your terrorist group, the CIA, me, the military of more than one country,…" "It's all smoke and mirrors," he said again softly, then returned to staring at the table near him. Mustafa and Jennifer exchanged glances, then shifted uneasily in their chairs. Each wondered if Mark was right, and afraid he might be. It was the only explanation that really fit, but it still didn't answer who, why or what. Well, at least they knew what it was they didn't know.

Once more, Jennifer broke the silence. "Mark, if nobody in London could have any reason for wanting me dead, then they were trying to kill you. I just got in the way." It was a statement, as well as a question asking why anyone would want to kill him.

"Why?" Mark voiced the question.

"Something you know, found out, or did had to be the cause," Jenn replied, "but what?'

They thought for a moment, then Jennifer's mind clicked into gear, "the murder." It was a statement of fact. "Mark, there was only one thing in your entire story that made you any different from the thousands of other tourists in London—the murder outside of your hotel." Both turned as Mustafa unexpectedly injected, "you did more than witness a murder, you tried to save the victim. You spoke with him, or were at least close to him. He was the son of an Sheik, a trusted emissary, and you were the last one to be with him alive." Mustafa stopped there. He wasn't sure what he was getting at, but he knew the Shadow World better than most, even better than Jennifer, since he lived in it all the time. Someone wanted something from Mark, or wanted to keep him from telling something he knew even if he didn't know he knew it, and passing it on. "Wheels within wheels," he thought. "Did the murdered man say anything to you, or give you anything?" Mark shrugged his shoulders, wanting to answer no, but no longer sure of how this game worked.

"What about you," Mark quizzed Mustafa? "Why would someone want you dead at the café?" Mustafa smiled.

"I can think of a hundred reasons, and a thousand people, but the only answer that makes any sense *this time*, is to prevent any possibility of the details of my recent mission from being brought to light." The implications were frightening. If the people who sent him wanted him dead, then he must have become untrustworthy in their eyes (not likely or he wouldn't have been given his last mission) or he had become expendable to prevent their secret from being exposed. If it was another faction, he couldn't think whom, and a country would have "taken him out," to limit civilian casualties. No, "it was my own people," he stated flatly, as he stared at a point in space about a meter in front of his head.

"This is crazy!" Jennifer's exclamation brought both of their heads toward her. "Different groups, for different reasons targeted you each for assassination, and I just happened to be with each of you when it happened. Is that what you are saying?" It sounded silly when put like that, but facts were facts.

Suddenly, as though a light bulb went on above his head in this deadly cartoon, Mark saw what the professionals did not, perhaps because they were too close to things, or too used to things. "Jenn." He stopped for a few seconds staring at her, then restarted, "Jenn, it *was* you who drew each attack." "But why," she asked again? It makes no sense because there would have been no reason. I hadn't had time to find out a thing. Nobody even knew why I was there beyond a handful of people at…." Her voice trailed off as surprise, and confusion crossed her face, mixed with just a smattering of amusement. The implications were unnerving, but they finally began to make sense, of a sort.

"Don't you see," queried Mark again? "You were followed by someone. After the murder, they thought I may have found something out, and they didn't want the information passed to you, so we were attacked at the earliest possible time when we were together. When you went to meet Mustafa, he had information that could never be shared, so when you showed up, you had to be eliminated. He was simply expendable, isn't that the word you use?" He hesitated, knowing that he may be sounding foolish and amateurish, but needing to finish anyway. "There is some connection between the murder, the man who was murdered, his mission, Mustafa's mission and the information you were sent to collect. Somewhere, the pieces fit together." He fell silent. It was the best he could do right now, and he knew it wasn't very good.

Mustafa looked at Mark with a hint of admiration, despite his disdain for the man. He could be right, of course, although he still saw no connection. Then he looked at Jennifer as if to confirm what Mark had said, and re-ask the question of what information she could have had, or been looking for, that tied everything together.

Jennifer looked from one to the other, then closed her eyes. Were they right?

Nothing more was discussed that night. Jennifer slept in the large bed, with each of the men taking a sofa in the adjoining room. While neither man trusted the other, they slept well because each knew that neither could harm the other until all of the questions were answered. It meant each of their lives.

The morning came and went, with no one awakening until well after noon. A night's sleep had revitalized them, but removing some of their exhaustion only emphasized the pain each of them felt from their bruises and wounds. Jennifer spent nearly a half-hour soaking in the bath, while Mustafa made his way down the seldom-used stairs to return with coffee and croissants. Then, after they had spent an hour talking quietly about trivia, each of the men took their turn in the tub, easing beaten muscles and soothing wounds and abrasions. At last, Jennifer and Mustafa were seated around the table in the "living room" of the suite, as Mark completed his ritual of returning his personal articles to his pockets from the perch on the dresser where he habitually laid them when undressing. It had never occurred to him that Mustafa would go though his things, because he really didn't care. He carried nothing that would interest anyone anyway.

Mustafa reached for his third cigarette of the day and, finding his lighter to be empty, turned toward Mark, "May I use a match?" "Sorry," Mark replied, "I don't smoke." "Then why the matches in your pocket?" Mustafa smirked, feeling self-satisfied.

Mark removed his right hand from his pocket where he had been depositing some of his "stuff," and saw, for the first time, the matchbook that he had unwittingly carried for so many days. He realized he must have picked it up somewhere, but didn't remember where and didn't care. "Here," he replied blandly as he tossed the matches to Mustafa, "I don't think you'll live to die of cancer, anyway," and he returned the smirk feeling smugly that he had gotten the better of the exchange. Mustafa caught the matches and, as he was about to remove one, stared quizzically at the cover.

"Where did you get these," he asked?

"Beats the hell out of me," Mark answered, and poured himself another half cup of the lukewarm coffee that was left before bringing a third chair to the table and sitting down. "Why?" Mark asked without really caring about the answer.

"Because these are from a restaurant in Kuwait City. I know it well," he answered slowly. "Were you there recently?"

"I've never been there at all," now Mark was becoming curious at the questions, and Jennifer's attention became more focused.

Mustafa didn't answer, but sat staring at the matches for nearly a half minute before walking into the bathroom and returning with a double edged shaving razor, the kind that had all but disappeared from the United States years earlier, but remained a staple among European men. As if in answer, he used it to meticulously separate the layers of paper of the cover, until the mid-portion of the back had been exposed. Peeling back the last part with his fingers, he laid the split book of matches in the center of the table in front of him, to display a small dark square centered there, and now exposed.

"Where did you get these." It was Jennifer this time. Mark stared at the split book of matches, and at the square of film that lay exposed, and had no answer. He never really knew he had them, although he had a tendency, like many men, to hoard things in his pockets, like some women hoard things in their purses. "The man who was murdered at your hotel," Mustafa paused then continued, "How close were you to him?"

"I was trying to revive him, for Christ's sake," Mark exclaimed! "I was close enough to be covered in his blood!"

"Then he was alive when you got to him?" Mustafa's questions were becoming more calculating, like a District Attorney ready to pounce for the kill.

"Of course," Mark answered, becoming more annoyed. "He was shot, and collapsed at my feet as I walked out of the door."

"Mark," Jennifer interjected, he turned toward her as she continued in an intentionally soft voice that was guaranteed to get anyone's attention, "he put them in your pocket."

"Excuse me," Mark asked?

"Don't you see, he needed to keep that piece of film safe, and you were the only one within reach. It was probably the reason he was shot, and perhaps the trigger for the events that followed." So far, no one had touched the tiny dark square laying exposed on the table. Each now turned to stare at it.

Now Mustafa grasped the square carefully with his fingernails, and lifted it off of the paper. Holding it to the light revealed nothing, but he knew that there could be an enormous amount of data on the film without any of it being visible to the naked eye. "We need a viewer or a microscope."

"What's on there?" Mark looked only slightly puzzled?

"Who knows," Mustafa replied in a whisper, sinking deeper into the same question, "who knows...."

The moment seemed frozen, like an insect in amber, but the mood was shattered when Jennifer stood up and began putting her jacket on.

"Where are you going," Mark asked in surprise?

"To get us something to examine that with." She was out of the door and gone before either man could stop her and, by the time they reached the hallway, she was gone. There was nothing for them to do but return to "their" room and wait.

Chapter 22

In the Oval Office, the President of the United States sat at the desk occupied by generations of chief executives before him. His back to Pennsylvania Avenue, he was plodding through three inches of paper that would become law with his signature. The light from the windows behind him was just slightly tinged with green because of the thickness of its glass, in place for strength to stop bullets and explosives. He had long ago failed to notice the difference. Having already made up his mind about this bill, he reached for the fountain pen protruding from its holder and signed, "Andrew Dalton," then affixed the presidential seal. HB 1245-01 was now law.

As he placed the thick, bound volume in the "out" basket, the LCD screen of the Laptop computer on his desk began to alternate from red, to blue, to green, and back again. Dalton touched the space bar, and the flashing was replaced by a bright red screen with diagonal white stripes with a white rectangle in its center labeled, "Enter Key." He typed a series of letters and numbers into the rectangle, which only displayed asterisks, and the screen again dissolved to be replaced by a menu, under which a flashing icon of an envelope let him know that he had email. The red color of the envelope on the screen informed him that it was of the most sensitive nature—"**For Eyes Only.**" He moved his index finger deftly over the touch pad until the arrow was positioned over the envelope, then tapped twice to open it.

After the header, which he failed to recognize, were three lines of "garbage"—an apparently random series of letters, numbers and spaces that indicated an encrypted message. He was puzzled. He was reading email that was listed as being of the highest security, was apparently directed toward him, yet his "key" failed to decrypt it. "Well," he thought, "I'll have one of the "crypto" boys go over it. He dragged the file to "Classified," and the screen changed to a much less impressive "File Saved." President Dalton returned to his work, leaving the computer to remind him to forward the message to the White House Cryptographers for deciphering.

In an office, not far away, the Secretary of State was also looking puzzled. A report on his desk indicated that there was movement of a Russian air wing toward the south, and an unusually heavy load of classified voice and data "traffic" in that direction, but no reason for it. Well, it didn't appear to pose any threat to American personnel or security, so he put the report aside in the box he maintained for things he wanted to look into, but were not immediate.

A few minutes later, in Langley, Virginia, a lower level intelligence officer placed a red and white striped folder into his own out basket, which would direct it to the superior officer he felt was appropriate. It contained information about a known terrorist named Mustafa Al Assad that was recently seen in New York, and later in Paris. Since he deemed it to be routine, it would not reach anyone important for another two days. By then the report, like the intelligence officer, would be irrelevant.

At about the same time a small man with horn-rimmed glasses and a mustache stood at the black topped table in the center of a room lit only by the bright glow of the overhead fluorescent fixtures recessed and sealed into the ceiling. A drop of sweat ran from his forehead to the right lens of his glasses, but there was nothing he could do about it inside the sealed suit protecting him form the deadly Anthrax he was working with. Slowly, his gloved hand picked up the test tube from the rack and, after checking the stopper to make sure it was secure, inserted the tube into the gleaming receptacle lined with Styrofoam. It wouldn't do to have any of these tubes break in transit. He sealed the top of the cigar shaped receptacle by screwing on the top, then added the pressure that would tighten the airtight seal, making the container as safe as the P-4 laboratory in which he stood. Once done, he placed the container into a box designed to hold one hundred such containers. This would make number seventy-three. It would not be long now. He retreated to the airlock where he could remove his suit, pass through decontamination, shower, and return to the rest of the world.

✷✷✷✷✷✷✷✷✷✷✷✷✷✷✷✷✷✷✷✷✷✷✷✷✷✷✷✷✷✷✷✷✷✷✷

High above the skies of Kazakstan, the last flight of MIG 31's turned toward the radio beacon that called toward them. Colonel Dimitri Papovitch banked his plane to 193°, knowing that the remainder of the flight was right with him. The evening sun caught the wings of the aircraft in their formation giving them a reddish glow that would make a few scattered people on the ground think a UFO passed overhead. The airbase toward which he was taking his flight lay ahead. Already in darkness, the runway lights glowed to show them the way. It had been a long flight, with three in-flight refuelings. He would be glad to stretch out on a bed, any bed.

✷✷✷✷✷✷✷✷✷✷✷✷✷✷✷✷✷✷✷✷✷✷✷✷✷✷✷✷✷✷✷✷✷✷✷

Mark and Mustafa sat quietly in their borrowed room, sipping tepid coffee and intermittently staring at each other. It was nearly a half-hour before Mark broke the silence. "She'll be OK," he stated flatly" "Jennifer is a professional," replied Mustafa, his voice belying his words, "she'll be fine." Mustafa rose quietly and walked to the curtained window, parting the heavy green drapes, and stared at the street below. Mark knew he was searching for Jennifer's return, and both knew she wouldn't be seen from their position, but Mark rose to join him at the window. Reaching for the other side of the drape, their eyes met for a moment, and each knew that they shared at least one thing in common.

It was nearly a half-hour later that the door opened and Jennifer walked back into the room clutching a bundle of cracked leather about half the length of her arm. Gingerly, she placed it on the round wooden table and proceeded to remove the cover, the last small bit raised with a flourish, "Ta da!" Her musical introduction left them staring at a microscope that must have dated from the Second World War. There was no lamp beneath the stage, only a mirror to redirect the light toward the lens that would focus it toward any specimen. The two men looked at the contraption incredulously, while Jennifer stood with a triumphant grin from ear to ear.

"The last time I saw something like that was in a museum," Mark chortled with a grin on his face. Mustafa said nothing. Its looks were irrelevant to him, if it worked. "Where did you get it without money?" Marked looked amazed.

"Oh, just shut up," chided Jennifer, mockingly, "and give me the microfilm." Mustafa, who had appointed himself "keeper of the film," passed the matchbook to her. She reached into a pocket of her jacket, and withdrew a small oblong package wrapped in tissue. Carefully, she unwrapped several glass slides and cover slips, and placed them on the table next to the ancient microscope. With a small tweezers, also contained in the package, she lifted the film from the matchbook, and placed in on a slide. Over this she placed a cover slip, and lay the entire assemblage on the microscope stage, with the black dot that was the film just visible over the lens.

"OK," she said, "open the drapes so we get some light." Mustafa moved quickly to the window, and drew the drapes just slightly apart, allowing a thin strip of bright sunlight to enter the room. Jennifer sat for a minute fiddling with the microscope. Finally, Mark could take it no longer, and gently moved her aside as he said, "here, let me do that. It's my business."

As he deftly moved the mirror, slide, focus and objective lenses at once, the dark shape began to define itself into several negative pages of writing and pictures. When he couldn't make out what was there, he flipped to a higher lens, and readjusted his focus until one of the pages became clear. He studied it for a few seconds, then moved on to the next page, then the next, and the next, without actually reading them all. "Well," demanded Mustafa? Mark said nothing, but quietly got up and moved to another chair, allowing the others to take a look through the 'scope. He was staring at nothing in particular as the others looked at the film.

"Some of these things look like kill estimates," said Mustafa, but I don't understand what most of this is." He looked up from the microscope then moved away to give Jennifer her chance to look. After a few minutes, she looked up and stared at Mark. She understood the pages with distorted concentric circles, they were the killing zones. They were all too familiar to her from nuclear scenario's. But these were not exactly the same, and she couldn't quite put her finger on why. The rest of the pages were filled with scientific "mumbo-jumbo" that someone else would have to interpret, and Arabic, that neither she nor Mark could read. Mark's face, though, told them both that he had seen something they hadn't.

"Mark?" Jennifer inquired. He sat there until she repeated his name and walked over to kneel in front of him, so that she was in his line of sight. When he looked up, there was anger in his eyes, which turned to revulsion as he looked toward Mustafa. "What is it," Jennifer asked, becoming worried? Mark stood, and slowly walked to stand in front of Mustafa.

"You…" The word trailed off into a silence that was about to explode. She understood the mood, and stepped between them before Mark did something stupid.

"Mark," more firmly this time. "sit down and tell us what you found." It was an order, however gently it was spoken, and he complied.

"You saw it," Mark replied. "You know." Jennifer pulled a chair over to sit in front of Mark, while Mustafa sat down in the chair facing the microscope. He knew to stay out of Jennifer's way. Mark had to be handled carefully.

"Yes," Jennifer answered carefully. "Those look like nuclear kill zones. We all understand that, and it is horrible, but we've lived with these scenarios for decades. It isn't that easy to launch a nuclear attack, trust me."

"No," Mark shook his head. "You don't understand." He sat quietly for a few seconds, then stood, walked to the window and after staring at the street for a few more seconds, turned to face Jennifer, ignoring Mustafa. "Did you see the page with the name *ATX-1204*?"

"I guess so," Jennifer was puzzled, "why?"

"That's a biological designation, Mark answered." Mustafa rose from his seat slowly, with more understanding than Jennifer, and fixed his gaze on Mark. "He knows," said Mark more loudly now, staring back at Mustafa! "Ask him!"

Mustafa stood, returning Mark's glare. Neither moved, and for a few moments the room remained engulfed in an explosive silence.

"Damn it," shouted Jennifer! "Will you two stop measuring your *dicks* and tell me what's going on?" Her face was becoming flushed with anger and frustration.

"Jenn..." Mark faced her and quietly began. That designation probably relates to an Anthrax strain used in warfare. It..." He stopped abruptly then found Mustafa and shouted that, "no civilized people would ever use it, only outlaws and terrorists!"

"Jennifer," Mustafa began again. "This looks like a plan to use this...Anthrax against several targets, and it even gives timeframes and probable downwind vectors of spread." His voice was even—unemotional. Jennifer understood now. She stood up, straightened her skirt, and asked,

"Where are they going to hit?"

"We don't know," responded Mustafa quietly, ignoring Mark's earlier outburst. The quiet that followed was broken a few seconds later when Mustafa, turning towards Mark said, "Look, I don't know any more about this than you do."

"What was it you delivered to New York, then," queried Mark, distrustfully? Mustafa stood quietly for a few more moments, then answered,

"I believe it was the reflective casing for a small nuclear weapon."

"What?!" Shouted Jennifer, turning to stare at Mustafa. "Are you telling us that you took a nuclear weapon to New York?"

"No," Mustafa said quickly. It was the casing for a weapon, not the weapon itself. I have long speculated that there would be a time when we would use the threat of a nuclear attack against the United States. We certainly don't have the weapon in place yet. At least I don't think so," he added reflectively. "In any event, I'm not even supposed to know about this. I was only a courier. Besides, we would not be the first to use such a weapon in a war, you are the only country to have used such a weapon." Mustafa stopped. They were both staring at him. He turned to the nearest chair and dropped heavily into it, cradling his head in his hands.

Now it was Mark's turn. He arose, walked to the window again, looked briefly down towards the crowded street, and then turned to address Jennifer. "This doesn't fit." He stated it flatly.

"Why," asked Jennifer? She had ambiguous feelings about the conversation with Mark. He was a civilian, untrained, and knew nothing about the world that she partially shared with Mustafa. "Still, she thought, "he seems to have grown into his role." She listened.

"Because," Mark answered, "If they were going to use a biological weapon against a target, they certainly wouldn't use a nuclear weapon also. It would destroy the Anthrax along with the target. Besides, talk about redundancy!"

Mustafa looked up from his chair with increasing realization in his eyes. He had rationalized the use of a small nuclear device against New

York, in his mind. It was the only thing the Americans would understand. They had killed enough of his people. They had given weapons to the Zionists and protected them even against UN sanctions. They needed a lesson in humility! But now the landscape was changing. If the PLO wasn't using a biological weapon, who was? What was the target? Why had there been no word?

"He's right," Mustafa found himself telling Jennifer. "There is another player here. I think that's the message the film represents. But who is it, and where was the message intended to go? If we find that answer, we will also know the target."

"Jesus!" It was all Mark could think to say. "You put a nuclear weapon in New York, and now you're surprised that someone else is using a biological weapon somewhere else? You people make me sick!" He kept his stare at Mustafa, so it would be obvious to Jennifer that she was not included in his remarks. "You son-of-a-bitch!" "Who the hell do you think you are, playing with millions of innocent lives like that?" He began moving toward Mustafa, who began to rise in his turn, but Jennifer abruptly stepped between them and pushed each away with a hand. "STOP IT!" She screamed the words, then stopped herself and quieted down. "Stop it," she said again. "Sit down, both of you." Each hesitated, then Mark turned and walked back toward the table where the microscope still sat, while Mustafa collapsed back into his chair. "God! That's enough." She turned toward Mark, crossed the few paces toward him, and gently rested her left hand on his shoulder. "Please, sit down." He sat.

"Look, each of you, don't you see what's happening here?" She looked back and forth between them, but each reacted without understanding. "Mark," she turned back to face him, "we were nearly killed, probably to prevent that piece of film from ever reaching it's intended destination. Then," she turned toward Mustafa, "you and I were nearly killed by the bomb intended to either keep you silent about your mission, or keep me from telling you about a piece of film

I didn't even know we had." She stopped then, and realized something. Then, with a slightly dazed look on her face, she looked back and forth between them again, and said quietly, "My people were the only ones who knew we were meeting, knew about Mark, and might have an idea where we would be." She sat on the sofa and, leaning forward, stared at the floor. "My own people..." she repeated.

"Don't be ridiculous," Mustafa rose to face her. "My people could just as easily have found us at the café. Why assume it was yours?" They stared at each other now, each wondering whose superiors ordered their execution.

It was Mark, though, who broke the silence. "Humph!" They turned to look at him. "Jenn, didn't you say that there was unusual Russian troop movement recently? Wasn't there an air engagement you told us about between American and Russian planes in the Persian Gulf? Wasn't there a missile attack on shipping in the Gulf? Doesn't it appear to you that there may be *other* governments involved in this?" He stopped. They were waiting for more. Nothing came.

"What are you getting at?" Jennifer returned his gaze with a quizzical look. He was no longer the scared man who ran with her from the restaurant in London, but she wasn't sure what he had become. Mark walked back to the window, then returned to his chair but didn't sit. Instead, he turned to Mustafa.

"Look," he began, "I don't have to tell you that you and the things you do disgust me. You are vermin, to be squashed by civilized people." Contempt encased each word, and Mustafa rose to meet him, but Mark turned and broke eye contact before returning the stare, thus defusing a potentially violent situation. "None the less," he continued, circumstances seem to have forced us together in this. We are each hunted, and we don't know by whom." He paused, allowing Mustafa time to cut in.

"So, do you actually have something to say, or is this simply the rambling of fear." This time Mark raised his eyes and smiled, but his smile carried a chill.

"Are you familiar with Sherlock Holmes' famous axiom?" Mark waited, still smiling.

"What is this nonsense?" Mustafa looked annoyed.

"It is a rule of logic. When you have removed all of the possible explanations for a phenomenon, whatever remains, however improbable, must be the truth."

"Riddles, American?", Mustafa retorted.

"Fact," answered Mark. "The simple fact is that there are people out to get all of us and, for the moment, we are all in the same boat. We don't know who is chasing us, we don't know why, and we don't know what to do about it. In fact, we know only two things…" they waited and, after a short pause for effect, he concluded. "First, if it seems like we're all being attacked by different people, but we can't figure out how or why, then we're probably all being hunted by the same people, even if we don't know who they are. Secondly," he continued, "the only people we can trust right now is each other. No matter how we feel about one another, none of us can solve this puzzle alone, and therefore none of us can survive without the others."

"He's right," Jennifer said quietly. "We need each other right now." There are pieces of the puzzle that none of us can find or put together alone." She was looking at Mustafa. "You know it," Jennifer reiterated. The silence lasted for more than a minute, then Mustafa, like Mark before him, walked to the window, looked down at the people walking below, and answered in an equally quiet, but venomous voice, "For now."

Chapter 23

Date: Sunday, 15-Jul-01 03:18 Zulu

>

> From: plo_1\num_1_usa@terra.gov

> To: rus_1\ num_1_rus@terra.gov

> cc: usa_1\ num_1_usa@terra.gov

>   uk_1\num_1_uk@terra.gov

>   prc_1\num_1_prc@terra.gov

>   ind_1\num_1_ind@terra.gov

>   iraq_1 \num_1_iraq@terra.gov

>   iran_1 \num_1_iran@terra.gov

>   jpn_1\num_1_jpn@terra.gov

>

> Subject: Re: Outlaw

>

> Strike unsuccessful. Will need to reschedule. Postpone operations.
  New strike will be undertaken once subjects located. Unable to
  ascertain degree of knowledge, but doubt any significant penetra-
  tion. Will notify upon completion.
>————————End Message. No reply needed.————————

Porter sat once more in front of his secure computer connection.
"Imperative you locate subjects as rapidly as possible. Terminate." Well,
there it was. It had been more than a day since his people had lost Mark,
and nearly that long since anyone knew where Jennifer and Al Assad

were. They had assumed that one or more of them had been killed in the blast at the café, but none of their bodies were found. He had gotten a call, patched through to him through several relays, from the Sureté, demanding to know what he knew about it. He could honestly answer that he knew nothing. This annoyed the French, which pleased him until he remembered it was true. He hadn't asked when Jennifer was ordered terminated, and it left him confused. She really didn't seem to know anything at their last meeting, but he was a soldier and followed orders, however much it hurt—he liked Jennifer Lynch.

Without allowing the revulsion he felt to surface, Porter lifted the handset from its cradle, pushed the red button at the upper right corner of the telephone, and a voice, higher pitched than he was ever able to get use to, flatly answered, "Yes." "I'm calling from home," began Porter, "continue," directed the voice at the other end. "Subjects and most recent data and photos are being transmitted. You are directed to…" he hesitated for a moment, "…terminate subjects as soon as possible. This is a Code Alpha Alert." This last meant that the listener was to drop whatever he was doing, and get on to this assignment. "Reception complete," the voice answered without emotion, "understood and acknowledged." The line went dead. Porter stared at the screen for a few moments, then turned away, went up the stairs to the dining room and had breakfast. "Life goes on," he repeated silently to himself.

✳✳✳✳✳✳✳✳✳✳✳✳✳✳✳✳✳✳✳✳✳✳✳✳✳✳✳✳✳✳✳✳✳✳✳

In a large room, nearly 30 meters on a side, with tapestries suspended against the walls, President Saddam Hussein sat in a comfortable chair with only one other person present. In front of him, spread out on an ornate table, were scattered photos and documents that he had already finished looking through.

"So, my friend," Saddam began as he looked up to face his personal security chief, "what is your recommendation?" "The thin man in his Iraqi uniform sat opposite his President, the table between them.

"It is imperative that we eliminate these people before any of this goes further."

"Hmm.." Saddam looked down again. "I have no problem with that," he replied, "but what of the microfilm?"

"When they are gone, it will be also," the man answered, knowing that this was a formality. Hussein had never failed to follow his advice before, especially when it involved eliminating people. The President considered himself the rightful heir to the great rulers of Persia, and everyone else a potential threat. Each person he eliminated was one less to bother him in the future. Many fewer people bothered him now than a few years ago.

"Do it." With these two words, the President stood and left the room. He was due to move to another Presidential Palace today. One couldn't be too careful, could one?

✳✳✳✳✳✳✳✳✳✳✳✳✳✳✳✳✳✳✳✳✳✳✳✳✳✳✳✳✳✳✳✳✳✳✳✳

In his office in the Kremlin, the President sat contemplating his next move in this very dangerous chess game. He loved Chess, and thought of all politics as an extension of it, rather than the other way around. He couldn't allow things to follow their present course because too much could be exposed before he was ready. Still to move too precipitously was to invite disaster. Neither he, nor any of his predecessors had ever really forgotten Kennedy and Cuba. It was a mistake that would never be allowed to occur again. He reached for the plain black telephone on his desk, pushed a single button, and stated flatly to the tinny voice at the other end, "Keep the planes armed, but out of the air until you hear from me." He hung up, assuming his orders would be carried out, but not entirely sure in these days. If things moved too prematurely, there would be hell to pay.

✳✳✳✳✳✳✳✳✳✳✳✳✳✳✳✳✳✳✳✳✳✳✳✳✳✳✳✳✳✳✳✳✳✳

In Tehran, the Ayahtolla knelt on his prayer rug, making his daily ablutions. He had just completed meeting with his military advisors before coming to the mosque. "Stand down the missile batteries," he had told them, "but keep them manned and ready to be activated immediately." For the moment, shipping in the Straights of Hormuz would be left untouched. Tomorrow…?

✳✳✳✳✳✳✳✳✳✳✳✳✳✳✳✳✳✳✳✳✳✳✳✳✳✳✳✳✳✳✳✳✳✳

In a small "Bed and Breakfast" in Ireland, Sean Leary sat with three of his compatriots. In front of him sat a steamer trunk, it's lid folded back with it's contents exposed. A metal box covering what used to be part of a microwave oven sat just to one side of many rows of high voltage capacitors, with a length of coated PVC pipe extending from the box in the other direction. A small circuit board was barely visible under the setup. Sean and his companions stared at what was to be their greatest and most unstoppable triumph—a *HERF* gun. *H*igh *E*nergy *R*adio *F*requency weapons had been worked on by governments all over the world. This was the "Terrorist Erector Set" version, but it and its cousins would be powerful enough to bring down a large part of the Air Traffic Control System over England. Now they had been given the order to stand down. He was angry.

✳✳✳✳✳✳✳✳✳✳✳✳✳✳✳✳✳✳✳✳✳✳✳✳✳✳✳✳✳✳✳✳✳✳

Mark, Jennifer, and Mustafa sat around the table in the "Salon" area of the suite. They stared at the table, then at each other, then back at the table. "OK," "someone has to begin this," thought Mark, and asked, "what now?" There was no answer. Each glanced around the table at the others, and back at the table again.

"Well," Jennifer was the first to break the silence, "let's begin with who we know is not doing any of it." Mark and Mustafa waited. "We know that the U.S. isn't likely to be bombing itself, and has neither the desire nor the need to use biological weapons."

"They would use them if it benefited them," Mustafa protested.

"Yes, *we* probably would," Jennifer's use of the pronoun "we" indicating that Mustafa needed to remember to whom he was speaking, "but there would be nothing but "downside." There would be no way to contain the effects. I think they (she was back to "us and them") can be eliminated at this point.

"What about the Russians," asked Mark? "They could have funded the nuclear device, and then been able to blame it on terrorists."

"A good thought," Jennifer continued, "but once again it makes no sense. Russia needs western help in rebuilding its economy, and support for whatever government is in power. They would have no reason to attack the US, and every reason not to."

"Well, that leaves us with everyone else." Mark sat looking annoyed.

"Look," Mustafa walked across the room to stand between Mark and Jennifer. "Let's keep this simple. No matter who funded it, I think it's fairly certain that the PLO is planting the bomb in New York. That leaves the biologicals, their location, and source for us to discover."

"Right," Mark answered, "as well as who funded each because they are probably the ones who are after us."

Jennifer stood and, like the men before her, looked out of the window before she turned to look from Mark to Mustafa and then back to Mark. "What makes you say that?"

"Isn't it obvious," Mark answered? "Who else would know both who we are and what we might know? Also, who else would have access to our locations at the times of the attempts on our lives?"

"It could have been a lot of people," Mustafa stood as he answered. I'm sure the Mosad would happily have me killed if they could, as well as the Americans, the British…" He was interrupted by Mark sniggering quietly.

"What's so funny?" Mustafa was in no mood for an ignorant American laughing at him.

"It could have been the Easter bunny, also."

Jennifer had been listening to the exchange between the two with a mixture of interest and amusement. Now, it was time she intervened in to calm things down. "Look, you two, I'm tired of constantly having to break up arguments between you." Each stopped and waited for her to finish. "Dav…", her voice trailed off as she realized she was calling Mustafa by a name that was no longer him. "Mustafa," she continued, "I think Mark is right. There has to be an explanation for the way we became targets, individually and together, as easily as we did." She paused, partially for effect, and then continued. "There is no one person or group who would know where, or even who all of us are, but collectively, there are a lot of people. What we need to figure out is whether they are each acting separately, or if there is collusion among them."

"I think that the idea that all of these people are working together just to kill us is absurd! Pure paranoia!" Mustafa stood as he spoke, pacing to the bedroom door and back again. We are victims of coincidence. Each attempt was aimed at one of us, and another of us just happened to be there. It's as simple as that." He sat, again, looking smug.

Mark had been uncharacteristically quiet during this exchange. He seemed to be staring out into space through most of it, but finally returned in time to answer Mustafa before Jennifer had time to.

"Look, I know I'm not the expert in these matters, that the two of you are, but it seems to me that we can sit here and speculate for days or weeks, and be no further along than we are. We need more concrete information, and the only way to get it is to set a trap for whoever is trying to kill us, using ourselves as the bait." Both Jennifer and Mustafa waited. "OK, listen. Each of us will get in touch with our own people, or in my case, I'll simply call home. It's probably being monitored. We'll let each know that we will be at a particular location at a specified time. When someone shows up, we'll know who they are, and begin backtracking from there. It's not much different than making a diagnosis. You do the appropriate tests and, when you see which ones come up positive, you follow those leads." He kept quiet now, waiting for the inevitable arguments. They never came. Instead, a thoughtful Mustafa asked, "how will we know who is trying to kill us if more than one shows up?"

"Yes," added Jennifer, "and how will we know that they weren't sent by more than one group, even if only one shows?"

"Maybe we won't," said Mark, but do either of you have a better idea?" Silence. "OK, then, let's make some plans."

✶✶✶✶✶✶✶✶✶✶✶✶✶✶✶✶✶✶✶✶✶✶✶✶✶✶✶✶✶✶✶✶✶✶✶

Less than 2 hours after the conversation in the Lancaster, Jennifer stood at a pay phone about a half block from the Champs-*Elysées*, with Mustafa standing across the street, and Mark at the corner, each watching people approach from various directions. It was agreed that each would dial their calls in private. Because of the lack of trust among them, no one in the group wanted the others to know the number they called. When a strange voice answered the phone at the safe house that she had so recently visited, Jennifer spoke quickly and urgently. She identified herself and asked to speak with Porter. "Yes?" The voice was unmistakably that of her old friend.

"I've run aground," reported Jennifer.

"Did you manage to get the information from your friend?"-Porter's query took no official notice of her announcement of being in difficulty.

"Some of it," Jennifer responded, looking at her watch to make sure that there was enough time for a trace. It had to be "just enough." If she stayed on too short of a time, they would be unable to trace the call, and couldn't react even if they were the ones involved. If she took too long, they would smell a trap, and not show up either.

"It's time to come in," Porter said firmly. He knew she wasn't coming, but had to say it anyway.

"Not yet, answered Jennifer, but suggested that they meet at a café about 6 blocks from where they were. Porter hesitated, then said he thought it would be safer if she "came to dinner tonight."

"No," Jennifer responded equally firmly, "I'll meet you there in an hour, and don't let your wife know" ("spook-speak" for "come alone"). Porter agreed, and Jennifer hung up the phone then quickly disappeared across the street and into a shadow-protected alcove to watch for approaching people. None came and, after about 10 minutes, the three gathered to go over strategy for the café meeting. After a brief discussion that simply reviewed what they had already agreed to, they walked a few blocks toward the café and the same scene was repeated with Mustafa at the phone. This time, however, he made sure to hang up before any trace could be made. This is what would be expected of him. His meeting was set for later that day with an unknown contact. There would be code words exchanged and then he was to give his information to the contact and return immediately to a safe house he was aware of.

Mark's call came last, and was the most difficult for being both overseas, and to Meredith. He didn't look forward to speaking with her, despite his desire to find out how the boys were. He knew she must have been told something or read about it in the newspapers, perhaps that he was dead or missing. He was also remembering a perfusion of blonde hair on the pillow next to his, and feeling guilty. Well, that was something that would have to wait for a better time to think about it. He heard the phone ring at the other end, and the mildly agitated, "yes?"

"Hi, Love," Mark began.

"Where the fuck are you!?" Mark looked toward the ground in sadness. Not "how are you?," or "are you OK?," just that demanding question in an accusatory tone.

"I'm in Paris," Mark answered after a moment's hesitation. "Listen, I don't know what you've been told or heard, but I'm OK if that matters to you (he muttered the last under his breath). I have to meet someone at a place called "Café Finále" a few blocks from the Champs-*Elysées* at about 6:30 PM our time. After that, I should be able to come home," he waited for the questions he hoped would follow, about his welfare. "Who is it?" A man's voice asked in the background. Mark's heart sank, realizing that it was no one he knew, and that Meredith was not waiting to find out if he was alive before beginning (continuing?) with another man.

"Now you listen to me…" Meredith began her attack. Mark hung up the phone. He didn't intend to deal with his situation here and at home at the same time.

The three met at a pre-arranged coffee shop near the *Arc d'Triumph*. Each remained silent until they had seated themselves, looked around, and ordered coffee.

"Well, it's' done." Mark stated the obvious. They sat silently, thinking about the next few hours. Each believed that the others were being attacked, but would admit, if asked, that they weren't sure about themselves. The discussion meandered through different topics, with all three trying to avoid discussing what they feared might happen, or whom they thought was responsible. Eventually, after running out of meaningless things to say, they sat for a few moments, until Mark broke the ice.

"Look," he began. "I can't stand this anymore." We MUST be able to figure out something about who is after us with all of the information we have!"

"We've been through this before," Mustafa said, a weariness in his voice that even he hadn't realized he felt until now.

"Then let's go over it again." Mark got a fresh napkin from the holder, took a pen from his pocket, and began to draw a diagram. "OK," he began again, let's see what we really know." "Jenn," he said, as he drew a circle around her name, "who knew you were coming here and what you were looking for?"

The discussion went back and forth until the time to go to the other café was near. "*L'addition, sil vous ples.*" The check paid, they walked briskly toward the "*Café Finále*" (they chose it partially because of the irony of its name) but separated when they were within a block of it. Mustafa looked more pensive than he had before. It was his turn first, and he was usually the hunter, not the hunted. It disturbed him not to know who the hunter was.

At 1630, Mustafa sat at the small round table on the sidewalk. Mark and Jennifer were nowhere to be seen, but he knew they were there. Quietly, he sipped an espresso and, trying not to seem obvious, allowed his eyes to wander over the entire area. Somewhere out there might be someone who wanted him dead. Lots of people wanted him dead, of course, but this was a special someone—an ally.

Mustafa felt his presence before he saw him slide into the seat across from his.

"Good afternoon, my friend." Mustafa looked up at the man sitting across from him. He was dressed in a gray business suit and dark red tie. His neatly cut and combed hair, and manicured nails added to his appearance as a well mannered gentleman. In this rather elegant part of town, no one would ever remember seeing him.

"I didn't expect it to be so warm today."

"Yes, but it's warmer at home." Codes exchanged, the nameless man smiled and asked, "where is the film?"

"Film?" asked Mustafa.

"Let us not play with each other," the smile never faded.

"Who sent you?" Mustafa was getting annoyed. For a few moments, his predicament was replaced by his anger. He was beyond these childish games. He had proven himself to his comrades many times since his youth. He had risen within his organization. He was not about to stand for this.

"I was instructed to ask for the film; nothing else," replied the well dressed but nameless man.

"Well I've been *instructed* (Mustafa made sure to emphasize the word) not to give anything to anyone without the answer to my own question."

"I see," the man said quietly, and stood to walk away.

"Just a minute…," Mustafa whispered through clenched teeth. Quietly, slowly, the man turned to face Mustafa. His lips curled into a slight sneer as he interrupted.

"You have become a liability. Goodbye my friend."

He turned slowly, and walked along the street in the direction opposite that from which he had come. Mustafa sat at the table knowing that Jennifer would follow him. After about 2 minutes, Mustafa rose, placed a few bills on the table, and began to walk away as a small area of the tabletop exploded. The bullet ripped the tablecloth and dug into the wood beneath, leaving splinters visible through the material. He dove, and rolled under another table to arise at the curb crouching, search the street for his assailant. At the extreme periphery of his vision, Mustafa noted the glint of what he thought may have been a weapon. He turned, and raised his own gun, withdrawn from its holster as he rolled, when the rapport of another gun from behind him and to his right was heard. As he watched, his assailant rolled slowly forward and fell off of the low roof he was on. Turning, he was just in time to see Mark disappear into a darkened alleyway. So, the American had saved his life. This angered Mustafa. Now he owed Mark something he may never be able to repay. It was unacceptable.

Mustafa ran to the man lying at the base of the building from which he had fallen. He could hear the police claxons in the distance, and knew he had to work quickly. He rummaged through the pockets stuffing anything he found into his own without examining it. There would be time for examination later. Then, as the police rounded a nearby corner, Mustafa faded into another shadow, and headed for their rendezvous point. Mark awaited him, but Jennifer hadn't yet arrived.

"Thank you," Mustafa grumbled grudgingly.

"You're welcome," Mark returned, but without any smile or hint of pleasure.

"You are not happy you saved me?" Mustafa was annoyed.

"It's not that," Mark said without emotion. "I've never killed a man before." Mustafa smiled broadly, then patted Mark on the back.

"Welcome to the war," he offered. "You'll get used to it. Besides, he was trying to kill me. What choice did you have?"

"I don't want to get used to it," Mark stated in a worried tone.

"So, what's the matter now," asked Mustafa, more irritated than before?

"That's just it," Mark answered flatly, "I don't feel anything. It felt more like swatting a fly." Mustafa saw Mark differently this time. He had that feeling each time he killed, but never expected to hear it from this American. He was, indeed, becoming a dangerous man—someone to be watched.

During this exchange, Jennifer returned. She was sweating and out of breath. "I lost him about 2 blocks from here. He got into a blue Toyota and vanished."

"Too bad," said Mustafa, "but I managed to collect some things from the pockets of the man on the roof. He won't be needing them anymore." Mustafa's smile bothered Mark more than Jennifer.

They made their way to another café about two blocks away, sat at another table with another checkered tablecloth and, after receiving their coffee, Mustafa spread the contents of the dead man's pockets on the table. There wasn't much. "There shouldn't have been anything," Mustafa mused mentally. "OK," he said aloud, "let's see." There were two keys, a few hundred franks, some scattered change, another clip of ammo for his gun, and a pack of cigarettes. It was only these that interested Mustafa. They were Turkish. He stared thoughtfully for a while, and then gathered everything but the cigarettes back into his pocket. These, he pushed toward Jennifer, ignoring Mark.

"Turkish," stated Jennifer flatly.

"Right," Mustafa was glad to see that she understood.

"So?" Mark looked puzzled.

"Mark," Jennifer began, after glancing toward Mustafa to see if he was going to explain. "People in this *business* are trained to have nothing in their pockets in case they are caught or killed. Morcover, it's unlikely that Muslim terrorists would be smoking Turkish cigarettes. They are usually transported toward the south, and sold to the Kurds in northern Iraq, Pakistan, and India. Finally, this is a nearly new pack of cigarettes. That means that he couldn't have been here very long or he would have had to buy cigarettes, and there would be a French import stamp."

Mark smiled. "That's a lot to get from one pack of cigarettes."

"Elementary, my dear Watson," she quipped, returning his smile.

"OK. I guess it's my turn," stated Jennifer looking at her watch, and they all rose together to return to the café, expecting the police to be gone by now.

The tape reading "Police Line" in French surrounded the area where the unknown man had fallen earlier, but that was about a half block from the café, and had no real effect. They had forgotten to allow for this possibility, and were grateful they had gotten away with their omission. Jennifer sat at a table only about a meter from the one Mustafa had occupied earlier, while Mark and Mustafa assumed their places.

At the appointed hour, Porter showed up and sat across from Jennifer with a grim look on his face. "What's going on, Jenn?" he asked solemnly.

"Well, I found out that Al Assad was, indeed, in New York, and made a drop, but he, himself, isn't sure what it was."

"That's not what I mean," answered Porter, tiredly. "You've been ordered Terminated. Why?" Jennifer sat looking stunned, then began glancing furtively around hoping to catch a glimpse of her assassin, but knowing that she would never see a professional. Should she confide in

Porter, she wondered? He didn't have to tell her about the termination. In fact, he shouldn't have. She sat quietly staring into Porter's eyes for a few moments, then decided that they could be in no worse trouble than they were, and they could use any help they could get.

"Nigel," she began. His eyes drilled into hers. He couldn't remember the last time she, or anyone, had called him by his given name. "I'm going to tell you a story. I'm not sure I should, because you are apparently on the other side in this, but you didn't have to tell me about the termination, so I'm choosing to trust you. What I have to tell you is bizarre, but true, and I...(she began to say "we" but stopped herself) need any help you can give me."

"I'll do what I can, Jenn, as long as I don't feel I'm acting against the best interests of the United States."

"I understand," she answered, and launched into a description of the salient parts of what they now knew, leaving out anything personal, or injurious to either Mustafa or Mark. When Porter commented on their notable absence from her story, she answered that she wouldn't go into their part. After a short "harrumph", Porter smiled briefly, then thought for a few moments.

"Jenn, I don't know any more than you do, less in fact, but I'll do what I can for you. For now, however, I suggest you leave before me and disappear. Call me at my personal number in the morning, and we'll talk." She understood. They wouldn't shoot if Porter were in the way. Not because he might be hurt, but because they didn't want to compromise him. Glancing quickly from corners to rooftops, she rose from her chair and disappeared into a nearby shadow, all in one fluid motion.

Once more, they sat at the table at the first café. Once more, they seemed to have no more answers than they had a few hours earlier, except that Porter appeared not to be a part of whatever plot there was.

An hour later, Mark sat at a table only about two meters from the one that hosted Jennifer's meeting with Porter. He was holding a copy of the day's "L'Monde," looking around the edges and searching for someone he couldn't identify anyway. More than either Jennifer or Mustafa, he was at risk both because of his inexperience, and his inability to identify anyone at all. Still, it had to be done. It was his idea.

Almost an hour had past without anyone even approaching him. "Well," he thought, this was a waste of time," folded the paper, and began to walk slowly in the direction of the first café again, where they were to meet. He hadn't walked more than a few paces when a heavily accented voice, from behind, instructed him to continue walking slowly without turning around. This was emphasized with something hard being jabbed between his shoulder blades. He couldn't be sure it was a gun, but he wasn't about to try to prove it.

"Turn into the next alley on the right, doctor," the voice sounded surprisingly civilized. Mark made the turn as instructed, and saw another figure at the other end of the alley. He and his unseen captor approached the other figure at an almost leisurely pace. The light was fading, and it was hard to make out faces, but he was sure the other man was about to speak when he suddenly collapsed, falling forward onto his face. Behind him, he heard a thud and turned to see Mustafa standing over the crumpled figure of a man in a black leather jacket. He stood there, unable to move for a moment, as Jennifer rounded the far corner.

"Let's get him to the room where we can have a more *private conversation*," Mustafa's smile held the ice that Mark first remembered. Following Mustafa's lead, he helped support his would-be captor under his arms, dragging him as though helping an inebriated friend. The four of them (Jennifer joined them now) stumbled a bit, as from too much alcohol, until they reached the *Lancaster*.

"I don't think the lobby is a good idea," Jennifer whispered.

"You're right," Mustafa whispered back, and led them around the back of the hotel to the Service entrance. Opening the door, Mustafa explained to the dozing security guard, in perfect French, that they had to get their drunken friend to his room before his wife came back and found him. He held up the key to the room to prove that they belonged there and, as he suspected, the guard offered a conspiratorial smile and waved them to the elevator. Less than four minutes later, they were ensconced in their borrowed suite, with their prisoner lying bound and naked on the floor.

Jennifer and Mustafa had meticulously removed all of his clothes and the contents of all his pockets, as well as cutting the lining from each garment, and the heels and soles from his shoes. They even tugged firmly on his hair to make sure it was real. When they were done, all they had was a wallet with a few hundred francs, a small photo of Mark, and one coin found in his pants pocket. Mustafa held it, turned it over, then turned it over again. It was a 500 Fil coin. "Iraqi," he stated, "and not a very bright one to have carried this with him." If he were one of mine, he'd be executed for making such a mistake. Mark believed him.

"I don't understand," Mark began, "why would anyone in Iraq want to kill me?"

"They didn't." Mark turned to stare at Jennifer. "If they wanted you dead, you'd be dead."

"Then what…"

"They wanted information, or the microfilm, or both, and they couldn't kill you until they had it." Mark collapsed back into the chair. He wasn't sure he could take anymore of this. Then he looked at Jennifer sitting at the table, holding the coin she had taken from Mustafa and looking thoughtful. He could take it as long as he was with her.

Slowly, the man on the floor began to regain consciousness. As his eyes focused, his fear became palpable, and the smell of it betrayed him to the others. His eyes focused on the shoes of the people around him, then he began to look around. As he moved, Mustafa stepped toward him and placed his foot on the side of his head, sending bolts of pain into the man's neck and face. Seeing the grimace, he leaned harder on the head, then asked in a conversational tone, "who sent you?" Only a soft grunt escaped the clenched teeth as the man held his silence. "He doesn't seem to want to talk with you," smiled Jennifer. Mustafa rolled the man over with his foot and, seeing Jennifer, he seemed to suddenly become aware of his nakedness and actually blushed. It was then that Mark realized that Jennifer was not the soft image he had in his mind. There was something in her that he hadn't seen before. The smile never left her face as she stepped forward and placed her heel into the man's scrotum and began to step harder onto his testicles. He would have screamed if Mustafa hadn't kicked him in the mouth to prevent it. "Now, now," he said. "We must not make noise, just answer questions." "Now," he began again, "who sent you?" The man seemed to be getting breath to begin speaking, when he spat toward Mustafa, cursing him in Arabic. Once more, Jennifer leaned on his testicles, this time with a twisting motion that sent searing pain throughout his body and caused him to pass out again. Without speaking, she sat, waiting for him to awaken. Mustafa walked into the bathroom, returning with a glass of water that he threw into the man's face. Blood ran from his ear where Mustafa's foot had been, and he once again regained consciousness. Mark felt revulsion but, remembering that he was just a target to this man, knelt beside him, wiped his face with a tissue, and spoke quietly. "I don't think my friends like you. "He sounded like a grade "B" movie actor, but continued anyway. "We don't need you dead, only your cooperation. Answer our questions, and we'll leave you where you are. You'll be found by the maid in the morning, and we'll be long gone."

"Fuck you!" The man's accent was thick, but his command of English was adequate.

"That's enough," said Mustafa, and shoved a large washcloth into the man's mouth to ensure his silence. "That's all we'll get from him. Let's take another look at that film and see what else we can make out." With this, he stepped over the man as though he wasn't there, and walked to the table where the ancient microscope sat in its case. Once more, they gathered around the table, with Mark staring through the monocular eyepiece at the light that now came from a lamp. More than an hour passed, as each took their turns examining frame after frame until they were bleary-eyed and agreed that they had gotten all they could get with the primitive equipment at their disposal. The film described projections of biological warfare strikes, some of the agents to be used, and even some time references, but they were unable to proceed further. They needed more.

Jennifer walked to the telephone and stood, staring at it. "Porter could have turned me over to the assassins, but he didn't," she stated to no one in particular. We need help, and there's nowhere else to turn." She lifted the handset and waited for Mustafa or Mark to stop her. Neither said a word, nor made a move. A few seconds later, she heard Porter's voice on the other end.

"Hi honey," she said quietly, "I'm coming home." With no more conversation, they packed up their accumulated belongings (including those they had appropriated from various sources) and walked to the door. As Mark reached for the knob, he heard a gurgling sound from behind him. The bound man lay with his life gushing from the wound where Mustafa had cut his throat. The knife was left at his side, and Mustafa brushed past him, opened the door and asked both of them, pleasantly, "coming?"

Chapter 24

Ibrahim stared bemusedly at the gleaming cylinder on the table in front of him. It didn't seem very impressive. Lying there quietly, less than a half meter in length and only 10 cm across, it began to acquire an almost surreal quality. He had been chosen to complete the construction of the bomb because of his background in nuclear engineering. He picked up the cylinder from a locker a few days ago, and already had the enriched uranium in his possession. It was not difficult to put the two together into their final, lethal form. "Enough!" Ibrahim visibly shook himself out of his state of reverie, lifted the cylinder off of the table, and very carefully lowered it, into the foam padded aluminum briefcase that would be it's new home. His instructions were clear. The case was to be taken to the Empire State building and left among the exhibits in the "Ripley's Believe it or Not" exhibition. There were so many places that things could be left there it would never noticed. Somehow, it seemed fitting that this building and all that it symbolized should become "Ground Zero" for the greatest attack on the enemy's soil that had ever been launched. "Well," he thought, "time to get started."

He was dressed in a dark business suit and, as he walked passed the mirror in the hallway, he glanced sideways and liked what he saw. He was 37 years old, and was being entrusted with this most important mission. Without further thought, but with a tingle of apprehension, he walked out the door of his apartment for the last time. He would miss New York. He felt alive with the excitement that never died at dawn, among a people who were so unaware of their own power and the actions of their government, that he felt sorry for their untimely end. "Perhaps if they really knew..." His thoughts trailed off as the elevator door opened and he stepped into the small cab to descend to the ground floor. Small beads of sweat formed on his forehead, and he felt slightly flushed as he looked around at the three other people in the elevator with him. There was a moderately obese man whom he recognized from having seen him in the elevator before. They had never spoken, but he always seemed nice. The middle-aged woman in the stark business suit reflected his own manner of dress. They were headed off to work on Wall Street, or some other equally likely area. The final passenger was a young woman whom Ibrihim had seen several times, and would have liked to approach, but hadn't the courage to face the probable rejection. She was tall, had nearly black hair with deep blue eyes and a magnificent figure that she always emphasized with tight blouses and sweaters, and tighter skirts that rose more than half way from her knees to her hips. He continued to stare at her from behind until the door opened and spewed them into the lobby. "Oh well..."

It was only a short walk to the subway stop where he took the crosstown train to a stop from which he could walk to his destination. Paying his money, he joined the rear of a jostling crowd in their tour of the bizarre. When he reached the exhibit which used mirrors to hide portions of what looked like a beach, he waited until there was no one in sight and carefully placed the locked suitcase behind the wooden wall and under a bench that no one could actually see from the viewer's position. It was about as inconspicuous as one could get. This done, he completed his tour of the exhibits, and walked at a reasonable pace through the door where he hailed a cab. "JFK airport, please. He hesitated for a moment, then added, "Air France." The meter flag dropped without the driver saying anything, and they spent the next half hour wending their way to the airport. Ibrihim was glad the driver didn't want to talk. He was relieved to be free of his package, yet remained both anxious about getting away, and guilty about what he had done. He believed in his cause, but questioned this act. It would certainly draw the world's attention to their cause as nothing else would, but it was insane.

Two hours and thirty eight minutes after having placed an aluminum briefcase behind a wooden partition and under a service bench, Ibrihim was relaxing in a coach seat on his way across the Atlantic. "Miss," he asked the flight attendant politely, "may I have another glass of orange juice, please?"

Chapter 25

The buttons on his uniform tunic glistened, as they had for 23 years since he entered the Royal Air Force. Air Marshall McCallister settled quietly in front of the video terminal waiting the few minutes until the conference was to begin. It was extraordinary. He remembered only three other conferences like this one, and he felt uncomfortable as he waited. This was dangerous. He had been assured that conferencing over the Internet was safe, being almost impossible to intercept or trace unless one knew what was happening, where, when, and through which servers. They were even using individual satellite uplinks rather than hard wiring. Still, he understood the risk as well as anyone, and was anxious.

✶✶✶✶✶✶✶✶✶✶✶✶✶✶✶✶✶✶✶✶✶✶✶✶✶✶✶✶✶✶✶✶

The white metal shed sat unobtrusively behind his house, blending into the foliage covering the interior of the large stone wall surrounding his deceptively large home. General Chang Li sat in front of his monitor, the small inverted umbrella to which it was connected by a cable, angled toward the unseen horizon. It was night in Beijing, long past the time when most of his compatriots would have been in bed. He had told the guard at his door that he couldn't sleep, and was going to take a walk. If it seemed unusual, there was no sign of it in the guards eyes. It was frequently healthier not to questions such things.

✶✶✶✶✶✶✶✶✶✶✶✶✶✶✶✶✶✶✶✶✶✶✶✶✶✶✶✶✶✶✶✶

In this dacha outside of Moscow, Marshal Pietre Sherbekov sat at a similar terminal waiting for the appointed time. Like his counterparts around the world, he was anxious about this meeting, despite the lack of any likelihood that it would be discovered. His new PC, with "Intel Inside," sat with the Cyrillic version of Windows and Microsoft Netmeeting lurking behind the changing colors of his screen saver. On the wall, the anachronistic analog clock inched its way toward the appointed time. He straightened his tie in anticipation, and repositioned the small video camera atop his monitor to allow for a more flattering picture of himself.

✳✳✳✳✳✳✳✳✳✳✳✳✳✳✳✳✳✳✳✳✳✳✳✳✳✳✳✳✳✳✳✳✳✳✳✳

It was afternoon in Washington D.C. when Stewart Hallsey punched the button on his new laptop. He smiled as the brilliant 15" screen came to life, slid his index finger to double-tap the NetMeeting Icon, and faced directly into the small video camera. It took some doing to make sure he wouldn't be disturbed for the next few minutes, but the importance of what he was doing was never far from his mind. The digital clock that comprised his screen saver reached the half hour, and he touched the "Enter" key, with the name of the server, "ils.terra.gov," already entered, and the address of the first person to be called in the line below. After a few seconds, Marshal Sherbikov's face appeared in miniature on the screen, soon followed by several others. It had long been agreed upon that English, being the most ubiquitous language in the world, would be the language of these infrequent conferences. Those who did not originally speak it had to learn.

When everyone who had been invited to the meeting was present in cyberspace, Admiral Hallsey called the meeting to order.

"Gentlemen," there were no women in this club, not yet, "we have a problem."

"Admiral," the heavily accented English made everyone aware that the speaker was from Moscow, "tell us what we do not know."

"OK," Hallsey's face looked strained, even in the low resolution of the small videoconferencing picture. "They're working with Al Assad."

"Illogical." This was the first they heard from General Abdhulla Mamet, Chief Military Advisor to Saddam Hussein since he first rose to power. He commanded the armed forces of Iraq and, as such, probably held more real power than Hussein himself. "He is being paid to work against them. His whole life has been dedicated to destroying them. Why would he change sides now?"

"An interesting question. Are there any answers, Colonel Bin Josef?" Bin Josef, the PLO commander, had been sitting quietly, with a worried look on his face. He hesitated before he answered, choosing his words carefully.

"There was...," another hesitation then he continued, "...it seems that there was an order issued to eliminate Al Assad."

"Why?" Mahmet looked puzzled.

"Because he was involved in the New York thing and when he was seen with the American Woman in Paris, he was considered a liability." He paused once more, "it was...expedient."

Hallsey's eyes rose to stare at the ceiling. "What is the probability that we could be compromised?" By "we" he clearly meant the group represented by the men sitting in front of him.

"I don't think that's possible. After all," continued Bin Josef, "none of them really know we even exist. Without a trail..." He allowed his voice to fade, then shrugged his shoulders.

"We need them all eliminated now." Mahmet's interjection surprised Hallsey who was beginning to think in terms of containment.

"Why?" He asked.

"We don't really know how much any of them know, or how much they are able to deduce. Remember, they have information about the nuclear weapon and that may be traceable back to us. Besides, I'm getting pressure from Saddam. Let's end this thing." He was clearly agitated, but living under Saddam Hussein's rule could do that to anyone.

"I'm not sure that we should have any continued contact with them at this point." Hallsey expressed what they all felt, that there was no real trail, and further exposure would be unjustified.

"No!" Mahmet's forcefulness surprised them. They must be eliminated. Either we do it as a group, or I will have it arranged, but I can't take the chance of my discovery, and you should all feel the same way. This is a small price to pay." There was a short silence then by acclamation, they all approved.

"Right, then…" McCallister began, "what about the New York thing? When is that to be discovered?"

The meeting lasted twelve minutes longer, then their screens went blank. In a small room, in one of more than seventeen Presidential Palaces in Iraq, Abduhlla Mahmet sat with perspiration dripping from his forehead onto his tunic. He wiped his face with a handkerchief, swallowed with difficulty, then calmed himself and picked up a telephone. Within minutes the assassinations of the three had been arranged. He would feel better knowing this had been accomplished. There was too much at stake now to risk exposure. Behind him, the door opened and Saddam Hussein entered the room. "How did it go?"

"Well, I'm sure of it," Mahmet answered.

When Mahmet was alone, he returned to his computer screen and checked that the funds in his Swiss account were intact.

Chapter 26

When the door to the safe house opened, Porter stood there with a Cardigan sweater smiling as though his distant cousin had just shown up to visit. He showed no surprise, at all, seeing Mark and Mustafa behind her.

"Jennifer," he said warmly, "how wonderful to see you again." She brushed past him and he extended a like greeting to Mark. His smile ended with Mustafa, however. He held the door open for him to follow Mark into the brownstone, but made sure to follow closely behind as they turned left and entered the sitting room. When they were all seated comfortably, Porter asked, politely if anyone wanted any tea. No one did, so they sat for a few more seconds before Porter began. "You gave us quite a start, you know," he said, looking at Jennifer. He then began to address Mark, when Jennifer stopped him.

"Porter," she began hesitantly, "we need to talk somewhere secure." He was quiet for a moment. Jennifer wasn't following the "rules." She directly asked for a secure room, and was making no pretense of anything. He hesitated for a few moments, wondering what to do. "Well," he thought, "in for a penny…" then rose, turned toward the hallway, and after a quick look back over his shoulder, said simply, "follow me."

The secure room was in the basement, again, but in a different area. Nobody was there at this time of day. Porter stood in front of a red rectangle which scanned his iris, then he placed the palm of his right hand on a glowing plate and stated his name. The thick pocket door slid open, and they entered a room that looked like any other, but wasn't. The walls and ceiling were double, with a small area of vacuum between them and the interior surface covered with a special paint and wallboard, behind which was a layer of anechoic material. The floor and ceiling were covered with similar material, while more than two feet of concrete lay beneath. The entire room was flooded with "white noise." It sounded like a low hiss upon entering, but quickly became unnoticed. There was a "living room" type of furniture grouping at one end of the room, and a conference table at the other. Lamps were scattered about on tables, but the room was now flooded with fluorescent light, giving everything a harsh and sterile appearance. Porter was in no mood for any further attempt at amenities at this point. His own ass was on the line for doing this, and he was only here because of Jennifer. He sat at one end of the conference table, and the other three followed suit. "Ok." Porter waited.

The three of them sat along the same side of the table, with Jennifer between the two men. "She reached into the pocket of her jacket, pulled out the pack of matches to which the microfilm had been returned, and placed them on the table. For the next fifteen minutes, she recounted their recent episodes in relative detail, leaving out extraneous and personal parts, like the animosity between Mark and Mustafa. Porter listened intently, without emotion, although occasionally glancing at each of the men when their parts in the tale were mentioned. When she finished, she pushed the book of matches to the center of the table. "The microfilm is in here. You need to see it."

Porter sat quietly, without moving, digesting the story. He knew there were gaps, but decided that Jennifer probably told him everything he really needed to know. She knew she had placed him in a dangerous position, but must have thought it was worth it and wouldn't have left any important information out. Without saying a word, he arose from the padded chair he occupied and walked to a wall where he touched one of a line of square buttons. It lit briefly, then subsided as a section of wall slid aside to reveal various electronics. Some were simple like radio equipment, while others had functions that were difficult to divine. Porter took the book of matches, separated the cover and removed the microfilm with soft tipped forceps, then placed it on another glowing square and stepped back to a seat at the head of the table. A panel flipped up in front of him, and with a few manipulations, a video screen on the opposite wall came to life, showing an entire page of the microfilm.

"Primitive." It was all Porter was prepared to say at this point. The three stared at the page, then Porter switched it to the next, followed by the next, and so forth. Where necessary, Mustafa translated the Arabic, and Mark some of the biological and chemical references. There were more than twenty geographic scenarios, most of which they had been unable to see with the microscope they had at the hotel and none of which were instantly identifiable. They were just turning to the last page, when Jennifer yelled, "stop!." Then she stood up, a little embarrassed by her outburst, but still needing to see something. She moved closer to the screen, and asked Porter if he could enlarge the middle of the page. "Sure," he answered, and as he manipulated the controls in front of him, a square appeared in the center of the screen, which then expanded. in front of them until the writing became blurred.

"Now," Jennifer said, staring at the screen, "can you reverse the coloring?" Curious, Porter played with the controls in front of him again until the screen changed to a slightly grayish-white and the writing became dark. Jennifer stared for another few seconds, then turned with a triumphant look on her face. "OK." Porter waited a few seconds, then followed with,

"What is it?"

"There's a seal there. Almost like a watermark, but darker. They strained their eyes, and could begin to make out the outline of what she was referring to.

"Wait," Porter walked to the apparatus on the wall, and the design began to grow darker as the writing and diagrams began to fade. Soon, they were staring at a seal. There was the outline of a bird, an eagle, its beak turned to the right with a shield on its chest from which hung three black bands. It sat on a band with some indecipherable Arabic on it. Mark looked confused, but the others stared, then returned to the table and sat quietly.

"What is it?" Mark felt left out. Each of the others looked at each other, then Jennifer finally broke the ice.

"It's the seal of Iraq. This is an Iraqi document describing a plan for a CBW attack. We don't know where, we don't know when, and we don't know how, but it's coming."

"That's nuts!" Mark leaned on the end of the table to stare directly into their eyes at their seated level. "An attack of this magnitude could not only cause millions of deaths where it strikes, but potentially spread around the world wiping out most of the population! Even if someone thought they had the antidote, there would be no guarantee that the agent wouldn't mutate into another strain that they couldn't control!"

Porter then noticed a small blinking rectangle on the small screen visible only to him in the panel rising out of the end of the table where he sat. "MATCH COMPLETE," it read. "OK, the computer seems to have overlaid the grids from the first location on the microfilm with a location. Let's see where it is." The larger screen with the microfilm went white for a second, then was replaced with a satellite photo that no one could mistake. There was the Chrysler building, the Empire State Building, and the twin towers of the World Trade Center. The Statue of Liberty was off to the right.

"Wait a minute," Mustafa was thoughtful. Perhaps this is just a contingency plan. Since they help finance many of our operations," he hesitated for a moment, realizing what he was saying then continued. "Why would they plant a bomb in a city that would be destroyed by this plague?"

"A better question," returned Mark, even more thoughtfully, is why plant a plague in a city that was about to undergo a nuclear detonation?

It would sterilize the area and prevent any damage from the plague. This makes no sense whatever!"

"I'm afraid you're both right," Porter sighed, but where does that leave us?"

"You know the answer to that one," Jennifer replied. They would have smiled if it weren't for the confusion and fear they all felt. Jennifer stood and paced up and back for a few seconds, then asked Mustafa, "do you still have any contacts in Iraq that you can trust?"

"Ah, trust…" Mustafa's voice trailed off, then he continued, "that is the problem, isn't it?" He looked straight at Porter, and everyone in the room understood.

"Look," Porter stood and leaned on the table so that his face was uncomfortably close to Mustafa's. "I don't like you, I don't like what you stand for, and I'll always loathe the indiscriminate killing that animals like you do, but right now, we are on the same side because we have to be. If we don't succeed, my career, your lives, and perhaps the lives of several billion people on this miserable planet will end, and my feeling for you, or yours for me won't matter." He sat back down, ran his fingers through his hair, then looked directly at Mustafa, "will it?"

"This is getting us nowhere," Mark stood to get the kinks out of his back, and leaned on the back of his chair. "Mr. Porter, do you have a blackboard, or something that we can keep notes or track of ideas on?"

"It's just "Porter," the "Mr." isn't necessary, and I think we can do better than that." He touched the panel in front of him and the wall on the opposite side of the table from where Jennifer, Mustafa and Mark were sitting came to life. It was a dull whitish sort of glow rather than any bright light—soothing, actually. "Here." He reached into a drawer and took out a flat black rectangle with a few buttons scattered on it, and handed it to Mark. "Just touch the "On" button at the bottom left." When he did, nearly the entire center section lit up." Porter handed each one a similar electronic pad, and explained how to use them. Everything they wrote on the pad showed up on the wall. Each entry could he highlighted and edited, erased, etc. using a plastic stylus attached by Velcro to the side of each pad. "OK." Porter looked at Mark, "there's your blackboard." He smiled, then sat and waited. He was beginning to like this amateur. He seemed to have an ability for cutting through bullshit.

Mark took the pad, and drew a horizontal line near the top, that appeared at the same location on the wall. He then drew several columns (his lines weren't straight, but the computer made them look perfect) and labeled each one at the top. "Prince Killing," read the first, "Restaurant Shooting," read the second, "Café Bombing" read the third, and so on, ending with the nuclear device in New York and the presumed bacteriological attack. He then drew several horizontal lines from the left and labeled the first line, "Objective." "OK," he began, let's try to narrow things down a bit.

"Well," began Jennifer, "I think the killing of the Sheik's son at your hotel was certainly to prevent him from delivering the microfilm to someone. Unfortunately we don't know how he obtained it, or to whom he was to deliver it."

"OK," Mark looked around the table, "is there any discussion or disagreement?" Hearing none, he printed the word "Microfilm" in bright blue letters in the appropriate location, intuitively understanding the use of the pad. "Now what about the shooting involving Jennifer and myself at the restaurant in London?"

"Obviously they were still after the microfilm, Mustafa answered in a bored tone. "Jennifer was just in the way."

"Was she," asked Mark? "Perhaps they thought I was going to pass it to her, and they wanted to get both of us at the same time." Mustafa's attention perked up.

"But how would they know you had it at that point?"

"They wouldn't." This was Porter's first entry into the discussion. He had been sitting back listening, enthralled. "They might have known that the police didn't find anything on the body, that there was nobody else near him before he died, and surmised that you had it. It would have been more prudent, from their point of view, to eliminate the two of you than to wait to find out if they were right."

"Yes," added Mustafa, but they may also simply have wanted to prevent Jennifer from finding something out that they thought she was close to, and not have had anything to do with the microfilm at all."

"OK," Mark said, let's add both to the column and move on for now." He made a similar entry in blue, but with a diagonal slash between the 'ideas. This continued for more than an hour, as each block was filled with entries. Mark had decided on Blue for assumptions, Green for acknowledged facts (there weren't many green entries), and Red for pure speculation. When they were finished, the stared at the wall,

"Curious…," Porter continued staring at the screen.

"What," asked Jennifer?

"There doesn't seem to be any pattern at all with regard to who may have initiated the attacks. They seem to have come from all sides, including ours."

"So?" Jennifer was uncertain what he was getting at.

"Don't you see, the events appear to be connected. The passing of the microfilm, the shooting in London, the bombing of the café, the planting of the bomb in New York, and so on, yet the attacks on you seems to be unrelated. Curious…" Porter's voice trailed off again, and he seemed to be looking past the screen.

Mustafa and Jennifer looked at each other somewhat quizzically, but Mark was staring at the screen much as Porter was. "Occam's Razor," he stated flatly.

"Excuse me?" Porter seemed to have been jerked back into the room.

"It's an old rule of logic that states that all things being equal, the simplest explanation tends to be the correct one. Whenever you have to bend your theory out of shape to encompass all of the facts, then junk the theory and come up with a simpler one that explains the facts."

"What the hell does that have to do with anything?" Mustafa was becoming increasingly annoyed by this pedantic meandering.

"Don't you see," Mark asked? "If there appears to be a lot of unconnected sides out to get us without any obvious reasons, then all things being equal, the simplest explanation is that they must be connected in some way we know nothing about."

"Yes," Porter reflected. "I agree. It's the only thing that makes sense."

"Do you know what you're saying," asked Jennifer?

"Yes, Porter answered quietly, "and it scares the shit our of me." We don't know what the connection is, but its implications are staggering!"

Mustafa had been sitting there listening to the discussion, but now had to add the obvious. "None of this explains the combination of the CBW plans of the Iraqis and the nuclear weapon in New York."

"No, it doesn't," replied Mark, "but it's a beginning."

"OK," Jennifer added to the conversation, "where do we go from here?" They were quiet for a while. Mark went to the coffee service and poured himself a cup, asking if anyone else wanted any. They all sat at the table for the next ten minutes, chatting idly, but with their eyes always returning to the screen. Where was the connection? What were they missing? It was Porter who finally ended the staring and banal conversation.

"We're getting nowhere," he opened the next round. "We need more information."

"Yes," replied Jennifer," but where do we get it?"

"I have an idea," said Porter, and he rose from his chair with a swiftness that they hadn't seen in him before, and walked to the wall housing the computer interface. After sitting, and entering his password, the screen before him cleared, and he began to type.

ENTER QUERY> terrorist and (bomb* or kill*) and date

The computer blinked for a few seconds, then several columns of data began scrolling down the screen. With the touch of another button, this was transferred to the larger screen across from the table, and they stared at the information trying to make some sense of it. As they did, the small computer began to "ping," repeatedly, and the screen turned to red with a flashing white band in the middle. "Incoming," it read, then was followed by an announcement that a 'Nuclear Device" had been discovered in New York. Suspicions were that an Arab Terrorist group had planted it. It had been diffused, and there was no further danger, but this was classified at the highest level—NEED TO KNOW. If knowledge of this leaked to the press, there would be a call for the bombing of countries known to support terrorism, as well as "copy cat" bombings. There would certainly be calls for a beefing up of internal security in the United States. Porter remembered seeing an appearance of Admiral Hallsey before a Congressional oversight committee to ask for the funds to form units to fight these kinds of things, but had been turned down. "The ending of the Cold War doesn't mean the end of danger," he had stated. There followed interviews with various congressmen and Senators, who seemed divided among themselves over the issue. Their constituents were asking where the "Peace Dividend" was. They expected the end of the "Cold War" to mean that they didn't have to choose between "Guns and Butter." Porter didn't share these thoughts with the others, only the news.

"They could not yet have known of the bomb," Mustafa said. We hadn't yet sent them any demands or made them aware. I do not believe the bomb was even armed. How could they have found it so quickly in a city the size of Manhattan?"

"Well," said Jennifer softly, I can tell you how they knew about it. I called Porter with the information as soon as I learned about it from you," she said facing Mustafa. "You didn't expect me to just stand by and watch millions of innocent people die did you?"

Mustafa brushed that aside and asked, "yes, but how could they find it so quickly?"

Mark had been silent throughout this exchange. He had been staring at the columns on the wall, then at the announcement on the smaller screen then back to the wall.

"Has anyone noticed anything odd here?" they seemed to have forgotten about Mark for a while, but now turned toward him.

"Yes, Jennifer said, "everything."

"That's not what I meant," he said. "Look at the dates for the terrorist activity in the last year. There have been a few peaks and troughs, but the pace, around the world, has been fairly steady. We probably don't notice this because each country tends to report only events involving their own country, or the most major of international events, like aircraft bombings."

"Get to the point," Mustafa said brusquely. He was tiring of Mark's tendency to lecture.

"Well," Mark began, trying to be more succinct, "look at the number of incidents in the last week." They stared for a few moments, then Porter instructed the computer to arrange the information sorted by date, and plot the number of incidents against the dates on a graph. It was graphically startling. During the preceding week, the number of incidents had dropped to a mere 8% of their usual number. It was as though someone had flipped a switch, and turned everything off. "Since our arrival in Paris, world terrorism, even international confrontation has almost evaporated." Mark walked to the table and sat down feeling smug.

"You're right," Jennifer answered tentatively, "but it doesn't explain it. Why should our predicament affect the rate of terrorism or military confrontation?"

"Why indeed," Mustafa queried? "In fact," added Porter, it seems to have dropped as soon as the three of you dropped out of site."

Minutes flew by, and each sat, then stood, then paced, then sat again as they continued to examine the enormous amount of data in front of them. Mark was first to break the silence, "Occam's Razor, again." He paused, realized that the rest were waiting for him to continue, and so he did. "We already decided that there was evidence that there must be some connection among the various groups that were trying to kill us." He paused, then continued, "now it appears that there are some, possibly the same factions, controlling the incidence of terrorism." They continued to stare at him with a questioning look in their eyes. "Don't you see?" Mark's voice began to rise. "When they failed to kill us, they turned off terrorist and military activity, afraid of what we might have found out, and what we might be able to reveal."

"Yes," Mustafa added thoughtfully, "that would certainly account for the rapid discovery of the nuclear device in New York." Porter stood quietly, thinking, but Jennifer's eyes widened, and she began to sweat.

"Do you realize what you're saying?" They waited. "That would mean that the United States government has ties to terrorism, along with nearly every other government in the world. It's the only way they could have discovered the location so quickly."

"More than that," Mustafa added, it means that they, along with England, France, Russia, China, and so on have taken an active role in directing attacks against their own countries and citizens. It means we've been had!" His "we" obviously meant his own terrorist group.

"My God," said Porter quietly, if that's true...." His voice trailed off, then, "It doesn't make sense."

"Yes, it does." Mark walked to the small screen on the wall where the news items had scrolled, and pointed to the item involving Admiral Hallsey. "There's the common factor—money." They waited. "With the end of the Cold War, most governments have been cutting back on their funding for the military and intelligence sectors. The only way they could keep the money flowing was to create an enemy to fight."

"Isn't that sort of Machiavellian," asked Jennifer?

"Yes." Mark simply stated the fact. "But give me a better, more logical theory that explains the facts. It even explains why all sides have been trying to kill us. They've been working together."

"But why us," Jennifer asked?

"Because of two things," Porter interrupted. "To begin with, this is the first time that a government agent and a terrorist seemed to be exchanging information, if not working together. More importantly, though, you had the microfilm. That combination seems to have scared the hell out of them."

"That brings us back to the microfilm," Jennifer changed the subject. I don't see the relation."

"Nor do I," answered Porter, but it must be there. If everything else fits, it must also." Mark sat in one of the easy-chairs at the other end of the room, feeling as though a weight had pushed him down. He felt drained. Porter looked at him, at the others, and walked to the wall from which the computers were controlled. He reached forward, touched a key, and all screens went blank. "Let's get something to eat and some rest," he said. "Unfortunately, this won't go away while we rest."

Chapter 27

High above the atmosphere, in a polar orbit that would allow it to be over most areas of the Earth at some point in time, the highly reflective surface of MRS—42 glinted brightly, reflecting the sunlight back into space. The military recon satellite slowly rotated and began its usual photo run over the Persian Gulf area. This wasn't a special mission. With the situation being chronically tense, photos were always made of this area. They were then transmitted back to an Earth station where they were downloaded into the NSA computer/graphics system. There, other computers noted changes from previous photos, and any significant differences reported either in one of four daily printouts, or in an electronic "**Alert**" sent as an email to the designated people.

Today, there were only small changes so no Alert messages were sent. The minor movements of troops and aircraft were noted and reported. There were two reports of "questionable asset relocation" (read, "their moving something and we don't know what it is...") and that was about all. As these photos were being analyzed and stored in the bowels of the NSA Graphic Analyzer, other reports of increased radio, telephone, and electronic/data traffic in the region, were being downloaded from millions of sources into another NSA computer system which would compare voiceprints and basic speech patterns. Once again there was an insufficient change in patterns to raise any alarms, so things hummed along pretty much as usual.

As all of the reports were collected and collated, they were dispersed to the various "desks" within the scattered intelligence communities— CIA, NSA, Military Intelligence centers, FBI, Secret Service…The list goes on, but each received its "SINTEL" (Satellite Intelligence) report in due order, and each passed the appropriate information to its various branches. It was like a clock that had been wound up after the Second Word War and never ran down.

Andrew Dalton sat in the middle of the conference table in the briefing room at the White House. To his left was Secretary of State, Arlo Kirkpatrick and National Security Advisor, David Wellington III. To his right was Mitchell Avery, the White House chief if Staff, and Admiral Hallsey , Chairman of the Joint Chiefs. Facing him across the table were FBI Director Matthew Gregory, and the Director of the CIA, Brett Manheim. The President had called the meeting after receiving the news of the nuclear device found in the Empire State Building in Manhattan. The light was diffuse, the acoustics were perfect, and the President was livid.

"How the hell could someone get a nuke into New York! I want some answers, and I want them now!" Each looked around the room at the others, measuring who would speak first and who they could pass the blame to.

"Sir," It was Matt Gregory who spoke first, "anyone could have done it. Getting the plans and materials is no trick, only the Plutonium would be a problem and," he paused then finished, since the old Soviet Union broke up…" Gregory looked around, waiting for understanding and agreement.

"He's right, Mr. President." Dalton turned to look at Stuart Hallsey. "We've known that it was just a matter of time before someone put things together to try this. Was there any call or demand?" Hallsey flushed when the President answered, "No." He turned to look at Gregory but before either one could speak, President Dalton looked over at Brett Manheim and asked, "PLO?"

"We think so, sir, but we have no proof. No one has called yet, or taken responsibility."

"Mr. President," Gregory's bass voice returned the president's attention to him. "The bomb had a radio controlled arming switch; a very sophisticated one. It hadn't been armed when we grabbed it, so maybe the people responsible don't yet know that we have it."

"How did you find it," asked the President?"

"We were, um," Manheim paused for a moment to search for the word, "tipped off, Mr. President."

"By whom?"

"Well, sir," he hesitated again, it came from Jennifer Lynch."

"Jennifer!" roared the president." He stood for a moment, then sat back down. "Where is she now?"

"Sir," Manheim said sheepishly, "we don't exactly know."

"What do you mean you don't know?"

"Well, sir, she called one of our assets in France to report that the bomb had been planted, apparently getting the information from a terrorist who took part in the operation, a Mustafa Al Assad." He paused, then continued, "but she never told us where she was, and we were only able to find the bomb with the help of the military anti-nuclear teams that Admiral Hallsey dispatched."

"Sir," it was Hallsey this time, "we've rehearsed this scenario for years. We've developed special equipment that can sense even small amounts of nuclear material, and, well, I also took a few lucky guesses."

The President was quiet for a few moments. He seemed to be bordering between anger and anxiety. "Gentlemen, where is Ms. Lynch now?"

"Mr. President," Manheim again, "I told you, we don't know. "We know she was involved in a shooting along with some American tourist in London, and they disappeared. Apparently, they both surfaced later, in Paris. Coincidentally, Al Assad had arrived in Paris a day or two before, from New York. We wanted to know what he was doing there, so we asked that, because of a past association she had with him some years ago, she locate him and try to get the information." He paused for a drink, then continued. "The next we heard, was that she was probably killed in a café bombing there, along with Al Assad, but we had no confirmation of that because the bodies were too badly destroyed for any rapid identification. Then, we heard from her later, stating that she wanted to "come in" but somehow, an order was issued for her," he hesitated, afraid to say it, "termination, because of her new association with Al Assad…." He was unable to continue because the President slammed his hand down on the table with a look of uncharacteristic rage.

"YOU DID WHAT?" The veins stood out on the President's neck as he faced Manheim.

"No sir, I didn't. And neither, apparently, did anyone else we can find. We have been unable to trace the origin of the order."

"How can that be?" It was the first time the calm voice of David Wellington was heard at the meeting since the introductory greetings. "Every order can be traced to its source, can't it?"

"Well, normally, but this was sent as a priority order via our computer network, and the user with whom the order originated is unknown to anyone. In effect, our system was compromised. Someone used the "root" password to create another user with the same privileges as the system administrator, then deleted the user and all logs after the order was sent. We've purged all passwords and access files, re-matched all files against known users, etc., and we believe that we're clean now, but we have no idea how they could have gotten into the system to send such an order."

The room was quiet as President Dalton rose and walked to a window to look out. He was staring across the White House lawn as he asked calmly, "David, are you telling me that someone could send out a Presidential Order, using my name and access codes, to anyone, anywhere, and it would be indistinguishable from one that I sent myself?" The space of time between question and answer stretched to infinity for most of the people in the room before Wellington answered.

"Yes sir. That's exactly what this means. But there's more."

"Yes?" the President's eyes never came away from the window?

"We have the most secure computer systems in the world. If they can do it to ours, it would be child's play to do it to the Russians, the Chinese…, anyone."

"Who are they," asked the President as he faced the others around the table? "Are they hackers?"

"No sir, we don't think so. Most hackers are playful, or mischievous, but not directional. If anything, they hate secrets and authority, and do things to expose them and make them look silly."

"Go on." The President remained standing where he was.

"We believe that this order had to come from someone in the loop. Someone high enough to have top level access, and well above suspicion."

"That could be you, couldn't it David?"

"Yes sir, Mr. President, it could, and I couldn't prove it wasn't."

Andrew Dalton, President of the United States, returned to his seat at the table, ran his hand through his hair, rubbed his eyes, and looked carefully at each face at the table before he said quietly,

"It could have been any one of us. It could even have been me." The antique clock on the mantle ticked quietly, it's sound being drowned out of the President's ears by the pounding of his own heart. He was alone.

Chapter 28

Mark lay in the darkness in that half awake, half dream state that exists right before we are truly awake. He knew he was still dreaming, but he wanted the dream to continue because it provided him relief from the world that awaited him when he opened his eyes. Well, he was awake, so he might as well open his eyes.

With his pupils still dilated from the absolute darkness of sleep, the light filtering through the door jam and outlining the door actually allowed him to make out the shapes in the dormitory style room that he had been assigned by Porter. Jennifer, he knew, was next door, and Mustafa across the hall. These were not like the rooms they had occupied upstairs. There was no beautiful furniture, no antiques, and no fine china. Each room, only a few yards down the hall from the Secure Room they had met in earlier, was outfitted with a bed, a nightstand with a digital clock and lamp, a table with three chairs and a desk. The carpeting on the floor was an industrial strength burbur, with little padding. There was a white telephone on the desk, but no buttons adorned its face because there was only one thing you could do with it—answer.

The room was remembered, only the glowing numerals on the clock were visible. "O300:00." "God," thought Mark, "what am I going to do now?" He wasn't sure if he meant tonight, or in general, but the question applied equally. As he swung his feet out of the bed and onto the floor, a feeling of claustrophobia began to touch him. He had felt it only once before in his life, but was now feeling as though he couldn't get a satisfying deep breath. He knew there was nothing physically wrong, and as he stood, he forced himself to calm down. He was in his underwear, and was enjoying the cool feeling of the processed air against his skin. Slowly, and deliberately, Mark walked to the door of his room, and stepped out into the hall. The fluorescent lights in the ceiling gave a harsh appearance to the bare hallway that he hadn't noticed when he went to bed. He walked back into his room and put his pants on without turning on the lights, then went back into the high tech meeting room they had been in before. Walking directly to the small kitchenette that occupied a small part of one wall, he punched a few buttons to make himself some tea in the microwave then sat on the sofa, placed his cup on the coffee table in front of him, and stared at the blank screens. From there his eyes wondered to the scattered art prints that occupied places on several of the other walls. It was an unsuccessful concession to esthetics. The clock on the wall read "0314:00." It's going to be a long night," he said to no one in particular.

He had been sitting for only a few minutes, when the door to the room opened, and Mustafa walked in.

"I'm not the only one who can't sleep, I see," and he too walked to the kitchenette and made himself a cup of coffee. Neither said anything else for a few minutes as Mustafa sat across from Mark in a leather easy-chair.

"You knew Jennifer before, didn't you?" Mark broke the silence with the first question that had come to his mind. It wasn't about world threats.

"Yes." It was a simple answer to a simple question, but not enough for Mark.

"Were you...," he thought for a moment, "close?" Mustafa was annoyed at being questioned by this American about things that were none of his business, yet he somehow, felt compelled to answer.

"Yes, we were. Very."

"Look, I know it's none of my business..."

"You're right, it isn't." Mustafa stopped him cold, and enjoyed doing it. They were both silent for another minute of two, when Mustafa put his coffee cup down and stared into Marks eyes. "How well do *you* know her?"

Mark stared at the gun in the holster attached to Mustafa's belt. He obviously never went anywhere without it, and Mark wished he had brought his own. It would have made him feel more "Professional." It didn't stop him from responding in kind, "that's none of *your* business." Mark glowered back at Mustafa, and was about to attempt another response when he was surprised by a broad smile that cracked Mustafa's face for the first time he could remember since they met. Was it really only a few days ago? His mouth began its automatic response but he fought it. He hated this man, despite the fact that they seemed to be in this together. He just wasn't sure whether he hated him for the right reasons.

"You're right," Mustafa's smile remained, as he stood and walked to the conference table, turned and looked back at Mark. "Have you been married long?" Mustafa remained smiling, but the warmth had evaporated as quickly as it had appeared.

"Let's stop fencing with each other," Mark answered. "It's obvious you had a relationship with her years ago, but leave her alone now. In the end, you'll only get her hurt, killed, or destroy her, emotionally."

"And what business is that of yours?" Mustafa's manner remained confrontational. Mark stood to face Mustafa, defiance swelling within him.

"It's my business. That's enough." They stood, facing each other, for a few seconds that stretched into hours in their minds, when Mustafa finally walked to the Kitchenette, threw his Styrofoam cup into the trashcan, and walked toward the door.

"That's an issue we may have to decide, between us, one day." Then he turned, and walked out of the door and back to his room.

Mark stood there for a few moments, his nerves remaining on edge, and his hands clenched. There was a slight trembling throughout his body that wasn't fear. Then, like Mustafa before him, he threw his cup into the trash and walked back to his room. He wished he had a TV or something to read.

As he opened his door, the light from the hall flooded into the room, outlining a figure sitting on his bed. "Hi."

He could sense her presence, smell her, and taste her before she said a word.

"I see you couldn't sleep either. Were you and Mustafa enjoying each other's company?" He could see her smirk in his mind, despite the darkness. He walked to the bed, sat next to her, and gently stroked her hair.

"Wait," she took his hand and held it in her own. "There are some things you need to know about before you go further."

"No there aren't," he said. "I know about you and Mustafa from years ago." He stopped for a moment then continued, "Do you still love him?"

"No…" she hesitated then continued, "…I don't know…" The words just didn't seem to come to her. "Look, it was a long time ago…"

"In a galaxy far, far away?" he interrupted." He felt, more than saw the smile, as she answered.

"Something like that; I can't say I feel nothing at all around him." Mark began to stand up when she pulled him back onto the bed, "but I'm here in your room, not his." Now it was her turn to stroke his face, feeling the stubble on his chin, and resting her hand on his chest. "What about your wife?" He knew the question had to come sometime.

"Jennifer," he had rehearsed this speech a hundred times, but none of the words came. "My sons are the most important things in the world to me, but Meredith and I haven't really been what anyone would call married for years. We're sort of legal roommates." He paused. "I've thought about divorce, I know she has, but I guess I had nowhere else to go, and was afraid of losing my sons. But you…" He wasn't quite sure whether to continue, or if he could even express what he felt. "I…," he stammered again, "I…" She put her hand over his mouth.

"It's alright. I understand. This is all I want…for now," she added.

Together, they lay back on the bed. She was wearing only her panties and a T-shirt, and his pants came quickly off. As they lay together on the small bed, there was none of the urgency that had characterized their earlier lovemaking. They kissed each other gently, soothing pain that was more emotional than physical. He had never known anyone that made him feel the mixture of respect and protectiveness he felt whenever he thought of her, and he was different than the men she had known. She had seen him react better than some professionals in his situation despite the fear that she knew he must be feeling. Most of all, though, there was a vulnerability within him that made him seem stronger, not weaker for having it and leaving it exposed. For reasons she might never be able to explain, she felt drawn to him. She wanted to nurture him (a feeling she never thought she'd feel about a man), yet she felt safe around him. As though he would let nothing happen to her.

Their kisses were accompanied by the roaming of their hands, and they were soon rising and falling as they remembered from the Inn, but more slowly, gently…When they climaxed, it was the least important part of the experience for both of them. For the first time in either of their lives, they understood the idea of two people "joining." They lay in each other's arms for the rest of the night, with her returning to her room just before they thought Mustafa might awaken, leaving Mark to lay in a pool of emotional warmth he had never experienced before. He fell asleep dreaming of Jennifer. He awakened in a pool of sweat. He couldn't remember why, but the feeling of dread stayed with him as he showered, dressed, and walked back into the Secure Room where Porter, Mustafa and Jennifer were already waiting for him, the conference table already set with breakfast.

They finished eating. Mark hadn't realized how hungry he was. He had never been a breakfast eater, but that seemed to be changing lately. He had eggs, pancakes, sausage, bacon, and juice, along with two mugs of strong coffee and cream. The dishes, except for the coffee, were placed on a service cart and sent upstairs to disappear somewhere, then they sat back down at the table in the same positions they had occupied the night before, and Porter began.

"Well, I hope everyone slept well." He looked around with a twinkle in his eye that seemed to say that he knew everything about everyone, but wasn't telling. Then he became more serious. "So where do we go from here?" Mustafa was about to say something, when Jennifer interrupted him before he could begin.

"Porter, yesterday we spoke of trust."

"Yes," Porter answered.

"Well I thought about it, and there is one person on our side I still believe I can trust." She paused, for effect, they all knew, but when she began again, the effect was complete, "Andrew Dalton." They were all quiet for a moment. They had forgotten that, while she lived in their world part of the time, there was another world of which she was a part. She walked the halls of power with a familiarity that none of them would ever be likely to know.

Porter sputtered for a moment, then asked, "even if that's true, how would you get to him? Besides, since the order to terminate you came from our side, what makes you think he would believe anything you say?"

"I don't know," she answered slowly, "it's just a feeling. But do we really have that many options?"

"How would you contact him?" Porter, despite his disbelief, was being drawn into the scenario.

"There is a way. We've used it several times when he wanted us to be able to discuss things without anyone being aware of the discussion. There are tapes of the Oval Office, there are tapes of the telephone conversations he has, and he is rarely ever alone."

"Yes, we know all of that." Porter was interested, but Mark and Mustafa were transfixed. How was she going to simply talk with the President of the United States, from here, without being detected?

"Is your computer tied into the National Security Net?"

"Of course," Porter replied. "Satellite direct, scrambled, encoded, the works. It's as secure as we can make it."

"OK. You said they gave the order to terminate me. Then maybe they didn't bother to take out my access codes yet." With that, she walked to the wall where Porter had accessed the computer the previous day, and sat down at the keyboard. "Gentlemen, I know this sounds silly after all we've been through together, but I'm going to ask you to wait over there," she inclined her head towards the sofa, "until I'm logged on."

"Wait," Mark stepped toward her and took her right wrist. "If you send it to him this way, he'll know the origin of the message, and be able to trace us here."

"Yes, he will," replied Jennifer softly. "But if he's in it also, then we haven't got a chance anyway." She withdrew her hand and waited for Mark to cross the room with the others. It was ten o'clock here, so the President would just be starting his morning. She pictured him sitting in front of the desk in his private office, papers piled high, the Notebook computer he favored blinking in front of him. He liked the early morning. He got things done before the politics began.

"LOGON:" read the screen.

LOGON: JLynch

USER ID: pieceofass It was a personal joke between the President and her.

Password: ***************

The screen turned deep blue with a red and white border, and the characters in the menu that now appeared were white. She chose "EMAIL" from the menu, then send, and the computer then asked her "Alias:" "Bossman" she typed, and an email message window opened. "Bossman" appeared in the "TO" window, she hesitated over the subject. "WWIII" she typed. Then moved to the body of the note. "OK, she said, you can come back now." They returned to stand behind her, as she typed:

Mr. President:

I am not dead. It is imperative we exchange information about the nuclear device that was found and other more dangerous things. Trust no one on this yet, except me. If you agree, reply with "OK" and I'll send you more information later.

Me.

They weren't quite sure about the signature, but she clicked on the "SEND" button, and the email disappeared. She logged off, and decided to wait on the sofa. She would check her email in about an hour to see if there had been a reply.

The hour moved slowly for all of them. They weren't sure whether to expect a compliment of Marines coming down the hallway, or a ping on the computer screen telling her she has mail. Slowly, the digits on the clock advanced, punctuated by occasional banal conversation. First to 10:15, then 10:30...to 11:00. She rose and walked to the terminal, sat staring at it for a moment, then logged in again. In the lower right corner of the screen was a flashing envelope. She had mail. Of course, it could be just the departmental junk mail that accumulates each day. She moved the arrow over the envelope icon, and clicked the left mouse button. A window opened with a list of mail waiting for her. Using the arrow as a pointer, she scrolled her eyes down the line of emails until it rested on the one she was hoping to see. *bossman@whitehouse2.gov*

"Whitehouse2," asked Porter quizzically?

"Yes, it's a separate server he keeps in his private office. Everything on it is encrypted, and only he has the password. I'm sure it can be broken, but so few people know of it that it's not likely." "OK," she thought, this is it!" She clicked on the message, and a second window opened.

Who is this? How do I know that It's you? If I receive no satisfactory answer within 3 hours, no further communication will be accepted.

There was no signature line.

Jennifer thought frantically. How could she convince him if the simple fact of her having this access didn't. She looked at the clock, "11:44." There wasn't much time.

"Well," asked Mark? "What are you going to write?"

"Shut up! Give me a minute to think." Porter, Mustafa and Mark sat at the conference table, at the other end of which, Jennifer sat at the computer console, her back to them. They waited as she thought. It was nearly noon when a small smile brightened her face and her fingers began to move. They never saw what she typed, being too far away, but within 5 minutes, there was a reply from the President:

Our computers have been compromised. The order to terminate you did not originate with us. We have been unable to trace the origin of the problem, but we suspect, from intel we have, it has occurred in other computers around the world. Unable to know whom to trust. Situation very dangerous. Please advise me when you have any more information. Be careful.

They stared at the message. There was an element of panic in it that wasn't consistent with what Jennifer knew of Andrew Dalton.

"There's more going on there," Jennifer began slowly. "He's scared, and he doesn't scare easily." She stood and began pacing up and back next to the conference table.

"What are you talking about?" Mustafa rose also, and approached her.

"I'm not sure," she paused, then added, "but somehow, this fits together. We just don't see how, yet." Porter now stood and walked toward the door to the room.

"Look, I have an idea, but I need a few hours to check it out. Wait here and, whatever you do, don't leave. I've put a security seal on this area from upstairs so no one from there will come down here, but it's important that you be here when I return."

"Where are you going?" Mark entered the conversation. "I have a...," Porter paused to chose the right word, "...counterpart with whom I have occasionally shared operations. I need to speak with him, *very* privately. I'll be back as soon as I have." With that, Porter turned and walked through the door, and toward the elevator.

Jennifer, Mark and Mustafa remained standing where they were for several seconds, without speaking, them Mark walked to the sofa and sat. Jennifer and Mustafa looked at each other for a moment, then they too moved to the "living" area of the room and the three sat quietly for about ten minutes. They were weary, all of them. Mark sat with his hips forward, and his head resting on the back of the sofa. His eyes were closed, and his mind drifted back to his home for a few minutes. He wasn't thinking about Meredith, although somewhere in the deep recesses of his mind the warm young woman she had been still lurked. He thought of his boys. He remembered little league baseball and Sunday afternoon football games. He had a great relationship with his sons. It was the one remaining point of balance in his life.

Suddenly, he opened his eyes and sat upright. There was a fleeting thought, an idea that was there and then it was gone, but he knew he had to recapture it. As he stood, Mustafa looked at him and asked, "what's wrong?"

"Nothing," he answered softly, "I just want to see something," and walked back to the computer display controls, pressed a few buttons as he had seen Porter do, and the columns of data and ideas they had worked on the day before appeared on the large screen. He stood in the same position, staring at them for nearly five minutes before Jennifer asked what he was looking for.

"Nothing seems to be connected to anything else," she said. "That's why we left it alone yesterday."

"I know, he replied, but there is something that is bothering me, and I can't quite put my finger on it." As he stood searching up, down, and across the rows and columns, Mustafa joined them. Together, the three stood staring once more at the data they had collated yesterday. It hadn't changed.

They had taken several breaks, including one for lunch, but each time they returned to the screen and stared some more. Perhaps it was just that they needed to feel like they were doing something, but they were standing and staring when Porter returned. It had taken him about three hours to complete his meeting, but he had an odd expression on his face.

"Well?" Jennifer couldn't stand that look. "What did you learn?"

"I learned," Porter replied slowly, "that the Russians are trying to figure out how a flight of MIG's were ordered to engage a flight of US aircraft without any idea of where the order came from. They're chalking it up to their faltering bureaucracy, but their President is hopping mad." He paused then asked, "and what have you been up to?"

"We were just reviewing the data from yesterday. We had to do something or go nuts," Jennifer took the job of spokesperson for the group.

They walked back to the living room furniture, and sat down, but before they began to speak again, noticed that Mark had remained staring at the screen. "Mark?" Jennifer looked at him from the chair she had chosen. He didn't' answer. He just stood staring. "Mark?" She called him again, but there was still no answer. They watched him for a moment, and Jennifer rose and began walking toward him when he startled them by slamming flat of his hand on the conference table in front of him. The sound would have been even more startling in another room, but the walls absorbed most of it. Still, it stopped them where they were.

"Damn! That's it!" Mark turned toward them; his face showed more excitement, and his voice was more animated than either had been in some time. He loved solving puzzles, and this was the "Mother of all puzzles."

"What's it?" Jennifer asked, baffled. Mustafa rose and looked at the screen, then at Mark.

"OK, what's it?" he repeated Jennifer's words.

"Look at it," Mark said. He looked like a child who had just discovered how to turn on the TV. "It was there in front of us all along, but Porter's information brought it into focus."

"What!…" Jennifer was getting frustrated with the mystery, and her voice rose, "…what is it?"

"Come over here," Mark took her hand and drew her over to the table facing the screen. "Do you notice anything about each of the incidents, where they occurred, who was involved, who might have gained by ordering it, and so forth?" They stared, but nothing seemed to come.

"OK, old man," Porter looked puzzled, but was beginning to catch the spirit, "I give up."

"Me too," Mustafa said sarcastically.

"Look again," Mark commanded, "each incident appears to be isolated, individual and that's the part that doesn't make sense because they all seem aimed at us. But if we add one element, it all makes sense."

"And what, pray tell, is that?" Mustafa was getting tired of the theatrics.

Mark smiled, "control."

"Excuse me?" Jennifer looked at him with a lack of understanding. "Suppose they were not individual incidents, but subject to some central control, some command structure?"

"You are a crazy man," Mustafa laughed, "and you have no idea what you are talking about. These are all separate groups, and most of them hate each other, and are fighting each other."

"Yes, I know. Beautiful, isn't it?" They were all looking at him now. "Look, he said again, "suppose each group is acting independently, but on orders that, without them being aware of it, are all coming from the same place?"

"And where is that?" Mustafa remained unconvinced.

"Damned if I know," Mark answered, "but it makes sense, explains the facts."

"Occam's Razor," murmured Jennifer.

"Exactly," returned Mark. "And it explains why orders that were never issued caused events that weren't intended, both at home, and in Russia, as well as among these terrorists groups. It explains things, don't you see?"

"And whom do you see giving these orders," Mustafa asked, "and why, and how...?"

"Hey," Mark turned to deflect this verbal attack. "I don't have all the answers, but this theory at least fits the facts. If you have a better one, I'd be happy to listen." There was no answer, so Mark continued. "I kept thinking that this had to fit together somehow, but I couldn't put my finger on it. When we read that email from the President, something began to gel in my mind, but I still couldn't quite get a grip on it, but when Porter's source confirmed that the Russians were having the same problem, it came together. Unfortunately, there are still some large pieces missing, like your *who, how, and why*."

"Mark," Jennifer was standing and listening like the others, but now walked to the computer console, picked up the book of matches from which the microfilm had been extracted, and tossed in on the table. "It doesn't explain this, or the nuclear device in Manhattan."

"No, it doesn't." Mark looked worried.

"Well," Porter interrupted, "we'll just have to begin with what we do have, and go from there."

"OK." Mark turned to look at Porter. "Where do we go, then? We can't go talk with the President in person, and we can't get to the Russian President, and I think..." Mark was interrupted by Mustafa.

"We begin with me and my people. They're the only ones we actually know how to reach." The looked at each other, waiting for someone to come up with a better idea and, when none were forthcoming, gave in by unanimous consent.

"So how do we begin?" Mark was resigned.

For the next couple of hours, they discussed how to approach the terrorists (Mustafa insisted upon calling them a Liberation Army). It was clear that since Mustafa, himself, had been a target, he could not simply walk into headquarters and say, "hello." Also, the heads were not at headquarters, but somewhere else. The sound of that grating voice rang in his head, along with his last glance of a burning cigarette in the dark receding behind him. No, they would have to be contacted through channels, but not given enough information to find them before they were ready.

It was more than 36 hours before any sort of plan developed. None of them knew how much information each group held. Did Mustafa's "Liberation Army" think he was dead? Did the Americans (Andrew Dalton excepted) really believe Jennifer and Mark were dead? Would New Scotland Yard stop looking for them? And then there was Saddam…They had to move carefully, and as a team.

Chapter 29

The small, partially destroyed house in central Beirut was one of hundreds that stood as a testament to generations of warfare that left some parts of the once beautiful resort city untouched, while others looked like bombed out remnants. The three of them had arrived by a small boat and landed on a deserted shore. This was not the first time Mustafa had made this trip, and the facility with which he maneuvered them through various road trips, airline flights, and boat excursions lent testimony to his knowledge and proficiency. Once there, they took a bus to the heavily populated Al Batrakiyah district center, and walked to the house they now occupied. When they arrived, nothing inside was visible through the boarded-up windows. The worn green wooden door swung open with a creaking sound, and they found themselves in a dusty, darkened hallway. Only the thin shafts of light that managed to penetrate the boards covering the surprisingly unbroken glass of the windows showed them the way. Mustafa led them down a short hallway, and through a low door at the rear of the stairs. Jennifer seemed to remain unworried through their trip, and was now relieved to be able to loosen the thin black fabric covering her face. The Arab custom of having women cover everything but their eyes, was an easy cover for a tall American blonde, but she was glad to be able to remove it. It felt cooler that way, even if it wasn't. Mark was tired. He looked over his shoulder at every turn, not trusting Mustafa's motives. He tried to sleep only when Jennifer was awake, without making it too obvious.

Nonetheless, Mustafa grinned at him each time he awakened and Jennifer was asleep. It was a sort of, "I could have killed you anytime I wanted to," grin. Mark eventually relaxed a little, but his senses once again became heightened here in Beirut. He neither spoke nor understood any Arabic, and there was no question as to his fate if caught.

As they descended to the basement, it became slightly cooler, and when Mustafa swung a darkened door open, the welcome feeling of conditioned air greeted them. The lights were switched on, and the room they found themselves in, while not the equivalent of Porter's safe house in Paris, was more surprising. It was clean, and brightly lit, with walls painted in a pale green. Around the room were scattered various pieces of furniture. A sofa was nearly where it had been in the Parisian safe house, with another along the left wall. Each had a coffee table in front of it, and chairs facing it. Two other doors were visible besides the one through which they had entered. One led to a kitchen and dining area, less modern and equipped than they had become used to, but stocked with provisions. Another door seemed to exit from this room. "We always allow for two exits," Mustafa seemed to read his thoughts. The other led to a hallway with several small, dormitory style bedrooms on either side of it. At the end of this hall was another door. This one was metal, heavy, and locked.

"What's in there?"

Mustafa was about to answer when Jennifer replied, "the armory."

"You've been here before?" Mark asked, surprised.

"No," Jennifer smiled. Mustafa walked to the door, fiddled with a combination lock built into the door, and swung it open as he stepped aside with a flourish. What this safe house lacked in electronics, it made up for in armament. The room into which mark looked was small, but stocked from floor to ceiling on every side with weapons. Rifles of all kinds, hand guns, grenades, rocket launchers, RPG's, stacks of C4, timers, detonators,…The list went on and on. Mark didn't recognize everything, but he understood what usually went on here. He didn't like it.

They all walked back to the "living area," leaving the armory door open. Mustafa and mark put their packs on the floor and sat heavily, as Jennifer removed more of the Arab clothing, revealing shorts, a tee-shirt, and long damp blond hair which she ran her fingers through as she tossed her head slightly to loosen it. They sat quietly, not talking at all for about ten minutes, each with their own thoughts, and each trying to relieve the weariness that they carried with them since leaving Paris. Finally, Mustafa reached into his pack and retrieved a bulky looking telephone with an oddly large antenna. It was a satellite up-link. The call could only be traced to its source with very sophisticated equipment designed especially for that purpose, and would require access to the satellite codes. It was possible that the people they were going to contact would have such equipment, but not likely. Their trail would stop at the Satellite itself. Mustafa looked at the two of them, with the question unspoken.

"Go ahead," Jennifer voiced the approval for both she and Mark. Mustafa sighed heavily then raised the antenna and dialed the number he had memorized long ago. The phone rang several times before the raspy voice that Mustafa remembered so well answered. Neither Mark nor Jennifer understood the conversation. Mustafa hung up after about three minutes, saying simply, "it's done." They waited. "I will call back in 12 hours, at which time I will be given a time and place to meet."

"Then what," Mark asked.

"Then," Mustafa shrugged his shoulders, "we shall see."

The time passed slowly. They wouldn't leave the safe rooms under the ramshackle house, there wasn't the electronics that they had in Paris, not even a TV, so they slept, ate, talked about trivia…They always avoided the topics of conversation that would put them into conflict. They needed each other right now, and didn't want to strain their relationship any further than they had to. Mustafa looked at his watch frequently, finally announcing that it was 02:00. He picked up the telephone and dialed the number once more.

"Al Assad." He announced himself and, as was usual, simply remained quiet and listened. When he lowered the antenna and pressed *END*, he looked at Mark and Jennifer, then sat in a chair before going on. "I am to meet them at an area just outside of town in one hour."

"Do they know about us?" Jennifer asked.

"I don't think so, but I can't be sure."

"OK, she said, let's get ready."

"Wait a minute," Mustafa stood and looked at her. This is Beirut. You can't go wandering around out there at night. You'd be too obvious."

"Leave that to me," she said. Together, they walked into the armory and looked around again. Mark hadn't felt more out of place since he and Jennifer raced to beat the police out of London. Was that a day ago, a week, a year…he couldn't remember. Jennifer and Mustafa were examining weapons, and choosing their own. Having no real understanding of what he was getting into, nor what he would need (but being unwilling to seem helpless in front of Mustafa) he looked around himself. On the wall was a larger version of the 9mm Glock he had used in Paris. He took it from it's hook, along with a black "pancake" holster to hold it, and a belt pack that would hold three more clips each with ten rounds. He placed the Glock, the holster, the spare clips and the ammo on a small tabletop next to him, and looked around some more. Hanging about two feet from the Glock was the largest semi-automatic handgun he had ever seen. He thought he remembered reading about it in a magazine—a 50 Cal. Semi-automatic Colt. He reached for it instinctively. If he was going to need a weapon, he wanted the biggest. All the ammo he chose was hollow nose. He may not have been the expert each of them was, but he knew he wanted to kill, not wound, if the need arose. He placed the 50 Cal. on the same table along with its ammo and a shoulder holster and, once more, three spare clips. Still, he continued looking. There, on the opposite wall, was a MAC 10. He recognized it, once again, from it's publicity in the U.S. It was the weapon of choice for many of the drug gangs because of its small size, and rapid firepower. Gun, clips and ammo were placed on the table once more, along with two very nasty looking knives and sheaths and six grenades. He kept looking. There, he saw what he wanted, a Kevlar vest that he could wear nearly undetected under his clothes. He guessed he was finished when he spotted two more that he wanted, an AK-47 "Kalishnikov" assault rifle. He had never fired one, or even seen one off of a television screen, but by reputation, he wanted it. Finally, near where he had picked up the Glock, he found a very small 32 Cal. Barretta. He wasn't sure why he chose it, except for some dimly remembered stories he had read, but he added it and it's ammo to the pile. Mustafa and Jennifer had already left the room, with a small smirk at the mound of weaponry he had assembled. They knew what he hadn't yet grasped—that it was the person who was dangerous, not the weapon. Alone in the room, Mark took the 32 Automatic and, chambering a round, slid it into the front of his pants, clipping the holster in front of his genitals. He remembered, now what he had read, that most men rarely frisk another man in the genital area. He next slipped one of the knives against his left calf, and used some tape he had found to attach it to his leg. There would be hell to pay when he removed the tape from his leg hair. The pancake holster with the Glock he placed at his right hip, with the pack of extra clips, now loaded, just ahead of it on his belt. The other knife rested in its sheath against his right side, and a third, he had just chosen hung along his left, under the shoulder holster holding the 50 Cal. Colt. He had already slipped the kevlar vest under his shirt, and was now hanging the MAC 10 from his right shoulder when he noticed a rack of silencers on a shelf. He tried screwing several into the Glock until he found one that fit, then returned it to its holster. Finally, he hung a web halter over his shirt, from which he hung the grenades. He was finished. He put his outer jacket back on, picked up the AK-47 and put two spare banana clips in his jacket pocket. When he walked out of the armory, Jennifer and Mustafa were waiting for him with smiles on their faces.

"What?" he asked.

"Do you think you have enough guns?" Mustafa grinned. "Can you still walk?" But neither of them made any move to make him leave any behind. "I guess they figure if I feel better with this stuff, why not have it?" he thought but feeling silly, decided to leave the MAC-10 behind.

They had a last few scraps to eat, a few sips of some tepid coffee, and headed upstairs to a jeep that was in what appeared from the outside to be an abandoned garage. Jennifer wore black pants and sweater, and her head was covered with a black cap that, in a pinch, would roll down over hear face and neck to form a type of ski mask. Beside them on the back seat, Mustafa had placed three sets of night vision glasses and another black cap for Mark. He seemed to have thought of everything. Mark hoped so. Before they left, Mustafa turned on a small map light, and turned to the others to show them a map of the area. He pointed out where he was to meet the man with the raspy voice, were he would drop them, and where he thought they should try to position themselves. When he was sure they understood, the garage door slid silently open, and closed behind them as they left. There were butterflies in Mark's stomach and a ringing in his ears. Each of the other times he had to fight, it was thrust upon him in an instant. No time to think. Now he felt he was going into battle, and the fear welled up into his mouth with the acid from his stomach. He swallowed hard, and couldn't have said anything even if he wanted to. He didn't.

Chapter 30

The jeep bounced along the increasingly rough roads as they left Beirut for the suburbs and beyond. This was a kind of "no-man's land." All of the myriad factions in this country were represented out here, and one never quite knew where the shifting lines were at any given time. About twenty minutes after leaving the house, Mustafa stopped the jeep to allow Mark and Jennifer to get out, then drove on. They would work their way diagonally through several blocks of houses and a wooded area, to arrive at the point were Mustafa and whoever he was meeting would be. It was a dark night, which should have been to their advantage, but one could never tell. They moved quickly, using mostly pre-arranged hand signals to communicate, until they reached a wooded area where the two lane road took a turn to the north. Using their night vision glasses, they scanned the area, but could find no evidence that anyone else was there, so they slid down next to a large boulder for a few moments to gather their thoughts.

"Mark," Jennifer continued glancing around as she talked. "We need to split up and create a cross-fire."

"I don't want to leave you here alone," he replied, realizing how silly that sounded but being unable to stop himself.

"Don't be stupid!" She lashed out at him, then stopped herself and added much more softly, "we're safer this way than together. Including Mustafa, we have three points of fire, and two separate people to help if the third gets into trouble." Then she added, "I'm sorry for what I said. I guess my nerves are shot. I didn't mean it." He looked into her soft eyes, kissed her forehead, and answered, "I know."

After a second look around, Mark pointed to a large tree on the other side of the road. "I'll work my way across the road to that tree. It should give me a good vantage point and decent protection. Watch through your scope for my hand signal that I'm there, and return the signal so I'll know you saw me. OK?" He began to move when she touched his shoulder, raised her mouth slightly to brush his cheek and quietly added, "be careful." "Trust me on that one," Mark said, then smiled and moved off toward the road.

Mustafa had parked by the side of the road, a little way from where he had dropped them off, to give them time to get into position. They had left a little early to allow for this. As he drove off after checking his watch again, he hoped he had allowed for enough time, and that his superiors had not counted upon Mark and Jennifer being a part of this.

At the bend in the road where Mark and Jennifer lay quietly, a car glided silently to a halt only a few yards from where Mark was hiding. After a few seconds, it turned into an area of the woods adjacent to Mark's position and was visible only through the night glasses when the headlights were turned off. Through the glasses, though, there were clearly three men. One waited in the car, one took up a position behind a tree about 30 yards from Mark, and the third walked to the road, lit a cigarette, and waited. Only a few minutes went by before Mustafa's jeep rolled around the bend in the road, and with a slight squeak of the brakes, rolled to a stop. He was on the shoulder of the road, opposite where the man was standing, and nearly in front of Jennifer's position. Mustafa got out of the Jeep and walked across the road for the meeting. As he did, the second man, behind the tree, turned slightly to get a better vantage point. Mark could see that there was a gun in his hand, and that he was covering his compatriot. He decided that Jennifer may not have seen this man, but would certainly be covering the other, so he lowered the sights of his Glock, the silencer extending the barrel, and rested the butt on his knee as he sat. If it had to be, it would be a clean shot. He hoped Jennifer had the same. He decided to use the silenced gun because he didn't know what the third man in the car would do, and he didn't want to give away his position. Time crept slowly forward. The conversation of the man at the road with Mustafa was barely audible, and what was heard was in Arabic and thus unintelligible to either Mark or Jennifer.

Minutes dragged on, and Mark was beginning to believe that the meeting would be concluded without incident, but he maintained his gun sight on the man behind the tree. So concentrated on his target was he, that he never realized the man in the car was no longer there until he heard a hammer cock behind his head and a soft voice demand that he drop his gun. Slowly, quietly, he lowered the Glock to the ground, and the man kicked it to the side, along with the Kalishnikov. Then, without further conversation, he felt a rag stuffed into his mouth and his hands were dragged behind him and some sort of tape wrapped around his wrists, then his ankles. Finally, a dark hood was placed over his head, and the right side of his head erupted in pain as he was struck with something hard. He was left in that position as he heard the footsteps of the man slowly disappear in the direction of the road. It seemed like hours until his head cleared enough for him to begin to think. Was his captor nearby? Would they hear if he moved? Had they already attacked Jennifer and Mustafa? He had no answers, but he suddenly remembered all of the hardware he was carrying that his captor hadn't bothered to look for in the dark. Painfully, he twisted his wrists so that he could reach the knife taped to his leg, and removed it from its sheath by extending the leg. A few twigs under him snapped, and he stopped for a few seconds to see if anyone came. When he heard no further sound except the muffled conversation in Arabic, he slowly twisted the blade until it faced the tape and, holding the flattened edge of the blade with his hand, moved it up and down as far as he could. With each stroke, the tape gave more, until he found his hands free. Before removing his hood, he freed his feet, then slowly, without a sound, he removed his hood and gag.

The pitch-blackness under the hood left his eyes sensitive to even the soft glow of the evening sky, and he could clearly make out the man still waiting behind the tree. "So," he thought, "it hasn't been that long after all." As he looked around, he found no evidence of the third man, but it was obvious he had moved on, no longer considering Mark a threat. There was too much at stake now. They knew about him, and they might guess that there were more, perhaps even where Jennifer was. He looked around, but couldn't find the silenced Glock, and he knew he could afford no noise. He realized that he had never really killed a man. He had pulled the trigger in Paris when he had to, but it was at a target, a silhouette. This was different. The side of his head was caked with dried blood that he could feel but not see, and each movement brought searing pain to his head and neck, but he forced himself to ignore these as he inched toward the man behind the tree. He circled slightly so that he could get to his feet without being heard, and realized that the man at the tree was as deeply engrossed as he had been. He had no tape, and trying to knock him out would cause a commotion. Besides, he wasn't sure he would know how to do it effectively. He knew anatomy, though.

The grass in front of him was soft and lush as he moved slowly forward, trying to even avoid breathing, lest me make a noise. He would put pressure on the Crico-thyroid cartilage to cut off the man's air until he collapsed. Then he could proceed. He was within two feet of the shadow's hulk when it began to turn towards him. He couldn't run, he couldn't strike out, and his previous plan was of no use. Without thinking, his left hand pushed against the man's mouth and nose, while his right hand slashed across his throat with the serrated blade of the knife, opening it from one carotid artery to the other. There was a slight gurgling sound that couldn't be heard more than a foot or two away, and the man collapsed. Mark grabbed him and held him as he fell to prevent a thud. He could barely see the man's face, but he felt himself covered with the warm flow of blood as the man's life drained onto the ground. There was a look, not of fear, but surprise. It stayed with him as he lay there turning the ground an unseen crimson. Mark stepped over the body and peered past the tree. His hands were trembling, and he felt the bile well up into his throat. He was going to he sick, but he forced in back down. "Later," he thought, and watched as Mustafa turned to walk back to the Jeep. There! About ten yards to the left of where the two men had been speaking was thc man from the car. His arm was extended, resting against a tree. Mark guessed that his hand held a gun. His? He was frantic. He knew Jennifer couldn't see him, and Mustafa didn't know he was there. "Fuck!" His thoughts raced, and he reached for the 50 Cal. Colt that his captor had forgotten to look for. Like his prey, he steadied his arm against the tree and squeezed the trigger. The resulting explosion turned a small portion of the woods into daylight, and startled everyone into a petrified stance, then each dove for the ground. His prey dropped also, but most of his head and neck were gone before he hit the ground. Mustafa dove behind another tree, and the man with whom he met lay flat against the ground, nearly invisible.

"Freeze!" he heard Jennifer from the other side of the road. "Wait!" Mustafa wasn't sure who she was yelling at, or who had fired the shot.

"It's me," Mark yelled from behind the tree. "Don't shoot." Slowly, he rose to his feet and even more slowly, he walked forward toward the man on the ground. When he was in clear view, Mustafa rose from behind the tree, and walked toward them, gun raised toward the man on the ground. Spitting an Arabic epithet at him, he ordered him to lie still, and soon the three of them stood looking down at the man who had yet to speak his first words.

"Wait," Mark said again, and ran to the tree where he was captured, then returned with the tape and the hood. He taped the man's Mouth shut, then his wrists behind him, and his ankles, as he had been, finishing with the hood. Jennifer and Mustafa said nothing during this ritual, but looked at each other. Mark was becoming efficient, and professional. To their right was the partially decapitated body of one assassin. Mark inclined his head in the other direction, and Jennifer and Mustafa walked the few yards to find the exanguinated body lying with a gaping opening in the throat. They walked back and watched as Mark completed his task. They were still staring as he turned to his left and began to throw up on the ground. Again and again, he heaved until there was nothing left in him, then collapsed against a tree and closed his eyes. Only the face of the man whose throat he had cut remained in his mind. It would be there for years, he knew. *They* couldn't see the face, but Mark was tortured by it.

Gently, Jennifer knelt beside him, stroked his face, and said quietly, "Come on, we have to go."

"It's time," added Mustafa, "the police will be here soon, or worse, some of their associates."

Mark rose slowly. He replaced the Colt into it's holster, thought about the knife and nearly wretched again. He didn't want that knife. He felt weak, but he helped Mustafa drag the bound body to his own car. He would drive the car, a large Mercedes 500 SEL, while Mustafa and Jennifer rode back into town in the Jeep.

Before they left, Mark asked Mustafa, "well, did you find anything out? Was it worth it?"

"It will be," answered Mustafa, and walked to the Jeep. "Follow me," he told Mark, and began the drive back into town.

It was nearly 04:00 when they arrived back in the city, still more than a kilometer from the safe house. The streets were deserted except for the occasional patrol that they managed to avoid. Mustafa pulled the Jeep to the curb, with Mark following him. Quickly, Mustafa got out of the Jeep, and walked to the rear of the Mercedes while Mark "Popped" the trunk, got out, and followed him to the rear of the car. Together, they lifted their captive and carried him to the Jeep, were they threw him into the back seat.

"What happens when they find the car?" Mark asked Mustafa.

"They'll probably begin searching the area. Hopefully, we'll be gone by then."

There was no conversation as Mark and Mustafa lifted the bound man from the Jeep and carried him into the house and down to the lower level. The three of them collapsed onto the sofa and chairs, temporarily forgetting everything but their exhaustion. Mark lay back, his head resting on the sofa, and his eyes closed. Once more, the face floated in front of him, the gaping rent in the neck seeming to grin at him. He opened his eyes with a start, and sat up. "OK," he began, "what now?" "First you need to get cleaned up," Jennifer said, "meanwhile we'll begin having a chat with our friend." She nodded toward the man on the floor, and Mark looked down at his blood soaked shirt. Once more, his stomach turned, but once more he forced it back down, and began stripping his clothes off as he headed for the shower.

By the time he returned to the common area, the prisoner sat in a comfortable chair. They had removed the tape from his mouth, but had replaced the hood. His clothes had been cut away, leaving him naked, and he was restrained to the chair with nylon chord. He was going nowhere. "We've been waiting for you," Mustafa told Mark. Our friend here has confided that his name is Ibrahim. That's all we've gotten so far. I think we can persuade him to be a little more communicative." Mark watched as Mustafa picked up a small knife from the coffee table in front of him, reached forward, and made a small cut on the man's left thigh. It wasn't large, and didn't bleed much, but the man drew air in through his teeth as it was made. About 30 seconds went by, when Mustafa made a similar cut on Ibrahim's left arm. Once more the man inhaled deeply through clenched teeth. "What do you want?" The raspy voice sounded angry, frustrated. Mustafa didn't answer, but repeated the small cut on the right abdominal area. "What do you want, Damn it!" Ibrihim's voice was rising in pitch. The next cut was in the genital area. It was small, like the others, but this time Ibrihim yelled and cursed in Arabic. There were still no questions. Mark moved forward, but Jennifer placed her hand on his shoulder and stopped him. Her look said to wait and see what would happen. There were three more small cuts, each about a minute apart, when Ibrihim finally broke down and screamed.

"Perhaps we're ready to begin," Mustafa said, and pulled another chair alongside of the naked prisoner. "Who gave you your orders tonight?" "I...I don't know," stammered Ibrihim. Mustafa didn't answer, he simply made another cut along the left cheek. The prisoner screamed, and again Mustafa's voice was calm—"Let's begin again. Who gave you your orders for tonight?"

It was another three hours before Mustafa was satisfied that he had extracted all of the information that Ibrihim had. More than half of it was unintelligible to Jennifer and Mark, being in Arabic, but when it mattered, Mustafa translated. It wasn't everything they wanted to know, but it was a start. Ibrihim's orders came not just from the top of his movement, but he believed they originated from outside the organization. He had been in the room when the discussion had occurred and he thought he heard someone speaking Chinese. This had implications that none of them had yet considered. How were they involved? It was another piece of the puzzle that needed to be fit into place. They also learned that the bomb in New York had, indeed, been found only hours after it had been planted. No one in the organization understood how that was possible. They were sure they had been penetrated, but since only a handful of men knew the whole plan, they couldn't imagine who it could have been.

They were finished here. This was all they would get form Ibrihim, and there was no way of going higher now, so they had to move to their next target. Sleep, they decided, was another imperative. Each went to a room, after making sure that Ibrihim was secure, and slept for more than nine hours. When they awoke, each found their way into the common room were Ibrihim lay, himself asleep, with rivulets of dried blood over much of his body, and a pool of urine at the base of the chair, where he could no longer hold it. Coffee followed, as each offered sug-gestions as to where to go next.

"I wish I could get to Langley said Jennifer. Someone issued an order to have me killed, and not even the President knows who. We need to find out."

"Yes, but I don't think that's a viable option right now," Mustafa held his head in his hands, and stared at the table.

"Maybe we don't have to," Jennifer answered. "Remember, all of these computers are tied together. It's all one big net."

"But how can we get access?" Mark understood, perhaps better than Mustafa because of his own computer background, but also understood that they had to have access before they could find anything out.

"Leave that to me," Jennifer said. "We need to get back to Paris and Porter's terminal."

They arose, gathered together some extra clothes, and various weapons of choice from the armory, and met at the door.

"You realize that now that they know we're not dead, they'll be searching for us at every airport and train station, don't you?" Mustafa had to be the one to bring them to earth.

"Can you get us to a small airport?" Mark asked.

"Sure, why?" "Let's borrow a plane."

Finding a Cessna that Mark knew how to fly wasn't too difficult, it was tied up in a private field. Fortunately, the panels of light aircraft are made to be accessed easily, so "hot-wiring" the plane took no time at all. After piling into the plane, Mark went through a partially remembered checklist and hoped he hadn't left anything important out, then taxied the plane onto the dirt airstrip, lowered one notch of flaps, and pushed the throttle forward. Slowly, the plane began to accelerate, gaining speed. He watched the Airspeed Indicator, and was thankful that it was marked in both Km/hr and Knots/hr. He allowed an extra few knots to build up before rotating the nose upward. As the plane rose, he pushed the yoke forward to lower the angle of attack, then raised the flaps. They were airborne. Hopefully, the plane wouldn't be missed for a while.

They had only been flying for a few minutes, when the talk again shifted to their predicament. Mark had set the GPS points in the autopilot to take them across the Mediterranean into Greece, hoping that the owner of the plane had kept it in good shape.

"OK," he said as he turned to face Jennifer in the right seat, and Mustafa in the back. "We seem to have some time on our hands, so let's go over what we know." They looked at each other and decided that as they, indeed, had nothing else to do, they might as well give it a try.

"OK," Jennifer began. "Our computers in the US defense grid have been compromised by someone who knows the system well enough to issue orders that appear real, and remain undetectable."

"Yes," added Mustafa, "and our people have been compromised also, otherwise the Americans could not have found the bomb when they did. Someone in the group is also working with the Chinese, or at least it seems that way,"

"Don't forget," added Mark, "that the President also believed that there were other computer systems compromised, more particularly it sounded like the Russians." "But who is doing it?" Asked Mustafa. "There are too many things happening at the same time. There are also too many players showing up that don't belong." Mark wasn't sure if Mustafa meant him, but he chose to ignore it.

"Is it possible that all of these things are happening simultaneously, by coincidence?" Jennifer sounded disbelieving, even as she said it.

The talk went on for some time, never reaching any real conclusion, but never straying too far from the facts. Soon, the Greek coastline passed under them with the trees much too visible. Mark had kept them at less than 160 meters on the altimeter to attempt to avoid radar. He had kept the transponder turned off, and kept his fingers crossed. It had seemed to work. Still, when he looked at the fuel gauges there wasn't too much left. "I think we had better find a place to land," Mark announced as he turned forward and pushed the button to turn the autopilot off. They had left the coast behind, and were crossing the hilly terrain that characterized this area, with Mark beginning to sweat trying to find someplace to land before the airplane did it for them. Just off to the left was a relatively straight road. It went through some hills, but there appeared to be room to land, so he pointed the plane toward it until the Directional Gyro read 272°, pulled back on the throttle, and reached forward to the flap lever, lowering full flaps. The nose of the plane angled downward, and they began descending at what he hoped was about 65 knots. Gradually, he eased the nose up as they approached the ground. He was slightly "crabbed" against a crosswind, but not enough to worry about. Sweat beaded on his forehead. He hadn't flown in quite a while, and he quietly prayed that landing was like riding a bike. The plane touched down on the road while still turned a few degrees into the wind, and immediately straightened out as mark reached forward and raised the flaps to decrease lift, then pushed the rudder pedals forward to apply the breaks. He had done it. They were safe on the ground in Greece, and undetected, or so he hoped.

The three climbed out of the plane, and looked up and down the road. It was a two lane asphalt road with no cars coming in either direction. "OK," Mark said, I've done my part, now how do we get to Paris?" First they pushed the plane off the road. It would still be visible, but wouldn't obstruct traffic, and that may buy them some additional time before it would be reported. They began to walk north, hoping to be able to find a ride.

Chapter 31

About 30 minutes after they landed in Greece, a large truck with the Mercedes "gun sight" in it's grille pulled alongside and the driver, smelling of garlic, offered them a lift. They spoke no Greek, and the driver apparently spoke neither English, nor Arabic, nor French, but the ride was appreciated none the less.

They were climbing into the cab of the truck. Mustafa entered first, then Jennifer placed her foot on the running board to climb after him when mark felt a sharp pain at the base of his skull, and the world disappeared. When he awakened, the three of them were apparently in the trailer of the truck, bound, gagged, and lying on the wooden floor as the truck bounced along. Mustafa was awake and staring at him, while Jennifer remained unconscious. Mark had no idea what time it was or where they were. The only light in the truck came from a single light bulb in the ceiling. Looking around, he saw that there were two men sitting on cushions toward the rear of the truck. They were speaking softly, but it was unmistakably a Slavic language, Mark guessed Russian. By this time, Jennifer moaned softly, and looked around at Mark and Mustafa. None of them could speak, so each lay with their own thoughts.

There was no attempt to interrogate them by the men in the back. Their weapons seemed to be gone, including the knives mark had on him. He wasn't going to cut his way out this time. Hours seemed to roll by. Twice the truck stopped, and the guards changed shifts. The last pair, to Mark's surprise, seemed to be speaking Italian. He could catch a few phrases from his knowledge of Spanish, but not enough to make their conversation intelligible. Still, the change in language was remarkable. What seemed like one more hour rolled by when the truck stopped again and the rear door was thrown open. Three men with Uzi's stood on the ground as a fourth climbed into the truck and cut the bonds holding their feet. "Andiámo!" They were to come with these men. There was no brutality, as there had been before. They were helped from the truck, and led down a narrow path to a manner house that appeared to be sitting at the top of a hill. To their left was a magnificent view of the sea, but they were given no time to enjoy it. The sound of the truck driving off as they were pushed inside of the house was a reminder that this could well be their final destination. Somehow, the word final kept repeating itself in Mark's head, and he didn't like it.

Through the house, down a flight of carpeted stairs, and into a well appointed, masculine den they were led until finally each was pushed down into a deep leather chair, and their feet once again bound. Shortly, two of the men returned with three straight backed wooden chairs. These were placed in a semicircle, and one by one, Mark, Jennifer, and Mustafa were placed in them. Their wrists were unbound and then rebound to the arms of the chairs, their ankles bound to the legs, and several turns of wide gray tape around their torsos held their backs firmly against the backs of the chairs. Finally, the gags were removed, and the men left the room.

Mark looked at the watch that was now visible on his wrist. It was more than 14 hours since they had been offered a ride in the truck. They could be anywhere by now, but there was something familiar about the short glimpse of sea he had before being led into the house. He couldn't quite get it to the front of his mind, but it was there somewhere.

"Is everybody OK?" Jennifer asked. Mustafa began to answer, but had to clear his throat and spit out a few fibers from his gag before he could.

"I'm OK," he answered, "How about you?" He looked at Mark.

"Great," answered Mark sarcastically. "Now what?"

"Now we wait," answered Mustafa. Not only had he been trained to resist torture if captured, and taught how to behave, but he had actually been captured once by another faction of the PLO, and had not only survived without divulging anything useful, but managed to escape. Jennifer had some training, but it was years earlier, and she never actually expected to need to use it. Mark's only training was from movies. Perhaps he wasn't as frightened as he should have been.

"We must not show weakness," Mustafa told the others. Mark chuckled through the pain that still remained in his head and neck.

"Weakness? "Why, you stupid asshole, what are we protecting?"

"Now look," Jennifer began, but her words were interrupted by a singularly unattractive redhead entering the room, followed by two very large men. She walked to the plush leather chair, facing them, in which Mustafa had been placed earlier, and sat quietly as the two men assumed positions behind them. Without saying anything, she rose again, went to a bar along one wall of the room, and poured herself some tonic water over ice, then returned to the chair and sat back down. She had consumed nearly half of the glass before she spoke for the first time.

"My name is unimportant," she began in perfect English, but with a distinctly Russian accent, "and I know yours, so I won't bother asking you what they are. You are probably troubled by many questions at this point, and most won't be answered, but let me at least tell you that we followed your flight from the time you took off, until you landed, then arranged to pick you up before you could slip away again." She paused, then took another sip of her tonic water. "Antonio," she addressed one of the men behind them. "Our guests have come a long way. Please take them, one at a time, to the bathroom where they may relieve themselves, and get comfortable." As she ordered, they were each cut loose in turn, taken to a bathroom, and allowed to use the toilet and the sink before being returned to their chair and rebound.

"What..." Mark's question was cut short by a wave of the redhead's hand, and so they all sat quietly until the last of them had been returned to their seat.

"Let me begin again," the redhead intoned softly. "Mustafa Al Assad. You are a middle level officer in the PLO splinter group "Bloody April." You were sent on a mission to New York to bring the reflectors into the country so that a nuclear device could be completed by your group. You accomplished this, and decided to return to Paris to enjoy a few days there before returning to your camp." She took another sip, then continued. "The woman you killed there, by the way, was never traced to you." Mustafa's eyes widened, despite his training. They seemed to know his every move!

"Jennifer Lynch," her attention turned to Jennifer. "You are an advisor to President Dalton, but were not always so. You spent more than five years working with your intelligence agencies. Four of them were with the CIA, and one with the NSA. It was after you presented a briefing paper that President Dalton took notice of your abilities, and asked you to work with him, where you've been ever since." She paused for effect, "until now." "The president was concerned about certain troubling inconsistencies in events occurring in the Middle East, and Eastern Europe, and hoped that with the combination of your new status, and your previous background, you could uncover additional information to shed some light on these." At this, she arose, walked back to the bar, and poured some more tonic water into her glass, then turned and began to speak as she returned to her chair.

"Mark Harmon." She stated the name flatly. "You have been the wild card in this game. You are a physician, with some substantial financial difficulties and an unhappy marriage awaiting you at home. Many people believe that you are a sleeper. I, for one, do not. I believe that you have found yourself in a situation that is beyond your understanding and control, and have acted out of instinct. I think you have been drawn into this by circumstances beyond your control, and would like to get out. Perhaps that will be possible, perhaps not. Wc shall see." There was a long pause, during which no one said anything, then "Red" began again. "We know about your escape from London with Miss Lynch, but we lost you shortly after that. It wasn't until you both turned up in Paris, along with Mr. Al Assad that we were able to begin to trace your movements again. We thought we had succeeded in killing all of you at once in Paris, but you managed to escape. That is a pity, as it would have saved us a great deal of difficulty and time. We knew you needed information, and the PLO seemed the logical place for you to start, so we followed you through several of our more highly placed operatives in your own organization, Mr. Al Assad. We were not there when you met, but we were not more than a few minutes behind. Again, no one has been able to trace the bodies to you, but once more, we lost you for a short while. We picked you up again as your flight began to cross the sea. It was one of several anticipated routes you would take, and we were prepared for all of them."

She now placed the glass on a small table next to the chair, and leaned slightly forward, looking at each of them in turn. "I'm telling you all of this so that you understand that there is no secret about your past, your government, or your present missions that you need to protect. We do not require your deaths, although if you fail to cooperate, they may prove convenient. If you do cooperate and give us the information we want, and it is verifiable, we will allow you to walk out of here. You can prove nothing, and know nothing of us, so you will be no threat. If you return to your organizations and tell them what you told us, their knowledge of it will change neither it's use nor it's value. So you see, there is no reason for you to die, or suffer."

Red looked at each, in turn, then said to Mark, "we will begin with you." Once more sweat beaded on his forehead, as he felt a chill make his body shudder. Red nodded at one of the men, who placed his gun on a nearby table, reached into his jacket pocket, and tool out a small leather case. When he had unzipped and opened it, Mark saw several syringes and sundry other pieces of equipment, and knew what was coming. His left sleeve was slit to his elbow, a tourniquet placed around his upper arm, and a needle inserted into the Anticubital vein. With the tourniquet released, mark could feel the slightly warm sensation of the drug entering his system, and spreading throughout his body. He was floating. He felt better than he had felt in a long time. His surroundings didn't seem to matter, although he was puzzled by his inability to move. "What the hell," he thought, and smiled at the pretty lady across from him. She seemed nice.

"How do you feel?" The feminine voice floated into his mind and lifted his spirits.

"Fine," he heard himself answer. He wanted to describe the feeling but she had only asked him how he felt, so that was all he seemed to want to say.

"Tell me," the voice continued, "who do you work for?" Mark considered the question and it's answer.

"Myself," he answered, and smiled at the thought that he actually worked for his family, his patients, the government, the insurance companies...

"Are you working for the American Government?"

"Only when they pay me," Mark answered, "which isn't often enough." Once again he smiled to himself at the irony of the question, but wasn't sure if the smile was actually visible on his lips.

"Now we're getting somewhere," the silky voice continued, "which branch do you work for?"

"HCFA." His answer was short and to the point.

"Hickva?" The Red sounded confused. "Are they part of the CIA?"

"No," and once again Mark felt a sort of inner smile forming about a joke that she didn't get. But then, she hadn't asked the right question.

"What is this Hickva?"

Mark knew his speech was a little slurred, and made a concerted attempt to speak clearly as he pronounced, "the Healthcare Financing

Administration." That seemed to puzzle Red, and she thought for a moment before beginning again.

"What do they have to do with the New York bomb, or Terrorist financing?" Now it was Mark's turn to be confused. The question seemed to have no bearing on the otherwise pleasant conversation, and he thought for a few seconds before answering, "nothing that I know of."

"So why are you here?" Red seemed as puzzled by his answers as he was by her questions.

"I was brought here." It was a straightforward answer to a straight-forward question.

"Let's begin again," Red said. "You are a doctor, is that right?"

"Yes," Mark answered in a straightforward manner.

"You have a wife and two sons?"

"Yes."

"Are they part of your cover?" Now Mark was unable to answer. That seemed like a "do you still beat your wife?" type of question. No matter how he answered it, it would come out wrong, so he decided that he would simply remain silent until she asked a question he could answer truthfully. "Well?" She seemed impatient. He still had no answer, and so said nothing. Red was getting frustrated. "This is getting us nowhere, he's too well conditioned." She turned to the man with the syringes, pointed to Jennifer, and said, "She's next."

Now it was Jennifer's arm that was laid bare, and the serum injected. After a few minutes, Red began again with her.

"Miss Lynch, what is your job."

"To advise the President," Jennifer answered truthfully.

"Then why are you here?"

"I was brought here." once again a truthful, if unsatisfying answer.

"What is your connection with Dr, Harmon?" Jennifer thought for a moment. It took her that long to realize that Red was referring to Mark.

"He ran with me when they shot at me in London," she answered, the added, "and he has saved my life several times."

"Do you know who shot at you in London?"

"No." Jennifer wanted to add that she wished she did, and to ask if Red knew, but it wouldn't come out.

"What are the two of you doing together now?" Jennifer reached for the most truthful answer she could give, while something deep inside of her fought to prevent her from revealing any secrets. Somewhere in the darkest recesses of her mind she remembered doing this before, in training, and the type of answers she was expected to give.

"We're searching for the people who are trying to kill us, to find out why." It was 100% truthful, if incomplete.

"Are you on a mission for your government now?" Jennifer thought again. Actually, she wasn't. Not officially.

"No."

Once again, Red was getting frustrated, with the answers, so she had Mustafa injected. With each question that Mustafa answered, Red became even more angered. He was giving her answers she already had, but adding nothing to what she knew. She asked him about why he was with Jennifer and Mark, and his answer so closely followed Jennifer and Mark's that she began to wonder. Looking up at her companions with the guns, she said to no one in particular, "They've either been exceptionally well trained, or they're actually telling the truth." She thought for a moment, then instructed the men to wait with the prisoners until she returned. After a few minutes, she re-entered the room and announced that they were to be held here while she awaited further orders, then disappeared again. The slightly groggy prisoners were cut free of their chairs, one at a time, and rebound in the leather chairs they had originally occupied. Then the two guards, then, took up positions against the opposite wall and stood with their backs against it to provide some support.

It was nearly forty minutes later that the drug began to wear off, and the three began to become aware of their situation.

"Are you OK?" Jennifer asked Mark.

"Yes," Mark answered, thinking that the question should have been his. "How about you?" The question was repeated to Mustafa.

"OK," he answered.

"Quiet!" the guard on the left leveled his weapon at Jennifer, "No talking!" His accent was indeterminate, but his meaning was clear. The three looked back and forth at each other. It was about ten minutes later, when Jennifer stated, "I have to go to the bathroom."

"Excuse?" The guard's English seemed poor, and he apparently didn't quite understand he request.

"I have to pee," Jennifer managed to sound sweet and exasperated at the same time.

One guard looked at the other, then the first said, haltingly, "you wait." He then opened the door, and came back in a few minutes. "She is not taking you now." Then thought again for the right words in English. "She is coming soon."

"Please," Jennifer pleaded, "I have to go now!" She began to squirm.

"If I take you, I must watch." The guard smirked as he said it. Either way she answered, he would feel like a winner.

"If that's how you get off, let's go."

He smiled at his partner, and whispered something to him that Mark didn't like the look of, but was powerless to stop, then rested his weapon against the sofa as he drew a knife from his pocket and cut the thin chord that held Jennifer's ankles together.

"Let's go," he grinned again, and pulled her to a standing position, then pushed her gently to get her moving toward the hallway where the bathroom was located. As they began their trek to the bathroom, Mustafa stretched by arching his back. Mark turned from Jennifer to Mustafa, just because of the movement, and caught the movement in Mustafa's eyes that said for Mark to watch for a chance to follow his lead.

"Hey, you!" Mustafa yelled at the other guard. "If your partner hurts her, I'll kill you both."

"Really?" the guard seemed appropriately amused, and walked slowly to stand in front of Mustafa, sitting bound in the chair. "And how do you intend to do that?" he chuckled.

"Just remember it, pig!" Mustafa spit the words at him with a venom that the guard could not mistake, even in a second language. With that, the guard's mirth changed to a look of Sadism. He transferred the weapon he was holding to his left hand, leaned close and slammed Mustafa across the face with the back of his right hand, then leaned even closer to spit in his face. It was at this moment that Mustafa's bound feet shot forward, catching the shins of the guard before he could respond. The guard began to fall backwards, but tried to catch himself and slid sideways with his head landing just in front of the chair where Mark sat. Without thinking, Mark lifted his bound feet and slammed them into the guard's right temple, sending him sprawling against the coffee table. The sprawl wasn't far enough, and Mark straightened his legs, once again bringing his feet into contact with the guard, this time at the bridge of his nose. He then edged forward in his chair, and managed to throw himself forward onto the top of the guard to hold him momentarily to the floor as Mustafa raised his own feet and slammed them into the back of the guard's neck. Mark was close enough to hear the bones crack as the guard's body went limp.

"OK," Mark asked Mustafa, Now what?"

"He must have a knife or something in his pocket also," Mustafa answered, and like Mark, managed to lower himself onto the floor next to the body of the guard. As he reached with his bound hands to try to get into the guard's pocket, there was a muffled sound coming from the hallway where Jennifer and the other guard had disappeared. Mark and Mustafa looked at each other, and redoubled their efforts to find some-thing with which to cut their bonds. They couldn't allow that goon to touch Jennifer. It was as they were searching that they heard footsteps coming down the hall. With trepidation, they looked up to see Jennifer standing above them, a knife in one hand and an Uzi in the other.

"Are you two still playing around?" she giggled. "Here," she offered, let me help you big strong men..." She reached forward and cut Mark's feet and hands free, since he was closer, then gave him the knife to cut Mustafa's bonds as she went to the other door to listen for the return of Red.

"How did you get loose?" Mark was amazed.

"I told him I needed my hands in front of me when I went to the bathroom. After all, I'm not built like a man. He complied and bound my hands in front, then stood there grinning as I pulled my pants down to sit on the toilet. I tripped, he grabbed me and tried to grab a "feel" at the same time. It was the last thing he felt." She was smiling, and looking through the crack in the door as Mustafa arose and grabbed the weapon, an Uzi. "I really did have to go, too." Sorry about the extra time." The grin never left her face.

"We have to get out of here," Mark stated flatly. That woman will be back soon, and probably with more help. We don't know what she heard."

"If she had heard us," Jennifer spoke softly, she would be here by now. What we need to do is find her and get some information from her." Mark had taken the knife Jennifer had given them, and added the dead guard's Barretta from his shoulder holster to it. He hadn't taken time to search for extra ammunition, or anything else.

Jennifer eased the door open just enough for her to look around and, seeing no one, tread softly into the hallway, with Mark behind her, and Mustafa bringing up the rear. He gently closed the door behind them so that someone looking down the hall would not know that anything was amiss. He then walked behind them at an angle so that he could see where he was going, but the main area of his gaze and his weapon was pointed behind them. A few feet beyond the room they were in, a staircase led up.

"Well," Jennifer thought out loud, "I guess it's time to go upstairs and say hello." She gently eased herself up the stairs one at a time, putting most of the pressure on the edges where she knew there was support and less likelihood of noise. When she reached the top, there was no door, so she just put her head down to the level of the last step and gingerly poked it out into another hallway, at either end of which was sunlight pouring into other rooms. Slowly, gingerly, she climbed to the next level, and moved to the right along the wall, as Mark followed her, followed by Mustafa. When she looked back, Mustafa held his first two fingers to his eyes, then pointed to her and then the room at her end, then pointed to himself and pointed in the other direction. She shook her head in affirmation, and began to move to the right, gliding soundlessly along the wall, as Mustafa did the same to the left. Mark was left to decide his own direction. He followed Jennifer.

They edged their way slowly up the hall to find themselves in a light, airy kitchen. There were windows and skylights around the room, with most of the cabinetry being white while the furniture was of a light colored wood. The effect was a happy one, reminding Mark somewhat of the kitchen in his house. There was a table in an eating area with windows surrounding it and a door leading to a deck that overlooked a vista, perhaps a hundred feet below them, of beach and sea. This was the first time in days?…weeks?…that Mark had stood in bright sunlight and basked in the glory of a beautiful day. For just a moment, he forgot where he was until Jennifer brought him back to reality with a tug on his arm. She was moving past the island in the center of the kitchen toward another room that appeared to be a dining area. Once more, Mark was caught by her appearance. Her blonde hair, dirty and somewhat matted, still caught the sunlight steaming through the skylight and she seemed surrounded by a golden glow, almost a halo. Mark's emotions nearly bubbled to the surface, as he watched this vision move into danger before him but like the fear and revulsion he fought to control earlier, he pushed these down also. "Another time, another place," he told himself, and followed her into the next room.

For the next ten minutes, they wandered around, finding no one and finally walked back to the area toward which they had left Mustafa walking. He sat in a chair in a study, waiting for them, smoke curling around his head.

"Well," he asked, "have you had a nice tour?"

"There's nobody else in the house," Jennifer answered in a tired voice. "Where's the woman?"

Mustafa nodded to a corner of the study next to a book case. She was crumpled there, in a heap.

"You killed her?" Jennifer was angry. "We need answers, and she was the only one left to give them to us!"

"She turned on me with a gun as I entered the room behind her. I wasn't left with much of a choice." There didn't seem to be any answer to that, so Jennifer sat on the leather sofa next to Mustafa, while Mark was forced to take one of the high, Wing Back chairs facing them.

"We have to get out of here," Mustafa said as he crushed the end of the cigarette he had taken from the woman's body into the ashtray beside the sofa. "We don't know when they'll be back."

Jennifer looked out of the shuttered window to their right, and answered, "perhaps we should wait right here for whoever comes, and get some answers from them. After all, we do have the element of surprise."

Both were right, but Mark wasn't listening very carefully. He was staring past them at a more familiar sight. Sitting on a desktop to the side of the sofa was the ubiquitous computer that seemed to adorn everyplace in the world today. On the screen, Mark could see the rounded cube slowly bouncing from one edge of the screen to the other as it changed colors. His eyes never left the screen as he asked Mustafa, "Where was the woman when you came into the room?"

"At the desk," he answered. "She turned to pick up her gun as I entered, and I just had time to reach her before she could turn and fire. She was good, for a woman." He looked at Jennifer as though he wished he hadn't said that, "but I had to..." He was cut short by Mark jumping to his feet and crossing the short distance to the desk.

"I wonder…" he reached forward and touched the space bar, and the screen came to life with a partially answered email on the screen. He was surprised, both the email and the answer were in English. "Look at this," he called to Jennifer and Mustafa. "She must have been in the middle of something when you surprised her." The email that was being answered instructed her to hold them until the sender arrived. "They'll be here in about six hours." Mark said as he continued reading. The answer was simply an acknowledgement. It had yet to be sent. "I think we should send this," Mark said. "If we don't, they will either get suspicious."

"Send it." Jennifer didn't even wait for Mustafa to agree. Mark was right, and they both knew it. Mark sat in the chair, pulled the keyboard toward him and typed the last few words of the sentence that remained incomplete. He was about to click on send, when he stopped.

"Hmmm…" he stared at the screen.

"What is it?" Jennifer asked.

"I wonder…" Mark clicked on the gray box with the horizontal line in the upper right corner, and the window with the email reply dropped to the bottom of the screen. Behind it had been the original that was being answered, not in a regular email window, but in a separate word processing window. Mark minimized that to find the original email window. "Gotcha!" he exclaimed with a smile on his face. On the screen was a window filled with seemingly random characters from border to border. "It's encrypted," Mark said. If we had sent that email as it was, they would have known something was wrong."

"But how do we encrypt the reply without knowing the encryption scheme?" Mustafa looked puzzled by Mark's lack of concern.

"Watch and learn, children," Mark answered. He looked at the "From" line on the original email. "*2034@terra.gov*" it read. "Interesting Domain name," Mark quipped, then brought up the unsent reply. He highlighted the entire text in the window, clicked on "copy" and then minimized it again opening a new email window by clicking on the "Reply" button on the original. Then he opened a new

Wordpad window, and clicked on the small icon in the lower right of the screen that looked like an envelope with an arrow circling behind it. A menu appeared, and he chose "Encrypt Clipboard" from the top. A list of public keys appeared, from which he chose the one matching the sender's email address, and the screen was filled with more garbage. Once more, he highlighted the garbage and transferred it to the reply window, the clicked on "Send." He then closed all but the original email window, looked up and said, "there, it's done." Getting no answer, he explained, "They're using PGP. It's a double key encryption scheme...nearly unbreakable if the key length is long enough. I simply found the public key matching the sender, and used it to encrypt the message. We should have about six hours now." He thought again and said, "well, maybe five and a half."

Jennifer gave mark a peck on the cheek and said, "I'm impressed." Mustafa made an unintelligible sound and straightened up.

They were about to walk away when they noticed that Mark hadn't left the computer.

"What are you looking at now," Mustafa seemed slightly agitated.

"Did you pay attention to the Domain name?" Mark asked.

"The what?" Mustafa remained agitated, now more so because of his own ignorance.

"Look, I don't have time to explain it all, but every point on the Internet is located on some computer called a server. That server can have one, or a million computers or terminals connected to it called nodes. In order to find each node for file sharing, email, etc., each node is assigned an address on the network, which itself has an address on the Internet. These are numerical addresses, but in order for people to keep them straight, they are also given names called Domain names. These are usually related to the Internet Service Provider through which they are connected to the 'Net, and give you some idea about who they are. In the U.S., commercial addresses usually end in "com." Internet related addresses tend to end in "net," and so forth. Well most government addresses in the US end in "gov," or in a national identifier in most other countries, like "uk" for England, etc. Look at the address of the sender," and he pointed to the "From" line.

"Terra.gov? Where's that?" asked Jennifer.

"Exactly!" Mark looked triumphant. "Terra is Latin for "Earth." According to this designation, the sender is part of the government of Earth."

"That's crazy," Mustafa had forgotten his pique, and was concentrating on the problem at hand.

"Yes, it is," Mark agreed, "but let me try something." He opened an Internet Browser window, and typed a vaguely remembered URL into the address line. The background was black, with deep blue columns of text across the screen. He clicked on the words "whois" in the lower right corner and a second browser window opened with the words," Enter Domain:" Mark typed "terra.gov" and was rewarded in a few seconds with a numerical address. He copied this to a notepad screen, then looked around in the drawers and finally found what he was looking for—a blank disk. He copied the address to the floppy disk, along with the PGP public key ring from this computer. He then began searching through directories, copying retained email files, whole word processing directories, anything he could find that might be worth looking into when they had more time. It filled six disks when he was through. He labeled each one carefully, and placed the pile into an envelope he found and stuffed them into his pocket.

"We need more resources than we have here to find out what is going on here." Mark thought for a moment, then asked," is there a car outside?" Mustafa left the room for a minute, then returned to answer that there was a Range Rover in a garage attached to the house. They found the keys on a key ring in the woman's pocket.

"Let's take the whole computer with us," Mark suggested. "They'll already know there's trouble when they get here."

"No!" Mustafa reached out and held Mark's wrist to prevent it from beginning to disconnect the computer. "They will know that we escaped, nothing more. Not if we leave this in place. Mark thought about it and wanted to kick himself for being so stupid, but at least Mustafa was not. On the other hand, that thought didn't please him much either. He wished he could make a complete backup of the hard drive, but they had no time for that, so they settled for what they had. He closed all of the open programs, and left the computer on. He wasn't sure if that was the right thing to do, but since it had been on, he took the chance.

After taking one more look around the house before leaving. They took the weapons from the dead guards (Mark now took the shoulder holster and extra clips for the Barretta) and collected whatever money they had. When Mark and Mustafa returned from their search of the upstairs bedrooms, after deciding that they would be a little less conspicuous if they shaved, they found Jennifer in the kitchen. She had made about a dozen sandwiches, and placed them, along with several liters of club soda, Coke, and wine into a paper bag. Each smiled at the scene.

"A picnic?" asked Mark. Jennifer just glared at both of them.

"Not a word!" she commanded, feeling the moderately chauvinistic character of the remark. Then she softened, realizing that she didn't need to be defensive here, with them. "Sorry," she added. "Old habits are hard to break. I was hungry, and thought we all would be, so…"

"You're right," they both answered in succession. Then Mustafa said, "let's go," and they followed him to the garage where Mark climbed into the driver's seat while Jennifer got into the passenger's side. Mustafa lifted the garage door, allowing them to drive out of the garage, then closed the door and climbed into the back seat along with the weapons and food.

Once into the short driveway, Jennifer looked around. "Well, which way do we go?" She looked in the glove compartment and found a folded map of Europe, but that didn't tell them where they were.

"We want to go to Paris, don't we?" Mark asked as he pulled into the street and turned left and down the hill.

"Sure," answered Jennifer. "We have to get to the safe house again. But we don't know where we're starting from." Mark smiled.

"Yes we do." He finally remembered where he had seen the vista of the sea before. "This is the Riviera, around Cap de Ferrat." I've been here before. He urged the large Range Rover forward. "Now," he thought, "should I take the Corniche Superior...?" and he smiled.

Chapter 32

The ride from the south of France to Paris was long but uneventful. They rotated the driving, with Mustafa now asleep in the back, snoring gently. As the outskirts of the city approached, Jennifer, reached across and nudged Mark, who appeared to be sleeping in the passenger seat.

"I'm awake," Mark mumbled. "I was just going over things in my mind. There Hasn't been much time for reflection or thinking lately."

"No, there hasn't," Jennifer agreed.

"What have you been reflecting on?"

"Everything. I was trying to piece things together, I've been going over how I wound up here, thinking about home…" He paused, then added, "…and about us."

"Look, Mark…" Jennifer glanced briefly his way then continued, "I'm not sure there is an *us*." She paused, not sure exactly what she felt, or what she should say. "You have a family to return to. What we felt…Sometimes, when people are thrown into a dangerous situation, things happen…" She stopped, knowing she was talking nonsense. Mark was looking at her as she spoke, and when she stopped, he answered her.

"It wasn't just being thrown together. I love my kids. They will always be the most important people in my life, but you know what my relationship with Meredith is. Mostly, it isn't." He stopped as he heard Mustafa stirring in the back, and wondered how much he had heard of their conversation, then changed the subject just in case. "We need to get all of that data on the disk to Porter's computers. We need to see what all of that is about." He was talking for the sake of talking, he knew it, and finally just kept quiet.

"Hi," Mustafa raised his head. "How far are we?"

"Nearly there," answered Jennifer. "Did you have a good nap?"

"Yes, thank you," Mustafa answered seriously. "I needed it." "You were speaking about the information on that computer disk," Mustafa said. Mark turned to look at him, wondering how much of the prior conversation he had heard. He would never know from Mustafa. At least not yet.

"I was just talking," Mark answered. "I remember as I was copying files, and looking at some of the email, there was something that struck me, but I can't quite put my finger on it. There was a trend, but I can't seem to bring it into focus."

"Forget about it my friend," Mustafa said. "It will come to you when you are not concentrating so hard."

Jennifer had just turned into a small street and parked the large car between two others. "Wait here," she said, then got out of the car and walked about a half block to a public telephone. They couldn't see her well in the early evening darkness, so they just waited. When she returned, she sat back in the driver's seat and said, "OK," "we're only about four blocks from the safe house. Walk individually two blocks down and two to the left. It's the only house with green shutters. I'll go first, and leave the front door open, just walk in and shut the door behind you." She didn't wait for a reply, but simply reopened the door and began walking. Mark was about to get out of the car after about a minute, but Mustafa held his left shoulder.

"Not yet. Give her another few minutes, then I'll be along a few minutes after that." Five minutes had gone by when Mustafa said, "now," and Mark began his walk to the safe house.

About twenty five minutes later, the four of them had resumed their seats in the lower level of the house, with a feeling of Dé-Ja-Vu. Porter listened intently for about a half hour, as they relived the time since they left him. Each had a slightly different version, but the whole was consistent. When they had finished, Porter asked, "…and where are these disks now?" Mark reached into his pocket, and held them up.

"Can I use your computer?"

Porter answered with a nod of his head toward the wall where the computer station was, and Mark got up and walked over to it. The others followed, looking over his shoulder as he inserted the disk and listed its files. There was a long list, with each file being no more than a few kilobytes. There were long lists of email messages from various unknown people to others, equally unknown, as well as scattered encrypted files that they couldn't access right now. As Mark looked down the list, he realized that this was going to take time.

"Look, how about getting some coffee while I look through these? I'm going to be a while." Jennifer brought him a Styrofoam cup with fresh coffee. He was inwardly pleased to note that she had made it the way he liked it, from memory.

After more than an hour, and with his eyes bleary, Mark got up from the chair and walked, with his cold coffee, back to the sofa. He sat heavily, looking at the others. "Look. I can't find anything definitive. Most of the email messages end in the same domain name, but there are several that are obviously from the US, Ireland, Libya, Iran, Syria, Russia, and China. There was one suspicious thing, though." He took several pieces of paper from the table where he had placed them when he sat down. He handed them to Porter. "Those are some of the emails I uncovered on the disk. They were among the few I had time to decrypt before we had to leave. They all refer to transfers of large sums of money to numbered accounts. What bother's me," he continued, "is that the sources of the funds comes from governments all over the world. It's as though everyone is contributing, but there isn't enough here that I can decrypt to give me a real handle on it."

Mustafa was staring at the floor, deep in thought. As Mark finished, he lifted his head with a quizzical look on his face. "It may make more sense than you think." Mark was confused, but said nothing. "Look, my organization must go through millions of dollars every year between basic expenses, training, weapons, travel, payoff's...I never really questioned where the money came from. I guess I just assumed that it all came from other Palestinians, Colonel Kadafy, our friends in Damascus and Baghdad.... It made sense then but when I was just thinking about it, most groups, no matter which side they're on, seem to be as well funded as we are. The same people can't be paying for everything. Why would they pay for both sides of the same fight? It didn't make any sense unless the money is coming from different sources. Perhaps each side is funding their own groups, and we are just fighting their wars for them." Mustafa was becoming angrier as he spoke. The thought of being used as a pawn because he was expendable, so that countries wouldn't have to go to war with each other made him furious.

Throughout Mark's revelations, and Mustafa's diatribe, both Jennifer and Porter remained quiet. Now Jennifer rose, walked slowly to the coffee that sat waiting for them in the black Braun coffee maker, and took her time mixing it to her taste. No one spoke. Mark sat back on the sofa, at the opposite end from Porter, and Mustafa simply stood staring at a wall without seeing it, seething.

"You have it wrong," she said, turning with the cup of coffee in her hand. She sat in the deep chair next to the one that Mustafa had occupied earlier, and waited for him to return to it. When he didn't, she looked at him and gestured as she said, "come on, sit next to me. You are all missing what is really happening." He finally sat down, Jennifer took another sip of her coffee, and she began.

"About six months ago, I was at a meeting with the President at which he handed me a memo from the OMB in which they had informed the Secretary of Defense that there appeared to be some evidence of funds being diverted from several sources at the Pentagon. They were not large amounts, not more than a few million dollars at a time, and would not have been noticed in a normal audit, but they were conducting a study of the outflow of American money. They weren't really looking for anything but the usual military spending, but when they began to examine the computer printouts, there was a list of transfers of hard currency from the "Black" funds to a series of companies throughout Europe and Asia. When they checked, they couldn't find any of the companies except one, and that one occupied the second floor walk-up apartment of a very inebriated man in Ankara." She paused, took another sip, then continued what turned from a story into a briefing. She was in her element again.

"They had brought it to the attention of the Secretary just to get an explanation, but of course, it was never forthcoming. Instead, when he tried to find out where the money went, he was stonewalled. Records were missing, clerks transferred, account records "damaged" by computer hackers…There never seemed to be a way to get a handle on any of it, so he brought it to the President's attention. It was curious, but seemed more a symptom of oversight and negligence than anything else. I suppose that was why it was brought up at a meeting where I was present—it didn't seem very important at the time;" another sip of now cooling coffee.

"Is this going anywhere?" Mustafa asked. Mark just listened, and Porter knew Jennifer better than to interrupt. He knew she had a point, and that she would get to it when it was right.

"Yes," she continued, "each of the transfers were authorized by a lower ranking staff officer—either a colonel, or a brigadier general, but attempts to find them by the Secretary's office proved futile. The President was concerned, but it had gotten no further by the time I left for London." She paused for effect, then completed her thought. "Now look, clerks can resign or be fired. Papers can be misplaced, and records can be buried in eight inch thick budgets, but colonels and generals don't evaporate. It never made sense to me before but…"

Porter finally sat forward and finished her thought, "…those transfers went to terrorists groups, probably through an organization like
you uncovered. Maybe even the same one." Now it was Mark's turn.

"That's absurd! We spend billions each year in antiterrorist activities,
military preparations, covert operations…Why would anyone send
money to the very people we're fighting?"

"Exactly!" Jennifer shot back. "Don't you see the obvious?" She
paused for a second, then softened her tone. "No, you wouldn't. Not
unless you had been involved in both covert operations and the civilian
government the way I have. I've seen both sides. The reason we have
those billions allocated to the military, the CIA, the NSA, and all of
those alphabet organizations is that there is an enemy to defeat. When
the Cold War ended, they saw their funding slashed, their bases closed,
and their "turf" reduced. They wanted it back but, since there was no
credible enemy to fight, they had to create one." The storm clouds that
formed Mustafa's face now turned darker yet. In a fraction of a second,
he realized that the cause he thought he was fighting for, and the killing
he had justified in its name, were shams. He was not a "tool" being used
to fight someone else's war, he and others like him were puppets, whose
strings were being pulled by the very people he was fighting. Jennifer
saw Mustafa's expression and answered him.

"It is said that if the devil didn't exist, God would have to create
him." It didn't help. It wasn't meant to.

"You know," Mark broke in, "this is all very well and good, but it's
pure speculation. We have no proof beyond a few emails and some
speculation about some missing funds at the Pentagon."

"You're wrong, Jennifer stated flatly, "there are the computers that
have been compromised throughout the world. There are confronta-
tions that have occurred between Russian and American planes over the
Gulf that were ordered by people who don't seem to exist. There was the
attack by unknowns from within Iran and Iraq against shipping, using
Silkworm missiles, and causing a crisis situation for no apparent reason.

That, by the way, was the event that the President sent me to Europe to investigate. With each action, more money flowed to the military of each country. We've been in a Cold War against a devil that we created." They remained silent, waiting for her to finish. "Don't' you see!" Jennifer sounded frustrated. "They're all doing it! Countries all over the world are paying to support terrorism so that they will have someone to fight, and keep the money flowing. It's all about money. It always is. It always was."

"You mean," Mark asked softly, "that governments all over the world have been allocating tax money to pay others to bomb their own people?" His eyes were wide, but his face looked drawn and tired. The idea of his own government paying to blow up the World Trade Center turned his stomach. "And you trust that bastard, Dalton?" He spat the words at Jennifer with an anger that he hadn't felt before. Jennifer looked at him, then at Porter, who appeared to be thinking the same thing.

"You sent him an email from here." It was the first thing Porter had said through most of the discussion, and it was said quietly, and with resignation.

"Don't any of you understand?" Jennifer looked at Mustafa with the most surprise. "Surely," the thought, "he understood." His demeanor belied her hope. "It isn't Dalton, or the government. It isn't the Russian President, It isn't even Assad or Saddam Husein." She looked around again. "It's the military of each country. They're diverting funds from their budgets to fund these attacks. That, and the international tension that ensues justifies their bloated budgets. They've become shadows—unseen, unrecognized, and unstopped."

"Terra.gov," Mark's addition brought everyone's attention to him.

"Excuse me?" Jennifer asked. "What was that?" Mark began to speak, had to clear his throat and finally began again.

"It finally makes sense."

"What does?" asked Mustafa, more puzzled than ever.

"Everything." Mark paused for only a moment, then the words poured out like a torrent. "Listen," he looked at Jennifer and began again. "You said that you were able to email Dalton because he had his own private server at the White House that few other people knew about. Well, consider that on the Internet, if you don't know a server exists, then you aren't likely to find it even if you look. The reason that we've been attacked by all sides, at every turn is that they're working together. This military "Shadow" that you describe isn't some group within each government acting alike in each case. They've formed a real shadow government. Not within a country, but throughout the world. Terra.gov," he repeated again.

It made more sense than most of them understood, and sent a chill down Jennifer's spine.

"But that doesn't explain why they would risk exposing themselves to kill us," Mustafa continued to look puzzled through his anger. "If they hadn't made all of those attempts, we wouldn't be together, and we would never have reached this point. It still makes no sense."

"Sure it does," Porter rose and walked to the cabinet where the electronics were located. He took a few seconds to locate the controls he wanted, made a few adjustments, and the first page of the enlarged microfilm that Mark had in his pocket appeared on the wall screen.

"This is why."

"I don't understand," Mark answered.

"Neither do I," Mustafa this time. Jennifer simply waited. She knew Porter, and knew he would get to it in time.

"They attacked you for this."

"But I didn't even know I had it," Mark said in an exasperated voice. "Besides, however horrible that is, it's one more attack that they wouldn't risk everything for."

"You're right, said Porter, an impish smile beginning to brighten his face, "if they knew this was what you had. But suppose they thought that you were given something that would expose them. They would go to any lengths to prevent it."

"You mean that we've been through all of this because of a mistake?" Mark looked dumbfounded.

"Yes," Porter answered, "but now we know, don't we?"

"But we can't prove it." Jennifer was thinking about alerting President Dalton. "We need to get proof to bring this house of cards down."

"Well I, for one, won't be used anymore!" Mustafa rose and faced Porter squarely.

"Yes you will," Porter answered him in kind. "If you don't, they'll know we know and redouble their efforts. That will eventually lead them here, and then they'll be unopposed."

"Then we need to get the proof, and warn Dalton, who can then warn others we can't get to."

They agreed, and Jennifer composed a lengthy email to President Dalton, explaining what they had learned, and what they were going to try to prove. She also suggested that he let the other major national leaders know about the problem, but urge them to take no action until they had investigated further. This was sent, after one last look around to see if everyone agreed, and then they got down to how they would proceed.

After about three hours of suggestions that seemed to lead nowhere, Mark asked Porter if he was able to use the computer equipment they had to tap into the banking system.

"Sure, I guess," Porter replied, "although I'm not sure I'd know how to do it. But surely you don't think that a group like we're discussing would leave an obvious financial trail, do you?"

"Of course not," responded Mark. "Not intentionally, anyway. But remember, they don't' know that anyone's looking. Besides, no matter how hard you try, there always has to be a trail, if only from bank to bank."

"I have an idea," Porter said slowly, "but you'll have to agree to it."

"OK, what is it?" Jennifer asked for the group.

"I am acquainted with someone whom we've used several times to obtain information for us. He's way beyond being a hacker. I don't think there's any system in the world he couldn't get into given enough time."

"That may be…" Mustafa looked agitated. He was tired of talking, he wanted to do something. "…but," he continued, "time is something we don't have enough of. Besides, how do you know he can be trusted?"

"He doesn't have to be trusted because we're only asking him to find certain specific information for us. He doesn't have to know why. Searching for illegal financial dealings is done all the time. It would be a reasonable assignment for him. As for time, we can cut it short by giving him some of the passwords and security access we have." Jennifer was aghast!

"You mean give him access to the Pentagon's computer system?"

"It's a risk, I know. But can you think of any other way? Besides, codes can be changed later, and the nukes aren't on the same system so we don't have to fear that. Also, Dalton will be watching for unusual orders now, so we at least have some safeguard." They agreed, and Porter went into another room to make the call. He came back and said simply, "it's done."

"We have other things to do," Mustafa said, "I can't just sit here doing nothing." He cast furtive glances at the door, wanting to charge out and attack, but having no target.

"It's all there is to do." Jennifer placed a hand on his shoulder and tried to soothe him. He turned, ready to lash out in his feeling of impotence, but was stopped by the look in her eyes. He had imagined that she had all but forgotten him since meeting Mark, but her eyes told a different story. He wasn't sure exactly what they said, but he knew she cared. That was enough for now.

"Ok." Mustafa turned back toward the cluster of furniture and sat in one of the chairs. He suddenly looked tired. Even to Mark, who's dislike for him was intense, there was a pathos that he was sorry to see.

Porter bid them goodnight, and reminded them that their rooms were waiting down the hall. He also reminded them not to come upstairs unless it was absolutely necessary. They were, after all, wanted, and who knew about the staff...

They talked for another fifteen minutes, and finally agreed that there was nothing they could do for now, so each said goodnight and went to their rooms. Mark didn't remember when he had been so tired. He hardly had time to pile his clothes in a heap on the floor before he lay back and was instantly asleep. His dreams were troubled. He dreamed of home, then of Jennifer, then of people trying to kill them. He remembered knowing that he was dreaming, but still not being in control. The night wore on.

Jennifer tried for more than an hour to sleep, but it eluded her. Getting up, she slipped into a robe that had been left in the closet, and walked down the hall toward the common room to get something to drink. When she passed Mustafa's door, It was slightly ajar, and she saw him sitting on the side of his bed, his head in his hands. Somewhere, deep inside of her, he was still "David." She felt some of it that night at the hotel.

"David." Mustafa looked up.

"Jen..." He wasn't able to complete her name. He knew her calling him David wasn't a mistake. It was pity, the one thing he couldn't stand. Still, he sat on the bed without moving. Slowly, Jennifer moved toward him, sat on the bed, and put her arm around his shoulders. He had a pain she couldn't sooth, but she could try.

"I understand how you feel," she began.

"NO! You don't." Mustafa was not to be denied his anger. He had been used by his own people who in turn worked for the very people they were fighting. He wanted to fight. He wanted to kill. It was his way. It was a way she could never understand, that was why he never met her in New York. "Yes, I do," Jennifer leaned closer and lowered her head onto his shoulder, her right hand resting on his chest. He began to answer, then stopped. She had kissed him gently on his cheek and her right hand roamed over his face, turning it toward her in the process. There was a sadness in his eyes, that mixed with the anger and frustration. She wanted to help, but didn't know how, so she kissed him again, this time on his lips. He turned slightly more to his right, holding her face gently in his hand as he returned her kiss. Long seconds passed before their mouths parted and they stared at each other. Before either realized what they were doing, without a further thought, they fell into an old pattern. Their hands gently explored each other as they had at the George Cinc, and as they had on the beach in Tel Aviv so long ago. For Mustafa, Jennifer was a haven in a world he no longer understood. She was a point of stability. To Jennifer, Mustafa was the cause of her emotional turmoil. She didn't really want to be doing this, but his hand cupped her left breast inside of her robe, and urged her gently back onto the bed, and she lay there with the gentle breezes of the Mediterranean cooling her body as the sand cushioned her head. Time had reversed itself, and she was a world away once more.

Mark's dreams had become more confused and troubled, and he awakened with a thin sheen of sweat covering his forehead and bear chest. For a moment, the dark room produced disorientation, and he thought he was back in his own bed, at home, with Meredith at the other edge of the huge king sized bed. Then his mind regained its focus, and the barely visible walls of the small room reduced it's size to reality. For two or three minutes, he lay on the bed, not wanting to think about his situation, but finally realized that he was becoming more awake rather than less. Slowly, he pulled back the institutional blanket and swung his feet to the hard carpet on the floor. Without turning on the lights, he found his pants and put them on, deciding that a cup of tea, or perhaps something with a little more kick would urge him back to sleep. Wiping his eyes to clear his vision, he rose to his feet, put his shirt on without buttoning it, and gingerly opened his door so that his eyes could get used to the light in the hallway. In bare feet, he turned right, and walked a few feet toward the common room which held everything from the computer gear to the kitchenette and bar when he glanced to his left, through Mustafa's open door. The sight of Mustafa, leaning over Jennifer, her eyes closed, and her robe lying open with her naked breasts yielding under his grip as they had to his own caused a physical pain in his gut. His jaw hung open, and though he knew he should just return to his room, he stood transfixed. Through a swirling cloud, he heard a moan deep in her throat as Mustafa reached between her legs, his mouth covering hers as his body pinned hers to the bed. He felt dizzy. The hallway in which he stood began to tilt, and being unable to balance securely, he leaned heavily against the door jam. It was a small sound, one that would have gone unnoticed in other circumstances, but both Jennifer and Mustafa opened their eyes to see Mark standing just outside the door with his eyes closed and an expression somewhere between agony and disbelief.

Quickly, Jennifer pushed Mustafa from her, sat up, and said, "Mark?" He stood without hearing. "Mark," she said again as she arose and began walking toward him, "you don't understand…" Mark opened his eyes and, with an unmistakable look of revulsion, turned and walked back to his room where he closed and locked the door. He wanted nothing to do with the world tonight.

"Leave him," Mustafa said to Jennifer, "he'll be OK in the morning." She looked back at Mustafa with a look of disgust, but deep inside, she realized that it was targeted more at her than him. Quickly she closed her robe and walked to Mark's door.

"Mark?" She waited for the answer that she knew wouldn't come. "Mark," she knocked softly, but again there was no answer. "Look," she said to the blank door, I understand what you think of me, but it wasn't like that."

"Go away." It wasn't a command, or even a desire, but a statement of necessity. Perhaps he could deal with this tomorrow, but not tonight. He hadn't realized the depth of the feelings he had developed for her until now. In the back of his mind, she had always been a dream he was having, from which he would one day awaken. That illusion was shattered. "Go away," he said softly, once more, and she did. Walking back to her room, she passed Mustafa in the hall.

"Jennifer," he reached his hand out to her shoulder, and gently brought her to a stop. "We need to talk."

"No, we don't," she answered in equally soft tones, and continued walking back to her room letting his hand simply drop from her as she walked away.

She sat on her bed in the darkened room for less than a minute when she felt tears well up in her eyes. She promised herself, years ago, after "David" failed to show up, that she would never cry again, yet here she was with warm tears streaming down her cheeks. She did nothing to stop them, but simply sat and sobbed almost imperceptibly. She knew she had hurt Mark, but she hadn't meant to. He was vulnerable, and she knew it. What she hadn't realized was that she was too. She fell asleep with tears still running onto her pillow, while Mark quietly grasped his with increasing furor.

The night wore on. The hours slipped by without being counted, and Mark finally made a decision. It wasn't a conscious one, but it happened just the same. His tears were gone now. His anger was calmed. In fact, he was feeling nothing. With neither hurry nor hesitation, he reached into the pile of clothes next to his bed, and retrieved the small 32 caliber automatic that he had brought with him from the armory to which Mustafa had taken them earlier (a day, a year, he couldn't be sure). He gently pulled the slide until it would go no further, then allowed it so slide forward. He knew a round was in the chamber without looking. Without putting his pants back on, he walked directly from his room to Mustafa's. The prostrate figure lay in the dark on the bed. Mark walked easily to it's side, directed the muzzle at the barely visible lump that represented the head, and thumbed the hammer back until he felt, rather than heard it click into position. He stood like that for more than five minutes. There was no reason not to pull the trigger, he would end a life that wasn't worth living. He would avenge all of the innocent people Mustafa had killed through the years. He had killed men during the last week, men he didn't know, men who had been trying to kill them. This was no different. His grip on the trigger tightened, but his resolve fell apart. He had killed, but he was no killer. Soundlessly, he allowed the hammer to come forward, and flipped the safety forward, then turned and left the room, returning to his own where, like Jennifer before him, tears rolled from his eyes as he drifted off into a dreamless sleep.

Behind him, Mustafa moved slowly and quietly away from behind the door where he had been standing with the Barretta in his hand. Soundlessly, he pushed the pre-arranged pillows aside and slipped into bed, knowing for the first time tonight that he would awaken in the morning.

Chapter 33

In the absence of windows and doors, morning in the basement of the safe house in Paris was indistinguishable from afternoon or night. It was into this pocket of frozen time that Porter exited the elevator and walked to the secure room where, since it was after 09:00, he expected to find Jennifer, Mark and Mustafa waiting for him. Facing the empty room, he was unsure how he should proceed. Their rooms were just up the hall, a quick knock on the doors would arouse them. On the other hand, since he didn't know who occupied which room, he wasn't sure where to begin, or even if he shouldn't give them an extra hour or two after their recent trials.

Duty overcame sympathy and he had just begun to turn toward the hall when a last shred of conscience caused him to put some fresh coffee on before he left. to walk rapidly down the hall. There were six identical doors on each side, but he knew that only the initial three, two on the left and one on the right, were occupied. Two quick raps on each door, followed by, "09:00, time to get up," and he stood in the center of the hall and concluded loudly, "I'll give you a half hour and be back then." After looking at his watch once more, he walked to the elevator and went back to the public areas where he had another cup of tea as he read the Morning Post. It was a "rag," he knew, but a minor vice.

The chime from the Victorian Grandfather's Clock in the vestibule sounded once, and Porter looked at his watch to be sure it was correct, then put the paper down and descended three levels in the elevator. The walk across the industrial carpet to the windowless, electronically shielded room was less than ten meters, but in that distance one crossed from the trappings of wealth to the hidden world of power—governments, agencies, and rogues. Entering the room he had left the day before, Porter expected the three to be waiting for him, sipping the coffee he had been courteous enough to make for them. Only Mustafa, dressed in a fresh set of clothes, was where he should be.

"Good morning," Mustafa seemed cheerful enough.

"Good morning," answered Porter, somewhat puzzled by Mark and Jennifer's absence. "Were are they?" Porter had no need to be more specific.

"I don't know," answered Mustafa pleasantly, then rose to add another measure to his partially empty cup of coffee.

Porter looked at his watch. They were running short on time, and they needed to act quickly on the information he had. "Ill get them," and Porter turned and walked to the hallway where the other two doors remained shut. "Jenn," he called in a natural voice. "Come on, we have to get going." When no answer came, Porter tested the door and, finding it open, let himself in. Jennifer sat, dressed, on her bed. She was staring at the floor in a way that was not what he came to expect of her after all of these years. "What is it?" Porter was genuinely concerned. Not only was she absolutely necessary to correct what was going on, but he had known her for longer than either of them cared to discuss. She was a friend, or as much of one as one can have in their business. She never took her eyes from the floor. "Jenn?" His concern rose as her morose state began to register in his conscious mind. He sat on the bed beside her without making contact. "Come on. Talk to me." Slowly, she lifted her head and he could see that she had been crying. It was the first time he could remember seeing her like this, and it worried him for more reasons than national security. Again, "what is it?"

"I…I…" She stopped herself repeatedly, then stood, pushed the emotions back down where they would remain until she could deal with them and, wiping her eyes, answered, "…nothing. I'm OK. It's not important. I'll be out in two minutes, OK?" She smiled as she finished, but it was a smile that came from practice, not emotion. Having nothing else to do, Porter decided that Mark was his next victim.

Crossing the hallway, he knocked on Mark's door as he had on Jennifer's. "Time to get up, old man. We've things to do." He tried to be cheerful, but it sounded hollow as his mind remained with Jennifer. Before he had completed his last syllable, Mark opened the door. He was clean and dressed, but seemed little more rested than Jennifer.

"Coming," he said too brightly, and followed Porter to the shielded room where nothing could penetrate but their emotions. As Mark stepped through the door and faced Mustafa, he hesitated for a fraction of a second, unsure of what his reaction should be. He had considered this moment and reconsidered it all night, but It's reality only left him floundering.

"Good morning," he said to Mustafa, who turned and nodded to him without speaking. Mark went to the coffee maker, and poured himself a cup before sitting on the sofa.

"Did you sleep well?" Mustafa smiled as he asked the question of Mark. Gall rose in Mark's throat, but his lifelong habit of control rescued him, although he didn't' know how long he could keep it up.

"Like a baby," he lied. "And you?"

"Well enough," answered Mustafa, although I could have sworn that I saw someone sleepwalking in my room last night. I suppose it was a dream. I seemed to be standing behind the door when someone came into the room and pointed a gun at my bed. Strange what we dream when things are tense for us, isn't it?" They stared into each other eyes, neither willing to be the first to turn away, as Porter stepped between them.

"I wonder what's keeping Jennifer?"

It was less than ten seconds, but seemed like an hour, between Porter's question and Jennifer stepping through the door.

"Good morning," she said to everyone, and no one in particular. She walked to the coffee service, never allowing her eyes to meet anyone else's. She took one of the mugs from a small rack and filled it with hot black coffee, added cream and sugar, and lowered herself gracefully into a chair, carefully avoiding the sofa and any physical contact. There was no conversation among them. Porter could feel the tension, it was palpable, but it remained just below the surface. He began to ask about it, then decided that, at least for the moment, "discretion *was* the better part of valor."

"Well then," Porter began. "I have some news for you. I've had three people working since our meeting yesterday, rifling through computers at banks in Switzerland, the Cayman Islands, and Asia. They were able to locate three of the account numbers that were mentioned in the emails you found. When they accessed the recent transfers into or out of them, three locations stood out. The first was Iran. That certainly is no great surprise. They've been funding terrorist activities for years." He paused for a moment, remembering Mustafa, but finding no reaction continued on. "The second, and much more surprising, was a transfer from the Central Bank in Moscow. Nearly 30 million in US Dollars, and not more than three months ago." Another pause, a sip of coffee, and he launched into his final announcement. "The final transfer that we've been able to uncover was from a bank in Maryland. More than 75 million dollars had been placed into an intermediate account from the Pentagon's account, then transferred to the Swiss Account." He stopped for comments. For a few moments, quiet was pervasive, then Jennifer broke it with a quiet,

"The world's been busy, hasn't it? Do we have any idea who authorized these transfers or to whom they eventually went?"

"Well," answered Porter, "as for the second, we can be fairly certain from where you found the accounts, that they went to terrorist groups," Mustafa's affiliation was forgotten now, "although we don't know which ones. But as for who authorized them…" He shrugged his shoulders and remained seated on the arm of an unoccupied chair.

Mark rose, walked a few steps into the center of the room, and then turned to face the rest. He hadn't wanted to be the one to begin. Not today, but it seemed as though his experience was the only thing to get them started, and he was now tiring of being here.

"Can the people you used penetrate computers at the Pentagon and the Kremlin?"

"Possibly," answered Porter. "In fact, almost certainly, but I didn't think it prudent to ask them to do so under these conditions. We don't really know who we can trust, and they would certainly become suspicious if they were asked to penetrate a Pentagon computer." Mark waited for another moment before answering. He needed Jennifer's help, and didn't want to talk to her right now. Still, there was nothing to do but begin.

"Jennifer." She lifted her eyes to meet his, and he found a mixture of sadness and trepidation in them. He continued, "Can your access code get into the Pentagon computer?"

"Yes, I suppose so, if they haven't removed it yet. Why? I can't get at the files we would need."

"No, but perhaps I can once we're in." Mark remained looking at her. It was painful, but this was something they had to do.

Without speaking, Jennifer walked to the computer console and sat in one of the two chairs that faced monitors. "You realize that once I log on, they'll know we're not dead and exactly where we are within seconds."

"Maybe not," answered Mark. "Unless they're actually monitoring your account, you will be just another user logged on, and the transaction filed away in the transaction file."

"And if they are looking?" Jennifer looked up at him from the chair, the question hanging from her lips.

"Well then," Mark answered, "we had all better be prepared to get out of here. Remember, someone at the Pentagon with enough clout to transfer millions of dollars into a secret account wants the information to remain dead, and us with it." They looked at each other, then at Porter and Mustafa, the previous evening buried in the heat of the decision they had to make. Porter nodded his head, then all heads turned to Mustafa. His consent wasn't really needed, but somehow they all felt compelled to seek it. Like Porter, Mustafa inclined his head slightly, still feeling used and wanting to get at the people who had used him.

Mark sat next to Jennifer at the console as she activated her terminal and entered her user ID and password. The familiar red and white striped box appeared in the center of the screen, and began to flash, then was replaced by the Department of Defense Seal as "wallpaper," over which a menu appeared. Jennifer looked at Mark, said simply, "OK, we're in," and swung out of the way to allow him to replace her at her terminal. Mark studied the menu and the screen. He had to get past the user interface and into the operating system, but which system were they using, and did he know enough after all this time to really get in and get the information?

"This is one hell of a time to ask yourself that," he thought to himself, then stabbed at the "Ctrl" key and tried various combinations that he vaguely remembered. Somewhere above them, the god of computer hackers smiled, and within about 20 seconds, the screen went black except for a small "$ /usr/bin/jl" in the upper left corner. Mark could feel the flush in his face and the slight trembling in his hands as they played across the keyboard. He knew what he was looking for, but could he find it before they found him? He changed directories back to the "root" and began his search for the password file. Using the "grep" utility within the system, he began narrowing his search, but eventually realized that he was getting nothing. He sat for a moment, trying to think. "Where would they put it? There had to be a password file..." Then he remembered something he had read about a year earlier. In many secure systems, in order to prevent hackers from breaking into anything important, the password file was "shadowed." There was a "pwd" file that led to another file, and so on down the line until the real file was found. Even then there were additional protections, but most often they presupposed that they were dealing with an intruder who was not supposed to be in the system, not one with top clearances.

Another twelve minutes went by, with sweat dripping from Mark's forehead despite the comfortable temperature in the room, and his shirt clinging wetly to his body. No one else spoke, but he could feel the weight of their stare as they gathered behind him to observe. "There!," he thought. A file appeared with a list of user ID's, account codes and passwords. It was small though. Only about a dozen were listed, and there were hundreds of files. The sweat began to drench him now as he issued a system command to search these files for a "string" that would bring him the "root" password. It was another 15 minutes before he found it.

"Gotcha!" he said aloud, to no one in particular, then copied the password to a small white tablet in front of him, and logged off the system. The rest would be easier as long as nobody was on the way to capture them.

Once again, the screen remained dark, with only the word "Login" in the upper left corner. "root," typed Mark next to the symbol, and the word "Password" appeared below it. Carefully, Mark transferred the series of characters from the paper in front of him to the screen then pressed "Enter." "Authentication Failure," read the white characters on the screen, "Access Denied."

"Fuck!" whispered Mark at the screen. "This doesn't make any sense."

"What is it?" asked Jennifer.

"Sshh!" he needed quiet. He needed to think. Perhaps he had entered the Password incorrectly. He was about to retype it when he stopped. There would be no more than one or possibly two more chances to try before the system reported a repeated failure. He held the paper with the password up to the screen, and compared the characters. They were correct. "Then what is it? What am I doing wrong?" he wondered.

"What's wrong," Porter's voice came from behind him.

"Quiet!" snapped Mark. "Just hang on." He had to think. There were three possibilities. First, he could have chosen the wrong password from the list. Secondly, he could have copied it incorrectly. Finally, it could have been a "dummy" password to trap people like him who were trying to break into the system. If any of these were true, they were in deep shit.

Seconds, that seemed like hours, passed as he stared at the darkened screen. Suddenly, an idea occurred to him. There was a fourth possibility—that the user ID was wrong. This was a Unix system, and it would never tell you which part of the authentication was incorrect, but simply stop accepting input after a second or third attempt. He had automatically used the user ID, "root," as the one that usually came with the system. But it could be changed. "Sysadmin," he typed onto the screen, then carefully re-entered the password, slowly, one character at a time, comparing the screen with the paper at each keystroke. Without realizing it, he held his breath as he pressed the "Enter" key. "#/" It sat in front of him like a trophy. He felt his heart beating so hard that he could hear it in his ears. He didn't say anything this time, he simply began the job of tracking who had made the transfer of funds. If he had been a real hacker, he would have created another user with "superuser" authorities, then logged off, thus allowing himself repeated access to the account while not remaining logged on as the "root." He didn't have time for this. More time elapsed as he searched for the "transaction" file. What he finally found was huge. He realized, then, how many transactions occurred each day on this and other servers in a system of this size with this many users. He was becoming dejected, and ran his fingers through his damp hair.

"I'll never find it in this," he said quietly, then lowered his head into his hands, feeling the energy bleed out of him, and his lack of sleep begin to play with his mind. He sat like that for only a few seconds before Jennifer reached over and placed her right hand on the back or his neck, her thumb brushing his left ear.

"You can do it." Despite everything that happened the night before, he suddenly felt a burst of energy. Sometimes, when you are about to give up, it takes only a word to get you over the hump. Someone simply had to tell you that they believed in you. He raised his head and smiled at her, then returned to the screen.

He knew the transaction date, so he began there, searching for that string of characters in the file, and using the ">" character to redirect the list to a file. There were only 12 transactions that had taken place at that date and time. He redirected this list to another file, then compared this file to the contents of the user account file. Most of the names were unfamiliar to them, and it was doubtful that any of them would have the authority to transfer these types of funds. As they looked down the list, one name stood out—"Hallsey, S. A."

"My God!" whispered Jennifer.

Porter's, "Jesus!" followed, and fell nearly on top of her words. Quickly, Mark stabbed at the "Print Screen" button then, after a minute, began typing, and continued for another two or three minutes. Finished, he logged off. They sat quietly now, staring at the white paper sliding silently from the laser printer. Jennifer took it and looked at it again, then handed it to Porter. He stared for a few seconds, then laid it carefully onto the desk in front of Mark. Mustafa looked from face to face. He understood the emotion, but wasn't familiar enough with the American chain of command to understand the significance of the names on the list. "What is it?" he asked. Getting only silence, he reached for Porter's shoulder and turned him so that they faced each other.

"Damn it!" he shouted, "what is it?" Porter looked at him, then at the others, and finally at the floor.

"Those funds were transferred by the Chairman of the Joint Chief's of Staff." Before Mustafa could fully realize the import of what they were saying, Jennifer looked at Porter and, with the color draining from her face, she said, "it's true, isn't it?" Porter said nothing but turned away

- 292 -

and sat heavily in one of the chairs that surrounded the conference table behind them. Now it was Mark's turn to lack understanding.

"Look," he said. I know who Hallsey is, of course, and that this obviously reaches to the top, but we've had scandals before."

Jennifer turned to look at Mark, then at Porter who nodded almost imperceptibly for her to continue, and back at Mark again.

"You don't fully grasp this," she said quietly. "Hallsey's taken control of the entire system. He controls the entire military, and probably most of the civilian computers as well. He's effectively done what no one else has ever been able to do in our entire history—we've had a coup, and we never even knew it." Mustafa took a few steps back and looked at the group.

"You have all been so smug all these years. It could not happen in America? Well it has!" He was nearly as anxious about it's meaning as the others, but his hatred of Americans remained untouched. It was startling to the other three, who had begun to accept him as one of them, but they stood quietly looking at him before anyone else spoke.

The thick layer of quiet in the room was broken when Porter added the final icing on a very scary cake.

"Don't *you* be so smug," he said to Mustafa. "If we're right, we have an even greater problem." Mark and Jennifer turned to face him, trying to imagine what greater problem there could be. He didn't make them wait for the answer. "Some of those transfers were from other countries, including Russia. This isn't an American coup, it's a world coup. We're all being manipulated like pieces on a chessboard, and right now, there are only four people in the world outside of this "shadow" world government who know about it."

He stopped for just a second, then ended, "I think we all have a problem." Each realized that while this "shadow" government remained, they could never be allowed to live.

Chapter 34

"We have to get out of here now!" Porter moved quickly toward the door as he spoke. "I'm going upstairs and pack a few things for us. I'll be back in a few minutes. You finish up here." He disappeared through the door as quickly as his words faded, leaving the three of them standing alone.

"I'm going to my room to get some things," Mustafa walked down the hall and closed the door to his room behind him, leaving Mark and Jennifer facing each other in the conference room. For long moments they stood looking at each other without speaking, then Jennifer took a tentative step in his direction.

"Mark..." Her throat was dry, and her mouth had an acrid taste. There was no answer, just a look of rejection and pain in his eyes that burned into her. She stood still and began again. She had to say this, even just this once.

"Mark...I don't know what happened last night. Mustafa was dejected, I went to him to talk. I..., we...Well, you know that we once..."

"Yes, I know," Mark stated flatly. "It must have been wonderful reliving old times!" He wanted to hurt her, but couldn't stand that he was succeeding. Jennifer looked at his face, flushed with...what? Anger? Excitement? She wasn't sure.

"It wasn't like that. It was...a mistake." Then she stopped, looked up at Mark again and asked, "and what were you planning to do about your wife?"

It had been a long time since Mark had thought about Meredith. Even when he talked with her a couple of days ago, he was thinking of himself, Jennifer, Mustafa, finding answers…not her.

"I'm not in love with her, Jennifer." He stopped for a moment realizing that this was the first time he had articulated his feelings, and trying to find the right words, then continued.

"I love her. I always will. I will always love the young girl I married, the one who sat with me in the middle of the night in our first apartment when I felt defeated, wanting to share my pain as well as my joy. That woman will always be in my heart, but that isn't the woman I'm married to now." He stopped again to gather his breath, then sat on the arm of a nearby chair. "I will always care for her. Fifteen years and two wonderful sons can't be discarded, but I'm no longer *In* love with her. She killed that years ago, we just haven't held the funeral yet." There was a sadness in his eyes. She reached out to touch his face, and just as her fingers brushed his cheek, he looked into her eyes and the sadness was gone. He held her hand against his cheek for a second, then said, "we'd better go pack our stuff also." He urged her toward the door, and followed behind as they walked to their rooms.

Jennifer had been in her small room for less than 5 minutes, packing the few things she had accumulated into a small duffel that Porter had provided for each of them, when Mustafa entered and closed the door behind him. They stood for a moment, each waiting for the other to begin, with Mustafa breaking the silence first.

"Jenn," his eyes betrayed a desire that she had seen on the beach in Tel Aviv years earlier, and in his room at the George Cinc only a few days ago. Her heart, so recently aching for Mark, now cried out for Mustafa's touch. No matter what had happened since, he would always be "David" in her mind. Perhaps it was the ghost of his memory that haunted her emotions, but she felt the pull none the less.

"Jenn," he began again, "through all of this, you're the one bright spot. I know what you think of what I do, and I know you care for the

American," he couldn't bring himself to say "Mark," "but last night was real. Last week was real, Tel Aviv was real…" He paused, looking into her soft green eyes that were welling up with tears. "Come away with me Jenn. We can leave all of this behind and disappear. I've put enough money into a secret account for us to live happily forever." He stopped, and waited for an answer. "Dav…, Mustafa," the two kept getting mixed up in her head, "I've loved you since we first met. I don't think anything will ever change that, but…" He stopped her before she could finish.

"Don't answer me yet. Think about it for a while. Even if your answer is "no," I'll still love you and protect you." He paused for a few moments, then turned, opened the door and, looking back before he walked out, said quietly, "For me, it can be no other way." The door closed behind him, leaving Jennifer with a partially packed bag, and tears rolling down her cheeks.

Mark was already in the meeting room when Jennifer arrived. He wore a light leather jacket with a sweater underneath. Her flowing blonde hair was draped over a black silk shirt covered by a Navy blue jacket, slightly pinched at the waist. Porter had done his selection with his usual efficiency—the clothes fit fairly well.

"Well, I guess it's almost time to leave." Mark opened the conversation.

"I suppose." Jennifer was strangely quiet, a "far away" look in her eyes that Mark couldn't quite place.

"We have to get word to the President," Jennifer said. We have enough information for him to act upon. It isn't over yet." Mark nodded, and moved to the computer. "I'll do it," he said, and sat at the first console, flipping the switch to activate the monitor. She was about to protest that she couldn't give him the passwords that would give him access to the President's private server, but logic prevailed. They would have no evidence except for him.

"Here," she said, and walked to the white tablet that still lay on the desk, took a pen from the drawer, and wrote her ID and passwords on the top sheet, passing them to him.

He composed a letter from her to the President with the story of how they came to have the information, explaining their conclusions, giving names, dates, transactions, and attaching the file with all of the information downloaded from the Pentagon computer. He was a little vague about his own role in hacking into it, but it was essentially correct. When he had completed the letter, Jennifer added a short line to make sure that the President believed that it was from her—another of those personal details that no one else could know. That done, Mark clicked the "Send" button and watched as it sped to a White House that may not even have the power to act anymore.

"I hope he can still do something," Mark said.

"He will," Jennifer answered with conviction. I know him."

Mark was about to get up from his position in front of the computer when Porter entered the room with his own bag. He carried a larger duffel in the same hand as his smaller bag which, he explained, contained some additional supplies, a notebook computer, electronic equipment…The list seemed extensive for the size of the bag, but neither questioned him. Jennifer seemed tired, but resolved to win.

"What about the Iraqi data?" Porter asked. "Did you send that to the President?" Mark and Jennifer looked at each other, feeling stupid. They had missed the piece of information that had begun the entire episode, and perhaps the most important.

"Once the conspiracy is resolved, "Mark answered defensively, "won't that end the Iraqi threat also?"

Porter walked to the other console and brought the file containing the scanned microfilm back onto the large screen.

"Take a look at that," he said. "Jennifer, I'm surprised *you* don't see the obvious." While they were staring, Porter followed up his statement. "This is a plan to launch a biological attack against multiple targets around the world, including major cities in countries that are part of the "Shadow Government" we've been so concerned about." He looked at Jennifer and continued. "You told us about shipping being attacked by Iraqi gunboats operating out of Iranian bases. Look at a map," and he replaced the first page of the Iraqi documents with a map of the region. "If the Iraqis launch this attack and then move troops northwest while the Iranians move north, they'll be joined by more Muslim countries, especially those that broke away from the old Soviet Union. That kind of alliance would encourage Pakistan to attack India, perhaps provoking a nuclear exchange, and totally destabilize the Balkans where the only thing holding things together are the Peace-keepers in Bosnia, and the NATO troops in Kosovo and Serbia." He stopped as they studied the map. "Don't you see?" Porter was exasperated until he saw understanding dawning in both their faces.

"Jesus!" Mark turned pale and Jennifer stood frozen. "World War III." Mark said it quietly, but the words rang in all their ears.

"Right," Porter continued quickly, and our "Shadow Government" not only doesn't know about it, they funded it!"

"We have to get this to the President now, before we leave." Mark sat back down at the computer as he said it, and began typing a short follow-up note using Jennifer's ID's and passwords again, then attached the file containing the scanned microfilm. Jennifer sat in one of the large chairs, rearranging some things in her bag to kill some time, while Mark composed the message. Porter stood watching Mark type, glad that they were getting the entire message across.

Mark was just completing his typing and was about to send the message when he was startled by the distinctive sound of the slide of a semi-automatic pistol being pulled back and released. "Stop!" They hadn't noticed Mustafa standing at the door to the room. "Don't move, and don't send that message." They were staring at Mustafa holding a black Glock in his right hand, his packed bag at his feet.

"Are you crazy?" Jennifer began to rise out of the chair when Mustafa raised his weapon and pointed it at Mark. "Please, Jenn! Move, and I'll put a bullet through his head." It was a flat statement, but there was emotion buried beneath it.

"You can't be serious!" Jennifer was stunned. Mark remained frozen, staring at the muzzle of Mustafa's gun, as it seemed to grow in size. He began to imagine the bullet leaving the barrel and entering his head, and sweat began to bead up on his forehead.

"Don't you see what will happen if this is allowed to continue? We have to stop it." Jennifer was trying to reason with Mustafa. He was a terrorist, but not an idiot. Besides, she knew he would listen to her.

Mustafa never lowered his gun from Mark's head, but spoke with a conviction that none of them had heard in all the time they had been together.

"This is the day I've been waiting for." The words hissed from his mouth. "It is the day that Islam would unite and drive the infidels from our lands. We would take back what is rightfully ours, and I wouldn't let you stop it."

"But you won't get anything back," Mark said, "there won't be anything left after this war."

"Yes, there will. Listen to me. There will be many dead before this is over, and I am sorry for the blood of people who have done us no harm, but some must die. Allah would never forgive me if I allowed you to send that message." The intensity in his eyes was frightening. This was a man Mark had wanted to kill the night before but didn't. This was a man who had saved his life. Jennifer tried to reconcile the look in his eyes with the man she loved. Porter remained motionless.

"Now," Mustafa said to Mark, "you don't have to die. You must not send that message. Get up from the chair without touching the keyboard, and move over there." He nodded toward the area where Jennifer sat, without ever turning his head.

"Please Mark, Mustafa said urgently, I can't allow this, and I won't explain more until I am sure of something, but if you touch that keyboard, I'll have to kill you." His left hand was now steadying the butt of the gun, making sure that the bullet would find its mark. For a moment, there was neither movement nor breathing in the room. Then, without preamble, everything happened at once. Mark stabbed at the "Send" button and dove onto the floor to his right as the silent room exploded. Mustafa's body jerked to the left, and his head followed, collapsing against the door jam. The glistening red stain gave testimony to where he slid to the floor. A look of surprise and confusion hinted at his thoughts, and his gun discharged by reflex as he fell, missing Mark by a wide margin, but smashing into the computer console.

The acrid smell of cordite filled the room, and both Porter and Mark turned to see Jennifer, still sitting in the chair, trembling her left hand supporting the butt of her gun as Mustafa had supported his. For long moments, everyone remained frozen, then Mark rose slowly as Jennifer instinctively brought the gun to bear on him before regaining her senses. She dropped the gun on the carpeted floor and, as Mark reached her and drew her to him, the last vestige of professionalism evaporated. She collapsed against him, her body shuddering with sobs and tears flowing from her eyes. She had killed a piece of a dream, a man she loved. Was it to save the world or Mark? She neither knew nor cared. She made no attempt to hold the tears back, or even wipe them away, and Mark made no attempt to stop her. Only Porter seemed to be thinking well enough to check Mustafa's pulse.

"He's dead." But Mark saw a slight movement in the chest as blood spurted from the open wound. He ran to Mustafa, who looked at him and, as Jennifer arrived at his side, Mustafa managed to whisper, "…fake. The film's a fake….had to be sure…you can't…" He looked up at the ceiling, and his eyes remained open as the breath left his lungs for the last time.

"Mark," Porter called from across the room. We don't have time for this. Let's get out of here." Mark was not going to leave Jennifer in her condition, but she steadied herself and gently pushed him away.

I'll be OK, she said. The tears remained, but the sobbing had stopped.

"It's over," he said. He wasn't sure why he trusted Mustafa's final words, but he knew, without a doubt, that they were true. "The microfilm's a fake. We can find someplace to rest, and let the whole fucking world fix itself without us!"

"No." Porter faced Mark. He had been going through Mustafa's pockets and his bag. "There's one more thing we need to do. That original microfilm must reach the President. If it's real, they can prove it at Langley, but if it's fake, he must be told that. He needs to know before he commits any forces. He needs to know about the conspiracy. He needs to stop this war or end it." Porter's speech became increasingly urgent.

"Then take it to him," Mark answered defiantly. "We're finished."

No, we're not," Jennifer stated flatly from across the room.

"Without us there, he has no witnesses, and the microfilm won't be worth much."

Mark looked from one to the other, allowed another ten seconds to pass, then walked to the sofa and, lifting his bag from the floor next to it, reached for Jennifer's hand and said, "let's go." If she could continue, then so could he.

The three of them stepped over Mustafa's legs where they lay crumpled under him in the doorway and calmly ascended the elevator to the public level of the safe house. They left through the garage, after Porter pleasantly asked one of the kitchen staff to please have supper for three ready by six o'clock. They put all of their bags into the back of the white Lexus LX 470 that sat waiting for them and drove off. They would figure their next move once they were clear of the safe house. They knew all of those break-in's of the Pentagon computer would be traced eventually, and they didn't want to be anywhere around when the men from the "company" arrived.

Chapter 35

"Ping!" The barely audible tone alerted Andrew Dalton to the arrival of an email message arriving at the computer that sat next to his desk. This was his real office, the one the public rarely got to see. It was large, but the clutter of folders, papers, memoranda, and to-do items on his desk and some of the surrounding furniture made it seem deceptively small. He knew it was a private email because since he had his own server installed when he first occupied this office, he had given his "private address" to no more than a few dozen people. These were people he trusted, and whom he didn't want to have to go through official channels or expose unpopular ideas to third-party scrutiny. He wanted them to be able to speak plainly about issues or, in a few cases, they were old friends whom he simply wanted to be able to say hello without being "sorted" into a "private" directory by a secretary. He was reading a memorandum from Bob Schiener at the NSA about troop movements that had been detected within Iraq and Iran. The Iraqis and Iranians were both moving troops to the Northwest. More surprisingly, though, was that though the area toward which Iran was moving troops shared a common border with Iraq, their enemy, no Iraqi troops were moving to counter them. There was also movement of heavy equipment to three separate areas in Iran where Saddam Hussein was suspected of secreting missile sites, but UNSCOM had never been able to find them, so there was no proof. There was also a great deal of movement around an area about 100 Km Northwest of Baghdad. There was no question that this was a facility that was able to produce chemical and biological weapons, but two inspections had provided no evidence. The troop movements were puzzling, and there were several pages of "Intel. assessments" that followed, but no hard answers. "Well," President Dalton thought to himself, "we have two carrier groups in the area since that last attack, I wonder if it's time to begin moving additional ground forces into the area again." "But to where?" he wondered.

"Ping!" Another message arrived, and interrupted his train of thought. "OK," he said to the computer, as though it was a person sitting there, "let's see what's you've got for me." He pushed the "On" button of his monitor, and a moment later, the large LCD screen came to life. He hoped that no one got to see the screen saver he had—a "morphed" picture of his predecessor in a "compromising position." No one had yet been able to determine whether the Impeachment proceedings helped or hurt his party, even this long after his election.

In the lower right hand corner of the screen was the small icon of an envelope indicating unread email. He moved the mouse pointer to the envelope and clicked, causing it to expand into a window with a list of several emails awaiting his attention. He scanned the list. The first one he picked was from his old friend Alex. They had been in law school together, but took separate courses after graduation. He hadn't talked with him in months, but he remained his best friend. If he ever needed someone to just "talk to," Alex was the one he would trust. Reading his note brought back images of sitting in the apartment they shared during school, getting "wasted" and listening to endless hours of the Grateful Dead, the Beatles, Chicago…When he finished that note and filed it, he continued scanning the list until his eyes fell on the last two. They were both from Jennifer Lynch. He "double-clicked" on the first icon, and it expanded to fill most of the screen. They weren't encrypted, and he didn't think the style of writing was hers, but it arrived with her ID and password used. He doubted she would give them to anyone else, but since she was one of the few who even knew of this address, there would be nobody that would even think to ask. As he read, he knew it was written by someone else, but the remark about the time they..., well, there was no doubt that it came from Jennifer.

The first of the two notes was more than five pages in length. It described, in only minimal detail an improbable sequence of events. It began with Jennifer, and another American whom she had met, Mark Harmon, being forced out of London after killing several of their assailants, and ended with their aligning themselves with a known terrorist and hiding in the safe house in Paris, from which he had received her previous email. Most importantly, however, it contained a theory of the most wide spread conspiracy he had ever heard. It would have seemed absolutely preposterous had it not come from Jennifer. As he read, he forgot about the origin, the circumstances by which it came to him, and he found himself becoming increasingly absorbed. As irrational as the whole thing sounded, it explained many things that had been troubling him lately. There were orders that appeared to come from nowhere. A nuclear device no larger than a suitcase, planted in the largest metropolitan area on earth and discovered almost immediately, followed by the immediate call for more funds to fight terrorism. An air battle between US and Russian aircraft that should never have happened, and the order for which was vigorously denied, in private, by a Russian President who, himself, seemed worried about a loss of control. By the time he was finished reading, and the accusation that Stuart Hallsey was not only involved but may be leading the American branch of this conspiracy, perspiration was dripping from his forehead onto the desk in front of him, and the smell of it filled the room. It was a smell that mixed anger and fear. The attached files of transactions, he believed, could be confirmed if he could get to them before anyone else did. As he sat there, his anger turned to rage. He was a politician. He had spent a lifetime acquiring the power he had, but the people had given him it to him. Regardless of the political infighting, schemes to raise campaign funds, *Quid Pro Quo* deals and dirty tricks, he believed in his country and the system, and would never tolerate it's being destroyed from within, any more than he would allow a foreign invasion. He would investigate this now, tonight, and if it was true, and Hallsey was involved, he would see to it that he was executed for High Treason.

Without thinking about it, he double-clicked on the final envelope icon and though he subconsciously remembered its origin, was consciously surprised that it, too, was from Jennifer. He couldn't imagine what else she could have to say after the last note, but as he read on, his rage was replaced with a fear he hadn't known since he was a boy during the Cuban Missile Crisis. He felt flushed, but no sweat came. His jaw dropped, and his mouth became dry. He began to remember the NSA report he had read, the increasingly aggressive attitude of the Pakistani government, and the increased attacks on the International Peacekeeping troops in Bosnia and Kosovo. This wasn't a product of the conspiracy, even if it did exist. This was a real threat that needed t o be dealt with quickly. The attached file with the scanned Iraqi documents was more than convincing despite the fact that he didn't understand most of it, and had no idea of the price that was paid to get it to him.

It rarely took Andrew Dalton long to act when he felt it was needed, but this was becoming complicated. He needed to find out about the possible conspiracy, and even warn others, in Russia, in France, in England, Germany, Japan…the list went on. But it had to wait. It couldn't be done until this potential attack from the Iraqis and their new allies had been dealt with. He wondered if any pervious president had ever been handed a combination of catastrophic problems like this. Only minutes passed as he sat there thinking, when the telephone rang. Without even asking who it was, he stabbed at the intercom button and in chopped tones said, "not now," then pushed the button again to disconnect. Another minute, and he reached for the yellow legal pad on his desk, wrote a list of names down the left hand margin, and reached for the phone.

"Marge?"

"Yes, Mr. President?" her voice remained calm and pleasant despite his curt tone. She had been his personal secretary since he was a City Councilman, she followed him into the Governor's office, and then to the White House. He didn't know what he would have done without her.

"I've got a list of people I want you to call for me. I want them here for a meeting in two hours."

"Yes, Mr. President." She was unhurried and stable.

"Oh, Marge?" She was still on the phone. She never hung up before he did because she realized years ago that he frequently thought of one or two more things for her to do before he was finished.

"Yes, Sir?" Her stability helped him to remain equally calm.

"When you call Bob Wallace and Tony St. James, have them meet me here an hour earlier than the others, and let me know when you have Bob on the phone, I want to speak with him on a secure line before he comes."

"Yes, Mr. President." He hung up the telephone, knowing that she was already calling the first name on the list.

Standing up, he folded the printouts of the emails and files he had been sent by Jennifer, and took them with him as he went to the bathroom to splash water on his face. This was going to be a long night. Finally, he walked to the large desk in the Oval Office where his jacket had been hung over the large leather chair that he had brought from home and sat heavily, staring at the folded sheets. "A long night," he said to no one in particular.

He was still staring when the tone sounded on the intercom.

"Mr. President?"

"Yes, Marge?"

"I have Mr. Wallace holding on line 6, as you asked."

"Thank you," the President answered, paused for a few seconds, then picked up the phone. Scrambling technology had improved through the years, but there was still a trace of the hollow sound in the secure telephone line.

"Bob"

"Yes, Mr. President." Bob sounded more curious than excited, as though he were asking why he was being disturbed at this time of night.

"Marge told you about the meeting tonight?"

"Yes, Sir, although she didn't say what it is about." Dalton ignored the question, and responded,

"There's something I'd like you to do before you come. I'm sending you a file that was emailed to me. It appears to have originated in Iraq, and I need it's authenticity and information verified. Then, I need you to go to the office and bring all of the current "intel" and satellite photos of the entire Middle East region, including Iraq and Iran, as well as recon on Pakistan and the Balkans. I also want any evidence of military activity in China, Azerbajan, and Kazakstan." There was a moment of silence at the other end. He knew what Bob was thinking. "Look, Bob, I know this is short notice, and there is no way you should be able to do what I just asked, but do it anyway, OK?"

"Yes, Mr. President." There was resignation in his voice, but he could hear the wheels turning, trying to decide how he could delegate tasks to get it all done.

"One more thing, Bob" the President hated to hit him with this, but he had to. "Don't let anyone know what you're doing, what information you're gathering, or why."

A short silence was followed by, "but…" then a final, "Yes, Sir," and the line went dead.

Andrew Dalton hung up the telephone and sat with his eyes shut. He was preparing for the most difficult days of his presidency and, perhaps, the most dangerous the world had ever known. Would he be up to it? How would history remember him? Would there be history to remember?

The hour since he asked Marge to make the calls passed too quickly, and he was still formulating his approach when Tony St. John was announced by Marge, and entered the Oval Office. He was a large man, at least six feet three inches in height and more than 220lbs;

most of it developed muscle. His dark hair and eyes gave him an even more powerful look, and he fostered this appearance by wearing clothes that emphasized his physique, and making sure his booming voice tended to dominate any conversation. All of this tended to obscure his real value to the President, his overpowering intellect. Tony had received his Bachelor's degree from the Woodrow Wilson School of Public and International Affairs at Princeton University, followed by Law School at Yale, where he not only habitually made Law Review, but served as editor. He had known Andrew Dalton since working with him in many of his early campaigns, and had come to respect his intellect, dedication and direct approach to problems. He was happy to count him as a friend. The President rose, walked the short distance across the Presidential Seal in the carpet toward the door, and reached for his hand.

"Tony, thank you for coming on such short notice."

"Not at all, Mr. President. I know you wouldn't have called me if there weren't a good reason." He remained standing in the same location, appearing to wait for an answer, but President Dalton wasn't yet ready to share the problem, so he motioned for him to be seated on the sofa.

"Tony, what do you know about the situation in Iraq and Iran, especially with relation to "nukes" and CBW?" St. John was wary.

"Well," he responded softly, "I've read the reports of troop movements, and there have been stories of CBW manufacture and deployment for years, but nothing has ever been proven." He left it at that, waiting for additional clues to the nature of the problem. Dalton was pacing around the room, occasionally stopping to examine paintings.

"I have reason to believe that there is an attack planned against a number of western countries using nuclear, and biological weapons, in the immediate future."

"That's crazy!" St. John had risen to his feet to face the President. "They know they couldn't win such an exchange. We know they've been developing these weapons to use against each other, but they couldn't hope to win any kind of war against us." The President walked back to face St. John.

"Perhaps you and I know that, but suppose they don't. Remember, this is the same man that believed he could win Desert Storm. More importantly, suppose he has allies." St. John thought for another minute then answered,

"What about delivery systems? Where would they get them?"

"Come on, Tony," the President looked surprised. "They've been buying missile systems from the Chinese for years, and most of the nuclear information that China stole from us in the late '90's has been on the market since then also. Besides, how much of a delivery system does it take to get a few bacteria or viruses into a country? Anyway," he continued, "we'll have a better idea in a little while."

Without preamble, the President changed the subject.

"Suppose all of this is true and we need to take action against it. How do we present it to the country?"

"You'd have to tell them, of course, and don't forget about congress. Shall I ask the Speaker and the committee heads, as well as Senator…"

"No!" The President was emphatic. He paced for a short time, then sat on the sofa facing St. John. "Tony, there's another reason I asked you to come early." Once again Dalton was quiet for a moment, and St. John knew not to push him. "I want to tell you a story before the others arrive, then I want you to look at some evidence, and then I want you to say nothing to anyone about this until I tell you it's time." He paused for just a second, then continued, "I just want someone else to know about it and have access to the information." As he handed the email and copies of the transaction files to St. John, he added, "…and I guarantee the source of the information."

It took several minutes for the pages to be read and re-read. St. John wanted to make sure he had made no mistake in his interpretation the first time. When he had finished, he sat quietly, staring first at the sheath of papers in front of him, then at the President, then back at the papers again.

"Andy..." He hadn't used the President's first name in a long time, but the information in front of him shook him out of his role.

"I understand," Dalton answered. St. John stood, looking down at the President sitting on the sofa.

"We have to expose this. My god! This maniac has usurped the authority of the whole government just by using a fucking computer!"

"We can't do anything yet, Tony," answered Dalton, "we need him and his expertise to deal with Iraq. When that's over..." Dalton was still concerned about the look in St. John's eyes. "Look, it's important that you not let on to *anyone* that you know *anything*. I don't want you looking cross-eyed at Hallsey tonight. It's important." Anthony St. John, White House Chief of Staff and one of the President's oldest friends handed the sheath of papers back to the President and sat back on the sofa. A minute went by, and his face had visibly cleared, when he raised his eyes and answered.

"Yes, Mr. President."

Barbara, one of several assistant secretaries (now known as "personal assistants") wheeled a silver cart with a tureen of coffee and stacks of cups and saucers into the Oval Office after knocking and being invited in, then turned and disappeared back into the outer office. Each got their own coffee, and Dalton was sipping his from a mug labeled "Dad," when Bob Wallace was announced and entered. He hadn't expected St. John to be there, but showed no surprise at finding him there.

"Good evening, Mr. President, Tony..." They exchanged friendly greetings and, after getting some coffee for himself, Wallace sat on the sofa across from St. John, giving no indication of the contents of the large case he carried with him. He was nearly the opposite of St. John in stature, with fairly narrow shoulders and a receding hairline. At 57, his waistline showed none of the toning effect that St. John's did. He eschewed exercise in favor of lying on the hammock in his yard, and his idea of "low fat" involved lean corned beef. For all of that, no one doubted his intellect or strength of character. He had been recruited for the CIA right out of Stanford, where he had earned a Ph.D. in Mathematics, with a specialization in Cryptography. Despite his credentials, no one who wanted his attention ever called him "doctor." "When they stop giving doctorates in basket weaving," he would quip, "then I'll use it again." He spoke six languages fluently, and had served as a "spook" both in the Middle East, and the old Soviet Union before being tagged for an administrative job at the "Company." It was almost three years since he had been appointed Director of the NSA, and doubled as the National Security Advisor to President Dalton.

The President returned to his usual seat at the head of the facing sofas, and waited until the two had exchanged their pleasantries before he began to speak. Somehow, he sensed that maintaining some semblance of normalcy was imperative.

"I have some things that you each need to know, and we don't have much time before the others arrive, and you each need to be brought up to speed on what the other knows." He paused for a sip of coffee that was becoming tepid, then retrieved the folded papers from his desk and handed them to Wallace. He explained what they represented, who was involved...essentially everything he had told St. John, including the admonition not to allow even a hint of the knowledge until the time was right. Wallace looked as shocked as St. John had, but he knew that the president couldn't act now because of what he had in his bag.

When he finished, he asked Wallace, "did you get everything I asked for?"

"Yes, Mr. President," Andrew Dalton wasn't someone you disappointed.

"Before we go over any of it, Bob," the President continued, "let me fill Tony in on what it's about."

It took about ten minutes to rough out the details of the events surrounding the microfilm, and he had to stop several times because, for the sake of brevity, there were things that weren't clear to St. John. When he was finished, and convinced that he understood everything, Dalton turned to Wallace to ask,

"OK, Bob, what did you find out?" Bob Wallace opened what looked like a large sample case, and withdrew several folders and Manila envelopes, laying them carefully on the coffee table in front of him.

"Mr. President, I collected the information you asked for and found, as I think you suspected, that in the last week there have been significant movement of troops, equipment, and materials throughout the region. Also, both Sat-Tel and airborne assets confirmed similar movement throughout Pakistan and the Balkans." He stopped and withdrew a folded world map, on which the placement of various military assets was noted with a date next to each, and arrows explaining their movement to another position with a later date. This included, to the President's surprise, a slow movement during the last two months, of nearly 60 divisions from China's interior to the Manchurian Border. Russia, of course, had moved almost 20 divisions to oppose them, along with moving eighteen ships to the Chinese coast including two aircraft carriers and three nuclear missile submarines from their bases in Vladivostok and the Kamchatka Peninsula. When he got through with this preliminary information, Wallace pulled out the copies of the files that the President had sent him, and laid them on the table, on top of the maps.

"Mr. President," he paused, looked at Tony St. John, and continued, "are you sure of the source of these documents? I mean, are you sure they're real?"

"That's not in question," the President responded."

"Then whoever sent you these knows something about CBW, but they missed a lot. There is much more detail in these documents than I was led to believe. This is a description of a combination of a biological and nuclear attack against nine countries, the most devastating of which would be against the US and Russia."

When he paused to catch his breath, the President re-stated that he understood that the documents contained many of these things. Wallace looked at the President and tried to assess how much he actually understood of what he had seen, and decided that there was a very incomplete understanding, or he would be less calm.

"Mr. President, I don't think you understand, and I'm sure the source didn't really comprehend what this is. This includes plans for nuclear missile launches, ground attacks, and dispersion of biological weapons and, by its nature, reveals secret alliances, and even timetables." He watched Dalton's face as he enumerated the contents of the documents, and decided that he might as well hit him with everything at once. "The world is going to be at war within a week, maybe less, if nothing is done to stop it."

Through all of the descriptions and pronouncements, Tony St. John had remained silent. Now he felt compelled to enter the discussion.

"Mr. President," this can't possibly be true." He looked at Bob Wallace, "you're asking us to believe that we're on the brink of global holocaust, and we never knew it?"

"Not exactly," responded Wallace. We've been watching the troop movements for sometime, but they appeared unconnected. We've seen each of them from time to time during the last several years. It is the combination of all of them, along with this additional information that makes this believable."

The President ended this part of the conversation by rising, walking to his desk and telling Marge to reschedule the meeting he had called for two hours from now, and we'll hold it in the "Sit-room." Before she had a chance to answer, he punched the button to clear the intercom, and then turned to face the only other two people in the world who knew what he knew.

"Bob, I want you to prepare a presentation for this meeting. Tony, we're going to have to address the nation in about 48 hours. Once this initial meeting is over, I want a media plan on my desk in 12 hours, and a report on our preparedness to cope if the attacks that are described in these document actually take place."

The President rose, looked at each of them in turn, then added, "I'm counting on you, gentlemen. See you in the Sit-room." They understood that they had been dismissed, and knew that they had more work to do than they could possibly accomplish, so answered, almost in unison, "Mr. President," then turned and left the room.

The President sat alone in his chair, behind the large desk in the Oval Office. He stared at the paintings on the walls, the papers on his desk, and the flat panel computer display facing him and lowered his throbbing head into his hands. This wasn't going to be easy given the number of countries that needed to work together, and his only live witnesses weren't around. "Where are you, "Jenn?" He asked the empty air. "Where are you…?"

Chapter 36

Porter took over the driver's side of the large Lexus, with Jennifer remaining in the front passenger seat while Mark took his place in back.

"Where are we going?" Mark's tone was more resignation than question.

"We need to get back to the States, but we can't go through London or Shannon because the two of you are wanted there. We're going to take a flight from De Gaul Airport." He spoke intensely as he drove, never taking his eyes from the road, but unzipping the outer pocket of his equipment bag and taking out a brown envelope.

"Here," he handed it to Jennifer. "You are Lisa Mann. You and your husband Steven are returning to New York from a vacation in Paris." Jennifer opened the envelope and removed two US passports one with her photo, and the other with Mark's.

"You've been busy, haven't you?" Mark sounded surprised as he examined his new credentials. Jennifer remained quiet.

"You'll find money, passports, driver's licenses, and a few receipts in the passport wallets." They had arrived at the airport, and Porter stopped just beyond the terminal. "I'm on the next flight. We don't want to be seen together. Give me the microfilm."

"Why?" Mark asked.

"Because no one is looking for me, yet. If they find you, I can at least get the film to the President." Mark thought for a moment, found no help from Jennifer, so he reached into this pocket and withdrew the re-glued match book. It was amazing to believe that the thing he held in his hand had begun the entire adventure. He didn't know why, but it made him feel better to have it, so he replaced it in his pocket and explained to Porter that he intended to keep it himself.

"We haven't been stopped yet," he answered. Porter looked disturbed, and turned to Jennifer.

"Explain to him why I should carry it…please."

Jennifer looked from one to the other, and said nothing for a moment, then answered, "I trust him, Porter. Let him hold it." That settled it as far as Mark was concerned, and he got out of the car and opened Jennifer's door.

The walk to the terminal was without incident. They were tourists. Their baggage had been sent ahead, and check-in took only a few minutes. It was always a standing joke with his kids that Mark always set off the metal detector, but not this time.

Once ensconced in their comfortable First Class seats with the "stretch 747" accelerating down the runway, Mark looked at Jennifer, whose gaze out the window left him feeling jealous. She was thinking of Mustafa, and there was nothing he could do to fight a ghost. Her left hand had been gripping the armrest as she watched the ground disappearing behind them. He reached out and took it in his own, and cupped it in his other hand. She looked at him, and with her eyes watering, she lay her head on his shoulder.

The landing at Kennedy airport was uneventful, leaving Mark and Jennifer to get to Pennsylvania Station to catch the Metroliner to D.C. The cabs were queued in front of the Air France terminal, and Mark and Jennifer moved quickly toward the first in line. As they approached, they found themselves being hailed by a man in a dark gray pinstripe suit, matched with a University stripe tie.

"Mark! Jennifer! How are you?" They looked at him, and at each other, realizing they'd been made, but before they could even alter their route, Mark felt what he assumed was the barrel of a gun in his back, and a hand placed on his left shoulder.

"Keep moving," the man was dressed much like the man who had hailed them, but without the smoothness in his voice. "Walk toward the Mercedes, and get in." He directed them toward a large silver Mercedes 600 SEL, and opened the door for them. Once seated in the back seat, the second man slid in beside them, the gun exposed and pointing at the left side of Jennifer's abdomen. The first man walked to the front and got into the passenger seat, with the driver already in place. "Let's go," he said to the driver, and the huge car accelerated smoothly into traffic.

"Where are we going?" asked Mark. There was no answer, but the man in the front seat withdrew a phone from his pocket, punched a few keys, and talked quietly for a few moments, then handed the phone to Mark.

"Hello?" Mark spoke cautiously into the phone.

"Mark?" Hearing Meredith's voice at the other end was difficult, and there was tension there, but he knew what he had to do.

"Meredith? It's Mark." Somehow, although they had been married for fifteen years, he still felt as though she might not recognize his voice and so he had to identify himself.

"Mark…" her voice was tremulous. He was about to tell her that he was coming, when another voice interrupted his thoughts.

"Harmon?" A deep voice had replaced Meredith's. "Are you there?" the voice asked.

"I'm here," Mark answered confused. The deep voice spoke in clipped tones, as though his speech had been over-rehearsed.

"We have your wife and children here with us. Cooperate. Give us the microfilm. Once we have it, we have no reason to do anything to you or your family. You'll be free to go." Mark knew Jennifer couldn't hear what was being said, and he desperately wanted her to so he could ask her what to do. They were being brought along until the microfilm was tested and found to be real.

"We'll come quietly," he said, and handed the telephone back to the man in the front seat. He looked at Jennifer. "They have my family. If we give them the microfilm, they'll let us go. They can't be hurt by us after that." He looked into her eyes, and knew she understood and agreed. They would never let them live. As soon as they had the microfilm, they would kill everyone and there would be no trace. They couldn't allow anyone to find out what had really happened.

The car proceeded through the Holland Tunnel, and onto the New Jersey Turnpike.

"Were are you taking us?" Mark asked again. There was no answer, so he sat back to think. They could never allow the car to reach its destination with these men in charge. They were slowed in traffic about a half hour after leaving Manhattan, when Mark shifted in his seat. The man on Jennifer's left had relaxed, and with small touches he caused Jennifer to notice it. She was ready when he was. After everything they had been through, there was a bond between them.

Three more minutes passed. The car lurched forward for the fourth time, and was brought up short by traffic, but this time, Mark allowed his weight to be thrown forward by the movement of the car. At first, it seemed a natural, although inept movement, but in less than a second, his right hand had reached around the head to grab the chin of the man in the right front seat. He used his left hand to push his left shoulder down, then leaned back, pulling sharply around on the jaw until he felt the neck crack, and the man's body go limp. On his left, the man holding the gun on Jennifer had been caught by surprise. His indecision lasted only a fraction of a second, but it was enough. Jennifer grabbed the gun and the man's left hand, raising it toward the ceiling of the car as her left hand opened and slammed into his throat. The sound of his gurgling was masked as the gun exploded, shattering the back of the head of the man driving the car.

"Quick!" Jennifer said to Mark as the car drifted into the car in front of it in traffic. "Get around and drive!"

It took a second for him to recover, by which time, Jennifer had already opened the left rear door and pushed the gunman out as she exited the car and ran to the other side. Mark opened his door, ran around the back of the car, and pulled the driver out onto the highway as he got into the driver's seat. Jennifer had already pulled the other man onto the road and sat beside him in the passenger side. She fumbled with the body for a few seconds before closing the door, then yelled, "get out of here, now!" Mark looked around, and decided that there was only one option, He twisted the wheel and accelerated onto the shoulder of the road, feeling a bump as the rear wheel ran over the body of the man who had occupied the front seat.

As he approached an exit, Jennifer pointed and said, "get off here." Another three minutes and they sat in the parking lot of a Wendy's, taking deep breaths and getting themselves composed.

Mark felt relieved, but turned to ask Jennifer, "OK, what now?"

"We have to get to your family," Jennifer answered.

"But we don't even know were they're being held," Mark said plaintively.

Jennifer smiled, "yes we do." She reached into her pocket, and withdrew the pocket phone that she had removed from the man in the front seat. Flipping it open, she touched the "Recall" button, and the number appeared in the LCD display.

"All we have to do is call to find out where they are."

"No we don't," Mark answered, "that's my home number. They're at my house."

"Let's go get them," Jennifer said quietly, and reached into her pocket and withdrew two guns that she had taken from two corpses.

Mark looked at her, reached for her head with his right hand, and stroked her hair.

"You don't have to do this," he said. "Take the microfilm to the White House and I'll get to my family."

"No." She was firm. "We do this together." She turned in the seat and faced him. "Mark, I think you know how I feel about you, and I believe I know how you feel about me..." She paused, then continued. "You have a wife and family, and I won't be the *other woman*. I can't play that role, and I can't break up a home, so there aren't many options left." She pulled her hand from his, and turned to look out of the window again. Mark felt the pain in the pit of his stomach as she turned away and said to the window, "I won't fight ghosts. Lets get your family and end this thing, and then we can sort out the rest."

It was nearly over now. All they had to do was get the microfilm to the President and verify the conspiracy, and they could return to their lives, only...

"Jenn?" She looked back at him, her eyes red. "I told you, in Paris, that my relationship with Meredith ended years ago. I won't tell you that my sons aren't the most important people in the world to me, but there is no real "family" to keep together anymore. There is only a house and a roommate." He stopped, and looked at her before continuing. He couldn't quite place the look in her eyes, but it wasn't what he had seen before.

"I'll tell you what we're going to do," he said with resolution. "Porter won't be in DC until tonight. We were going to wait for him anyway. We'll head to my house, and somehow figure something out." He paused, then continued, "when this is over, I'm going to tell Meredith about us. I owe her that much. The boys will be there, so everything can be out in the open." He stopped and turned to face her. "I love you." He had said it so many times to Meredith without meaning, trying to hold their marriage together, that saying it now, to Jennifer, felt like lifting a weight. "I think I've loved you, from the moment I saw you, but never considered the possibility that you would,...could ever love me."

He paused, tears were running down her cheeks, and she was making no attempt to wipe them away. A moment passed, without a word, before Jennifer leaned forward, pulled his head down and kissed him with a depth he hadn't felt in years. It was a kiss that came, not from the heart, but from the soul. It was a kiss that said that the world could go to hell, and them with it, as long as they were together. It was the kiss he had dreamed of all his life. For long moments, they held each other. When their lips parted, their decision had been made. Still, his face was ashen. She felt the weight in his heart. They were holding his family, they couldn't call anyone, and he wasn't sure if they could do it themselves.

"Mark, listen to me! You know you can't just give them the microfilm," she reiterated, "and you also know we can do this. After all we've been through, you know that."

He did know, but damn it, it was his family...his sons...Now he felt anger grow in him as he hadn't felt it ever before. For the first time, he understood "fury." He wouldn't let them get away with this. They would pay, whoever they were! She waited for him to calm down, then began again.

"We also need to know who "They" are. How did they know you would be coming back here? How did they know you still had the microfilm?

Mark looked at Jennifer, wanting to hold her again, but the time was wrong. He wanted to tell her not to come, it was his fight, and he didn't want her to get hurt, but he knew she was right.

"I love you," was all he could get out.

"I know," And she smiled at him. "I need to let the President know I'm here, and that we'll be coming in with the microfilm after we take care of some unfinished business." She dialed the phone, and waited for an answer.

"This is Jennifer Lynch," she said to the secretary at the other end. "Put me through to the President." She knew she was taking a chance with everyone looking for them, but he had to know. Only seconds passed before she heard the familiar voice.

"Jennifer!" It was Andrew Dalton." "My God, do you know how many times you've been reported dead?"

"Mr. President," she began, glad he was happy to hear from her, but needing to get this done with quickly. "I'm on my way to the White House with someone, and something I think you need to know. We should be there tonight or tomorrow." She stopped, waiting for him to answer, but when he did, it was with concern.

"You need to get here now," he said. "We're downstairs. Do you understand?" She did. They were in the Situation Room, the "War Room." "Things will begin to happen in less than eighteen hours. We need you and that thing you have with you. I'm sending a chopper for you."

"No! You can't do that. It's important that we come to you our way. You'll understand when we get there. We'll be there on time, Mr. President." She was about to hang up, when she had one last thought. "Please, Mr. President. It's imperative that you don't take any action until we get there."

"I'll try," answered the President, but things may get out of my control." She hung up the phone and looked at Mark.

"We have eighteen hours, then it won't matter." She looked at her watch, it read just before noon.

"Eighteen hours…" The thought ran through both their minds as Mark restarted the car's engine, and headed back to the turnpike.

Chapter 37

Andrew Dalton returned to his seat at the middle of the horseshoe shaped table after the brief telephone conversation with Jennifer. She was back, and would be here soon, but asked him to do nothing until she arrived...and that was exactly what he couldn't do. There was too much at stake.

"Mr. President," Hallsey began a new round of conversations, and Dalton made a conscious effort to suppress his attitude toward the man as a traitor. He was still the Chairman of the Joint Chief's, and the best Strategist Dalton had ever known. "I think our next moves are clear. We have enough power in that area now to handle Iraq, and if we are in contact with Russia and some of the more moderate countries in the area, I don' think they will react."

Dalton waited a moment for Hallsey to continue and, when he didn't, asked, "OK, Admiral, how would you *handle* this situation?"

Hallsey paused for a few moments, looked back at the situation board, being updated continuously by the computer, and answered, "We know where the Iraqi missile facilities are. We know where their CBW plants are, despite their efforts to hide them. Three, low yield nuclear strikes would be enough to take out 98% of his capacity to launch this type of an attack, and a good chunk of his military with it. There would be some substantial collateral damage, of course, but given our proof of his intentions, I don't see how anyone in the world could do more than bluster. The very fact of our attack would quell any idea of retaliation by anyone."

The room was deadly quiet. Dalton sat with his head turned to the left, staring at Hallsey.

"Admiral, do you understand what you are saying?"

"Yes sir, Mr. President. I don't like it any better than you do, but it is the only way to eliminate the threat in one strike, before those weapons can be used against us. And if our intelligence is correct, that will be in a matter of hours, days at the outside."

"We'd kill hundreds of thousands of people, maybe millions!" Dalton's manner belied the mixture of anger, revulsion, and fear behind his words. "Besides, what if they launch, as we would, on warning of attack?"

"They can't, Mr. President. First, they haven't the warning systems we have, and secondly, a launch from a submarine would arrive at its target before its detection was ever relayed back to Saddam." He paused then continued, "It would be over before they were aware it had begun."

"Mr. President," broke in Warren ("Wes") Shoemaker. He was young to hold the job of CIA Director, but he had proven his abilities and his intelligence many times, and he seemed to possess a sixth sense about world affairs. He seemed able to have assets in place before things broke, rather than after. For that reason, Dalton had enjoyed better intelligence information through most of his presidency, than had his last several predecessors.

He continued, "I agree with admiral Hallsey's assessment of what needs to be done, but we haven't yet gotten any independent confirmation from our ground assets. All we're going on is Satellite and air Recon photos, computer analysis, and interception of electronic traffic by the NSA." He stopped again, looking around the table at the directors of the agencies involved. "I'm sure we'll get confirmation soon, but do you really want to be the one to launch a pre-emptive nuclear strike without confirmation?"

"Damn it, Wes," Hallsey broke in, "We can't wait for your spooks to get up off their asses and tell us what's happening! According to our "intel," this is going down now!"

"Mr. President." This time it was Bob Wallace calling for the President's attention. "I agree with the Admiral. We can't afford to wait until it's too late. Besides, there is a lot of diplomatic groundwork to lay before the actual attack."

Dalton looked around the table, waiting for other opinions.

"Tony?" He hadn't yet heard from St. John, and he wanted another opinion badly.

"Mr. President, I think we need to leave both options open. I've spoken with Secretary Daimler, and General Lakewood, and they believe that there is still a little time left before we have to push the button. Let's give Wes a chance to confirm or deny before we strike." Dalton valued the opinion of both the Secretary of Defense and the Army Chief of Staff, but the decision was his. Should he tell them that he wanted to wait to hear Jennifer's report before proceeding?

"Admiral," the President said, sitting straight up in his chair, "move the submarines into position, and target the Tomahawks, then go to Defcon 2." I'll be in my office upstairs. I need to brief some members of congress, and talk with President Yelenkov."

As he stood, everyone around the table stood as well. The elevator took him back to the West Wing of the White House, and he re-entered the Oval Office. There, sitting at his desk, he buzzed Marge and told her to ask the members of Congress on the list on her desk to come to the White House at 16:00. "Also," he added, "I want Adam Chernikov here within 30 minutes. I don't care where he is, or what he is doing, I want him here." He was the one interpreter that he trusted to give him a sense of the Russian president's feeling, as well as his words. He not only translated, he interpreted.

There was nothing to do now but wait. Would history record him as the man who destroyed the world? Would there be any history left? His head collapsed into his hands, his eyes closed, and his mind went blank except for the internal anguish he felt. For the first time since his election to the Presidency, he wished he had lost.

Chapter 38

They had driven more than 50 miles in relative silence. Mark wasn't sure what to say, and Jennifer wasn't sure what she wanted to hear, so both kept their thoughts to themselves.

"There," Jennifer pointed to a sign indicating I-276. "Get off there, it will take us into Philadelphia." Mark turned off at the exit without comment, and began searching for money to pay the toll when they arrived at the gate.

"Mark," Jennifer turned to him. "I'm with you all the way, you know that, but do you have any idea what you're going to do?"

"Not a clue," Mark confessed. "Look," he continued, there are probably not more than three or four men holding them. It wouldn't make sense to have any more for a woman and two kids, and I know that house better than the architect who designed it. We made changes when we built it. There are weaknesses that we always hoped no one would find out about, but now we can use them." He looked at his watch. "15:02" it read. His kids always joked about him using 24 hr time because of having to time things at his office and the hospital. "We still have plenty of time. I wish we could wait until dark."

"So do I," answered Jennifer, "but we don't have as much time as you think. The President let me understand that they were in the planning stages of an attack. We have to get to him before he commits—before it's too late."

Mark thought for a few minutes, then pulled to the shoulder of the road.

"Jenn, I need you to drive. I'm going to draw a map, and explain how I think we can approach the house, but I can't drive and do it, and we haven't much time." They slid across each other, with Mark sliding over the gearshift and then lifting Jennifer slightly so that she could change places with him. As the car left the shoulder of the highway, Mark searched the glove box and, finding scattered paper and a single pen, he began to draw. It was about 10 minutes until he was finished. "There," and he studied his handiwork. "OK," he said, and held the map so she could see it. "You can see it better when you're not driving, but I wanted you to have an overview as I describe it." He brought it back onto his lap, and studied it as he began.

"There is so much glass in the back of the house, that almost everything is visible, and the transom window makes the entire hill in front of the house visible to anyone who is looking." He stopped and thought for a moment, then added, "I would also put on the alarm system if it were me, that way anyone trying to sneak into an uncovered area would trigger it."

"That makes sense," Jennifer responded without taking her eyes from the road, but it doesn't answer how you intend to get us in."

"There are three points that are relatively blind. The first, is the approach from the cul-de-sac behind the house. It approaches the left rear corner of the house, and is nearly invisible unless someone is looking directly out of the small living room window at that direction. Even so, there is cover if you know where it is, and I do." He turned the paper slightly then began on what he thought of as phase II.

Once we reach the house, there are two ways in past the alarm system. The best is through the second floor. Because of the way the system was designed, there are no alarms on the bedroom windows. That allows people to sleep with the windows open, without having to skip a zone. It also assumes that there is no way to the second floor windows except over the kitchen, where the windows are alarmed." He thought again and added, "There is also no glass breaking sensor. If the windows or doors are not opened, no alarm will go off. We can also enter through the garage, which isn't alarmed, but the door into the house is. Finally, the telephone wires, and the power cables leading to the alarm are buried just about six inches below ground at the right front corner of the house. They're invisible, but easy to get at and cut, and the alarm box is just inside the closet in the basement."

Mark seemed to be thinking as he was talking so Jennifer let him ramble. He continued to study the diagram, then said, "we need to get to a hardware store before we go to the house. There are a few things we need to get in."

By the time they arrived in the city, Mark had a working plan. The problem was, he didn't really know how many people there were holding his family, where they were being held...

"Shit!"

"What's wrong?" Jennifer asked.

"This isn't any good. We don't know enough to make a plan, so this is an exercise in futility."

"No, it's not," Jennifer answered. "Look, I've been in situations like this before. It's true that we can't formulate a legitimate plan until we know more, but you can make a basic plan, then a couple of contingency plans, and if none of them fit, we'll just improvise, adapt and overcome" (a phrase she borrowed from the SEALS).

She made sense. "Besides," Mark asked himself, "what choice do we have?"

By 16:10, they were in a small, local hardware store not far from Mark's house. He didn't usually shop there, but it was on their way, and they didn't have time to go any farther than they had to. In 14 hours, the US, and maybe the world was about to go to war. It took about 20 minutes to find and buy the things Mark wanted. There were suction cups, a glass cutter, insulated shears, thick work gloves for each of them, and a small set of knives, screwdrivers, and pliers. All of these he placed into the small duffel that had held his clothes, and then got behind the wheel of the car.

"Are you going to share your plan with me, or am I supposed to play it by ear?" Jennifer asked, annoyed.

"Get in," Mark said, "I want to go to my office for something." She climbed into the passenger seat and shut the door before asking what he wanted.

"My gun."

"I have the guns from the men in New York," she answered, and reached into her purse to take them out. One was a Glock, which he liked. The other was a Browning "Hi-Power Practical." It's chrome frame and blue slide made it distinctive, while its rubber grip made it really easy to hold. Both were 9 mm, and both were loaded with hollow nose ammunition.

"Here," Jennifer offered him the Glock that she remembered he had always chosen before, and he took it but continued his journey. "I know it sounds nuts, but I want one I've used before This is my family we're talking about." She said nothing more until he emerged from his office building with a bulge in the front of his sweater. When he got into the car, he withdrew a stainless steel Ruger .357 Magnum.

"You keep that in your office?" Jennifer chuckled. "Expecting a war?"

"You never know when some addict will come into the office strung out on something." On the way to his house, Mark made one final stop. Jennifer waited in the car as he emerged from the Sharper Image with a small but very powerful set of binoculars.

It was only a few minutes from Mark's office to his house. It was approaching 17:00, and it was still light at this time of the year. It was the first time he remembered wishing for winter. They drove up the hill, and cruised slowly past the cul-de-sac, at the end of which his house was located. Jennifer held the binoculars to her eyes as they passed the street. There he was, as Mark had predicted, a man sitting on the stairs looking out of the transom window above the door. He continued driving to the next cul-de-sac where he turned in and drove slowly in a circle. From this vantage point, the garage, study, and one of the bedroom windows were visible, as well as the deck. There were no cars parked at the house, so either their car was in the garage, or it was somewhere else. As they drove around the circle, Jennifer could make out one man sitting on a patio chair, looking out across the woods that bordered the rear of the house. "Well, she said, that's two."

They parked on a street leading into the development, from which they could see the corner of the house at which Mark planned his "attack." He was sure they wouldn't be seen from the house, but he wasn't so sure about the man on the deck not hearing them. As they sat there, he now pulled out the diagram again, and carefully explained his plan to Jennifer.

"I doubt they'd be holding anyone in the basement, because the visibility would be poor, and accessibility too good. So, it's my guess that they're being held in the Family Room. That way, they would have almost complete visibility, access to the kitchen area and a bathroom, as well as the TV for news, the computer in the study, and the telephone. It would be ideal for them, and the worst possible place for us."

"I'm glad you figured that our for them," she said, "now what do you have in mind for us?"

"We can get to the left rear corner of the house—there," he pointed as he spoke, and Jennifer followed his finger to the house. "From there," he continued, "we can work out way up the side of the house and cut the telephone and alarm cables. That way, even if we trip the alarm, the police won't show up and get us all into a battle." He stopped for a moment to regroup his thoughts, then continued, "after that we need to get under the deck and into the basement through one of the windows. It won't set off the alarm if we cut the glass and remove it, and they wouldn't have set the motion sensors with them in the house. Once we're inside then the hard part begins because if I'm right about where they're being held, there's no way to get to them without being seen."

"Great," Jennifer interrupted. So you have us in the house where we can't do anything."

"No, I have *me* in the house where I can't do anything. That's where you come in. I'll create enough distraction that they'll come to get me. Perhaps I can take one of them out, perhaps not, but they won't kill me until they have the microfilm. As I'm doing that, you have to take out the man on the deck, and come in through the glass doors. Between the two of us, we can create enough distraction that we should be able to take out most if not all, but at least get my family out." He waited for the obvious answer, and she didn't disappoint him.

"Mark," she paused and put her hand on his arm. I know how much you want to do this, but what you're proposing places them in the line of a cross-fire." "Let me make another suggestion." He waited.

"Cut the phones, then, on cue, take out the men on the deck and the stairs. That will only leave two, maybe three." She paused, knowing his reaction to her next statement, "then let yourself be captured." He looked incredulous. "Once inside, you can make a better assessment of the situation, and they'll have to post at least one person in either the stair or the deck position, probably the stairs because it's less vulnerable. If I can get around front and take him out, that will leave only two. They don't know you, or me, or what we can do, so I'll give myself up also, and we'll work from the inside."

"That's nut's! Mark's reaction was what she expected.

"Look," she said. "I know what I'm doing." He was still looking at her with suspicion, so she touched his chin with her hand, kissed him gently, and softly urged; "trust me." He did.

It was past 18:00 when the phone lines were cut. They had to move slowly and carefully because of the man on the deck. Within ten more minutes, they had synchronized their watches and moved to their respective positions. It was decided, by Jennifer, that Mark would crawled to the top of the hill facing the house, where he could lay on his stomach, and rest the butt of his gun on a small rock next to a large tree. He would be nearly invisible, and the Magnum would be able to penetrate the glass without losing much of its trajectory. Meanwhile, Jennifer crept slowly next to the deck, avoiding the gravel that lay underneath so that she wouldn't be heard. She was in position at the end of deck with two minutes to spare. Each watched the seconds tick away until the appointed time. "I'd never believe I'd be doing this," Mark thought to himself. Then a thought struck him, "what happens if someone in the neighborhood calls the police, and they are arrested or, worse, this became a hostage standoff with the police?" It was too late. As he sighted down the barrel of the Magnum, the countdown timer on his watch beeped, and he gently squeezed the trigger. The sound of Jennifer's gun was lost in the explosion that erupted from the Magnum. As though in slow motion, the glass over his front door shattered, and the man on the steps was thrown back, striking the stairs behind him, then forward, tumbling down the remainder of the stairs.

Mark Jumped to his feet and ran forward, about to allow himself to be seen and captured, when an idea stopped him. With a burst, he ran to the left, out of sight, then smashed the long vertical window at the front of the garage and went through it with only minor cuts to show for his efforts. He made his way past their cars to the garage door, and slowly opened it about three inches. To his surprise, there was no alarm. Perhaps they hadn't thought of that after all. The thought of his enemies making such a simple mistake gave him courage. If they made those kinds of mistakes, they weren't invincible after all. He could see through the darkened pantry and the opposing door that the man he had shot lay at the bottom of the stairs, a pool of blood and shattered glass collected around him. A small man, slightly balding, stood on the fourth step, crouched, holding a gun in his right hand, and periodically peeking above the, now open, transom. From inside the house, he heard a man shouting orders, and the sound of footsteps running.

Then the sound of a slap, and a brusque, "shut up!." He wanted to charge in, but he knew better. With agonizing slowness, so that he made no noise, he swung the door open just a few more inches, and rested the gun on the pantry floor, it's sights on the second man on the stairs. Before he had a chance to cock the gun, he heard the sound of glass breaking, and knew that Jennifer would be coming though the glass doors in the study. The man turned to the sound, and his mouth opened as he saw the barrel of Mark's gun extending through the crack in the door. He crouched lower and swung his weapon toward Mark, but not in time. Mark squeezed the trigger three times before he was sure the man was dead, then rose and stood against the pantry doors, waiting to hear Jennifer give herself up.

It was less than ten seconds before he heard the sound of a struggle, the sound of someone being struck, and the same man's voice calling to Mark to come out before he began killing people, beginning with Meredith.

"OK," he yelled, having little hearing left these few moments after shooting the Magnum in the confined space. "I'm coming out. Don't shoot."

He walked through the door and out into the hallway. Blood was running along the grout between the Terra-cotta tiles, and broken glass crunched beneath his feet. He held his hands high, with the magnum dangling from a thumb to show that it wasn't accessible. "Don't shoot," he said again, as he rounded the corner. The man he faced was more than four inches taller than him, and outweighed him by at least fifty pounds. The gun seemed to be nearly smothered in his right hand, while his left nearly encircled Jennifer's neck. The muzzle of his gun pointed at the back of her head. His two boys sat tied and gagged on the leather sofa against the wall, while Meredith sat bound and gagged in one of the large leather chairs that faced the television, her back to the glass doors leading out to the deck.

"Come in, join us." The man nodded to the other large leather chair, and Mark carefully placed his gun on the floor next to the kitchen counter, then sat in the chair. There was a frantic look in his wife's eyes, and terror in his son's.

"It will be OK," he said, looking at the boys. "Trust me."

"Where's the microfilm?" the gunman demanded.

"I don't have it," Mark answered. "It's coming with someone else who took another flight. We knew you'd be looking for us, so he took it to the White House."

"Is that right?" he asked Jennifer, without releasing his grip.

'Yes," she said softly, the pain in her neck keeping her from speaking properly. Still, before he sat down facing in the other direction, he had seen Jennifer begin inching to the side to position herself for a quick kick or thrust with which she might free herself, and give Mark time to reach for the man's gun. His mind was racing. He had to be ready to act quickly when she made her move. She had been right, this had been the only way to save his family and stay alive. He heard her move once more, behind him, and was about to turn his head to try to see if it was time to move, when a chill ran down his spine, and all hope seemed to vanish.

"I don't think so, old man." From the living room, where he had been waiting with another companion, Porter walked slowly toward them, a smile on his face. "You should have given me the film in Paris," he said, and motioned to the first man to release Jennifer.

"You would have killed us anyway," she was stunned, but couldn't keep from responding.

"I thought you were on the next flight," Mark said questioningly. "How did you get here so quickly?"

"The Concorde has excellent service," Porter answered, "perhaps you should try it someday." He paused for a moment then added, "but of course, you won't get that chance now, will you?" Once more he nodded to the first man, who produced a roll of adhesive tape with which he bound Jennifer's hands behind her, and pushed her down on the sofa next to the boys, then bound her feet. He then moved to Mark, and did the same thing. When he was finished, Porter asked politely, "Now, where is the microfilm?" Mark didn't answer, so Porter reached into Mark's jacket pocket where he had seen him place it in Paris and, sure enough, it was still there.

"Thanks, old man," and Porter placed the matchbook into his own pocket.

"Why?" Jennifer asked. "Why do you want a war? What will you gain by it?" Porter sat on one of the stools at the kitchen counter, and faced the group of prisoners.

"OK," he said, "why not." He reached into his pocket and got out his pipe and tobacco pouch, and began the ritual of filling his pipe as he spoke. He was a professor lecturing to a class, imparting information without emotion.

"You were right about the "Shadow Government," you know. But it is much more extensive than you can even imagine. We control the computers, and the computers control the world. There was no way we could be discovered using the Internet and Satellite relays. Besides, who would be looking?" He paused to take out a silver metal pipe tool, tamp down the tobacco, and then begin again. "It began with the simple objective of keeping the funds flowing to the military while not letting terrorism get out of hand. It was a self centered motive, to be sure, but it did serve the purpose of controlling many violent groups that could have easily gotten out of control. After all, we held the purse strings.

Fighting terrorism wasn't enough, though. You don't fight terrorists with billion dollar aircraft, million dollar Tomahawk cruise missiles, and submarines, so an occasional war became necessary. The Gulf War was a gift because Saddam did that all by himself. We could expend all our energy on fighting him. When that was over, though, all we were managing was the occasional bombing raid to blow up a suspected Chemical Weapons factory." He paused again, drew on his pipe several times as he held the butane lighter above it, then continued as he exhaled the smoke. "Then there was the occasional confrontation between Russia and the US. A few aircraft ordered into the wrong area..." We had to keep tensions high, although there was never any real danger of war since we controlled both sides.

"Bosnia came next, followed by Kosovo. We were glad that a butcher like Milosovic was in power in Yugoslavia, because it made it much easier to convince the politicians at NATO that he was moving troops toward Bosnia, then Kosovo. They bombed the hell out of Serbia and, when it was done, Russia convinced Milosovic to consent to an International peacekeeping force in Kosovo, thus raising their stature in the world and re-stabilizing the region, all at the same time." He smiled again. Mark was beginning to hate that smile more than anything in the world.

"During all of this time, of course, we had an underlying plan. Scattered terrorism and brush wars were OK, but it takes two real enemies to provide stability in the world. Just think how things have come apart since the end of the Cold War. We found that enemy in China, a country with an ancient sense of greatness, and a modern inferiority complex. We encouraged their agents to infiltrate the American scientific and bureaucratic infrastructure. And even prevented any real action from being taken to prevent their espionage until they had stolen enough to reach scientific parity with the U.S., despite the fact that the FBI and Justice Department were aware of the theft. That made them feel safer, made the U.S. more wary, and began the next arms race."

"Finally, we found out that Saddam was planning to invade Iran again, and his generals, some of whom are with us, were unable to stop him. Now, it isn't that we love Iran so much, but we couldn't allow a renegade state to exist. Still, it wasn't likely that any country would voluntarily interfere with that war, so we had to come up with something. We began with missile attacks on shipping that appeared to be Iranian, followed by Iraqi gunboats operating from Iranian bases. We planted the information about Saddam's planned nuclear and CBW attack, and let it fall into the hands of the Saudi's. When the Sheik sent his son to deliver the microfilm to the U.S., he was killed to make it appear as though the Iraqis were trying to prevent the information from reaching us. Unfortunately," he paused to take a few puffs from his pipe in a leisurely manner, "you came along. When you met with Jennifer, some people thought that it had been pre-arranged. I'm sorry I didn't know about it at the time, or I might have saved all of us a great deal of trouble. Most of the rest of the story you already know, except that Mustafa was apparently told, at his meeting in Lebanon, that he was being manipulated, and that the film was a fake. He just wasn't sure whom he could trust. Pity…"

He turned to Jennifer and saw the look of anguish in her eyes. "He had to die, my dear. If you hadn't killed him, I would have found an excuse to. That message had to be sent."

"Andrew Dalton isn't stupid, you son-of-a-bitch! He isn't going to war over an email!" Jennifer barked at Porter.

"No, you're right, he wouldn't. But he's seen troop movement in Iraq, Iran, and several other countries. So have the Russians, and even the Chinese. Remember where that *intel* comes from…" he waited before answering his own question—"computers. They control the satellites, they make the photos, they eavesdrop on electronic transmissions all over the world, and we control them. The president is now looking at intelligence data that appears absolutely real, because it came from real sources—the NSA and NSC computers. Director Wallace brought it to him this morning, and who wouldn't trust him?" His smile turned cold as he said that.

Another puff on his pipe, and Porter stood up and moved toward the hall. "Well, I guess that's all." He motioned to the second of his companions this time, who reached behind the kitchen counter, and picked up a paper bag. From it, he withdrew a large can of gasoline, and began spreading it over the floor, the macramé vertical blinds covering the windows, and the walls. "When they find you, they'll know it was arson but," he shrugged his shoulders, "who cares?" As he talked, he unrolled two more strips of tape and placed them over Mark and Jennifer's mouths. "…Besides," and he smiled as he re-lit his pipe while his two companions went out to the garage and opened the door, "you're a wanted man."

Porter dropped the wooden match he was using instead of the lighter, and the gasoline on the floor immediately caught fire. "Bye," and Porter joined his companions in the garage, backed the car out, and drove away.

Mark knew that the fire company would be there soon. Their alarm had been deactivated, but the neighbors would call them. Unfortunately, they would never make it in time to save this room and his family. He had to think. He strained at the tape, trying to twist it, make it looser, but to no avail. He saw Jennifer trying to get to the floor to reach him, as the boys and Meredith silently screamed. "Think!" his mind raced along. Eventually, the bonds would be gone, but not until after they were burned along with them.

Suddenly, it came to him. Harder and harder, he began to rock the chair he sat in, getting it to tilt further and further back until it fell over backwards. Mark's head struck the floor, momentarily stunning him. As he came around, he could feel the flames closer, near his head, but he had to ignore this. With all of the effort he could muster, he rolled the rest of his body onto the floor and over the flames. The heat seared the hair from his arms, and his sweater began to catch fire. The pain became unbearable, but there was no choice…for him, for his family, or for Jennifer.

By the time the tape on his wrists had burned away, there were large blackened areas of skin on his arms. He hoped they weren't full thickness burns but he ignored them and the pain as he pulled the tape from his feet.

"Stay calm," he yelled through the smoke on which everyone was beginning to choke, and he ran to the counter where Meredith kept the knife block, withdrew the first knife he came to, a steak knife, and ran to cut the others loose. He began with the boys and when they were free, he threw a kitchen chair through the glass doors and told them to run, then returned. The smoke had already become so thick that there was little chance of taking the time to cut anyone free. He wasn't sure there was time to do more than carry someone to safety, but who?

Through the smoke, Mark could see Jennifer lying on the floor, struggling with her bonds and coughing against the tape over her mouth. Just to his right, Meredith was screaming something unintelligible. There was no time…Mark stood frozen by indecision, but instinct took over. Fifteen years of marriage and the mother of his sons couldn't be forgotten. Besides, she didn't belong in this situation. She knew nothing about it. Ignoring the pain from his burns, he lifted Meredith over his shoulder and as he carried her through the broken doors to the driveway, paused for just a second to search through the smoke for Jennifer. Meredith was coughing from deep in her lungs as he deposited her on the cement.

Flames shot through the shattered doors of the family room, and his own lungs felt seared from the smoke and heat, but there was one choice left for him to make. He raced back onto the burning deck and ran once more through the broken glass of the doors. He fought to breath, and the heat from the flames made his already burned skin feel as though thousands of needles were being pressed through his arms and body. Slowly, he felt his way to the overturned chair, then toward where he had last seen Jennifer. There, through the smoke, she was laying, still. The only thought racing through Mark's mind, was that he was too late. By now, he no longer felt pain or noticed the smoke.

Never stopping to find out if she was still alive, he lifted her limp body onto his shoulder, as he had Meredith. Through the flames that danced around his legs, he carried her across the deck, and to the cement, where he laid her down on the soft grass beside the driveway.

The fire engines, whose sirens he had heard in the distance, finally arrived and the firefighters went to work, and so did he. He ripped the tape from her mouth, reached the first two fingers of his right hand through Jennifer's mouth and into her throat, making sure the airway was clear, then tilted her head back, and lifted her chin. After taking a deep breath into his own lungs, he pinched Jennifer's nose with his left hand, and covered her mouth with his as he exhaled, and watched her chest rise, then fall as he withdrew his mouth. On his third attempt, she began to cough violently, then rolled to the side as she threw up on the grass. His body was too exhausted to show it, but in his mind, he was laughing with joy. By the time she began to sit up, Mark had removed the tape from her hands and feet, and was cradling her head in his lap.

"What the fuck is going on here?!" Meredith was screaming at Mark, demanding answers that he didn't have time to give.

"Look, Meredith, there are lots of things you need to know, but not now."

"You brought those men into my home! Get out!" Mark looked down at Jennifer, who was now awake, and getting to her feet. When she was standing on her own, he turned and walked to the fire truck where his boys were being examined.

"Hi guys."

"Daddy! What happened? Who were those guys? Did you kill them?" Their questions would have gone on but Mark had to stop them.

"Listen guys. Those men have been doing some bad things to hurt our country, and they still are. They need to be stopped, and I have to leave for Washington for a little while. Are you guys OK?"

"We heard on the news that you killed someone. Did you? Mommy said you weren't coming back."

Mark thought for a minute, "some of it is true, some of it isn't. You know your mother and I have been having problems..." His older son, Steven, interrupted him.

"Daddy, Mommy said she doesn't want you here anymore. She said you're a loser. Does that mean that we won't see you again?" He was fighting back tears as he spoke. Mark's eyes began to water also, as he knelt beside his sons.

"Boys, if there is one thing I want you to remember, it is that there is no one in the world I love more than you. Your mother and I may split up, but *we'll* always be together, at least as much of the time as I can." He looked at them, rubbed their heads, and said, "I have to go now, but I'll be back, I promise."

When he stood up, Meredith was standing behind him. "Are you finished your lies? Where have you been? I didn't hear from you for days, then these men break into our house, and you show up with that woman...Who is she?!" The shrillness of her voice could be heard above the din of the firefighters.

"Meredith, that's Jennifer." He hesitated then walked back to where Jennifer was standing next to the EMS van. She insisted that he allow them to bandage his arms, despite his protest that they didn't have time. When they were covered with Silvadine cream, and wrapped, he pulled his sweater sleeves over them, ignoring the twinges of pain.

"Let's go," he said, looking at his watch. We have less than six hours left to get to the President." Somehow, the words didn't seem to fit here, standing in front of his house. It was like talking about a movie.

"I know," she answered, and they began to move, as inconspicuously as possible, toward the car. Eventually, the firefighters and police would discover the bodies in the house, and there would be days worth of questions to answer, and there wasn't time for that now.

As they walked, Meredith ran after them, and grabbed Mark's arm, causing him to wince in pain. She seemed oblivious to anything but her own thoughts.

"Where are you going? You can't leave me here like this! Wait until my father hears about this. Wait till you hear from my lawyer!"

Mark held his arm where Meredith had grabbed it, looked sadly at the ground, then back at the house he had loved as his home, and answered simply, "I'm in love with Jennifer, Meredith," and walked slowly toward where they had parked the Mercedes.

Jennifer stood there for a moment, staring into the angry, dark eyes that were the soul of Mark's wife. She hadn't understood before, but now..."I love him too," Jennifer spoke with a quiet strength that stopped Meredith's ranting, then turned and began to follow Mark toward the car when she turned toward Meredith one last time and, without warning, slapped her across her left cheek, leaving a red mark and a stunned look, then turned and kept walking.

Chapter 39

Andrew Dalton sat in the situation room under the White House, his "team" surrounding him, staring at "The Wall." Together, they watched the large screen reflect troop, ship, and aircraft movement. The room had been quiet for the last few minutes. After everyone had given their opinion on the best course of action, the decision still fell to Dalton. He continued to stare. "Why me?" he was asking himself. "What makes me more qualified than them to make this decision? How many lives is it OK to take?" He wished he had better answers.

Yelenkov had not only understood, he confided that he had noticed orders given in his own country for which no source could be found. Their radar and computer analysis was showing the same as his, and while he had too much to contend with between China and the Moslem countries that used to comprise the southern republics of the USSR, he would bluster and threaten, but take no action against the US. Dalton felt reassured, but hardly safe. The lines were being drawn on the map in front of them. The US and Russia, along with most of Europe were targeted by Iraqi, Iranian, and Chinese missiles. Russia once more felt surrounded, and was threatening to launch a pre-emptive strike against China if he didn't hear from Dalton before time ran out. The Chinese had moved troops toward Russia in response, while India moved troops north and Pakistan South to face off against each other, once there was no one else to interfere. The Balkans was threatening to flare again, and

Greece was making ominous accusations against Turkey, who answered in kind.

Perhaps the quietest place on Earth right now was the Middle East, and it too was on full alert with reserves being called up, air forces being placed on alert, and Israel finally making no secret that it could and would launch a nuclear strike against any invaders. It was all coming apart. Everything the world had worked for the last century to create was about to disintegrate, and the decision that would either trigger it or stop it was his. Once more he lowered his head into his hands and silently prayed.

"Mr. President," Hallsey sat in his usual place, and Dalton didn't even lift his head to answer.

"Yes, Admiral?"

"Mr. President, you have to commit. It's time." The President raised his head, then stood, leaning on the polished wood in front of him and looked at the man who would rule from the shadows.

"It's time when I say it's time, and not before. Do you understand me?" The two stared at each other across the table. There was a dynamic between them that only Dalton understood. Hallsey wasn't aware of his knowledge of the conspiracy, and those who were, didn't have to make a decision that could end millions of lives, and begin a chain of events that could plunge the world back into a new Dark Age. Jennifer had been adamant that he do nothing? What was he waiting for, and where was she?

"Look, Mr. President," Hallsey began again, "if you…"

"No!" Dalton slammed his hand on the table, shattering the silence, but thickening the tension. "If we're going to do this, I'll give the order, and not until I'm ready! Is that clear, Admiral?"

"Yes, Sir," Hallsey answered stiffly, and sat back down, gathering some papers he had in front of him into an unnecessary pile.

✶✶✶✶✶✶✶✶✶✶✶✶✶✶✶✶✶✶✶✶✶✶✶✶✶✶✶✶✶✶✶✶✶✶

Despite feeling weak from her ordeal in the fire, Jennifer drove the huge Mercedes to D.C. to spare Mark's burned skin the pain. He said nothing about it, but sat with his arms in his lap, trying not to move them too much with each bounce of the car.

"How much time do we have left?" Jennifer asked as she pushed her foot further toward the floor.

"Less than an hour," Mark answered, and painfully turned his head to look at Jennifer. Areas of her beautiful blonde hair were shortened and singed where the fire had done its work, and soot was still covering parts of her face. She was still the most breathtakingly beautiful woman he had ever seen. It never occurred to him to wonder what he looked like. Their speed was approaching 110 MPH as they approached D.C., and Mark once more raised his head and told Jennifer to "slow down." "I know we have to be there on time, but it won't help if we get killed or a cop stops us. You don't have enough ID on you to get us out of it, and I doubt he's going to call the White House from his squad car." She knew he was right, but there was something he didn't understand, and now seemed to be the right time to tell him.

"When I spoke with the President earlier, she began, "he told me that they were "downstairs." In other words, they were in the Situation Room." She stopped, looked at Mark, and translated—"The War Room," then continued. "Mark, if we don't get there and let him know that the microfilm was a fake, he's going to launch a nuclear strike against Iraq, and that could trigger a chain reaction that could mean World War III." Mark's eyes widened. He knew the situation was bad, but he had never imagined that the result could be that bad.

"Oh my God," Mark said softly to no one in particular. He remembered the visions of a post apocalyptic Earth from the movies of his Cold War youth. "For God's sake call him!" Mark was sitting upright now, the pain pushed into a corner of his mind that he would deal with later.

"I don't think it will work," Jennifer said, "but we can give it a try." She reached into the console between the seats, and removed the pocket phone that she had taken from the original occupant of Mark's seat.

"Here," and she gave him the private telephone number to the President's office. "He's out of the office right now," a female voice answered, may I take a message?" Politeness was the word of the day for her. She didn't know who was on the other end of the phone, but if they had the President's private telephone number, it was someone to be nice to.

"Listen to me," Mark began again, "this is Mark Harmon. He may not know me, but I'm here with Jennifer Lynch and we're on our way there now. Please," Mark's tones were nearly begging, "call him to the phone. You won't be sorry."

"I'm sorry Mr. Harmon, but the President can't be reached at this moment. If you'd like to leave..."

He never heard the rest because Jennifer snatched the phone from his hand, put it to her ear, and commanded, "This is Jennifer Lynch. Who is this?"

"My name is Mildred..."

"Millie, this is Jennifer. I have to talk with the President. I know he's downstairs, but I have to be put through to him. It's way beyond an emergency." The urgency in her voice was evident, but the hoarseness resulting from the smoke made her hard to recognize on the telephone.

"Ms. Lynch," Mildred responded, "so you've come back from the dead, have you?"

"Millie, please! It's me. Can't you tell?"

"I'm sorry miss, the President is occupied, if you'd care to leave a message..." Jennifer snapped the phone shut and threw it into the back seat.

"Fuck it," she said. "We'll make it," and their speed climbed back into the triple digits again.

✳✳✳✳✳✳✳✳✳✳✳✳✳✳✳✳✳✳✳✳✳✳✳✳✳✳✳✳✳✳✳✳✳✳

The President looked at the clock on the wall. He had waited as long as he could. He didn't know what Jennifer needed to tell him, but she couldn't know about this situation, and it wasn't likely that a few more minutes would make any real difference.

"Admiral Hallsey." Hallsey looked up at the President with anticipation. "Go to Defcon 1."

"Yes sir, Mr. President." The room became quiet as Hallsey punched a button in front of him and was immediately answered with, "Yes Admiral?"

"Pass the word along," he spoke calmly into the speaker phone, "by order of the President of The United States, we are *at* Defcon 1." War. They all understood, and they all prayed. "Mr. President," Hallsey turned back to Dalton, "we are at Defcon 1. All assets are on station."

Dalton thought for a moment, "Which ship is going to launch the missiles?" he asked.

"There will be two ships, Mr. President. The USS Truman, a guided missile frigate, and the Tiger Shark, a Tomahawk equipped Submarine. Both are on station and awaiting orders to commit." Dalton paused, then quietly asked to be put through to them. He wanted to say something to the men and women aboard those ships. Less than a minute went by when Hallsey nodded to the President that he was "on."

Dalton stood, as though he were addressing the sailors in person. He looked at the Wall, showing their position, and down at the dark speaker built into the table in front of him.

"Ladies and gentlemen," he began, "in a few moments, you're going to be asked to do something that you've trained all of your lives to do perfectly, in the hope that you would never have to do it at all. Some of you will have doubts about whether you can accomplish your mission. You can. Remember, you may be turning the launch key, but I, and I alone, am giving the final order." He paused and added a final thought,

"We all hope that this will be the end rather than the beginning. We are hoping to prevent war, not start it." A last pause, then, "God bless you all, and keep you safe." He touched the button in front of him, and the line went dead. There was no movement in the room for nearly a minute, then Andrew Dalton, President of the United States, did what only he could do. He turned to a young Major sitting only about ten feet behind him, with a black briefcase handcuffed to his wrist.

"Bring me the case, son."

✳✳✳✳✳✳✳✳✳✳✳✳✳✳✳✳✳✳✳✳✳✳✳✳✳✳✳✳✳✳✳✳✳✳✳✳

Their speed was a mere 50 miles per hour inside the city, as they raced through traffic lights and stop signs. Cars slammed on their breaks, horns blew, but to their great relief, there were no police around to stop them. When they reached the White House, Jennifer remembered that the street had been blocked several years ago due to bomb threats, and she had to drive around to the guard station. She didn't have her ID with her, but she prayed the guard would be one who would recognize her. As she approached the gate, the Marine guard walked to her side of the car and looked in.

"Miss Lynch?" He looked incredulous. "We thought you were dead."

"Well I'm not, Sergeant, so let me in."

"Ma'am, I'm sorry but I need to see ID's, especially from the man you're with. I have my orders."

"Look, Sergeant, you know who I am, and I vouch for this man. His name is Mark Harmon. We have urgent business with the President, and we haven't time to argue. If you don't believe me, call the President and ask him!" The guard looked young and confused. He knew Jennifer, and knew that she was a close confidant of the President who was never denied admission to the White House. On the other hand, he had orders to let no one onto the grounds until further notice, and there had been no exceptions.

"Wait here, he said, and re-entered the booth next to Mark's side. He picked up the telephone, and dialed the extension for guard headquarters. He explained the situation to someone, listened for a minute, then returned to Jennifer's side of the car.

"Ma'am, I've been told that the President left word that you were to be admitted immediately upon you arrival."

"Good!" Jennifer felt a wave of relief sweep over her. There was less than ten minutes before the deadline, but they would make it.

"But your companion will have to present his ID at the guard station and get a badge."

Jennifer stepped out of the car and, coming barely to the guard's shoulders, assumed a presence that towered over him. "Now you listen to me, Sergeant! You know I have clearance, you just confirmed it. Well I'm giving this man clearance. If we're not inside that building in eight minutes, you can look forward to getting your chance to fight in World War III. Now give us badges, open the fucking gate, and get out of our way!"

The guard remained unsure for a second, then snapped to attention, saluted and answered, "Yes Ma'am!" and in less that 30 seconds, they were wearing badges and driving to the Working Entrance of the White House.

Mark looked at the watch he had strapped over his bandages—"eight minutes," he said, and they leaped out of the car and headed for the door.

✶✶✶✶✶✶✶✶✶✶✶✶✶✶✶✶✶✶✶✶✶✶✶✶✶✶✶✶✶✶✶✶✶✶

President Dalton opened the thin back briefcase, and withdrew a red plastic covered three ringed notebook. He placed it on the table and opened it to its only page—a plastic sheet with two pockets, and withdrew the two red and white striped plastic covered cards, one from each pocket.

"Admiral, please verify that I have removed the launch codes from their binder"

"Verified, sir." Hallsey was beginning to become anxious. He knew all of this had been pre-arranged, but what if something went wrong? What if someone didn't get the message, and decided to launch a real strike against them. What if…? He was interrupted by the President.

"Admiral? Are you OK?"

"Yes, Mr. President, I'm fine."

"Hang in there Stuart."

"Yes sir," answered Hallsey.

The President broke open the first card. Inside was a blue card with plain white block lettering. There would be no mistaking letters or numbers on this card.

"Admiral, enter the following series—Alpha, Tango, Zulu, 3, 7, 3, 5, 1, Charlie, Charlie, Foxtrot." Each digit was repeated by the Admiral as he pushed the buttons on his console.

"Entered, sir." The president passed the card to the Secretary of Defense, both State and the Vice President being aloft in Air Force One as called for by protocol.

"Mr. Secretary, will you verify the series?"

"Yes, Mr. President," and he read the series again, but without the phonetic pronunciation the President had used. Once again, the Admiral read them back.

"Verified, Mr. President," the Secretary of Defense stated with resignation.

"Verified, Mr. President," Admiral Hallsey stood partially facing the President, and partially the panel in front of him. There was no further discussion in the room. Every face was turned toward Dalton as he cleared his throat, took a deep breath.

"Execute."

The Admiral touched the "Send" button, and every head turned to the Wall.

"How long until target, Admiral?"

"Seven Minutes, Mr. President." Neither he, nor the President sat down.
✶✶✶✶✶✶✶✶✶✶✶✶✶✶✶✶✶✶✶✶✶✶✶✶✶✶✶✶✶✶✶✶✶✶✶✶

When Mark and Jennifer reached the door to the Working Entrance to the White House, they were challenged again by another Marine Guard. This was always a minor annoyance for her in the past, but each second was precious now. He was a "spit and polish" Marine, shaved so close you could probably see your reflection in his chin if you cared to look. This time, however, since he recognized Jennifer, and they were both wearing badges, he overcame his skepticism at their appearance and let them through. Mark followed Jennifer down several corridors until they reached an elevator. They were almost there. This time, the guard checked not only their badges, but the log in front of him.

"I'm sorry, Ms. Lynch, but you're not on the list for the Sit-Room today." Mark looked at his watch.

"It's too late anyway, he said, dejectedly. "No it isn't, Jennifer said there is always a cushion available to abort." There were two guards at the elevator today, the senior was a lieutenant.

"Lieutenant," Jennifer said with quiet urgency, "call downstairs and find out if we are cleared. It will only take a moment, and we'll wait." They had gotten this far, they couldn't fail now. Mark kept looking at his watch. Another minute passed before the guard handed each of them another colored badge to add to the first one, and pressed the button on the elevator for them. It took only another few moments for the car to arrive, and for them to enter. There were only three buttons. The top was for the Residence, the middle was where they had boarded, and the lower was for the Situation Room. There was no other use for this elevator.
✶✶✶✶✶✶✶✶✶✶✶✶✶✶✶✶✶✶✶✶✶✶✶✶✶✶✶✶✶✶✶✶✶✶✶✶

Aboard the USS Truman, Captain Adam Ross looked at the series of letters and numbers on the screen in front of him. Reaching for the metal safe, that sat at eye level, he flipped the combination knob until he had opened it, and withdrew a red binder that, unknown to him, was nearly a duplicate of the one in the White House. "Mr. Detrich."

"Yes sir," his Executive Officer answered. Do you confirm reception of a launch code?"

"I confirm, sir." The captain broke open the red and white striped plastic card, and withdrew the blue card with white letters from within. He put his reading glasses on and looked at the card.

"Please confirm launch code, Mr. Detrich," and he read the sequence just as the President had a few moments earlier.

"Do you Confirm the code?"

"I confirm the code, sir."

He then handed the card to his XO, who repeated the sequence, reading to the Captain, who entered it into a keypad, then answered, "I confirm." The XO placed the card gently on the counter in front of him, and reached inside his shirt, at the same time as the Captain, each withdrawing a key on a chain.

"Insert your key, Mr. Deterich." And the Captain and XO each raised the red covers from the key slots, and inserted their keys. Sweat was dripping from the XO's forehead. The Captain seemed calm, but it was an illusion he hoped his men never penetrated. He had been in the Navy more than eighteen years, and always wondered if he could turn the key if he had to.

"Prepare to rotate, on my command," and the Captain began to count—"Three, two, one," he paused for just a second, then added "rotate." Each turned their keys clockwise.

****

Almost a hundred miles away, the sequence had been carried out nearly simultaneously aboard the Tiger Shark, were the Captain now gave the command, "Initiate Launch Sequence."

"Launch sequence initiated," the weapons officer replied, embarrassed that his voice broke as he answered.

✶✶✶✶✶✶✶✶✶✶✶✶✶✶✶✶✶✶✶✶✶✶✶✶✶✶✶✶✶✶✶✶✶✶

"Launch in 60 seconds," Lt. Commander Detrich stated as he watched the seconds count down on his screen. It was automatic now. They could abort, but failing that, the ship would launch the missile now, even if they all suddenly died.

✶✶✶✶✶✶✶✶✶✶✶✶✶✶✶✶✶✶✶✶✶✶✶✶✶✶✶✶✶✶✶✶✶✶

All eyes in the Situation Room remained glued to the Wall, as four red triangles appeared where the ships were, and from speakers around the room, the words echoed twice in everyone's ears—"Launch Confirmed."

✶✶✶✶✶✶✶✶✶✶✶✶✶✶✶✶✶✶✶✶✶✶✶✶✶✶✶✶✶✶✶✶✶✶

Mark and Jennifer stepped out of the elevator, and ran to the heavy metal door to the Situation Room. There were closed double wooden doors behind it, but it was meant, like the room. to ride out anything but a direct hit with a nuclear weapon. Jennifer had never paid much attention to it before, but it loomed large in her mind right now.

The guard in front of the door was courteous. He had been told that they were coming down, and that the President had authorized it, so he stepped back and opened the door for them. Jennifer ran past him with Mark struggling with his burns to keep up.

"Mr. President," Jennifer ran toward him. "You have to stop! That microfilm I sent you a copy of was a fake. There is no plan to attack us. It's only a plan to get Iraq out of the way." She was puzzled when nobody moved, then looked at the Wall. Four blinking red triangles were moving swiftly from the sea toward Iraq.

"Mr. President, the whole thing was a set-up. You have to abort!"

"This is ridiculous," Hallsey shouted. "Get her out of here!"

"How much time do we have to abort?" the President asked. Four minutes and twelve, eleven, ten seconds," someone answered.

"Mr. President," Bob Wallace came around behind Mark and Jennifer to face the President. "The Admiral's right. We're committed. We can't take a chance that she's wrong."

Jennifer looked at the President. She had to convince him somehow. "Mr. President, remember the first email I sent you, well that's confirmed, and it involves Mr. Wallace, also." It was a big gamble. Bob Wallace was as trusted by the President as they come.

"Think about it, Mr. President, who are the people who are most in favor of this attack?"

"Mr. President," Hallsey stepped forward indignantly, I don't know what she's talking about, but even if you forget that material you showed us, look at the evidence on the Wall! Look as the Satellite photos! Look at…anything!" He was sounding exasperated.

"Mr. President," Jennifer said with a look of fear in her eyes, think about it. Where do all of those things come from—computers! Do you have any independent confirmation from ground assets? Has anyone in the area confirmed these things?"

"Three minutes to detonation, Mr. President." It was an Air Force Colonel, sitting at a console, that was counting down.

President Dalton looked at Jennifer, without even seeing the burns. He looked past Mark, not even knowing who he was, and turned to look from Hallsey to Wallace, and back again. Suddenly, his decision was made. He turned toward the table, picked up the second plastic card and snapped it open.

"Colonel," he snapped, "issue the abort code immediately. Then began to read—Tango, Charlie, Xray, 3, 4…"

"No!" and Hallsey grabbed for the card. The President held it away in his right hand, and held Hallsey at bay with left.

"Guard!" the president shouted, but before he did, Mark launched himself at Hallsey, taking both he and the Secretary of Defense to the ground. When the guards ran through the door within a few seconds, the President was shouting.

"Admiral Hallsey and Mr. Wallace are under arrest. Take them away!" Then, without giving any of them another thought, he returned to the blue card and completed the sequence.

The Colonel read it back smartly, following it with, "90 seconds, Mr. President."

"Execute!" The President, with everyone else in the room, stood watching the wall.

Unlike the launch order, the abort order went directly from the Situation Room to the missiles via satellite. It was only ten seconds later that each of the four red triangles disappeared from the screen. They all remained standing for a few more seconds, then the President sat heavily in his seat. Without moving, or turning his head, he told the Colonel at the console to "Take us to Defcon 3." He was standing down, but not all the way. He was a politician who learned long ago to leave all options open, even the possibility that Jennifer was wrong.

On the Wall, things remained static, but he wouldn't really know where things stood for another day—until they had independent confirmation one way or the other.

Two days later, after having spent that time being thoroughly de-briefed, Jennifer and Mark were shown into the Oval Office, where the President and Mrs. Dalton, the Vice President, and Mrs. Javits, and the Secretary of State awaited them. This time, they were well dressed and ushered into the room by Tony St. John. They all stood, and the President walked to Jennifer and kissed her on the cheek.

"You look a hell of a lot better today," he said.

"Thank you, Mr. President," she answered. Then he moved over to Mark and held out his hand. Mark shook it gingerly. He had been re-bandaged at Bethesda Naval Hospital, at the order of the President, and, between the new bandages and the Percocet, his pain was much less now.

"I understand we have you to thank for much of this, Doctor," Dalton said. "Your country…the world is grateful." Mark felt like he deserved every word of the praise, but somehow, it didn't matter anymore.

"Thank you, Mr. President, but I just, kind of got caught up in things."

"That's not quite the way I hear it," he said, looking at Jennifer who was smiling at Mark.

"Well," Mark answered, "some people have a tendency to exaggerate other people's roles, at the expense of their own." It was the first time he had ever seen Jennifer blush. He hadn't thought she could be more beautiful than she had been the first time he had seen her, but he was wrong.

The President now walked to his desk and returned with two cases. His demeanor now became very formal. "Mark Steven Harmon," he began, and Jennifer Ann Lynch." He paused for effect. "By order of the President of The United States, you are hereby awarded the *Medal of Freedom*. This is the highest civilian award our country offers." He opened each case, and removed the medal and ribbon, placing one around each of their necks and handing them the cases. "You've earned them."

"Thank you, "Mr. President," each said in turn, and they were congratulated by the First Lady, the Vice President, and each person in the room as they filed by. Then the President spoke again.

"Of course you realize that you can never tell anyone how or why you earned them. The official documents read, "for service to your country in the highest tradition of democracy and freedom."

"We understand, Mr. President." He paused for a second, then looked at Mark.

"You wouldn't be looking for a job, would you?" There was a sly smile on his face.

"No thank you, Mr. President, I think I've had enough "cloak and dagger" to last me for a while.

"Well," he smiled again, you never know when you might change your mind…"

Chapter 40

A notice appeared in the Washington Post that the President regretfully accepted the resignation of Admiral Stuart Hallsey, who had to retire for reasons of health. It had been more than two months since Bob Wallace resigned due to "irreconcilable differences" with the White House.

Martin LaMont was buried in a cemetery in Queens eight weeks earlier. No more than a handful of people knew that the tombstone should have read "Porter."

Around the world, various high ranking military officers and public officials either resigned, were arrested, or disappeared, according to the customs of their countries, and in Geneva, a new round of talks about bringing peace to the Middle East began, with Russia and the United States jointly hosting them. There was much speculation as to what would bring about so much cooperation between the two, they were sure that the very large amount of money that Russia received from the IMF had something to do with it.

In a sheltered marina on Paradise Island, the 70 foot sloop, "Valkyere," sat tied to her dock, her Teak and chrome polished until it was hard to stare at her on a sunny day, and it was nearly always sunny here.

Abaft the helm, in a comfortably soft lounge chair, Mark Harmon lay with his face to the sun. His wounds had healed, and the few scars that remained were covered by his tan skin. His eyes were closed, and he felt the soft breeze play over his nearly naked body as the music from the nearby restaurant floated toward him. Hearing a soft sound, he raised his head to see Jennifer, much as he had first seen her, but with the sun reflecting from her smooth skin creating a sort of halo around her. She wore a thong bikini that could just barely be called clothing. She was so beautiful it hurt.

He pretended to be asleep as she approached with two Piña Coladas, putting hers down, and gently touching the ice cold glass of his to the side of his chest. He twitched, grabbed the glass and, after placing it gently on the table, he drew her toward him and held her body against his as their lips met. She rolled over onto the wide lounge chair beside him, their bare bodies sliding as the perspiration lubricated their movements. Their mouths met again, and as they reached inside each other, their souls entwined with a feeling of joy that neither had ever expected to know.

Hours later, or so it seemed, they disengaged long enough to each take a sip of their drinks, then lay back to enjoy Paradise.

"Mark, Jennifer began softly, her lips still tingling from the kiss, "I've been meaning to ask you something."

"Yes, my love?" Mark answered. She paused for a moment, unsure how to phrase the question, or even if she should ask, but knowing that she had to.

"You're a doctor," she said tentatively.

"Yes?" he answered, turning his head and looking into her Kelly green eyes.

"Well, I know you weren't making that much when we met…, and I wouldn't care if you didn't ever have a shirt on your back…" she added quickly.

"Yes, Love…?" he knew what was coming. He had been expecting it before now, but he waited for her to ask.

"Well, it's just that I don't understand how you can afford this boat, the house, our trips…" Mark smiled and turned over without answering, knowing it would annoy her into asking again. After all, it was her brilliant mind that he loved as much, or maybe more, than her beauty.

"I'm serious!" she laughed as she hit him with a pillow. "How can we afford all of this?" Mark turned back to her, lifted himself up on his right elbow, and looked for all the world, to Jennifer, like the "Cheshire Cat."

"You remember when I was hacking into the Pentagon mainframe for those transactions, and found the ones we needed to prove our case?"

"Sure…," she replied hesitantly.

"Well, while I was in there, I sort of figured…, well…the money was already gone, so I simply redirected one of the transactions into a different account—mine. I figured that if I lived, it was owed to me anyway."

"But some of those transactions were in the hundreds of millions," she gasped. 'How much did you…redirect?"

In answer, Mark kissed her again. The question and the answer melted into one for each of them\enough."

✶✶✶✶✶✶✶✶✶✶✶✶✶✶✶✶✶✶✶✶✶✶✶✶✶✶✶✶✶✶✶✶✶✶✶

The tropical sun was just leaving a burnished rust color on the sea and sky where they met at the horizon. Mark was still asleep on deck, where Jennifer had covered him with a large towel to prevent sunburn.

She had slipped below to shower and change before awakening him for dinner, and now stood without clothes in front of the full length mirror in the main stateroom. She paused for a few moments to admire her image, and was pleased with what she saw. She never doubted the effect she had on men. She had known it since she was a little girl, but Mark was the first one whose approving stare gave her that warm glow she never tired of. She loved him with all her heart.

Wrapping a towel around her damp hair, and allowing a short satin slip to slide over her shoulders and onto her body, she glanced at the ship's clock. "17:00," it read. Without hurry, her bare feet carried her soundlessly to the small desk where a notebook computer sat. Mark had been using it to try his hand at writing.

With a single practiced motion, Jennifer sat and lifted the lid, bringing the screen to life, then clicked on the email icon, followed by "Compose Mail."

To: *num_1@terra.gov*
From: jlh
Subj: Missing funds
Funds accounted for. No need to search. Location unimportant and unreachable.
Do not expect further contact for an indefinite period.

Finished typing, she clicked on "SEND," and closed the program, leaving the screen as she had found it, then put her white skirt and shear blouse on before she went back up on deck to awaken Mark for dinner. "It's a dangerous world," she thought to herself, "and someone has to hold it all together."

As she passed the computer, she couldn't avoid reading what he had been working on. He made no attempt to hide the fact that he was going to write a book exposing the whole affair. There, in front of her, was the last page he had worked on. "*It was unusually warm in London, today,...*" the page on the screen began. She smiled. He could write his book. After all, it was only fiction? She closed the lid.

Once back up on deck, she smiled as she leaned forward, awakened Mark with a kiss, and whispered, "time for dinner." "Hmmm...," Mark opened his eyes and, looking at his new wife standing over him, drew her down to the lounge again, kissed her, and ran his hand lightly along her face and neck. "I'm not very hungry right now," he said softly. He had other ideas.

Epilogue

Saddam Hussein sat at the ornate round brass table, rotating it first clockwise, then counter-clockwise to get at the particular piece of food he wanted. Sitting about a meter to his right was General Abdhulla Mamet, whose smile was only blunted by his chewing.

"Well, my friend," Hussein said, reaching for another grape. "What have you got for me?"

Mamet said nothing, but took a folded piece of paper from his left breast pocket and handed it to Saddam who looked at it and smiled, as well.

"When would you like to begin?" asked Mamet, "they want to know."

Saddam tossed the short Laser printed note onto the table in front of Mamet.

"We'll give it a couple of years so they can become comfortable. Besides, that will give us more time to build and prepare."

Mamet's smile widened, and he reached for the paper. It couldn't be left on the table.

TO: Iraq_1
From: prc_1
Subject: Timetable

Canisters loaded onto missiles. We have at least 20 targets within reach around the world. We will be able to build at least 20 more in the next year. Understand that our combined arsenal now includes

30 nuclear warheads as well. Our troops ready also. Can proceed at your discretion.

"Yes," thought Mamet, "he's right again. Another year or two should be enough."

About the Author

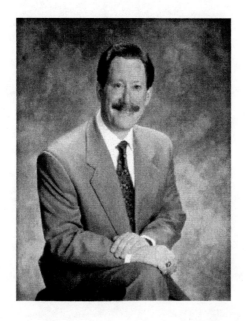

Eric Shore is the 21st Century equivalent of a Renaissance Man. Born and raised in the Philadelphia area, he achieved his childhood dream of becoming a physician, began his practice of Internal Medicine and Geriatrics, and remains on the faculty of two area medical schools.

Not content with the ordinary, Dr. Shore completed his M.B.A. in 1997 and is currently enrolled in law school where he will earn his J.D. and enter the practice of Health Law. Lest anyone think that academics is all he knows, he has held a pilot's license since his internship, has a black belt in karate, sculpts, and plays the piano and guitar. When not engaged in any of these activities, boating or writing (including a short volume of poems), he engages in weight training, golf and tennis, and is active in local politics.